Swell

Lauren Davies

ISBN-13: 978-1495986178

Los Angeles

One

I was a British writer of moderate success. Some would say three novels published in three years was something to be proud of, but I felt little pride in writing books few people had read.

'Have you written anything I would know?' people asked politely at parties.

After years of embarrassing silences when I uttered the titles, I finally resorted to the line, 'No, I have an underground following.'

I desperately wanted to be a bestseller. To hold book-signings that would have people queuing in the rain for my autograph. I craved the sort of deals I read about in the Press: an eye-watering amount of money for one book, film options, bidding wars, one million pounds for the reality TV star who could hardly string three sentences together let alone write a book. My guess was, they didn't.

I worked hard and my career meant everything to me. It had been my sole focus for most of my adult life, yet the overwhelming feeling I had when I reflected on my 'achievements' was guilt about the waste of trees. I had made a mediocre amount of money, so I had to continue pursuing that bestseller in order to pay the bills. It was either that or throw in the towel and admit I had been dreaming to think I could keep myself clothed and fed by way of my creative efforts. My motivation, however, was waning by the day. I wanted to inspire but I could not even inspire myself. An exceptional idea for my fourth book was proving to be the most elusive yet. The more I focused on finding a subject I felt passionate enough about to spend a year of my life writing about it, the more my mind went as blank as a shaken Etch-a-Sketch. I feared my grasp on literary success was slipping and I was about to plunge headfirst into the remainder bin along with my back catalogue.

According to my publisher there was always a reason my books had not topped the charts that was beyond their control. The cover was the wrong shade of blue. The market was down. The dollar was up. The supermarkets were only buying the ghost written autobiographies of halfwits, recipe books written by people who had never been to chef school, or guides to surviving on monkey spit in the jungle.

I had considered taking a risk and changing the genre of book but I had never been one to relish risk-taking whether in my career or otherwise. I had never dyed my hair outlandish colours, or been skinny-dipping, or had a one-night stand.

'Stick to fiction, that's what you're good at, darling,' my agent, Tristan, a true English gent advised, 'and if we decide you're no longer good at it, we'll find you a bit of ghost writing.'

'An autobiography of a half-wit,' I groaned. 'Did you not once tell me that is the road trodden by failed novelists?"

'Did I, darling?'

'Yes, Tristan, I believe you did, several times. A year ago I was, according to you, too talented for ghost writing.'

'Oh and you are, darling, supremely talented.'

I don't think he even convinced himself with that statement,

'If I'm that talented why is my royalty cheque a negative value? I *owe* money to my publisher, Tristan. That is not the definition of bestseller.'

'Bestseller means anything we want it to mean, Bailey darling. Look, don't fret. I am positive the right thing will come along,' he said while ushering me out of the office past a waiting author who was evidently worth his expensive breath. 'We just have to hope it comes along soon or I fear your publisher will drop you like a buttered baby.'

Motivational speaking was not his forte.

In need of a holiday to escape the four walls that seemed to mock my lack of inspiration, I headed to L.A. to visit my old friend, Jon, who worked in the film industry and had been begging me to visit him for years. Like a moth to a flame I was drawn to the place where money talks out of the mouths of perfectly sculptured people, all of whom are either a success or well practised in pretending to be. The trip was intended to kill or cure. I would either be inspired to write the best book of my life or I would realise I did not belong in the club for creative geniuses, allowing me to finally let go of my dream and, as my mother had said all along, get a proper job.

Jon took me straight to an 'industry' party, said with the mimed inverted commas.

'This is just our weekend house,' said the host who was an acquaintance of Jon's, not for any reason other than she was something in the film industry, which, I soon realised, was how L.A. worked. People were friends if they were either useful or connected to people who were useful.

If she weighed more than seventy pounds I would have been surprised.

'We also have homes in Vail, Hawaii and, oh I forget.'

I felt like impaling myself on the jewel-encrusted champagne glass that probably cost more than my flat.

'Have you met Ashlee? She just got back from her latest tour.'

Seeing my blank expression, Ashlee, who looked like she should have been at home playing with her Bratz dolls, raised both manicured hands as if I were about to shoot and squealed – 'Don't tell me you haven't heard of me? *Gaard* I am like totally famous. My music is huge in Japan.'

'Big in Japan,' I mused, 'you should be very proud.'

Ashlee eyed me suspiciously.

'Sorry,' I said to the self-proclaimed musical megastar, 'I stopped listening to music when Genesis split up. It broke my heart.'

I thought she was going to throw up on my shoes. Musical Barbie and my skeletal host tottered away twittering like canaries.

'Genesis,' said a voice behind me, 'that was funny. So tell me, did you have a crush on Phil Collins?'

'Didn't everyone have a secret crush on Phil Co...?'

I almost choked on the Collins when I turned around to see the face of an angel staring back at me. A bronzed, broad-shouldered, blond haired, edible angel with the most spectacular silver eyes I had ever seen.

'Phil Collins,' I said again, well aware my cheeks were burning with the intensity of rescue flares, 'and of course I had a crush on him. Most girls my age did, even if they didn't like to admit it because he was a ballad singing baldy dwarf.'

The angel smiled. His teeth, of course, were as white as coral and straighter than the Queen's guards, this was America after all. He ran a hand through his own thick, sun-bleached hair that almost sighed as it relaxed back over his smooth forehead. He slowly pushed the same hand into the pocket of his jeans and leaned back against the wall.

'I had a crush on Tiffany.'

'I think we're alone now,' I sang.

He placed a warm hand on my shoulder. I jolted like a schoolgirl caught passing notes in class.

'Sorry, do I make you nervous?'

I brushed my shoulder dismissively.

'Not at all, I've just got a thing about personal space.'

'Is it not better with me in it?'

'Wow, you've got a ticket on yourself haven't you?'

'Not at all,' he repeated mockingly, 'although I do have two VIP tickets for the Jack Johnson gig in town tomorrow night. It's not Genesis but I think you could easily develop a crush.'

'Are you asking me out?'

Five minutes earlier I had been questioning my attendance at this ego-fuelled bash. Now I was standing in a dark corner sipping champagne alongside easily the most handsome man in the room who had just asked me on a date. I hoped Ashlee was within earshot.

'Yes I am asking you on a date. You're cute and you're funny. Why waste the opportunity, right?'

His very un-British directness was rather appealing.

'But you don't even know me,' I said, flicking my long hair over my shoulder in a rather obviously flirtatious move that made me want to poke myself in the eyes, 'and I don't know you.'

The look on his face was enough to tell me I should.

'Oh God not another one.'

Raising my hands in an Ashlee manner, I squeaked – 'I am like totally famous. Don't you know who I am?'

It was his turn to blush. The modesty suited him.

'Is it me or is everyone famous at this party except me?'

'This is L.A., babe, get used to it.'

The 'babe' made my legs tingle.

'My name's Jason,' he said, extending a hand, 'Jason Cross.'

'I bet you are.'

Rather than punching myself in the face, I took his hand. His skin was smooth and warm. The tough skin on the ends of his fingers suggested he played guitar.

'Bailey Brown,' I said, shaking his hand confidently, 'are you a musician?'

A group of men walking past laughed out loud.

'She's either bullshitting you or you've found the one girl in L.A. who won't let you get laid just by saying your name, J.C.,' one called over his shoulder.

Jason laughed along, his eyes shimmering.

'I wish I was talented enough to be a musician but no, I'm not.'

'So if you're not a budding Phil Collins, what do you do?'

I leaned back against the wall and tilted my head towards him.

'You first,' he said.

'I'm a writer,' I said, almost swallowing the last word.

'A writer? Cool, what do you write? Screenplays?'

'Like every waiter in L.A.?' I smiled. 'No, I write books. I'm a novelist.'

The word always sounded precocious but I secretly enjoyed using it.

'A novelist? I'm impressed. How many novels have you written?'

'Three.'

'So you're published?'

I nodded and looked at my feet. My toes wriggled inside my wedges.

'And modest too. I knew you were smart when I first saw you.'

'How? Because I'm holding my champagne glass the right way up?'

He laughed. The sound warmed my body, which was already glowing from the pleasantly mild temperatures for early November.

'You're funny,' he said.

My toes wriggled again.

Funny was a start but I would have preferred 'sexy' or 'unfathomably gorgeous'.

'Thanks. I'm British, we always seem funny to Americans.'

He grinned and, as he did so, he winked, which would in most circumstances have made me cringe but those silver eyes had the power to pull off a wink.

'So, Bailey, these novels of yours, would I have…?'

'No,' I said, pre-empting the dreaded question, 'I have an underground following.'

'Sounds intriguing, I'd like to read one.'

Good luck, I thought to myself, Amazon might have one wedged under a wonky desk.

'So what about you?' I chirped, moving the subject on, 'You're here with the who's who of L.A. so you must be a "someone"' – I made inverted commas in the air – 'but you're not a musician, so what are you, an actor?'

'No actually I'm a "surfer".' He copied the motion with his fingers.

'A surfer? Is that a job?'

He laughed out loud. I saw a few heads – predominantly female – turn to look at us.

'Now that was a very British question and the answer is, yes it is a real job.'

'So you're a professional surfer?'

'Yup.'

'Gosh that's a very twenty-first century job title. And judging by the fact that you're rather well put together' – I looked him up and down, which I rather enjoyed – 'and that you're not hanging out in the car park in your VW campervan smoking spliffs and listening to the Beach Boys, I am guessing you're a successful professional surfer.'

'This may be news to you, Bailey but the Sixties are over. I'm afraid we're athletes these days.'

I looked at him questioningly and smiled.

'So?'

'So what?'

'So you didn't give me an answer. Are you a successful professional surfer, Jason Cross?'

His silver eyes met mine and sparkled.

'Before I tell you, how about that date?'

I studied my nails and shrugged.

'Sure, but if it turns out you're a complete loser I might decide I'm washing my hair.'

He smirked.

'I am twelve-times champion of the world.'

I had died and gone to heaven, on a platinum surfboard paddled by an angel.

'Oh,' I whistled, 'just twelve times?'

'Yes, twelve. I'm chasing my thirteenth title in December in fact.'

I crossed my arms and caught Jason's eyes moving swiftly over my chest. I tried to control the tremor in my voice caused by the seismic activity between my legs.

'Lucky for some.'

'Hopefully for me. So, are twelve titles enough to get me a date, Bailey Brown?'

Now Brown was such a dull name in Britain but the way he said my name made me sound quite delicious.

'I suppose the date is on.'

'Great. Tell me where you live and I'll pick you up tomorrow at seven.'

I told him.

'Perfect. Now how about I show you where I live?'

The second I met his gaze I knew exactly what he meant. Back home where I was sensible Bailey Brown who avoided risks at all costs, I would never have considered sex on a first date. Sex *before* the first date would unquestionably be the most dangerous thing I had ever done, far outranking my previous personal best of eating magic mushrooms at the age of sixteen. Well, I say 'eat' but to be honest, it was more of a lick. It still counts. I had felt distinctly woozy for at least thirty minutes.

It was either the effect of the grab-opportunity-with-both-hands attitude in L.A., or the fact that I felt my life was running downhill to a non-climactic finish that gave me the sudden urge to be impetuous. Whatever the reason, before Jason had the time to say please and with my head pounding as loud as my heart, we were heading for his car.

Two

'Jason you bastard!' the girl screamed, leaping towards him like an attacking panther.

She was another of the party's lollipop girls - big head on a stick-like body too petite to contain vital organs - but she packed a punch. Before I could react, Jason Cross was lying flat on his back in the driveway, straddled by a Polynesian beauty who was hitting him about the face with a Jimmy Choo stiletto.

'Ouch, won't that damage the heel?' I shrieked, straining to see whether the man of my dreams still had both eyes.

'Get off me, Portia, you're crazy,' Jason shouted, fending off the blows.

'I'm gonna kill you.'

I had the feeling she meant it.

'Somebody help?' I suggested to the crowd that had gathered behind me.

They glanced at their fingernails, women and men alike, as if weighing up the cost of a manicure against Jason's untimely demise.

'I knew you were fucking someone,' yelled Portia. 'You told me you were gonna fix us and here you are leaving the party with some fucking whore.'

'Charming,' I said behind Portia's tiny back, 'at least I'm not a stiletto wielding psychopath.'

Still astride Jason, Portia whipped her head around and stared at me with cat-like eyes.

I flinched.

'Just for clarification purposes, I'm not actually a whore,' I said.

'English,' Portia spat as if that explained everything.

'Portia, please, let's talk about this,' Jason pleaded, straining to push her off him.

I was surprised by how much he seemed to be struggling considering my head probably weighed more than her entire body. She clearly had the strength of a woman scorned.

'I don't wanna talk, I wanna kill you.'

'No you don't, baby,' Jason reasoned, 'you love me.'

Her tears fell like hailstones on his grey cashmere jumper. I shuffled my feet, feeling more uncomfortable by the second as the chemistry fizzed between them, if a little too explosive to be healthy. Behind me, a chorus of gossip buzzed around the crowd. I could feel their eyes burning into me as they wondered about the trouble-making English whore in their midst.

'How can you fuck her as soon as I leave town?' Portia wailed. 'She's just a dumb groupie, Jason.'

'Groupie? I'm not a groupie, I didn't even know who he was.'

A laugh coursed through the crowd.

'Don't give me that shit. The whole world knows who he is.'

'Make that the whole world minus one,' I said.

'She's no groupie,' said Jason, grasping Portia's wrists, 'in fact she's a writer. You've got it all wrong, Portia. Bailey is…'

'Bailey? What sort of dumb name is that?'

'Pot, kettle,' I muttered.

'Bailey is actually a novelist,' Jason pressed on. 'She's working on a project here, with me. In fact she is actually my biographer.'

Genius, I smirked, aware my own street credibility had just jumped several storeys with the onlookers.

'Your what?'

'Biographer,' I repeated in Jason's defence. 'It's someone who writes books about people.'

'Huh?' she growled, whipping her head around again.

Even overcome with rage I had to admit she had the most naturally beautiful features I had ever seen.

'Books,' I said, 'they're funny little things made of paper. You might remember them from school.'

Only Jon's timely arrival and quick thinking saved me from having a Jimmy Choo implanted in my forehead. Which at least would have meant I owned one if not a complete pair.

'Jesus, Bailey, you've got a mouth on you sometimes,' Jon hissed, pulling me to one side.

'I couldn't help it,' I shrugged, 'she's far too pretty for her own good.'

The audience was visibly disappointed when a seriously tall, lanky young man with slicked back hair the colour of a Bordeaux red wine and a loud suit to match pushed his way to the front. An entourage of burly men followed.

'Back in your cage, Portia. Give J.C. a break you freaky bitch.'

He yanked her off Jason and plonked her onto her single shoe.

'Jason's manager, Chuck,' Jon explained under his breath. 'He hates Portia.'

'Chuck?'

'It's short for Charles.'

'Right. Maybe our own Prince Charles will become King Chuck.'

'There's only one King Chuck and it's that fellow there. He controls the affairs of the most legendary man in surfing. Jason can pretty much ask for anything he wants and Chuck will make it happen.'

I smoothed down my hair and watched Chuck drag Portia away from the scene into an awaiting SUV with smoky windows.

'Well this is one affair he won't be controlling because it's over before it began.'

'Glad to hear it.'

'Unfortunately,' I sighed.

I watched with dampened spirits while Jason regained his composure among his entourage who stood protectively around him. Crowded together they looked like a set of expensive leather luggage. Jason was a stunningly handsome, fit and evidently successful man but I might have known there would be a catch. I felt ashamed I had put myself in such a humiliating situation on the one occasion I had relished the chance to be impulsive. Now the promise of my first sexual encounter in months had lit me up like a firefly and I was struggling to douse the flames.

'I mean it, Bailey, don't get involved,' Jon warned, obviously sensing the hormones prickling my skin.

I flicked my hair as nonchalantly as I could manage.

'I don't know what you're talking about.'

Jon pushed his designer glasses up the bridge of his nose.

'Let me tell you about people like Jason Cross, Bailey. You don't come across many men like him. He's glamorous, adrenalin-fuelled, sexy and dangerous.'

'And the down side is…?'

Jon took my elbow and guided me away from the scene and back towards the house.

'These professional surfers are a law unto themselves, Bailey. They travel the world for ten months of the year. They're rich, they get everything they want for free, their office is the ocean and many of them, at least the ones that aren't married, have groupies in every port.'

Lifting two glasses of free champagne that had been flowing like tap water all night, Jon flopped onto a white leather sofa as soft as marshmallow and motioned for me to sit.

'Jason Cross is the kind of guy women leave their husbands for and then regret it when he's had his fun and moves on to the next bikini babe in the next destination, leaving them single and forever labelled as a desperate groupie. Please don't be one of those girls or I will have to reconsider our friendship.'

I shifted on the sofa.

'You sound like you know him well.'

'I know people who know him.'

'So in fact this could be pure speculation and idle gossip.'

Jon creased his face into a frown.

'I know people who have had their fingers and even more delicate parts burned.'

I crossed my legs.

'Personally, I think it sounds fascinating but don't worry about me, Jon, you know me. I'm far too safe for those sorts of shenanigans so you can rest assured that I am never going to sleep with Jason Cross. Largely because he has a girlfriend who probably kills baby animals for fun and but also because I have morals.' I paused. 'Although you must admit he is hot.'

'Hot as in you will be the next to get burned.'

I ran my tongue across my lips and grinned.

'Possibly, but just a quick sizzle would have been fun.'

Three

The party was once again in full swing. Impossibly perfect women draped themselves over the arms of rich, powerful and famous men. Those with a coke habit queued to use one of the seven bathrooms, leaving a layer of fine powder behind as if the CSI team had been in to fingerprint the joint. The networkers spun webs of influence around the house like spiders on the hunt for unsuspecting flies. On the one hand it all seemed incredibly fake but, on the other, there was a lot to be said for the opportunity to forge a bible of contacts at a single party. Mingling with the important and self-important people of L.A. I suddenly felt alive and within sniffing distance of opportunities that did not exist back home. There was a reckless world out there and I thought if I learned how to go with the flow, perhaps I could join them and start to live a little. As far as I could see, dwelling on negative Amazon book reviews from housewives in Hampshire was not living.

'This is a funny world you live in, Jon but I kind of like it.'

'Stay,' said Jon. 'Write a screenplay. You're talented and I know plenty of people in the film industry. See that guy over there…' - I glanced over at the man with glossy salt and pepper hair who was in the process of licking the salt to accompany his tequila slammer from the artificial cleavage of a cute young thing - '... he's the hot new director in town.'

'He should cool himself down a few degrees, she's young enough to be his daughter.'

'She is his daughter,' said a familiar voice.

I spun around to see Jason smiling pleasantly down at me as if Portia attempting to murder us both had been nothing more than a hiccup.

Jon groaned.

'Not really,' Jason winked, 'but knowing what goes on in this town, she could be and he just doesn't know it yet.'

Jason reached out a bronzed hand and took my empty glass.

'Can I get you another one?'

He had no qualms about ignoring Jon completely, which seemed to be a regular occurrence at this party. These people had neither the time nor the inclination to waste valuable conversation on people they had no use for.

'I don't know.'

I glanced at Jon who rolled his eyes at the ceiling.

'Please, Bailey, I want to explain,' said Jason.

Don't worry, I mouthed to Jon.

I won't but you should, he mouthed back before I followed Jason out to the pool bar.

As I walked behind him I felt the eyes of every woman we passed piercing my skin like sharpened daggers. This man was clearly their very eligible bachelor and I was an unknown quantity, doubtless disrupting their future plans to be Jason Cross' wife.

The stars reflected in the glistening pool as if they were floating on the surface.

'This is quite something,' I breathed, filling my lungs with air perfumed by sweet champagne and the scent of beautiful people.

'You're quite something,' Jason said softly.

I looked into his eyes that were just inches from my face. His lips were soft and full and his skin closely shaved. He clearly took care with his appearance but something told me it was not a difficult task to keep Jason Cross looking delectable. His breath was warm against my skin as he leaned closer. The hair on the back of my neck stood up like the fur of a startled cat in response to the aura of quiet confidence he exuded.

'You're unbelievable,' I said, lifting my hand and placing it between us on his searching lips.

'I know,' he winked.

'You're not suffering from low self-esteem, I'll give you that. Mummy must have told you every day what a special boy you were.'

'Mummy was dead,' he said.

'Oh I am sorry.'

He shrugged.

'Don't be. My life was not perfect but then it gave me the drive to get out of there and get to where I am today. I've got no regrets.'

Jason tilted his head at me and his fingers drummed the side of his champagne flute.

'But I do regret getting you caught up in all that crap before. Portia can get a bit crazy, but you must understand she's my ex. We're not...'

I lifted a finger to silence him.

'You don't have to explain, it's fine.'

'It's not, you're angry with me.'

'No,' I said, pausing to think, 'I just came to my senses. Sex after five minutes is never a good idea.'

'It's better than sex that only lasts five minutes.'

'Does it ever last longer?' I laughed.

'Would you like to find out?'

'Jason, I'm sorry but I am not going to sleep with you,' I said firmly. 'I make it a rule not to sleep with men who lie to their crazy exes to pass me off as their biographer.'

His cheeks flushed beneath his tan.

'Shame but I get it.'

'Good. Now we've got that sorted, you can either run away and find a girl who will sleep with you or we can stay here and have an interesting conversation.'

Jason pressed his lips together and then a smile spread across his beautiful face.

'I admire your honesty. You know I think I'm already having the most interesting conversation I've ever had at one of these parties so if you don't mind, I'll stay.'

We clinked our glasses together and drank. The combination of the expensive bubbles, the delightful company and the breathtaking surroundings lifted my mood so high above where it had been for the previous few months, I felt as if I were watching myself from above. So much so that when Jason asked me the question that had the ability to change my life forever, it seemed to reach me on a warm breeze.

'I've been thinking, Bailey, how great would it be if you actually were my biographer?'

'Pardon me?'

Before he could reply, Jason's eyes flitted over my shoulder. Half expecting to see Portia bearing down on me with a stiletto heel poised to strike, I spun around.

Instead I saw the man I recognised as Chuck. He beamed at me. I tried to smile back, but his aubergine hair was so startling, I just felt myself staring at the top of his head.

'Chuck's my manager,' Jason explained. 'Chuck, this is the girl I was telling you about, the writer, Bailey.'

'How's it going?' Chuck chirped.

He greeted me with a handshake so enthusiastic it made my bones rattle. His suit was as sharp as a lemon.

'Delighted to meet you, Chuck.'

'Likewise, dude,' Chuck whooped. 'Man, that is one cool accent. If I didn't know you wrote books I'd already be guessing that compared to the chicks Jason usually hangs out with, your IQ's actually on the scale, for shizzle.'

'Er, thanks I think,' I said, raising my eyebrows.

Chuck spoke at three hundred words per minute and shouted as if speaking into a strong headwind but he was friendly and interesting and bubbled with infectious energy. I did not come across people like Jason and Chuck in my everyday life. So even if I had found inspiration for two new book characters the party had been worthwhile.

'It's been a real pleasure,' I said bowing my head, 'but I should really get back to my friend.'

'Hold up, dude, what about the deal. Is it a no go?' Chuck hollered.

'Deal? What deal?'

Jason glanced at Chuck, ran his tongue along his lips and took a deep breath.

'Well I was trying to quiz you about being my biographer. I know you don't know me…'

'Must be the only damn person in L.A. who doesn't,' Chuck snorted. 'Ironic, I like it.'

'Look, I'll cut to the chase. Chuck and I have been trying to find the right person to write my book for so long but everyone here has a pre-conceived idea about me.'

'Half the writers in town have been dreaming about landing this job for years,' Chuck interrupted. 'For real, some of them have probably penned the whole damn thing already, just waiting for the call you know what I'm sayin'?'

My focus flicked back to Jason. I could hear my heart beating faster.

'So I haven't found anyone I'd be happy working with. Until now.'

I jolted under the intensity of his gaze.

'But you don't know anything about me, Jason. You haven't read my CV or any of my books.'

'Yeah OK I apologise for that. I've got a short attention span for books but I will read them.'

'Don't worry, I won't force you to,' I laughed.

He reached out and placed his hand on my knee. I wobbled on the barstool and caught a glimpse of Chuck's eyebrows disappearing under his fringe.

'I'm impulsive and instinctive, Bailey. I live my life according to ocean swells. I catch a sixty-foot wave based on my gut feeling about whether it will kill me or not. I take risks and so far it's paid off.'

I blew air up into my hairline.

'Gosh, you and I really are polar opposites. I would do none of the above.'

Chuck spread his arms theatrically.

'The perfect team,' he hooted.

I tapped the side of my champagne flute anxiously.

'I don't know. I did not expect this. When do you need an answer?'

Jason shrugged one shoulder.

'Now would be good. We work fast here in L.A.'

'I'm beginning to realise that. I feel as if someone pressed fast forward the minute I landed at LAX.'

I ran my hand through my long, black hair.

We had only known each other for a couple of hours and already Jason and I had met, flirted, had an affair, been caught out by a Choo-wielding maniac, had a fight, made up, become friends and started talks about going into business together. If this were England, I thought, we would still be eyeing each other awkwardly across the room and building up to a handshake.

'It's a guaranteed bestseller,' Chuck pressed on. 'This guy is massive.'

I blinked and suppressed the obvious comment.

'I don't know, my life is in England.'

'I understand but I could trade you England for Hawaii.'

I raised one eyebrow.

'Then Tahiti, South Africa, the beaches of Europe.'

I raised both eyebrows.

'A year on the professional surfing tour writing about my life on the world's best beaches.'

I stopped breathing.

Seeing the expression of disbelief on my face, Chuck threw his arms skywards and shouted – 'Welcome to L.A., girlfriend, the land of opportunities.'

I glanced at Chuck and started to laugh. My eyes then moved to Jason and past him to the glossy people networking around the party. They were not sitting back waiting for inspiration, they were out there grabbing life by the collar and dragging it to where they wanted it to be.

I gulped the dregs of my champagne and, for the second time that night, felt something fizz inside me that urged me to go for it. Tristan would disapprove of my choice but he was not the one who had to search the depths of his imagination and actually write a book. I had come to L.A. to find inspiration and here it was staring me in the face.

Slowly and with a certain amount of trepidation, I held out my empty glass towards Jason.

'Fill it up,' I said with a smile, 'looks like we have something to celebrate.'

HAWAII

Four

Only one month later I found myself in Hawaii for the final event of this year's tour where Jason was hoping to seal a thirteenth world title; lucky for some. I was there to get a taste of tour life that I would be embarking on in full the following year and to get to know both Jason and the sport. I was staying with Jason and Chuck on the North Shore of Oahu, the home of some of the world's most infamous big waves. Oahu was a place where grandparents surfed alongside their grandchildren. It was the birthplace of surfing and an intrinsic part of the culture. The missionaries in the nineteenth century had tried to ban the sport for being too sexual but it had returned with a vengeance and was deep in the blood of the Hawaiian people. The beautiful and fit male and female bodies emerging minute after minute from the surf, however, confirmed the sexual reputation. Six-packs were not something bought in the beer aisle of the supermarket on this island.

Our beachfront house was a cornflower blue, architecturally designed, wooden home nestling in a perfectly tended garden of towering palm trees and hibiscus flowers. A wooden lookout post like a childhood den hovered above the beach at the front of the garden. From there, Jason watched the deadly waves of the Banzai Pipeline crashing onto the reef. Sitting alongside him, I was aware of the searching eyes of the public and the lenses of photographers focused on us from the beach. I was a friend of surfing royalty, which meant I had the best ticket in town. The lifestyle I had tasted so far was indeed fit for a princess.

The previous few weeks had been a whirlwind. I had spent days convincing myself I was doing the right thing while brushing up on my surfing knowledge, or rather opening the book of surfing knowledge at chapter one and starting at the very beginning. I had to convince Tristan that I was not selling my soul to the devil by writing a surfer's biography but that I was simply selling my writing talent for *money*. Something he had thus far failed to grasp as an essential feature of my career.

Jason, Chuck and I had talked money and talked contracts and then his people had talked to my people. He was important enough to have an entire entourage of people. My 'people' numbered just the one. While on important international calls, Tristan had repeatedly forgot he was on speakerphone, shaking his head and saying things like – 'A surfer? A professional surfer? What's that? Never heard of him, darling.'

At the age of sixty-four Tristan was a very successful and respected agent but this proposal had left him flummoxed. Much of the problem arose from Chuck's use of slang and surfing jargon. One conference call I had witnessed at the end of the negotiations went something like:

Chuck – 'So basically Trist' the word is Bailey will follow Jason on tour. She's gotta learn the breaks, see it all as it happens. It'll be a buzz, for real. The reef breaks like Teahupoo are the danger on Tour, Trist'. Beach breaks in

Europe are heavy, man but that ain't nothing compared to Chopes you know what I'm sayin'?'

Tristan - 'I haven't the foggiest, Charles.'

Chuck - 'Yeah, man, you should come check it out. I mean, for real, Chopes is heavy but Pipe, you can never underestimate Pipe. That's where B will start the book, at Pipe.'

Tristan - 'What sort of Pipe are we talking about, Charles?'

Chuck – 'Pipe. The Banzai Pipeline, North Shore Oahu. Tell me you've heard of the Banzai Pipeline, man.'

Tristan – 'Can't say I've come across it in my line of work, Charles.'

Chuck – 'You haven't lived, Trist', man. Bailey will freak when she sees Pipe and then she'll roll with us around the world for next year's dream tour. It'll be a blast. You know what I'm sayin'?

Tristan had coughed and loosened his tie from beneath his sagging jowls – 'Frankly, Charles, I'm as lost as a sailor without a compass. Do you think we could just move this on to the money and get it over with?'

Their worlds were not even in the same universe.

The deal had been agreed while I listened, feeling at last like a writer on the front line, which also brought with it the fear of taking up arms and going into battle. I knew I was a talented writer but I could write my surfing knowledge on a postage stamp. Jason was taking a gamble in hiring me, but so was I in forging a new direction for my career. Deep down I was terrified the gamble would finish me, just as gambling had destroyed my father.

Tristan did little to alleviate my fears.

'Well if deciphering this surfer fellow's grasp of English is a task akin to listening to his buffoon of a manager then you will be climbing a bloody big mountain in your search to find anything at all intelligent to write, darling. But find it you must, Bailey, because if this book goes belly up, you will have alienated your publisher and your readers for nothing and that will be a shame. I very much doubt you have a bestseller on your hands but I can see the thought of sand between your toes has you convinced. I am warning you, darling, this is the last chance saloon and the exit sign is flashing.'

We had not popped champagne to celebrate the contract.

'What are you thinking about?' said Jason, sitting down beside me and scooping a spoonful of berries and granola into his mouth.

'Just looking for inspiration,' I said, tapping my pen on my notebook. 'What is that stuff you're eating again?'

'Acai. Miracle Brazilian berries. They're great for your body, full of antioxidants. They're from the Amazon and help to sustain the forests by giving the local people an alternative income to logging.'

I smiled. Tristan was wrong about the intelligent conversation.

'Gosh, breakfast and an environmental crusade all in one.'

'I'm a surfer. I have to care about the environment or else I wouldn't have a job left. No clean oceans, no healthy surfers.'

'Very admirable.'

'So, do you want to try some?'

I screwed up my face at the granola-topped sludge that was the colour of Chuck's hair.

'No thanks, I'll stick to my coffee and blueberry muffin but thanks anyway.'

I bit off a generous mouthful of sumptuous muffin and gazed out at the stunning beach that had become my home. A group of four girls in bikinis that were more string than bikini caught my eye. Before coming to Hawaii I had never known how toned a woman's body could be without airbrushing. These girls had probably never heard of cellulite. I swallowed my mouthful with some difficulty.

'I think someone might be trying to get your attention, Jason,' I nodded while trying to suck in my cheeks. 'Actually can I try some of those miracle berries?'

'Sure. Why are you talking funny?'

'Hmm?'

I released my cheeks and dug into the health food. The lean girls were now practising yoga stretches just inches away from our garden, glancing at Jason from upside down through their smooth legs.

'Bloody hell, if she gets that string stuck up there she'll need a doctor.'

Jason crossed his arms over his naked torso and chuckled to himself as I sank lower into the wooden chair.

'Jason, are you going to go over there and speak to them before they start taking each other's bikinis off with their teeth?'

'And stop the show? Why?' he teased.

'Do things like this happen often to you?'

'All the time,' he said with a nonchalant shrug.

I set the acai bowl on the floor and rubbed my hands together.

'Right, I think it's about time we got down to some work, Jason.'

'What brought that on?'

'Because we haven't even started yet.'

'Yes we have. We're getting to know Hawaii. We've soaked up the aloha vibe, we've checked the surf, we've de-stressed in the hot-tub.'

'De-stressed? Jason, if you get any more de-stressed, you'll be dead.'

Jason raised his sunglasses to hit me with his incredible eyes.

'Come on, Bailey, they may call the contest on tomorrow. I'm relaxing and watching the surf today. Today is not a work day.'

'Is any day a work day?'

'Sure, you'll see soon enough. It's not always like this.'

I clicked the anxiety from my neck.

'But I haven't even learned anything about your work.'

Jason stood up and extended a hand. I heard the girls groan loudly on the beach when Jason's nut-brown six-pack became visible. Keeping my eyes fixed above his hemispheric pectoral muscles, I accepted the hand and let him pull me to my feet.

'This is my work,' he said, placing one hand around my shoulders and pointing at the topaz blue ocean with the other. 'These waves are my office.'

'Not a bad office admittedly.'

'Now, Bailey, to understand my work, the best thing you can do is come to the office with me.'

I looked at Jason and then back at the churning, hollow waves pounding the reef at a decibel level that would have most neighbours complaining.

'What? Out there? Are you joking? I don't mind looking at your office from here but I don't fancy having a skyscraper landing on my head thank you very much.'

'Alright,' he smirked, 'maybe not at Pipe but if you look at those waves on the next break at Ehukai Beach Park they are fine for you. Small and mellow. I promise you it won't hurt. Are you regular or goofy?'

I arched my eyebrow.

'Goofy? Cheeky bastard.'

'It means do you surf with your right foot forward?'

'I have no idea.'

'How would you skateboard?'

'Jason, do I look like the kind of girl who skateboards? I know you live in this world where grown adults play in the ocean, eat Brazilian berries for breakfast and look presentable in beachwear but I am a novelist from England. As a general rule we don't skateboard.'

Jason lifted both hands in surrender and laughed.

'Hey, I'm just trying to turn you into a surf chick.'

I tapped my nose.

'Tell you what, why don't you stick to the surfing and I'll stick to the writing?'

'Fine by me.' Jason paused and glanced over at the beach. 'Speaking of writing, can I borrow your pen?'

Jason took the pen, turned and walked out of the garden and onto the beach. The reaction of the people gathered there was as electric as if the Dalai Lama had just sauntered into Tibet. Girls fiddled with their hair and hurriedly applied lip-gloss. Grown men walked boldly up and shook his hand. Pushy parents grabbed their children and shoved them to the front of the excited throng.

'He'll be kissing babies next,' I laughed to myself.

My smile faded when Jason moved on from signing autographs on everything from books to bodies and made his way towards the yoga-tastic bikini babes.

'Or more likely making babies,' I tutted.

I turned away and headed for the hot tub to spend yet more hours busily doing nothing.

Five

It was the day of the contest final. After a year touring the world to compete for the world title, Jason and his fierce rival, Cain Ohana from Oahu were nail-bitingly close on points. The crown was about to be decided in the final heat of the very last event and by the end of the day Jason could have claimed his place in the sporting hall of fame by winning a record-breaking thirteenth world title.

'So tell me about Cain,' I said to Jason that morning over a fruit smoothie and a bowl of muesli.

Jason chewed slowly and meticulously like a wise old horse.

'What's to tell? He's an arrogant prick who got lucky and won two world titles.'

'So he got lucky twice?'

'Yes and he thinks he's going to get lucky again.' Jason held up a finger and tilted his head. 'Correction, he thinks he is talented enough to deserve another world title this year but he's not and he won't.'

There was an angry edge to Jason's voice. I could instantly tell Cain Ohana was one competitor who, beneath Jason's calm demeanour, really had him riled.

'He's Hawaiian isn't he?'

'Yeah well sort of. He grew up on the west side, Makaha. They make them tough over there but Cain was a haole.'

'What's a haole?' I asked. The word was pronounced 'howly'.

'A white guy. He was an orphan from California but adopted by a Hawaiian couple. They brought him here and the dad taught him to surf. He took to it straight away, stood up first time and all that jazz. They had no money but the mom worked like three jobs so Cain could do the contests. He owes them everything, you know, but he's still got a chip the size of Texas on his shoulder. He's dark. On the inside and the outside. He's tanned his skin so much to fit in, he's darker than most of the locals.'

'Wow, that's quite a story,' I said.

Jason inhaled sharply.

'Really? You want to go write his story instead?'

'Of course not, I just need to know everything about you for the book and your rivals are very much part of that.'

He nodded and lowered his eyes.

'You're right, I'm sorry.' He paused. 'I guess I'm a little tense.'

'Understandable on a day like this,' I said, even though I still knew very little about what to expect from the final of the Pipemasters.

'Basically they love Cain Ohana on this island. I will definitely be the underdog today.'

'Interesting. A reigning twelve-times world champ as the underdog. How does that work?'

Jason moved his tongue slowly around his mouth and peered up at the ceiling fan whirring above our heads.

'Intimidation, tactics, local advantage. Cain has his posse on the beach who cheer and holler so the judges hear it and it influences their decision. The judging is subjective in these comps so often the local guy gets a bit of help if you know what I mean?'

'Isn't that cheating?'

'Sometimes it works for you, sometimes against you. I've just got to make sure I surf twice as good, right?'

'Right,' I smiled. 'No pressure.'

'Only what I put on myself. I'm fit, I do good at Pipe so I've got nothing to lose.'

Other than a world title and an alleged five million-dollar bonus, I thought to myself.

'By intimidation, do you mean they threaten you?' I frowned, pulling my legs up underneath me on the chair.

'It happens but I have to ignore it. If Cain wants to send his gang to break my legs I can't stop him but so far it hasn't gone beyond words. Apart from one time but I won't go into that. You know, I can deal with it. It always comes down to just the two of us face to face in the water and I can definitely deal with that. I was injured earlier this year in Tahiti, so Cain got a result there. He jumps in when my luck or my confidence slip. He's shrewd like that, but he doesn't yet have his talent honed.'

'Not that I know much about the technique yet but I have to say he looked talented enough on that DVD,' I said, testing him for a reaction.

'What DVD?'

'Over there on the television. I found it on the front step this morning.'

I nodded to an open DVD case. Jason pushed himself up from the table, his biceps bulging, and walked over to pick it up. He silently read the blurb on the back.

'Cain must have had it sent over as a gift,' he said, nodding sagely. 'Nice touch.'

Jason ejected the DVD and snapped it in two. He then returned to the table, plonked himself down and returned to his laboured chewing. I watched him for a while, making mental notes for my book. I decided I would have to interview Cain Ohana if I were to truly understand the rivalry but I chose not to upset Jason's mental preparation any further at a time of mounting pressure. He had been quiet all morning so I guessed he was nervous but I did not yet know him well enough to know what made him tick. I wanted Jason to win, certainly because a record title would be great for the book, but also because I was already growing fond of him as a friend. I could sense the result meant the world to him.

'Is there a champ in the building?' hollered Chuck from behind the screen door.

He burst into the room and immediately overwhelmed it with his presence. He was tall and skinny but everything about him clamoured for space from his huge personality to his loud voice and his even louder red and green Aloha shirt. Out of L.A., Chuck discarded the sharp suits for colourful fashions, looking as if he had dressed by falling headfirst into his washing basket.

'It's all firing up out there, dude. Ready to see this guy blow up, Bailey?'

He made a fist and jabbed it towards me. I self-consciously returned the gesture.

'It's time Jason. They're ready for you out there. Man the crowd is buzzing. I'd say the girls are so wet with anticipation the tide just came in. No offence, B.'

'None taken,' I grimaced.

While Chuck and Jason discussed the plan of attack, I took the opportunity to slip away and prepare for the day ahead. I smoothed on enough sunscreen to protect me from a meteor shower, pulled my liquorice coloured hair into a low ponytail and topped it with a wide-brimmed cowboy hat. Chuck had left the house and Tyler was nowhere to be seen. I intended to grab a glass of ice-cold pineapple juice and then settle down in the quiet sanctuary of the garden to concentrate on the final. However, a wave of noise hit me when I opened the door to the terrace as if a tsunami had suddenly crashed into the house.

Our garden was packed with entrancing people whose bodies were built to be flaunted in skimpy beachwear. They were sipping beers and glasses of champagne. I immediately knew I was among the movers and shakers of the surfing fraternity. The ego in the air was palpable.

'Who's that?' I heard a girl say.

She had the sort of squeaky voice that made fingernails on a blackboard sound pleasant.

Her friend turned to look at me, her cat-like eyes searching me up and down for a clue. Portia. I had not expected to see her again. My heart thumped as if I was the one about to surf Pipeline.

'Oh her,' said Portia nonchalantly, wafting a delicate hand in my direction, 'she's Jason's bio whatsit. I mean she's writing some story on him or whatever. She's nobody important.'

She had a way of making a girl feel special.

Angry retorts and smart comebacks fizzed and popped behind my eyes but I was too new to the scene to react in the way Portia deserved. Stamping her book for a later date, I raised my chin, looked straight through Portia and proudly negotiated my way through the intimidating collection of surf stars, rock stars, movie stars and people whom I did not know but whose sunglasses were too large not to be concealing a star of some kind.

I picked out Chuck just by the colour of his hair and took my place beside him.

'It's action time, B.'

He handed me a beer and clinked his own bottle against mine.

'It's gonna be a showdown to remember, you know what I'm sayin'?'

We looked out at the beach. It was packed with an eclectic mix of locals, travelling surfers, tourists and media all straining to see the waves over the pack of hungry photographers three deep on the shoreline. The contest arena was empty yet the majority of the crowd sat with their eyes trained on the breaking waves. I had of course seen waves before, lolloping onto the shingle of south coast British shores but Pipeline was like nothing I could have imagined. Having to look *up* at the crests of waves took my breath away.

The powerful barrelling wave broke on dry reef. Within this reef, I had been told, lurked a maze of dangerous caves that could trap a surfer while waves powerful enough to wash away houses landed on them from above. Pipeline claimed lives. Only two days before I arrived, a twenty-five year old surfer from Brazil had paddled out at dusk for a few last waves before dark and never returned. His broken surfboard washed up on the beach the following day but his body had still not been found.

'Our four surfers have five minutes to paddle out into position then they have thirty-five minutes for the final,' explained the commentator, Rock O'Rafferty, to the assembled crowd of thousands on the beach and the millions watching the live online broadcast around the globe. 'The wave is scored according to its size and the manoeuvres completed by the surfer in what we call the most critical part of the wave. The two best waves of each surfer count as their final score. Today we will mostly be seeing tube rides but surfers of this calibre can be full of surprises. How could we forget the perfect ten-point ride Jason Cross scored here in the Pipemasters' final last year? The best surfing has seen since the glory days of Kelly Slater. Hold on to your hats, ladies and gentlemen, the heat is on.'

A klaxon wailed from the top of the judging tower and what sounded like a Red Indian war cry erupted from a house further along the beach.

'What the hell was that?'

Chuck tilted his head down almost onto my shoulder and muttered - 'The Tiger Sharks, Cain Ohana's gang. Man those guys will have been drinking since dawn. They'll be so stirred up, if Cain goes down, they'll go off.'

I turned towards Chuck.

'*When* Cain goes down you mean.'

'Goddammit I hope you're right, Bailey Brown. If our guy loses it could be the end of my career.'

'What about his?'

'Yeah yeah, that too.'

'Don't worry, Chuck,' I said, glancing out to the four figures sitting on their boards in the ocean waiting patiently for a wave, 'I have faith.'

'I had faith too 'til that bitch turned up.'

He nodded towards Portia.

'She's got no business coming in here stirring him up before the final. Hell she's only here so she can get her stupid face in the Press if he wins.'

'For a stupid face, it's a rather pretty one.'

Chuck shook his head.

'That girl is living proof that real beauty is on the inside you know what I'm sayin'? She may have a pretty face, but once you get to know the inside, man is she ugly.'

I had underestimated Chuck. He was very likely the only man in the vicinity who was not even tempted to jump Portia's dainty bones.

I rubbed his arm reassuringly.

'Come on, Chuck, Jason won't let her upset the apple cart.'

'I got no clue what that means, dude, but I'm with you girl. You're on our team,'

We clinked our bottles together again and I suddenly felt part of something. Feeling like I belonged was comforting. I sipped my beer and caught Portia's eye. She gave me a look that would scare children. It seemed she not only had the bones of a bird and the eyes of a cat but the hearing of a bat too. Something about Portia made me very uneasy. I had the distinct feeling we would be having a second run-in before too long.

Six

Before I had even managed to grasp the complexities of the scoring, ten of the thirty-five minutes had flown by like a daydream at a bus stop.

'So Jason has scored a seven and an eight, right?' I said to Chuck.

'Yep you got it and Cain has only had the eight-point-five, Cory has two sixes and Hayden is sitting on a five-point-seven-five, so Jason is in the lead. It's decided on the best two scores of each guy, you get me?'

I nodded and scribbled notes, looking up every couple of seconds to make sure I did not miss a wave. When the horizon bubbled, I knew a big set was approaching. My heart jumped back up into my mouth where it had been hiding for most of the heat. Watching Jason throw himself off the lip of a wave several storeys high was awe-inspiring. Each set of waves seemed larger, louder and more powerful than the last. Every time Jason caught a wave, he had to contend with the life-threatening drop, the watery rollercoaster of a ride, the dangers of wiping out and the paddle back out through moving walls of water. His office may have been a tropical beach but paradise clearly had its disadvantages. Whatever they were paying him would not be enough to make me paddle out there.

'Cain Ohana is in the barrel,' Rock O'Rafferty whooped when Cain disappeared from view into an immense tunnel of water. 'Still in, still in and BOOM, there he is. No time to breathe and he pulls into a second barrel. One mistake here and Cain could be slammed on the reef but this guy is something else. He's still in there. Two perfect stand-up barrels at Pipe and a huge re-entry. Awesome. Cain must know that is one hell of a score.'

Cain punched the air victoriously.

'Prick,' Chuck muttered.

The second wave roared onto the reef and I nibbled my fingers as I watched Jason digging his arms deep into the water to propel him over the lip that was beginning to froth. It looked like an angry monster foaming at the mouth.

There was an audible intake of breath when Jason took off, jumped onto the deck of the board with the grace of a ballet dancer and free-fell through the air.

'You gotta watch,' Chuck laughed, pulling my hands away from my eyes.

At the bottom of the drop, Jason's muscular legs absorbed the impact. The wave peeled to his left. A second later, the jaws of the angry beast closed around him, consuming him completely.

'OH MY GOD!' I shrieked.

'An epic tube ride from the reigning champ, ladies and gentlemen,' Rock cheered, rousing the crowd, many of whom were already on their feet. 'Man, that is so goddamn big, a whale could fit in there.'

'Where is he?' I squeaked, my voice now only audible to dogs.

I grasped Chuck's arm when a jet of water blasted from the end of the watery vortex and Jason appeared, outlined in a halo of water with one arm pointing at the sky.

A cheer loud of enough to dislodge the coconuts from the trees enveloped Jason's garden party.

'It's two perfect tens from Cain and J.C., ladies and gentlemen,' Rock announced.

The crowd on the beach erupted. Jason and Cain were indeed putting on the show the spectators had anticipated.

I looked at my watch. Five minutes remained. I then looked at Portia, who was applying her lip-gloss in preparation for the presentation ceremony.

'Is she even watching this?' I said, nudging Chuck.

'Huh? Nope, she doesn't give a shit about the surfing. She just likes the bits that come with the surfing like the money, the fame and the six-pack, you know what I'm sayin'?'

I knew precisely.

I stood on my tiptoes and strained my eyes against the sun to see Jason sitting out in the water. In between the sets of waves, the ocean was surprisingly still, which was the sign of a perfect Hawaiian ground swell. In Hawaii especially, it was advisable to sit and watch the ocean for at least a quarter of an hour before committing to surfing or swimming. Even sunbathing was a precarious activity. I had seen unsuspecting families from Japan settling themselves down for a picnic at the water's edge during a lull only to have the entire family and the latest hi-tech video camera knocked into next week by the next set of waves.

'With the minutes ticking away, the situation is Cain Ohana is in the lead with a ten and an eight-point-five. Jason Cross is just point-five behind with that perfect ten and an eight. Cory Jones is sitting on two sixes and Hayden has only caught one wave, a five-point-seven-five.'

The other two competitors seemed to have lost faith in their own ability to beat Jason and Cain. The final was clearly a battle between two rapacious surfing warriors fighting for the same prize: the world champion crown.

'If the situation stays the same, we will have a new world champion,' Rock explained.

As if responding to Rock's announcement, Jason began paddling up and down in the line-up searching for a wave that would improve on his eight-point ride and push him into the lead.

'He needs to go big,' said Chuck, opening another bottle of beer and inhaling half of it in a single mouthful. 'There's only time for one more set. This is it, B. A happy start to the book or a motherfuckin' tragedy?'

He ended with a comical grimace.

The crowd fell eerily silent when the final set darkened the horizon. Only the whoops of the Tiger Sharks pierced the tense atmosphere, informing Cain, their leader, that the final waves of the heat were imminent.

'Come on, Jason,' I whispered, clasping my hands in prayer.

The set approached like a gathering storm cloud. The spectators were on their feet jostling for a better view. Suddenly Cain began to paddle towards Jason, forcing him to react and paddle further to our left.

'Cain's pushing Jason too deep into the impact zone,' Chuck warned. 'Don't take the first one, man.'

I wished Jason had an earpiece like the cyclists in the Tour de France so that Chuck could advise him in the dying seconds.

The wave built behind Jason, growing the height of a lamppost with each couple of seconds. The sound of the tonnes of water moving at high speed towards the reef was incredibly loud. To Jason it must have been deafening, which may have been a blessing considering the taunts and heckling coming from the Tiger Sharks' house.

'You gonna die, Man.'

'Fuck, check him out, he's losing it.'

'Yeah, Brah, Cain is doin' it.'

'I feel like going over there and telling them to shut up,' I growled.

'They'd eat you alive,' said Chuck.

Thrusting himself forward with two final powerful strokes, Jason took off. His take off point was so deep, however, the wave had already started to break and the drop was beyond vertical. Jason flew through the air, his feet loosely connected to the sliver of fibreglass that was the only solid thing between himself and a wall of water several times taller than him. I watched him fall. He was upright but even I could see with my limited knowledge of physics that the lip of the wave had sent him on a dangerously arced trajectory. The knuckles on my hands turned white, Chuck's body stiffened beside me and a gurgling cry burst out from my throat without warning when Jason landed at the bottom of the wall and was concertinaed into the reef. His body crumpled as if he were made of paper and he disappeared from view.

We ran. Chuck was ahead of me, forcing his way through the people on the beach like a bull running through the crowded streets of Pamplona. When we reached the water's edge, the lifeguards were already mobilizing, carrying a spinal stretcher that instantly brought tears to my eyes. In the ocean, the water patrol guard on his jet ski desperately scanned the water for a sign of life.

'Jesus, where is he?' I cried, my eyes searching for an arm breaking the surface to show us he was alive.

Out of the corner of my eye I saw Cain take off on a wave. There might have been a world champion drowning in the water beneath him but as far as Cain was concerned, the heat was not over until the buzzer sounded. He wanted that world title by default or otherwise.

'There he is!' someone shouted.

The throng carried me along, my feet hardly touching the ground.

I tripped and fell, sand covering my face. It scratched the surface of my eyes when I blinked. I scrambled to my feet and tried to see.

People were in the water now, wading towards Jason. I finally exhaled when I saw he was alive and slowly dragging himself towards land. I realised I had been holding my breath for an improbably long time and my head was spinning.

'Leave him!' a lifeguard ordered, yanking an overzealous citizen rescuer out of the water. 'Let us do our job, people.'

The lifeguards ordered Jason to sit down on the sand. I saw his legs crumple just before he elected to obey. I picked my way through the silent onlookers. Some were taking photos and videos on their phones. Social media would soon be playing out the drama.

I caught up with Chuck, who let me through the human security fence to see Jason. He was hunched over his knees while the lifeguards busied themselves touching various parts of his battered body. His Lycra rash vest was shredded as if he had been thrown to the lions. Blood seeped through the holes, diluted by the water.

'Jason,' I breathed in a funereal volume, 'are you OK?'

Jason looked up at me as a broken man. His usually lustrous eyes were as red as his sanguineous skin. He smiled weakly and when he opened his mouth to try and speak, Rock O'Rafferty's inappropriately jovial voice sang out over the P.A system.

'A perfect ten for Cain Ohana there on his final wave, ladies and gentlemen. Two perfect tens for the local boy. I have news that Jason Cross is fine so we can all relax. What a final, what a showdown and what a result. We have a new world champion, people. His name is Cain Ohana.'

'Not really,' said Jason in response to my question.

'Outta my way, whore!' I heard Portia scream.

She dragged me away from Jason by my hair.

'Baby, baby, are you OK? Jason, oh my God, what happened?'

'If you had been watching you might have seen it,' I seethed, rubbing the roots of my ponytail.

Portia rounded on me, her devil eyes inches from mine. She reacted like a rattled wasp in a jam jar when her temper took hold.

'Step back you English bitch, this world champion is mine.'

'He's not world champion anymore,' Chuck said, pulling Portia away from my face.

I wiped her spittle from my cheek.

'If you were concentrating on the surfing instead of your make-up you would have known that. So, do you still want him, *babe*?'

Portia looked from Chuck to me and down at Jason. If a photographer had not appeared at that moment to take a shot of the scene I swear she would have walked away. World champion or not, Jason had become my friend and I made a note to myself to sort out this mess. A devastatingly gorgeous millionaire and dozen-times world champion surfer he might have been, but his choice in girlfriends really sucked.

Seven

I did not see Jason for the next few days. Finding the Press intrusion and the boisterous, seemingly unending sound of partying coming from the nearby Tiger Sharks' house unbearable, Jason took a Hawaiian Airlines shuttle to the Big Island of Kona and vanished from the radar. Portia also vanished at precisely the same time, which in some ways was a relief but also made me concerned that she had her claws in Jason when he was at his most vulnerable. Chuck was busy drowning his sorrows in Hawaiian cocktails as the competitive year drew to a close and the surfing community celebrated or commiserated in an end of term manner. Knowing as I did very few people, I spent much of my time alone. Over the first two days I soaked for so long in the hot tub I sweated off a dress size, which would have been great had my skin not resembled used clingfilm. I then decided to follow the example of the locals and power walk on the beach but I was not in the same league as the Hawaiian surfer girls who had tanned, lean legs rippling with toned muscle. The day I was overtaken by a heavily pregnant girl in a bikini who resembled a supermodel with a Kinder egg attached to her six-pack, I realised I had a lot of work to do.

Oahu was both breathtakingly beautiful and rugged. The North Shore was the rural part of the island and had remained largely unspoilt while Honolulu grew as the city on the South Shore. Quirky wooden beach houses sat comfortably among the more recent millionaire dwellings that were still in keeping with the modest character of the Sunset Beach area. One of our neighbours had a tree growing through the centre of her house because she had not wanted to fell the tree to make room for her development. Sustainability of the environment was respected and protected because, as Jason had pointed out, many of the jobs relied on it for their future.

I explored the local village of Haleiwa, which had a charming marketplace as its centre, selling everything from black pearls to carved wooden Tiki Gods and surfboards. The sweet local delicacy was shave ice; a huge cone of crushed ice atop a dollop of ice cream and soft beans covered in a rainbow of sugar syrups. I ate so many on the third day I gave myself a multi-coloured nosebleed.

Every second shop in Haleiwa was a surf shop and it soon became clear I was in the very heart of the history of the sport. I wandered around the local surf museum run by a man who had enjoyed the Sixties to such an extent he had decided to stay there. He reminded me of Garth from *Wayne's World*. Although the museum was no larger than my mother's front room, he managed to string the tour out to an incredible three hours, largely because he spoke so slowly I could have fitted whole sentences between each word. I did, however relish the opportunity to view the surfing memorabilia that dated back to the 1900s. I learned every detail of the evolution of the surfboard, from the first bulky wooden door-like boards that were twelve-feet long, to the boards with a single fin as their rudder, on to the twin-fins, the three-finned modern board known as the 'thruster' and four-finned 'quads'.

The island vibe was so relaxed I met people as mellow as the museum curator everywhere I went. There was no unnecessary rushing around. The speed limit everywhere except on the one freeway into Honolulu was thirty-five miles an hour. The freeway limit itself was fifty-five. People surfed before and after work and talked about surfing when they weren't doing it. Of course stress existed in Hawaii but the North Shore locals seemed to either have the time or they made the time to enjoy life. The Aloha spirit was infectious and I soon realised my own reality was almost a distant memory. I hardly looked at my watch anymore and at one point I had to stop and think what day it was. However, I knew I was in danger of becoming too complacent and complacency did not produce best-selling books. Jason may have earned his break but I had not. I had work to do before the Christmas break with or without him.

Back home at the beach house I looked out my trusty notebook that had a pleasant crêpe feel to the pages. I had always enjoyed the sensation of pen on paper and still favoured this method for my note taking and first drafts. I grabbed a pen and my i-Phone and threw them in my beach bag. I then stood in front of the bathroom mirror and studied my reflection.

My face suited a tan and the sand and salty air had naturally exfoliated my skin. I was what one would call an English rose. My skin was usually chalk white in direct contrast to the deep black of my hair, which was my crowning glory. I had an oval face and big eyes that were as green as a leprechaun's jacket. Not having been blessed with thick eyelashes, I applied two coats of waterproof mascara and stepped back, stretching out my already wide mouth. I was neither pretty nor particularly beautiful but, as my father had always said, I had striking features in all the right places.

'Lip-gloss,' I muttered and applied a layer thick enough to catch flies.

My outfit was understated. A pair of denim shorts skimming my mid-thigh and a bright white vest top that clung to my breasts. I pulled my hair back into a knot tied at the nape of my neck and finished the look with a pair of thin silver hoop earrings.

'Not bad,' I said to myself.

I slung my bag over my shoulder, stepped into my sandals and strode confidently out of the house.

My confidence wavered somewhat when I walked up the path to the Tiger Sharks' house and my flip-flops noisily announced my arrival.

'Chick!' shouted a brute with a shaved head whose hair had been replaced by jet-black tattoos.

'Good observation,' I muttered. 'So are you the genius of the operation?'

'Huh?' he sniffed before returning to screwing the fins into his surfboard.

I stepped boldly onto the terrace at the front of the house and raised my arm to knock on the doorframe but it swung open before my fist connected with the wood. The unmistakeable sweet aroma of marijuana wafted through the fly screen.

'Who da fuck are you?' said another man through the screen whose tattoos had also crawled onto his face and neck.

I assumed he was assigned to door duty but if he had aspirations as a butler he really had to work on his greeting.

'I'm Bailey Brown,' I said with a forced smile.

The man looked me up and down and ran a thick tongue across his lips. They were outlined with a white residue that could either have been salt water or cocaine. I shifted my feet under his sexually charged gaze but stood my ground.

'Who is it, Brah?' said a voice from inside the house.

'Some English wahine called Bailey, Brah. She got a good rack.'

I glanced down at my breasts.

'Kind of you to notice. Now on a more professional note, I wondered if I could have a word with Cain Ohana. I'm writing a book on Jason Cross and I needed Cain's input.'

The screen slid forcibly across and Cain Ohana appeared behind the burly bouncer. In contrast, he was willowy and handsome with defined bone structure and eyes as black as my hair. He wore a T-shirt slashed at the shoulders to reveal muscular arms tanned darker than the true local. The fabric clung to his torso like the skin on a sausage. There was not an ounce of fat on his body. Cain shook his head as if he had hair but it was shaved so close to his scalp I could not tell what colour his hair would naturally have been.

'You need my input, huh? And what input would that be?'

'Your dick put in her mouth,' the tattooed oaf roared, finding himself hilarious.

'Shut up, Brah,' said Cain, smacking his friend on the arm.

He looked me up and down.

'You know people don't usually just rock up here uninvited asking for things and get away with it.'

I raised my chin.

'I'm not most people, Cain.'

He stared at me then a smile spread across his face, his teeth as white as the flesh of a coconut. He looked surprisingly friendly when he smiled.

'I like your style, Sista,' he said, then held out a hand and guided me into the house.

I kicked off my sandals at the door, as was the Hawaiian custom, and slipped past him into an open plan sitting room and kitchen. The first thing I noticed was the number of bodies slumped around the room, many semi-naked. Surfboards covered every spare inch of floor and walls. The faces of the Tiger Sharks and their girls turned to inspect the intruder. Cain Ohana slipped a warm arm around my shoulders as we made our way across the room and lowered his mouth to my ear. His voice made me shiver.

'Don't mind my friend, he's got a big mouth. Sure I'll give you my input. I heard about you and your book.'

'Really? How?'

'This surfing world's a tight knit community. We don't miss much.'

His attempt at cosiness unsettled me. I tried to force myself to relax and accepted a bottle of cold beer from the over-sized fridge.

'I just need to ask you some questions about your rivalry with Jason.'

Cain slowly swallowed his beer. His Adam's apple was prominent in his slim neck.

'Sure thing,' he said. 'Come out on the lanai and we can talk.'

I nodded and made to squeeze past Cain as he rested against the work surface.

'Talk first,' he said, burning into me with eyes so deep they made me gasp, 'get to know each other later.'

Eight

After a nervous start, we talked for over two hours uninterrupted by the crowd of people in the house who clearly thought midday was an appropriate time to start partying again.

'Are they your family?' I asked.

Cain lifted his legs onto the table in front of us. I noticed he had slightly webbed feet. I was about to comment on whether webbed feet helped him in the water, but he was already talking and I didn't want to interrupt his flow.

'They might as well be my family. They're my ohana, my Hawaiian family. They do better for me than my real family.'

'Do you know your real family?'

He shook his head fervently.

'Nah. My real dad sent me a picture of himself so I know what he looks like, but I don't know who he is.'

'Does he look like you?'

He shrugged, attempting nonchalance.

'I guess, a bit yes and a bit no. I don't care. Maybe one day he might knock on my door for my money or my fame but fuck that, I'll slam that door right back at him.'

I paused to let him collect his thoughts.

'But you were originally from California like Jason?'

Cain lowered his legs and spread his knees apart. He rested his elbows on them and leaned perilously close to me.

'Let's get this right, Sista. There ain't nothing the same between Jason Cross and me. Get it?'

'But you're both champions. You're both at the top of your game,' I said, taking my life in my hands.

Cain sat back, grinned and opened his arms wide. He turned his head from side to side.

'Well I sure can't see him up here with me. Jason's finished. Sorry to burst your bubble but he ain't a champ no more. He's running and he ain't coming back. It's my time now.' He leaned forward and tapped my notebook. 'Write that in your little book.'

Cain Ohana had a rawness about him that made me think he could kill a man one minute and celebrate with his nearest and dearest the next. He was calculated and somewhat fierce but stunning at the same time. His deep-set black eyes reflected the darkness bubbling beneath the surface. However, I wondered how much of the aggression was a mask he wore to hide any hint of a soft side. Of the pain his unsettled childhood had caused him. Cain was a fascinating character. He was complex and driven by a dark force. It was safe to say I had never met a man like him before.

'Thanks for talking to me,' I said when he returned from the kitchen and handed me another ice-cold beer.

'Actually I really shouldn't have another. I'm not great at drinking during the day.'

'As long as you keep drinking, I'll keep talking, Sista,' he grinned. 'I'm celebrating.'

I found him hard to refuse and by four p.m. I had a wealth of quotes for the book and a rather fuzzy head. At last I felt like a writer at work.

'Thanks for your help,' I said, 'but I should be going.'

'Where to, huh? Jason ain't there. No point sitting in that big house all alone now is there, Sista?'

For the surfer with a reputation as a gangster, he had been incredibly accommodating and welcoming.

'Come and party with us,' he said. 'We never had an English girl join the Tiger Sharks before.'

I put my phone and notebook in my bag and stopped to think. Voices inside my head told me to leave. Told me I was in the wrong camp and skating on very thin ice despite the blistering temperatures. Yet other voices told me to celebrate my own achievement of scoring an exclusive interview with the new world champion, who had very likely been misconstrued by people because of his fierce rivalry with Jason. Part of me wanted to do like the L.A. glamorous people and make the most of this opportunity. It went against my natural instinct but then taking this job had been unnaturally impulsive for me and that had been the right choice. Jason had sneaked off and left me to my own devices. Deep down I wanted to embrace the dangerous vibe that hung over Cain's posse and throw caution to the wind. After all, when would I ever be in Hawaii again celebrating a surfing world title with the new champion and his entourage? Besides, this was essential research.

'OK, I'll stay,' I said.

'Cool, but no more work. I gave you input, now it's time you gave me some.'

'I have no idea what you're talking about but OK. Show me how a world champion celebrates,' I grinned.

Cain opened the door and shepherded me into the party. The lifeless bodies from earlier were now upright and the atmosphere was electric. Punk music blasted out of the surround sound system. The house itself was a spectacular architecturally designed wooden pentagon with huge windows on four of the sides and a cinema screen on the fifth. Images of Cain surfing tropical waves flashed endlessly on the screen. A little egotistical, I thought, to play a movie of oneself at one's own party but judging by the adoring faces staring at the film, Cain's ego trip was welcomed.

'Bailey, these are my Brahs, the Tiger Sharks,' said Cain.

I turned to smile at the men lined up in the kitchen. The faces that greeted me were a mixture of ugly, hard and uglier.

'Junior.'

'Orca.'

'Rosario.'

'Maika'i.'

'Waipahe.'

They said, standing to attention.

'Maika'i means good looking,' Cain explained, placing a proud arm around Maika'i's hunched shoulders.

'Really? Gosh your parents had good foresight,' I lied, trying not to focus on Maika'i's crooked nose and derelict teeth.

'Waipahe means good-natured in Hawaiian,' Cain carried on just as Waipahe, the tattooed machine who had greeted me at the door, opened a beer bottle with his teeth and proceeded to chew the metal bottle top.

If Jason, as many people criticised, had chosen to surround himself with the beautiful people, then Cain had obviously done his level best to do the opposite.

'And Orca means…'

'Killer whale, I know that one,' I interjected, glancing nervously at the bull of a man whose eyes were towards the side of his very odd shaped head. 'Cain is there a bathroom I could use?'

I meandered up the vast, curved staircase that led up to the bedrooms and a bathroom so immense a real tiger shark could have splashed around in the bath. Three lithe girls were prettying themselves in front of the huge mirror that covered one entire wall, reminding me of a dance studio.

'Hello,' I said, slipping past them into the separate toilet.

'Hi,' they sang in response, their word somehow stretching to three syllables.

Their false smiles were wider than their waists.

I closed the door and sat on the toilet to reflect on the day so far. I had made progress, which I was proud of and I felt I had made a valuable contact in Cain. His M.O. was the polar opposite to Jason's professional and more Hollywood style camp but they shared characteristics in that they were both confident, successful, driven, determined to beat the other and, dare I say it, more than averagely attractive.

Long after I had finished I stayed there listening to the girly conversation outside the door.

'Yeah like we had dinner on Maui with Tiger Woods and some other tennis players.'

'Mimi, Tiger Woods like plays golf.'

'Serious? What*ever,* it's all the same to me. And that girl was at the party, the one in the new HBO series.'

'Oh my god, she is like a totally skinny double zero.'

'I know, Janey, and in person like she is sooo even skinnier. She is like totally anorexic.'

'COOL.'

'Totally cool. You know I think like if I was anorexic I still wouldn't get skinnier than a size two.'

'Worth a try though huh?'

I felt like stuffing a toilet roll in my mouth to stop myself screaming.

'So did you do it with Jason or not, Mimi?'

My ears pricked up.

'Um no he wasn't up for it, like totally weird, but I did do it with Cory and Josh.'

'At the same time?'

'Like yuh huh.'

They cackled like the Macbeth witches.

'So like who's the new girl? Do I have to worry?'

'I doubt it. You've seen her she's like totally pale and plain. Have you seen what she's wearing?'

I glanced down at myself and frowned.

'I know, tragedy. But who is she anyway? I don't remember her on tour before.'

'Like apparently she's Jason's new girl but God knows why, she doesn't even model.'

'No way, Kirsti. Is she a movie star?'

'Hullo, Mimi, does she look like a movie star?'

'Portia said she's some nerdy writer.'

I held in a gasp by covering my mouth. They were talking about me! Had they already forgotten I was just metres away or did they not care?

'But even if Jason is screwing her she is like so not Cain's type. Don't worry, Janey, he won't do her, she's too plain. I bet she doesn't even have a Brazilian. English girls are so weird like that.'

When I strode purposefully out of the toilet and squeezed between them to check my reflection, their faces froze back into their false smiles. Or that could have just been the effect of the Botox.

'Great acoustics in here don't you think?' I beamed. I leaned closer and ran a finger over my lips. 'Damn, I wish I'd remembered my lip-gloss. I've given so many blowjobs today my lips are quite raw. Oh well, every job has its disadvantages. Bye now.'

Turning on my heel, I left them with a smile and a sway of my hips. As I left the bathroom I heard the one called Mimi say - 'Oh my GOD, like did she just say that?'

'OMG she so did,' her friend gasped, 'but like what's a coostick?'

Nine

Cain was waiting for me at the bottom of the stairs. He was surrounded by a flock of blonde girls with silicone breasts who all looked identical to the ones in the bathroom. It would not have surprised me if the surfers routinely took home the wrong girl by mistake. Or perhaps the interchangeable chicks were part of their cunning plan. They could always plead innocence when they 'accidentally' picked the wrong one and got caught cheating.

The girls gazed adoringly at Cain and I noted a thin covering of white powder beneath their button noses. It was evident the coke I had heard being offered at the party was not the fizzy sort for the designated drivers.

'Sandy, Jenny, go see Orca huh?' said Cain.

He tapped two of the girls on the bum, sending them tottering away towards the Tiger Sharks. The others followed, their taut backsides wiggling in symphony.

'It's like human pick 'n' mix,' I said, finally alone with Cain. 'Sorry I didn't mean to say that out loud.'

Cain laughed.

'Yeah, Sista, you're right. They are kinda the same. A guy could get confused.'

He winked and I knew my theory had been proven right.

'But you, you're different. You're interesting. I like that.'

I clamped my back teeth together when Cain moved so close I could almost hear his blood pumping.

'I like like you,' he sighed.

'You like *like* me. Is that a double amount of liking?'

'Could be.'

I turned to look at him but he was too close for comfort and cross-eyed wasn't my best look. There was something very alluring about him. His body, his eyes, his face and his confidence ticked all the right boxes. I gasped when Cain's mouth closed on my ear and his tongue licked my skin. I squeezed my eyes shut as a ripple of wanting ran down from my neck to my feet and back again at incredible speed. When I opened my eyes, I was surprised the music had not stopped with the sudden scratching sound of a needle on a record because it was as if someone had pressed the pause button at the party. Every eye in the room was fixed on us. The Tiger Sharks stared open mouthed at their leader. The pick 'n' mix blondes clasped their bony hands to their overly made-up faces. The rock stars and movie stars smiled approvingly and returned to their debauched activities. Feeling like the first girl at the school disco to slow dance, I held my breath and felt a blush creep across my face. Cain obliviously continued kissing my neck. His breath was hot and I could smell the sweet scent of his body. He was so overpowering, he had the ability to make me feel small and weak, yet there was something about being with the man every girl in the room so desperately wanted that made my inner strength surge.

'Come upstairs with me,' Cain groaned into my ear.

I wanted to say no. I wanted to be the one girl there to turn him down. I wanted to think I was better than Janey and Mimi and the rest of the girls who were on their own version of the world surfing tour, bedding as many of the stars as they could. Yet when Cain took my hand and led me upstairs I followed. I followed because I hadn't had sex for so long and because I had never had a one-night stand and because I was in beautiful Hawaii where nobody knew me. I followed because, of all the girls at the party, he had picked me. I followed because deep down I wanted to win.

When we reached the top of the stairs Cain turned me towards him and traced his finger across my lips.

His eyes that had seemed so black and menacing now sparkled as if they were on fire, reflecting the heat between my legs.

One minute his lips were pressing against mine, the next I was lying in the centre of a four-poster bed the size of a limousine with his mouth tracing every inch of my naked torso. I writhed beneath his touch, his hands following his tongue, massaging me and making me feel so alive.

I pressed my eyelids together and let the sound of the ocean outside the open window cascade over me. The tropical breeze wafting across the bed cooled the heat of my body just enough to make his sensual touch bearable.

What am I doing? I asked myself. *This is not like me at all.*

It must only have been five o'clock on a Friday afternoon and there I was in Hawaii being licked all over by the surfing champion of the world when back in my real world I would have been sitting alone in front of my computer eating liquorice allsorts and hoping for inspiration.

There was not much searching to do. Inspiration had found me.

I opened my eyes and had to bite my tongue to stop myself crying out when I saw the naked body of Cain Ohana straddling me. He was lithe yet muscular and the colour of espresso. Across his firm chest was tattooed the outline of the Hawaiian Islands.

I groaned as he moved down my body and I offered no resistance when he pulled off my knickers. The only time my brain kicked into gear was when he moved to enter me without a condom.

'Sensible girl,' he said and reached for a condom but the look in his eye told me he was not used to being told what to do by a woman.

Finally he was ready and, judging by the feeling between my legs that was as moist as the ocean outside our window, I was ready too. He licked me then moved up my body and when our lips met, he thrust his tongue inside my mouth at the same time as he thrust himself inside me. I cried out but his mouth absorbed the sound.

'I don't usually do this,' I gasped while we moved together. 'I'm never impulsive. I'm not that kind of girl.'

'Sure you're not,' he said, thrusting harder.

He was vigorous and confident. He made me relax and he made me explode with lust. He was everything I imagined a champion of the world to be. When he came, he lay on top of me breathing heavily until his body fell limp. I did not climax but neither did I complain. It was admittedly a selfish outcome, but my body was celebrating nonetheless. For once, being impulsive felt fantastic.

We showered together then Cain returned to the party and left me to get dressed. I smoothed cocoa butter from the bathroom cabinet all over my skin, revelling in my own sensuality. The moment replayed over and over in my mind when I stood at the open window gazing out at the turquoise ocean stretching to the distant horizon. I smiled. It was not love of course, it was lust. I was not looking for love and neither was Cain but we had connected and enjoyed each other for what it was. I slipped into my clothes and took one more look at the horizon. Since arriving in Hawaii, life had felt so much bigger and full of prospects. Just seeing the sunset every night had opened my eyes to what was out there if I took a moment to stop and look. I had not, however, that morning expected to experience a moment of dangerous passion I would remember forever.

When I walked back downstairs, I watched Cain mingling comfortably with people I had only seen in gossip magazines. He walked with a swagger. He was desirable; he knew it and I had simply reinforced the fact. I allowed myself a smile. Squeezing past two girls who were comparing their real diamond belly button piercings, I poured myself a glass of champagne and enjoyed the fizz of the bubbles on my tongue.

'You know like you shouldn't be so stoked about what just happened. Cain only slept with you because you're Jason's girl.'

The bubbles popped. I turned to see Mimi and her entourage lined up behind me like a firing squad.

'Excuse me?'

Mimi pushed out her already pert breasts and spoke very slowly.

'I said, bitch, Cain only fucked you because you're Jason's girl and not for any other reason.'

'Gosh you do have a way with words but I have to disappoint you, I'm not Jason's girl.'

'Sure you are,' said Mimi with a well-practised pout, 'you live with him right?'

'Yes but only in a professional capacity.'

Mimi nodded towards the Tiger Sharks. They flanked Cain who was chatting away animatedly and laughing. When he began to add actions to his story, my stomach tightened sharply towards my spine.

'Then you're like totally his girl. You're part of Jason's crew and they love messing with Jason's crew. D'you get it?'

I stopped and watched open mouthed as Cain made unmistakeable gestures with his hands. I prayed he was not doing what I thought he was doing but he was clearly not playing charades.

'Yeah and like Cain totally hates Jason,' said Janey.

I turned mechanically to look at them, my face set in an expression of grim acceptance.

'He did you to get at Jason,' said Kirsti with a self-satisfied smile.

'He'd do anything or' – Mimi looked me up and down as if I was something on the sole of her shoe – '*anyone* just to mess with Jason's head.'

I had no witty response. I just blinked at them and shakily replaced my glass of champagne on the counter.

'And you like totally fell for it.'

'Yeah like hook, line and whatsit.'

'My God like how humiliating?'

Their laughter made my hackles stand on end.

'Shit, girl you have got like so much to learn,' said Mimi.

She clicked her fingers and turned on her Manolo heel.

'Sooo much,' said Janey, 'like totally.'

'Welcome to the tour, bitch,' said Kirsti with a wink. 'Just like Jason, you lose.'

She followed her friends like a proud little duckling. I could still hear them laughing when I grabbed my bag and headed for the door.

'Did the earth move?' Cain called after me over the noise of the party.

I froze, my hand shaking on the door handle. I pressed my lips together and forced myself to turn around and face him across the room. My eyes narrowed to hold his victorious stare.

'I didn't feel a thing,' I said nonchalantly and walked out of the house with my head held high.

Ten

I had never imagined an evening in Hawaii could be so utterly painful. The house was empty so I sat by myself staring at the four walls. I could not believe I had allowed myself to fall for Cain's charms. I was no better than Mimi and her friends whom I had been so ready to mock. Regret weighed heavily on my shoulders.

I resisted the urge to call my sister and confess all, which showed the extent of my desperation. We did not have the tendency to tell each other everything. In fact, my sister and I had the sort of relationship that could well have fizzled out were we not connected by DNA.

Joanna was ten years older than me and had a grand house in the neighbouring county, but lived a life several planets away from my own. She had trained as a doctor and had always been the power-suited career woman type until our father committed suicide when I was fifteen and she was twenty-five. My father lost everything we owned on a horse called Donkey Jacket. The clue was in the name.

Joanna subsequently married the first wealthy father figure she found who made her feel safe. Gerry was a pompous arsehole who did not deserve her. I suspected she knew this was true but could not admit it to herself. Her situation frustrated me but I still loved her. I also adored her son, my only nephew, Zac. As for Gerry, we had an understanding. He understood I disliked him immensely and I understood he could not give two hoots what I thought of him because I was wholly insignificant in his world.

I found my own security in deciding never to rely on a man for my happiness or financial means again and so I concentrated on my career. All that remained of my father were memories and an antique sports car that we had succeeded in hiding from the creditors. It was my inheritance and I loved it as if it were part of my father. I had also inherited a desire never to gamble the way my father had, which was why I had enjoyed a life free of risk. Right at that moment, however, I felt like my father's daughter. I had indeed gambled and lost.

Not being able to face Joanna's doubtless judgemental reaction to what I had done, I craved the company of someone completely self-centred who would not focus on the sort of day I had had. I picked up the phone and called Chuck.

'Chuck, where are you?'

'Bailey, dude, I was just gonna call you. I was in a hot tub enjoying myself with some bikini model chicks but now I am freaking out at the airport.'

'Why? What's happened?'

I was rather relieved to hear mine was not the only problem.

'What's happened? Man, Jason is totally tripping this time. He calls me this morning from Kona, says he's gonna retire, for real. RE-TIRE! I mean, goddamnit, how can he even think about retiring now? What the fuck is he gonna do, and, much more importantly, what the fu-uck am I gonna do, you know what I'm sayin'? How can he do this to me the selfish prick?'

I relaxed a little, pleased to be able to concentrate on helping somebody else.

'Well it must be hard to deal with losing a world title, not to mention a multi-million dollar bonus, Chuck.'

'What*EVER*. Like I lost fifteen percent of that bonus, but, you know, get over it, dude. Move on. Make a different few million. Don't just be a freakin' loser and give up.'

'Well I guess Jason has been doing this for a long time. He's been a pro surfer since he was, what, seventeen? He's won a dozen titles. Maybe he's just had enough and wants to relax for a bit.'

Chuck clicked his tongue.

'Bullshit, Jason doesn't do relax. This is his life, man. The fame, the competitions, and the travel. He's not ready to settle down and especially not with you know who. Without the tour, he'll fall apart, for real. B, if we don't sort this right now we are fucked with a capital F U C K E D.'

'We? What do you mean *we*?'

'Well for one you won't get a year on tour on the world's best beaches.'

'Bugger.'

'And for two if he can give up on the tour just like that he can give up on the book, you know what I'm sayin'? He's in a bad place right now and I know Jason. When he's in a bad place he closes in on himself. He's not gonna wanna go shouting about his life in some book.'

'OK I'm listening.'

'Portia's in his ear like the freaking devil on his shoulder telling him this and that and shit and asking him to quit the tour to go hang out in Hollywood. I know it, for real.'

I stood up and gazed out of the window at the view. The reflection of the full moon floated on the glassy ocean. I should have known a life like this was too good to be true, especially for a girl like me who was not genetically predisposed to tanning evenly.

The day was turning out to be a disaster but I was not willing to let Jason give up on our book just on a whim and I was damned if I was going to let Portia get her way.

'Portia doesn't like me, B, but she sure as hell hates any other woman having an influence over Jason. Especially one as smart as you,' Chuck said as if reading my mind.

'Well I am not giving up that easily Chuck. I need this job.'

'Now you're talking, girl. Look I'm at the airport collecting him from the Kona flight. Thank God the bitch has gone back to L.A. for Botox or an ass reduction or some shit. We'll be an hour then we'll swing by and treat you to dinner up at Turtle Bay. You gotta help me fix this thing fast.'

Dinner at a posh restaurant and a battle of wills was the last thing I felt like doing, but if I was going to salvage anything from the day I had to help Chuck.

'I'll be waiting,' I said.

I suspected changing Jason's mind about anything would be like trying to hold back the tide with my bare hands but I could be just as determined as him. My career was all I had and success was not going to find me like a bee looking for pollen on a sedentary flower. I had to be the bee and find my own sweet reward.

Eleven

We were shown to the best table at a beautiful open-sided restaurant on the beach. Flaming torches lit the ocean in the sheltered bay and relaxed waves drifted lazily onto the shore. Palm trees sheltered the glass ceiling like umbrellas that had been shredded in the wind. When Chuck walked into the restaurant the manager stood to attention. When Jason strolled in behind, the manager bowed so low I thought he might pull a hamstring. I was a nobody to them of course but I was happy to enjoy the kow-towing-by-proxy.

'Champagne, Madame?' asked the manager, proudly displaying a bottle of Cristal.

Would anyone refuse?

I sipped the golden liquid. It tasted as if each bubble had been individually wrapped.

'How much is this per bottle?' I whispered once the manager had finished lavishing us with complimentary small talk and had scurried away to bully his staff into making us feel even more special.

'That, oh I dunno about three fifty,' Chuck shrugged.

I spat the mouthful across the table.

'Three hundred and fifty dollars?'

Chuck hooted with laughter.

'Yeah so that's like thirty bucks you just spat out.'

Jason grinned.

We clinked our glasses together and drank a toast.

'To the team,' said Chuck.

'The team,' said Jason quietly.

We had all been unnaturally bright and jovial on the way to the restaurant, skirting around the issue we were there to discuss as if it were too hot to handle and we had to wait for it to cool.

I sipped what might as well have been liquid platinum and smiled my thanks to our waitress who nervously delivered a plate of raw fish poke to the table. A mouth-watering aroma of sesame and coriander wafted into my nostrils from the dish of thinly sliced tuna adorned with fresh purple orchids. I grabbed a generous portion with my chopsticks, popped it into my mouth and rolled my eyes at the taste that was nothing short of heavenly.

Chuck nudged my foot under the table and waggled his eyebrows, urging me to speak.

'Say something,' he mouthed.

I grimaced.

'Shame, I was so looking forward to sampling wonderful foods like this around the world on tour with you next year,' I said eventually.

I looked pointedly at Jason.

Sensing the intensity of my gaze, Jason lifted his head and looked at me through a lock of blond hair. He lowered his chopsticks to the table.

'So Chuck told you.'

'Yes Chuck told me. So let's talk about it.'

Chuck clapped his hands.

'Why do you want to retire now? Because you lost? I thought you desperately wanted the thirteenth world title.'

Chuck shoved a huge mouthful of poke into his mouth and his eyes bulged.

'I did want it but I don't need it. I've got twelve and that's enough.'

'Nine might be good, brilliant in fact but twelve is not thirteen. Thirteen is a record-breaking number; it's never been done before. That's what drove you. Pardon me if I got it wrong but I thought you wanted to do something remarkable.'

Chuck's eyes bulged even more. I was goading Jason on purpose because, from what I knew of him already, I thought I had to challenge him. I almost had to dare him not to retire to have any hope of changing his mind.

I took a sip of champagne. Jason weaved his fingers together and rested his elbows on the table.

'Are twelve titles not remarkable enough? Where does it end?' he said.

I shrugged. 'Of course. It ends when you want it to end but won't it be an anti-climax slipping away quietly after losing to your Nemesis?'

Tyler visibly bristled. 'It's not healthy to just focus on getting thirteen world titles. What if I never get there?'

'What if you do?'

Jason ran his tongue across his lips and stared intently at me.

'So you think you know how I tick already?'

'Isn't that my job?' I paused and took a breath. 'Or are you going to give up on that too?'

'No of course not. Retirement is the perfect time to release a book and anyway I am not giving up.'

He made inverted commas with his fingers.

I raised one eyebrow.

'Looks that way to me. What do you think, Chuck?'

Chuck looked like he might choke.

'Yes, Chuck, what do you think? It's not like you to be so quiet. Join the game.'

Jason's mouth was set in a firm line. The waitress approached the table to clear the plates but Jason raised his hand and said – 'Leave us, please.'

She scurried away as quietly as she had approached.

'This isn't a game, Jason,' said Chuck. 'Why do you wanna go listening to Portia at a time like this? Why give all this up?'

He waved his long arms wildly, almost decapitating a passing waiter who apologised as if it was his fault for taking up too much space in the world.

Jason sat back in his chair and smoothed his hands through his hair.

'I'll say it again. I am not just giving up and I sent Portia home. This has nothing to do with Portia.'

'Does too.'

'Does not.'

'Does too.'

'Does not.'

My God, how old were they, twelve?

'Whether or not Portia is instrumental in your decision to retire is not the issue here. We just have to make sure it's the right decision for you and that you won't look back and regret not trying for the title again.'

'I don't do regret.'

'Really? Or do you just tell yourself that?'

My toes curled at my own regret over what I had done with Cain just hours earlier. When I had first seen Jason in the car I had hardly been able to look him in the eye. He despised Cain and Cain's victory was the reason we were there. I had literally slept with the enemy and now here I was ensconced in Jason's camp, acting as his confidante. I was disgusted by my own disloyalty but I knew it was a moment of madness that would never happen again. I too would not live with regret.

We sat back silently while the waitress approached the table and cleared the plates for the main course. My choice was a succulent butterfish on a bed of sweet potato and edamame beans. The first mouthful was so utterly divine I closed my eyes and prayed we would be continuing our world tour.

'Look, I appreciate your efforts, Bailey, but my mind is made up. I don't just want to focus on the world title and keep getting my ass kicked at Pipe, I want a new challenge.'

I blinked at Jason like a chess master considering my next move.

'I understand but then I am a friend. People on the outside will probably see you retiring and put it down to the fact that you were defeated by a better surfer and you didn't have what it took to fight him back to the top.'

Chuck choked on a baby back rib. Jason leaned so far across the table his breath blew the steam snaking up from my meal.

'Cain is not a better surfer than me. He just got lucky.'

I casually brushed my hair back over my shoulder.

'For a third time.'

Jason inhaled sharply.

'Look, Jason, I do think you were unlucky but luck, talent, tactics, whatever it comes down to, Cain is still number one and you are number two. That is the way history will remember it. I just want you to realise that.'

A nerve twitched in Jason's left cheek.

'How do I know you're not just saying all this because you want a year on tour?'

'Because I am honest. I know you want to beat Cain more than anything in the world just like I want to write a bestseller more than anything. Of course another world title would be better for the book but that is not the point. The point is you are a winner, Jason and this is not your style. I am just saying what other people' – I shot a look at Chuck who was pretending to be engrossed in the wine label – 'might hold back from saying to you because that is who I am. You can trust me.'

The moment I met Jason's eyes I knew I had won him over. My victory, however, was fleeting because seconds later, a willowy man and his entourage of tattooed bruisers entered my line of vision and I knew there was trouble ahead. As Cain approached our table with a twisted smile on his face, my own words 'trust me' jumped back into my throat.

'Is this a private party for losers or can winners join in?'

Jason did not have to turn around to recognise the voice.

'Table for one is it, Cain, or do they serve monkeys in here?' he muttered, nodding towards Cain's cronies.

Cain placed one hand on the back of Chuck's chair and the other on mine. My skin crawled and I stared straight ahead while silently saying a prayer that he would not say anything. Jason tried to ignore the heckles of the Tiger Sharks who were circling us in the manner of the creatures they were named after. I held my breath but the minute Cain uttered my name I knew the game was up.

'So, Bailey Brown, you couldn't keep up with us, huh? Decided to go back to the loser's gang did you, Sista?'

Jason's head whipped up and Cain's laughter rumbled down my spine, connecting with each vertebra like a stick being dragged across a xylophone. He bent down until his mouth touched my ear.

'What's the matter, Sista, cat got your tongue or did you lose your voice from screaming so much when I screwed you?'

I felt sick.

Jason's chair legs scraped along the wooden floor and he leapt to his feet. Jason and Cain faced each other, their faces inches apart and I could sense Cain willing Jason to fight him. Cain knew how to fight; it was how he had got to the top.

Jason clenched his fists and breathed heavily. I stood up and placed myself between them. The hairs on the back of my neck bristled. I had never before truly wanted the ground to open up and swallow me.

'Just tell me it's not true, Bailey. That's all I need to hear and then I will sort this creep out,' said Jason, his eyes unblinking.

I searched my mind for a way out but there was only one direction I could take. The truth. I had told him he could trust me and now was not the time to perpetuate the lies. I said nothing. Jason slowly turned his head to look at me. The hurt in his eyes wounded me more than any words.

'I can't,' I said, my voice breaking, 'I'm sorry, Jason.'

Jason's head dropped. From the glint of victory in Cain's face, one would have thought he had won the world title all over again.

England

Twelve

'Bailey would you get me another G and T? I'm parched in here,' screeched my mother who had been sprawled in front of the television since the previous evening.

I unwillingly fixed her a drink in her disastrously disorganised kitchen and took it out to her with a forced smile.

'Are you going to get dressed, Mother? It's almost two and Jo and Gerry will be here soon.'

My mother glugged back the gin. She gasped as if she had been marching through the desert without water for three weeks when, in reality, not ten minutes had passed since her last gin and tonic. She handed me the glass with a nod. I stood and looked down at her.

'What? What are you staring at? Honestly, if a woman can't relax in her pyjamas on Christmas bloody Day when can she?'

'Every other day of the year from the look of you,' I muttered as I stalked back to the kitchen.

'I heard that.'

I had been responsible for shopping for the Christmas dinner, paying for the Christmas dinner and cooking it. Having flown back in to Heathrow the morning before Christmas Eve, I was still painfully jetlagged as I fought stressed out supermarket shoppers for the turkey and trimmings that were apparently turning to gold dust before our eyes. When a woman dressed head to toe in bronze velour threatened to fight me for the last remaining cauliflower I lost my rag.

'It's not a Willy Wonka golden ticket, it's a fucking root vegetable.'

I threw the cauliflower across the vegetable department, at which point my heavily veloured opponent launched herself after it like a desperate single woman trying to catch the wedding bouquet. Bewildered, I left the supermarket vegetable-less, stepping over warring shoppers fighting over everything from cranberry sauce to crap Christmas crackers. When I passed two women playing tug of war with the last copy of the latest reality TV star's memoirs, I hissed, - 'You should be ashamed of yourselves' – and purposefully knocked over the book display.

'They did it,' I said to the distressed shelf stacker boy as I made a hasty exit.

I was not, as Chuck would say, in a good place. I had come down to earth with such a bump I felt bruised. Waking up in my flat on a donkey grey Christmas morning with the realisation that I had ruined my chances of writing a bestselling book pounding in my head, my jetlag intensified. I missed the sunshine. I missed the ocean and I missed my new friends. I also missed the buzz of knowing my life was heading in an exciting new direction. Jason may have chosen not to live with regret but I was feeling enough for both of us.

I still reddened when I recalled the car journey home from Olas restaurant, which had been a silent penance. None of us had spoken until we were inside the beach house with the door closed, at which point Chuck sadly retired to his room to leave us to sort the matter out between us. Used to living under the scrutiny of the public eye, Jason was always careful not to create scenes that would attract attention. I knew it had taken every ounce of willpower he had not to wipe the smug grin off Cain's face in the restaurant. I had, therefore, expected Jason to shout and scream when we were back home but the cold disappointment I was in fact faced with was one hundred times worse.

'In your own words, Bailey, I trusted you,' he said sadly.

His eyes had lost their unique sparkle.

'And I made the biggest mistake of my life, Jason. I was weak and I let the thrill of being here and feeling part of the scene cloud my judgement. I thought he was genuine.'

Jason smiled weakly.

'Genuine? There is nothing genuine about that guy. I thought a girl like you would see through it.'

'I guess I got carried away but I can assure you it will never happen again. I am off professional surfers for life, I promise you. Romantically speaking. Sexually. You know what I mean.'

Jason lowered his eyes and sighed.

'No, it won't happen again, Bailey, because you're leaving. It's over. I'm sorry.'

I did not want to give up my dream because of one mistake. I was all too aware of how mistakes could destroy people and I could not let that happen. I had to go down fighting.

'Cain used me to get at you,' I said.

'And you let him.'

'And you are going to let him win. Yet again.'

There was a flicker of confusion on Jason's face but then the shutters came down and my fate was sealed.

'I made a mistake, Jason,' I said softly, 'and I am truly sorry I hurt you, but you had gone way with Portia and I was alone on a tropical island. I am not a bad person. I won't be made to feel ashamed. We all make mistakes, even you and from those mistakes we learn life's lessons. We all have to fail sometimes to recognise success, I thought you would understand that.'

He tilted his head and said nothing.

'Punish me if you want,' I carried on, 'but believe me I am the best person you will find to write this book. I am passionate about this and I would have risen to the challenge because I am determined, just as I believed you were. But all I have seen is that you are ready to give up on things at the first opportunity. You could win the thirteenth title and we could write the best possible book. We could beat Cain and both win in the end. I thought you were a winner but obviously I was wrong.'

I left the room, shaking internally from the effort of trying to stand up for myself. They were the last words I said to Jason before I left Hawaii on the morning flight.

I stared out of the window at the identical grey houses in the street standing in a row like sad little orphans waiting to be chosen by new parents and have some colour introduced to their lives. The sheet rain seemed to wash everything dirty rather than clean. I heard a loud sigh in the room and looked around only to realise it was my own.

I checked on the turkey that had been shivering in my mother's ancient oven for more time than it would have taken to cook it over a candle flame.

'Mother, did I not send you money for a new oven in September?' I shouted, feeling my blood boiling.

Something was rising above room temperature but it was definitely not the food.

'What? Oh I don't think so. I would have remembered that.'

'Maybe not after four-hundred pounds worth of alcohol,' I seethed, stabbing at a solid parsnip bobbing defiantly in a pan of tepid water.

'Only us, Mother,' Joanna called out, bursting through the front door with bags full of wrapped gifts.

'Merry Christmas, Mother,' I heard Gerry's plummy voice say.

'Mother,' I tutted under my breath while my head was in the fridge, 'you're practically the same age you fat bastard.'

'You said bastard,' gasped a voice behind me.

I banged my head on the freezer door handle and emerged to see my adorable nephew Zac beaming up at me with eyes as clear and blue as Hawaiian rock pools.

He was wearing a brand new football kit several years too big, complete with shin pads and boots.

'Hello, Zac, or is it Ronaldo?' I bent down and kissed him on his soft, pink cheek.

He grinned back at me proudly.

'Merry Christmas, Auntie Bailey. Did you lose your job?'

If adults got to the point as directly as children, political summits would be over in half the time.

'I did lose my job yes, Zac, but it's OK I'll just write something else.'

'Have you thought of anything yet?'

'No I haven't but inspiration may be just around the corner.'

I glanced out at the sky and immediately doubted it.

'Will you still be a famous author?'

'Auntie Bailey is not famous, Zachary,' Gerry bellowed from the doorway to the accompaniment of my mother's cackling laughter, 'and maybe now Auntie Bailey will get a proper job or at least get herself a man with a proper job who can pay for her pipe dreams.'

I bit my tongue and ignored the jibes for Zac's benefit who was too young to know, and perhaps would never know, what a complete tosser his father was.

Gerry lolled at the kitchen door with a glass of port in one hand and a yellow paper hat perched on the apex of his shiny head. His stomach arrived several seconds before the rest of him.

'Hello, Gerald' – I said his name as if I were saying 'raw sewage' – 'diet not working then?'

'I'm not on a diet,' he said before stopping to think.

I raised one eyebrow pointedly and, with a winning smile, turned to remove the turkey from the oven.

Thirteen

My heart leapt when I thought I heard the roast potatoes crackle but it was just Zac opening a packet of crisps.

'Don't spoil your appetite, Zac,' said Joanna.

She squeezed past Gerry to give me a tight little hug.

'Don't worry about appetites, this turkey won't be ready until Easter at this rate,' I said, hugging her back.

My sister was always well dressed and an obviously wealthy woman but she chose clothes far too mature for her years. Every time we met, her inner light had dimmed a little more. Her mousey hair was pulled tightly into a bun and had become distinctly salt and pepper coloured at the temples. The expression of sad resignation set deep in the lines on Joanna's face had appeared on the day of my father's funeral and had gradually become a permanent mask over the years.

All of us had lost part of ourselves when my father committed suicide. He was the mortar that held the bricks of our family together. Christmas had always been fun with him around. The last Christmas before my father died, every girl in the in-crowd was praying for the special edition puffer jacket as worn by Bros, the boyband of the moment. On Christmas Day, I had awoken at a suitably teenage hour of midday to find not only *the* jacket but a pair of jeans hand-ripped by my father and a shiny new pair of black DM shoes to the laces of which he had attached a pair of beer bottle tops, just like the ones the boys in the band and their fans 'the Brosettes' all wore. He simply understood how much it meant to a teenager to fit in and be liked.

'Any more customising that requires I drink two bottles of beer before noon, I'm your man,' he grinned when his Brosette daughter threw her arms around him and cried – 'I love you, Dad.'

Less than two months later he used the same beer to wash down a fatal cocktail of pills, which definitely took the shine off my new shoes. I was the one who found him. Having to be liked, it seemed, was also my father's downfall. Bob Brown did not believe anyone could like a man who had lost everything his family owned on a lame horse.

Without a father, Joanna had become a needy young woman who had signed up to a loveless marriage because she thought Gerry would not leave her penniless and alone as my father had. My mother had found solace in a liquid friend called alcohol and grown bitter towards his memory and the rest of the world. I had tried to reach her but I had always been a daddy's girl and my mother resented me for it.

Gerry eased his well-upholstered backside onto the edge of the rickety white table that had been known to collapse under the weight of beans on toast. My mother clattered in behind him on fluffy kitten heel slippers that looked as if she had kicked two bunny rabbits up the backside and kept on walking. She wore stained cow print pyjamas that were loose and misshapen but failed to conceal her expanding waistline. Her hair that was naturally as onyx as mine had been singed to a crisp by home peroxide kits and sprang at gravity-defying right angles from her head. My mother's appearance never failed to shock me even though it rarely changed. Deep down I think I still naively held onto the desperate hope that one day I would be greeted by the smart, intelligent woman I vaguely remembered from my childhood. Instead I was always met at the door by an angry drunk who could not wait, it seemed, for life to be over.

'Is the bloody dinner ready yet, Bailey, I'm starving to death in here,' she grumbled, finishing her sentence with a burp.

'Don't tempt me,' I muttered.

Zac giggled while trying to balance a fresh pineapple on his head. Joanna threw him a scolding glance.

'I give Bailey one bloody job to do and she can't even manage that.'

'Hardly surprising,' Gerry chortled. 'She doesn't have the best track record. Can't even write a book about a beach bum. What's the next big thing, Bailey, pop-up books or colouring in?'

I dug the fork into the turkey skin, wishing it was Gerry's stomach.

'I said she should find herself a rich man,' he announced, 'stop trying to be Little Miss Career Woman.'

'Quite right, Gerry,' said my mother while pouring herself a glass of whiskey from her stash in the bread bin.

'I thought you would be the last person to support that theory, Mother.'

'Bailey, don't,' Joanna mumbled half-heartedly.

Our eyes met and a flash of sorrow passed between us.

I turned away and a tear ran down my cheek, turning to ice on the turkey's back. I missed the life I had dipped into just long enough to tan my toes. Jason and Chuck would not be spending Christmas in a house full of lunatics waiting in vain for a decrepit oven to perform its sole purpose of cooking. They would be sipping champagne, probably with beautiful people in a spectacular house in between refreshing surfs in an azure ocean. It was hard to imagine that his world of sunshine and beauty existed simultaneously out there in direct contrast to the world I had suddenly returned to. Did wanting it make me superficial? I wondered. Or did it simply make me aware of what the planet had to offer if one went in search of a better life. I missed the startlingly fresh air. I missed the sound of the ocean. I missed Chuck's vibrancy and colourful presence. I missed the spontaneity. I missed Jason.

I sighed. Here we were like a group of people trying desperately to play a game of Happy Families with a pack of Tarot cards. I felt as if I did not belong.

'Look at me, Auntie Bailey,' Zac whooped, thrusting out his arms.

The pineapple balanced on his head for a second before toppling off and landing on my mother's foot. She shrieked and hopped towards Gerry, who tried in vain to catch her. There was the sound of cheap wood splintering before the table collapsed. Gerry sprawled on the floor like an upturned beetle with my mother remonstrating beside him. Joanna shouted at Zac who burst into tears and clip-clopped from the room in his football boots.

Just when I thought I could take it no longer, the sound of my phone trilling interrupted the sounds of the 1980s Christmas compilation CD. I ran to find it and grabbed the phone as if I was drowning and someone had thrown me a lifebuoy.

'Hello.'

'Merry Christmas, Bailey Brown,' said a voice I instantly recognised as Jason's.

I closed my eyes and I could almost feel the sun on my back.

'Hello, Jason. Merry Christmas.'

Now that was a contradiction in terms.

I said no more and willed him to fill the gap.

'Look I don't say this very often so I'm just going to say it once. I was wrong and you were right. I am an asshole.'

'I didn't call you an arsehole did I?'

'No but you had every right to. I was too quick to judge you when you had done nothing but support me. I made a mistake. I want the best girl there is to write my book and you are that girl. It may just be the Christmas spirit getting me all giddy but so what? I judged you and I had no right, I don't own you. I want you to come back. I... we miss you. Will you come to Indonesia in March?'

Christmas wishes did come true. I had my pride, but it was safe to say Jason did not have to ask me twice.

Indonesia

Fourteen

Jason did not retire and, while he spent two months in Australia opening his competitive season, I worked on ideas for the book and got to know him over the phone. That gave him time to refocus on his surfing and I found it an easier way to break the ice than facing him after everything we had been through. Telephone interviews also guaranteed I had his attention because his mind had a tendency to wander if he was bored, as if it was drifting away on the tide. I had fresh determination to make Jason's book exceptional.

Having spent years working as a writer, in my opinion there was no magic formula for writing a book. Every writer I had met used a different method of working. Writing a biography was new to me but the basics of creating a story that would grab the reader were the same, and the more I researched, the more passionate I became about the subject. I grew in confidence over this time that I could do a good job despite the efforts of my family to dampen my spirits and the resounding silence from my agent who was clearly having his doubts. I ploughed on and took my own advice that I often gave to budding authors when they asked me how to write a book: simply sit down and get on with it. Or alternatively, write a book on 'How to write a book'. It's a guaranteed winner.

With my groundwork done, I left for Indonesia at the beginning of March. Jason had booked the trip for me and I felt exhausted just reading the itinerary of the journey. Despite my initial buzz of enthusiasm when I took off from London, the solo flight via Singapore was tiresome. After I had watched two movies, read the in-flight magazine, completed the word search and cheated on the Sudoku, I ate a meal of congealed cheese and plastic pasta while the heady aroma of real food wafted into cattle class through the first class curtain. One stopover and fifteen hours later, I landed in Denpasar at Ngurah Rai airport in Bali.

'Backpacking?' asked a young girl while we waited for our bags.

Her short blond dreadlocks stuck out of her head like dry shredded wheat.

'No, I'm heading to Java for a surf contest,' I announced casually.

'Cool,' she said with a slow, considered nod of the shredded wheat, 'where are your boards?'

'I'm not actually a surfer, I'm writing about the surfers,' I said, struggling with my neon pink suitcase.

She looked disdainfully from me to the case and back again.

'Not so cool,' she sighed and ambled off to find somebody else to bother.

I momentarily wondered whether I was really cut out for the inherently cool international surfing circuit. One thing was certain; I was about to find out.

The first thing that hit me when I stepped outside the bustling airport was the heat. The second thing was the pungent aroma of Balinese gudang garam clove cigarettes.

It was an unmistakeable smell that would forever remind me of Bali.

'You want taxi?' a gaggle of enthusiastic little men shouted.

They waved their car keys and shouted prices in Rupiah that sounded expensive. Surely forty-five thousand of anything had to be a lot?

I was to stay overnight in Kuta, which was a death-defying three-kilometre taxi ride from the airport in a Nissan Vanette that apparently had neither suspension nor tyres on the wheel rims. The traffic was unlike anything I had ever experienced. Barely roadworthy cars jostled for space with scooters ridden by entire families. One scooter held a father, a toddler and a mother who was in the process of breastfeeding her baby while flying along at forty miles an hour. Four lanes merged into one then out again to six. Trucks carrying chickens and carpets raced head-on towards us. I gripped the seat belt, which had no buckle attachment and functioned as little more than an ornamental sash.

The hotel was in central Kuta and, despite being surrounded by the hustle and bustle, was surprisingly tranquil inside. The architecture was typically Indonesian with steep ornamental roofs and breathtakingly ornate woodcarvings. When I signed in at the outdoor reception desk, a gecko the size of my hand scuttled across the guest book and took refuge in the lap of a wooden Hindu God.

'I hope you have an enjoyable stay,' said the male receptionist with a respectful nod of the head and a smile so honest it made me feel instantly at home. 'My name is Wayan.'

'Thank you, Wayan. I go to G-Land in Java tomorrow so I want to make the most of my evening. Can you recommend any sights while I'm here?'

He lifted his smooth-skinned arm and wafted it in a balletic movement towards the street.

'Take a walk down Poppies Lane, meet the people, talk to the people, breathe in the aroma of Kuta, buy our beautiful goods and you will come back smiling.'

As tired as I was after the journey, I had to take a bus and boat to Java to join Jason and Chuck at nine o'clock the next morning so I wanted to make the most of my very short stay in Bali and be adventurous. I decided to take Wayan's advice and head out into Kuta. It was stiflingly hot and humid so I dressed in light clothes that also protected me from mosquitoes. I chose an embroidered cream cotton tunic and loose linen trousers in powder blue and pale blue sandals. Topped with a soft-brimmed straw hat, I was satisfied I looked like a character from *Out Of Africa*.

After half an hour battling my way through the hot streets of Kuta, the only thing out of Africa I resembled was a sweaty hippo. The roads were either muddy or dusty and the traffic whizzed manically in every direction whenever I dared step off the metre-high kerbs designed to cope with floods during the wet season. Exhaust fumes enveloped my new trousers in a smog of toxic smoke until I appeared to be travelling on my very own cloud. Pavements suddenly ended in swimming pool sized puddles of mud and I watched in dismay when one distracted Australian tourist disappeared from view into an uncovered drain.

While I battled my way nervously along the narrow streets with one hand over my mouth and the other on my wallet, diminutive Balinese women with leathery skin followed me like rats trailing the Pied Piper.

'You want massage?' they said in singsong voices.

'You want hair extension?'

'I give you nice nails pretty lady.'

'Plait your hair?'

I rushed past them apologising profusely.

'No thank you, I am too ticklish for massages.'

'No thank you, I like my hair as it is.'

'No thank you, I find long nails impossible for typing.'

'No thank you, I'm sorry but I really feel cornroll plaits from the hairline should only be allowed on black sprinters with incredible bone structure.'

A moon faced white girl who had just had her stringy hair yanked back into innumerable eye-watering plaits decorated with multi-coloured beads was my case in point. If I were her holiday companion I would be having her deported.

Finally exhausted and intimidated, I gave my pursuers the slip and hid in a dark corner of a restaurant on the main street, Jalan Legian.

'Hello lady, I am Wayan. This your first time Bali?' said the waiter.

He handed me a menu full of faded photographs of the dishes on offer.

I nodded silently, turning the menu over and over in my hands. I felt weary and dejected. I was not the unflustered international traveller I had intended to be. I was lonely and unnerved and I had only been in Bali less than four hours. I was convinced by the end of an evening alone in Kuta I would have been conned, robbed, and even worse, had my hair pulled into tiny plaits that would require a complete head shave to remove. I took a deep breath to calm myself. The restaurant smelled of gadang garams and satay sauce. Tracey Chapman played sombrely on the stereo. I exhaled slowly.

'You want snack?'

I nodded again.

'I think you like banana jaffle with peanut butter. Very good comfort food for sad lady. Also coconut lassi. Bring a smile to pretty face.'

I looked up at the second Wayan of the day, who smiled back at me with an almost childlike innocence.

'You will like Bali,' he said confidently. 'We are good people.'

'Are you all called Wayan?'

He laughed.

'No we have four names, Wayan for first born, Made, Nyoman and Ketut.'

'Gosh,' I said, relaxing back into the throne-like carved chair that I had only just noticed, 'and the girls?'

'Same,' Wayan said. 'Then for fifth born we start again, Wayan Balik, mean Wayan again.'

'That's fascinating. So you all have the same names? How do you distinguish yourselves?'

'By what we do and who we are inside.'

He tapped his pen against his sternum.

'My friends call me Beckham,' he winked before scurrying off to fetch my food.

The jaffle was a buttery toasted sandwich crammed with hot peanut butter and sweet bananas. I washed it down with a coconut and yoghurt drink.

'You were right, Wayan, that was perfect comfort food. I feel better already.'

'I am glad. Now go meet the Balinese people, they will be good to you. We love tourist. The bomb they keep tourist away for long time, but we do not deserve this. We must have tourist to live.'

'I understand. Well, thank you for being so welcoming.'

'What your name?'

'Bailey.'

'And what you do in Bali?'

'Actually I'm only here for this evening. I go to Java tomorrow to G-Land to write a book.'

Wayan gasped and pressed his hands together.

'Writer lady, you very lucky for me,' he said with a bow. 'You very clever, famous writer lady.'

'Well actually I'm not famous.'

'I am honoured, Miss Bailey. You write book about surfer in G-Land?'

'Yes. About a surfer called Jason Cross?' I said, expecting nothing.

Wayan shrieked with delight, which brought the entire kitchen staff (Made, Ketut, Made, Wayan and Ketut) running into the restaurant. Each one of them shook my hand and bowed. I could not help but laugh.

'We big fans of Jason Cross. Writer lady, we very proud, you must have food as gift.'

I held up my hands.

'No, Wayan, I must pay you, please.'

'No no, please just come back with your big book one day. I hope we see you again, English writer lady. You very nice.'

I thanked Wayan for making me instantly feel at home in Bali and when he wasn't looking I left a twenty thousand Rupiah tip. I then went out onto Legian with a new-found spring in my step. It was, I realised, so often the people who made a place, which was why leaving home had been nothing short of a delight.

By the time I returned to the hotel, I had met twelve more Wayans, eight Mades (pronounced Marday) and four Ketuts. I had bought a Bulgari watch from a man called Elvis and Gucci sunglasses from George Clooney. My nails had been manicured and painted with intricate blue and ivory orchids and I had relaxed with a massage expertly performed by a female Wayan who was known to her friends as Beyonce. I had gorged on a meal of chicken satay with rice, fresh papaya and coconut cocktails for the equivalent of three pounds and I had exchanged my sandals for a pair of leather ones allegedly from Prada. I was loath to condone counterfeit goods but they were so lovely and in need of the business, I was powerless to resist. I still drew a firm line not to be crossed at hair plaiting.

Stopping at the hotel entrance on the delightfully named Poppies Lane II, I was rummaging in my bag (Christian Dior) for my room key when I spotted a tiny bookshop on the other side of the street. Dodging a scooter driven by a child whose legs barely reached below the seat, I skipped across and peered in the door.

'You want book?' said the woman inside with a wide, genuine smile.

'Yes, I think I do,' I smiled back.

'English yes? We have many many.'

Made led me to the English 'department' of the ten foot square shop and showed me the shelves crammed with well travelled second hand books that had more dog ears than a dog pound.

'Thank you, Made.'

I proceeded to lose myself in the search for a book to take to G-Land. There were indeed many titles from England, Australia, America and Canada. Their pages were well thumbed and, as I flicked through them, I wondered about all the history squashed into one bookcase. Where had these books been and who with? How many people had read each one and what had the reader given as a review to encourage the next person to pick up that book? While I rummaged I felt the stir of my childhood adoration of books that had inspired me to dream of becoming a writer.

I clasped my hand to my mouth when my eyes fell on one of the books on a lower shelf nestling between a John Grisham and a Jackie Collins. It was like seeing one of my own children. Unmistakeably mine.

I reached out a shaky hand and pulled my first novel from the shelf. A rush of pride and disbelief overwhelmed me. This was my first day in Bali but part of me had been there long before. Doubtless brought in the hand luggage of someone who had read it and then, judging by the creases in the cover like wrinkles in a tumble-dried duvet, had passed it on to friends and fellow travellers. It was just one copy in a dusty second hand bookshop in Bali but it was the proudest, most heart-warming moment of my literary career so far. For a brief moment I felt like a bestselling novelist.

'I love Bali,' I pronounced to Wayan the hotel receptionist with a smile to match his.

'Good then you are ready for G-Land,' he said. I wondered what he meant.

Fifteen

My journey to G-Land began early the next morning with a twelve-hour bus ride from Kuta to the north of the island. The bus appeared to have been hurriedly put together from old baked bean tins and some sticky-backed plastic. The PVC seat stuck to the backs of my legs and a layer of grime added inches to the floor. The further we travelled from Kuta, the more uneven the road surfaces became and I had to peer out of the dusty window to check we weren't driving on a bouncy castle. The driver was a very pleasant Balinese man in his fifties who had just completed the twelve-hour inbound route but could see no reason to stop for a break before we set off.

'Tiredness kills,' I warned him as he lifted my case with ease and tossed it into the luggage compartment.

'My boss kills if I am late,' he chuckled out of the side of his mouth while balancing a gadang garam on his crusty lip.

He shepherded his passengers onto the bus.

If I had been concerned the driver might fall asleep and drive us to our deaths I needn't have been. He played the Rolling Stones on repeat for every minute of the twelve hours at a decibel level that rattled the windows while he sang along in words that were not strictly English. I had hoped my fellow passengers would complain so that we might rest for at least part of the trip but it quickly emerged they were all Australian surfers under the age of twenty-five with boundless energy and degrees from the school of how to shout for half a day without losing your voice.

En route we stopped in Ubud, a small town renowned for its production of silver Balinese jewellery. I bought two intricate rings and a bracelet of interlinked silver starfish while the Australians shouted at each other about the 'farking sick' silver surfboard necklaces.

'Do you sell silver muzzles?' I asked the lady. 'Silver earplugs perhaps?'

We re-boarded the bus and everybody around me sang *Jumping Jack Flash* for two hours straight.

The ferry across to Java was no better. The permanent tilt to one side, the holes in the floors and ceilings, the broken seats and the overflowing single toilet put me in fear of my life. The surfers found dodging a river of raw sewage hilarious and the hilarity grew further when the boat rolled dangerously mid-voyage and 'Robbo' from Wollongong spotted a family of sharks tailing us in the hope of a meal. Of course there were no life jackets onboard. Not that a layer of inflated plastic was likely to help when Jaws' Indonesian cousin decided to have me for dinner.

The bus journey from hell continued when we reached Java, taking us to the remote village of Grajagan from where we were to take a 'speedboat' to the surf camp at G-Land. From the look of the wooden boat bobbing apologetically just off the beach, I thought 'speedboat' was pushing the irony to the limits.

'We take eight then come back for rest,' said the emaciated skipper.

Eight of the biggest Australian men threw chivalry to the wind and crammed themselves into the boat, leaving six of us behind on the beach to wait in the baking hot sun. Two hours later the boat still had not returned and I was beginning to wonder how long it took to die of heat exhaustion.

'Do you have anything to eat or drink on you?' I asked one of the Australians sitting next to me on the beach.

'Nah mate but you could have a chew on that thing.'

He nodded towards my hand resting in the sand. I turned slowly and leapt to my feet.

'What the bloody hell is that? Is it REAL?' I screamed.

'Yeah, mate you betcha. It's a farking boa constrictor. Farking eat you alive that thing ay. It's dead but.'

'Get me out of this place,' I pleaded to the sky.

'No worries, mate, the speedboat's coming.'

'A bit of speed might be nice,' I hissed, backing away from the giant snake for fear of it suddenly springing to life.

It was easily eight feet long and wide enough to swallow a Chihuahua whole.

Two of the Australians lifted the dead snake onto their shoulders and paraded it around the beach.

'Careful, it might be faking it,' I warned, although it was safe to say I would not miss a single one of my fellow travellers and rather them than me.

I sat back and watched them until we finally heard the roar, or rather the putt putt, of the speedboat's engine. I was first in line this time.

'We must go now, high tide,' said the skipper, 'or else we must stay here all night.'

'Just start the sodding boat and get me out of here,' I growled.

The camp was situated on the edge of the Javanese jungle under a heavy canopy of rainforest. It was bordered by a white sandy beach that very few human footprints had ever disturbed.

'Welcome to jungle camp. Nama saya David Hasselhoff. My name is David Hasselhoff or the Hoff. Apa khabar?' said our host who met us at the boat dock. 'How are you?'

'Fine, thank you,' I replied somewhat shakily.

This was undoubtedly the most exhausting journey I had ever undertaken. I just wanted to get to my air-conditioned hotel room, close the door and regain my composure before I faced Jason and the work ahead.

As I was the only girl in the group, 'the Hoff' lifted my case and carried it to the camp. He was as lean as Bambi but tossed my luggage onto his shoulder as if it were empty. Which, judging by how this trip was progressing, it probably was.

We walked along a meandering jungle path through trees with leaves as big as garden parasols. I peered up at the treetops and noticed they were littered with debris. I could make out items of clothing, shoes and planks of wood.

'What is all that up there?'

Our host shrugged.

'Oh this is nothing. Just left from tsunami that wiped out camp before.'

'Before when?'

'Before before.'

'Long before?'

'Just before,' he shrugged nonchalantly.

'Well that's reassuring,' I sniffed. 'Are you expecting another anytime soon?'

'Who knows? Only ocean knows this,' he beamed and marched on ahead. 'Could happen any time.'

We came to a clearing that housed the main camp reception. It was a wooden pagoda structure open to both the elements and the wild animals of the jungle. Leather sofas held together with spit and string sat in one corner in front of a television screen that was playing a Hollywood movie with Indonesian subtitles and occasional dubbing. To my left a bar offered only Indonesian Bintang beer and Sprite. The door to the kitchen was at the far end of the pagoda and rows of benches and tables filled the centre of the room in the manner of a school canteen. Surfers milled around swigging from bottles of beer, many of whom I recognised from Hawaii. I looked around for Jason but a monkey swinging upside down from a tree behind the sofas diverted my attention. He appeared to be watching the television.

'Wow, do you see many animals?' I said, a smile touching my cracked lips.

'Yes yes. Many monkey and tiger.'

'Tiger?'

'Yes,' the Hoff nodded excitedly as if tsunamis and free roaming wildcats were the best tourist attractions in the world.

He really had to work on his PR pitch.

'Don't worry. Not so many tiger this season so you not be eaten. Probably.'

'Probably. Well isn't that just swell,' I replied, forcing a smile.

We were all given keys to our rooms. I managed to sneak a peek at the list of guests and breathed a sigh of relief when I saw that Jason and Chuck were indeed both on the island and this was not some nasty hoax to pay me back for sleeping with Cain. I was also pleased to note that the three of us had been allocated some of the 'luxury' bungalows in the camp. I glanced around again to see if I could catch sight of either of them but the man who caught my attention was the one man I really did not want to see. Cain was playing table football with one of the Tiger Sharks on the far side of the room. They both roared aggressively and I could tell Cain was winning. Something that he clearly made a habit of. Well not this time. He had not beaten me. I was back. I just needed a moment to collect my thoughts.

'Hoff, is there a restroom here, please?'

The Hoff pointed towards a small wooden cupboard on the edge of the pagoda. I squeezed through the crowds of surfers and photographers with my head down and slipped into the cubicle. The darkness consumed me completely as if I had dived into a bottle of soya sauce. I could not find a light and I could barely see where to aim but the pungent smell curling up from the toilet was unmistakeable.

Where was the paradise tour of the world's best beaches I had been promised? Where was the glamour and first class travel?

I clenched my thighs and squatted. My whole body felt suddenly drained of energy from the gruelling trek across Indonesia. I truly hoped the year on professional surfing's dream tour would not be as tough as this or I would never last.

It was then I heard a loud squeak above the voices of the men outside the door. I strained my eyes in the darkness. The noise repeated itself this time from around my feet. Still squatting, I peered down at the floor. There was a scuffling, a third succession of squeaks and then a very large, very furry, unmistakeably rat-like creature scratched over my flip-flop and settled its belly on the arch of my foot.

Yanking up my trousers I let out a scream that could itself have caused a tsunami and fumbled manically for the door handle. The rat hopped around my feet as if we were flirting at a disco. The door burst open and I tumbled out into the arms of the nearest man. I almost knocked him over but he wrapped his arms around me and held me tight. I could hardly breathe and tears bubbled on my eyelashes but I squeezed my eyes shut and steadied myself.

'Welcome to paradise,' said the man.

I took a step back and looked up at the bemused face of Jason.

'Bailey Brown, that was quite an entrance.'

Sixteen

'It was a test.'

I sucked up a noodle and scowled across the table at Jason.

'A test of what exactly?'

Jason smiled and a mischievous twinkle flashed across his eyes.

'A test of how much you wanted this job.'

'What? Of course I want this job, I've flown half way round the world haven't I?'

I glugged back the Bintang that was succeeding in washing at least some of the stresses of the day out of my tired body.

'Count yourself lucky I didn't turn around and leave you high and dry without a biographer.'

He gave a small bow.

'I am a very lucky man.'

'So if my eventful journey was a test, how did you two get here? You look far too refreshed to have suffered that trip.'

Jason and Chuck looked at each other and grinned.

'Would you call it a luxury boat, Chuck? Yeah I guess it was kind of luxurious.'

'It didn't have the best champagne, dude, but yeah I'd call it luxury. And fast too. Not even three hours from Kuta to the door, for real,' Chuck hooted.

'Tell me you are joking.'

Jason placed his smooth hand on mine.

'You wouldn't have liked it. It wasn't the true Indonesian experience. It was way too easy.'

'I think I might have to kill you both.'

Jason and Chuck threw their heads back and laughed.

'We had to initiate you into the world tour somehow and you have to admit I owed you one. We were worried you were too soft.'

'You passed, dude,' said Chuck, patting my hand, 'welcome back. We missed you.'

'Thanks,' I said with a wry smile, 'to think I missed you too.'

I shook my head.

'Look at the two of you buzzing like merry mosquitoes at your own joke.'

Jason waggled his index finger at me across the table.

'Speaking of mosquitoes, Bailey, I hope you've brought protection. They are really bad here for malaria and dengue fever and that is one initiation I would not wish on you.'

I nodded and reached into my bag.

'Yes I'm on a course of pills and I also did a bit of research and read that this is good for repelling them.'

I placed the plastic jar of Marmite on the table and unscrewed the lid to reveal the tar-like brown substance. Chuck lowered his naturally high brow and peered into the jar.

'Whoa what the hell is that?'

He recoiled at the smell.

'Marmite, it's a spread for toast in the UK. The vitamin B content is apparently released through your pores and repels mosquitoes. You either love it or hate it but I'm not taking any chances when it comes to tropical diseases.'

'Too right, B, I get where you're coming from, for shizzle.'

'No, you're not meant to…' I began but my voice trailed away.

'Man this shit is sticky.'

I settled back into my seat with a happy sigh while Chuck proceeded to smear Marmite over every bit of his bare skin. Revenge was sweet. Or rather savoury and decidedly pungent.

Over the course of the evening we settled into an easy companionship, thankfully as if the events in Hawaii had never happened. We were open and honest with each other and I learned that Cain's manipulation of me had left Jason so incensed after my departure that he had discarded his retirement plans and had vowed to teach Cain a lesson in the only place he could; the ocean. Driven by a new desire to win, Jason had steamrolled the new world champion in the first two events in Australia. Jason was currently leading the rankings and was already well on his way to regaining his world title.

I had of course been dreading the moment I came face to face with Cain for the first time and managed to avoid him for days. I had played many an awkward scenario over in my mind but as it happened I need not have worried. When we eventually came face-to-face one week into the trip while waiting for the boat to ferry us across the lagoon to the outer reef break, Cain reacted as if he had no recollection of what we had done together. I drew a line under the incident with my fake Prada sandal, stepped over it and moved on in the hope that my mistake would not resurface to haunt me.

On day three of what would eventually stretch to three weeks in the jungle, I met Jason's teammate, protégé and friend, Rory, who was on tour for his first year. He had flown in at dawn by helicopter at Jason's expense. When we met, Rory had just emerged from a surf at Speedies, the barrelling wave in G-Land at which the contest would be held when the swell was declared perfect. Rory wore nothing except a pair of purple board shorts slung low on his hips. He had a tiny waist in comparison to the rolling muscles of his chest and shoulders and his hairless skin glowed with the healthiness of youth. I guessed he was in his mid-twenties, his face not yet displaying the wrinkled map of life's ups and downs. Rory had a bright, special quality that made me wish I had a younger brother just like him whom I could proudly watch growing into a strong, successful man. I wondered whether my father would have stuck around for a son like Rory.

When Rory reached out to shake my hand his dark curls dripped salt water over his cheeks.

Jason introduced his protégé like a proud father.

'Bailey this is Rory. He's this year's tour rookie and is the future and first British world surfing champion.'

Rory laughed and shrugged one shoulder.

'Pleased to meet you future world champion,' I said as I shook his hand. 'Where are you from?'

'I was born in Newcastle, why aye,' he smirked.

'But I detect a hint of Australian.'

'We moved to Dunsborough, W.A. when I was fourteen to do the surfing thing, which did me a favour. I mean I am happy to be British. There are waves up in the North East of England that people wouldn't believe. But I'll admit it's bloody cold and the water is often as brown as the beer.'

I grimaced. Rory smiled and ran a hand over his chest that glistened like a varnished table.

'I wouldn't be getting myself a tan like this in Newcastle that's for sure and I definitely wouldn't be surfing in shorts. The surfers there are made of tougher stuff than I am.'

'Hey, darl', how was the surf?'

A girl carrying a pink surfboard under one arm appeared behind Rory and lovingly wrapped a beach towel around his shoulders with her free hand.

'Great, how was yours?'

'Perfect three footers. I loved it.'

She placed the board on the sand and beamed up at Rory while running her hands through her boyish cropped hairstyle that reminded me of Mia Farrow in *Rosemary's Baby*. The feathered blond cut flattered Ruby's elfin features and enormous innocent eyes. If I had attempted the same style I would have looked like a cancer patient. In contrast to some of the other girls I had met on tour thus far, Ruby had neither fake boobs nor a fake smile. She turned to me and beamed.

'Hey, you must be the famous Bailey Brown I have heard so much about. I am so excited to meet a real writer.'

I blushed and offered a handshake but Ruby pulled me into a tight hug.

'I know we are going to have a blast together on tour, you and I. A definite year to remember.'

It was one of the fastest friendships I had ever made.

Rory and Ruby had met in a coffee shop queue in Margaret River one day when they had simultaneously ordered the last chocolate chip muffin.

'We must be compatible,' was the first thing Rory had said to her.

Ruby had then offered to share the muffin and the rest was history.

'Have you got a boyfriend?' Ruby asked me while Rory lovingly entwined his fingers with hers. 'Are you and Jason you know…?'

I shook my head vigorously.

'God no, you must be joking. Jason and I are just friends. I'm his biographer and we have a professional relationship. I am one hundred percent not looking for love. Besides, he is definitely not my type.'

'Well glad we got that cleared up,' Jason laughed from very close to the back of my neck.

He picked up his surfboard.

'Bailey is off surfers for life, isn't that right, Bailey?'

'Absolutely.'

My eyes flickered over the pack of professional surfers on the beach in various states of undress. There were no ill-fitting elastic waist swimming trunks in this scene. The modesty of the glistening wet bodies of those who had surfed was protected either by a beach towel or by board shorts to the knee in light, quick-dry fabrics that caressed their thighs and hung precariously low on their hips. I had never known hips could be muscular but surfing gave these men muscles in places I had previously thought impossible. This new world I had entered was a feast for the eyes but unfortunately for me, not for the tasting. So much almost hair-free, medium to well-done skin. So many athletic physiques. So much sporting prowess and masculinity. It was like finding oneself locked in the world's most sumptuous chocolate shop for a year and being told not to touch or sample any of the treats on display.

'Absolutely,' I said again, pushing my sunglasses up my nose, 'I am not interested in the slightest.'

I was thankful nobody could see my eyes.

'Shame,' said Ruby, 'we could have had some fun finding you Mr Right.'

Seventeen

The morning of the competition, the island was buzzing with nervous anticipation. G-Land was considered to be one of the most idyllic and perfectly formed barrelling waves in the world. The contest had been held at the break in the past until political instability in Indonesia had made attendance at the event by foreign surfers unadvisable. However, with the threat of terrorism now existing almost worldwide, the sponsors had decided to return the contest to the left-hand reef break that made every surfer on tour dizzy with delight. The prize money for the winner had been elevated from the seventy thousand dollars it originally was, to one hundred thousand to encourage the surfers to participate but, judging by the monkey-like chattering emanating from the competitors' area, the surfers needed little encouragement to surf a wave they dreamed of.

The first round consisted of twelve half-hour heats with three surfers in each. Being the number-one seed as the reigning world champion, Cain surfed against the unfortunate lowest seed. Reluctantly ranked number two, Jason surfed in the other half of the draw. In the interests of pleasing the audience watching online around the globe, it was considered beneficial to have a system in place whereby the top two surfers in the world could only meet in the final.

As was the case in most of the contests, the winner of each heat in round one progressed directly to round three while the losers met again in round two. The loser in round two was then eliminated from the competition. It was a gruelling trip (less so for them than for me perhaps) to the Javanese jungle at great expense just to surf two half-hour heats and leave defeated. Do not pass Go; do not collect one hundred thousand dollars or valuable points.

At the end of the year the Tour waved goodbye to the bottom surfers in the table of the top thirty-two and welcomed into its ranks the top ten surfers from the lower league tour, the WQS. Any surfers who did not re-qualify saw their earnings plummet. It was an idyllic life in many respects but, as with every job, it had its own level of stress. The pressure to perform in death-defying waves every month of the year and not lose a heat to be able to pay the mortgage and feed one's family was stressful no matter how glamorous one's office.

As the contest progressed over the week, Cain and Jason defeated their adversaries with military precision. There was a nervous moment when, with five minutes to go in the semi-final, the surfer competing against Jason scored a nine out of a possible ten to scrape into the lead. Jason was left searching for an almost flawless nine-point-five to win.

'Damn,' I seethed, finding myself more and more engrossed in the action, 'a nine-point-five is almost impossible at this stage.'

'For any normal human, it sure is,' Chuck nodded calmly beneath his fluorescent orange trucker cap, 'but our guy is no normal human.'

Sure enough, as if by magic and with just thirty seconds remaining on the clock, the ocean rose up and morphed into a perfect wall of smooth water that barrelled along the reef. Jason's fellow competitors, Cain being the exception, whistled and cheered. Jason took off and rode the wave with a breathtaking display of brilliance. When the chips were down, Jason often seemed to perform even better. His calmness under pressure while surfing was the sign of a true champion.

Cain was rattled by Jason's last-minute victory. His jet black eyes burned into Jason while they waited to paddle out for the final but Jason simply nodded a good luck, making Cain even more disgruntled. Cain was trailing Jason at the start of his year as reigning world champion, which was a severe knock to his defence of the title, not to mention his pride. He wanted the number one slot so desperately it had knocked him off balance. The more effort Cain made, the more Jason surfed as if his feet were glued to the deck of the board. There was no danger of him falling or making a mistake. For those thirty-five minutes Jason reigned supreme.

'You won!' I applauded enthusiastically when he returned victorious to the beach.

'You bet,' he smiled. 'Did you ever doubt me?'

'I love you man,' said Chuck, embracing Jason with a manly hug while his eyes flickered with dollar signs.

'Three out of three,' said Rory.

He pulled Jason into a hug and then handed him a frosty bottle of beer.

'Best start to the year you could have hoped for, mate, let's celebrate.'

It was not a glamorous party, being as we were in the Javanese jungle miles from civilisation but I dressed up as seemed appropriate. Ruby advised the natural look but that was all very well when she had been blessed with perfect bone structure, a flawless tan and a body that displayed clothes better than a mannequin. However, life in the jungle was a lesson in embracing the natural. There were no hot showers and no electricity in the 'luxury' (to use the term lightly) bungalow after eight p.m. Even before eight, there was not enough power to heat my hair straighteners above tepid so I wore my hair loose in relaxed waves. I applied two layers of Mac mascara in extreme black, brushed my cheekbones with bronzer and finished with a natural lip colour.

Ruby rummaged happily through my clothes and selected for me a black and deep blue Marc Jacobs top with long chiffon sleeves to protect me from mosquitoes. I teamed the top with wide leg trousers and a pair of Ruby's black sandals. They were adorned with oversized gems that could well have been precious stones had I not known Ruby was a girl with unpretentious tastes. Ruby radiated the joy of a young woman who was happy with her lot as long as she had the man she loved and she was able to dip her feet in the ocean every day.

'You look beautiful, darl',' said Ruby when we made our entrance together to the contest party.

'You too,' I said, accepting the compliment with a squeeze of her hand.

A monkey gazed at us admiringly from a nearby tree.

'Whoa, chicks, you look awesome,' Chuck hooted, which attracted the attention of every surfer, surfer's wife and girlfriend (or SWAG as I had christened them), judge, official, sponsor and photographer in the vicinity.

Rory's eyes lit up when he saw Ruby. She gathered up the full skirt of her purple polka dot dress and perched on his knee. I turned away when they kissed and caught Jason's eye. He was looking up at me with his lips parted.

'B, you look hot, girlfriend,' Chuck whistled. 'For real, Jason, doesn't your biographer look hot?'

There was a pause during which I glanced across the room and saw Cain eyeing me with an expression of approval and something else I could not quite put my finger on.

'Yeah she looks good,' said Jason, bringing my attention back to our table, 'really good.'

'Thank you,' I said with a wink, 'now did anybody think to import champagne?'

We ate the same meal we had eaten nearly every day in Java of nasi goreng fried rice with vegetables but we did not care. The simplicity of jungle life was strangely comforting. There was nowhere to go other than into tiger territory and nothing to buy. Our only entertainment other than each other was the fantastic scenery and a few scratched, subtitled DVDs. We watched sunsets and waves instead of mind-numbing television and we made real conversation, forging deeper relationships in weeks than one would over years back home. The stresses of modern life seemed a million miles away and I suddenly realised I felt free of the constraints that had held me back. My mother was still a bitter alcoholic, my sister was still married to a man I despised and my agent still had zero faith in my ability, but I was living a new reality. I felt as if I could reinvent myself and finally be the successful, adventurous woman I had dreamed of being.

'Bailey,' Jason whispered over the plates of half-eaten fried rice, 'do you want to go get some air?'

I glanced around us at the wall-less dining room.

'Isn't there enough air here already?'

'I need to escape,' Jason shrugged. 'I'm a bit drained.'

I nodded and we slipped out into the darkness. The beach was bathed in the light of the moon and the quirky calls of unidentified jungle creatures competed with the constant drum of the ocean. We sat side by side on the boat jetty. I pulled the sleeves of my top down to cover my hands and curled my feet underneath me so as little skin as possible was showing for the mosquitoes to dine on. In the distance the waves darkened the horizon creating the effect of high walls enclosing a medieval town.

'Rory and Ruby are a lovely couple,' I said after a while.

'Aren't they great? They're just meant to be together, aren't they? A dream team.'

'Definitely. Have you noticed how they even look a bit like each other? Same smile, same mannerisms. I think really compatible couples often do.'

'So then I have to find myself a short, buff girl with weird coloured eyes and webbed feet.'

'You're not that short.'

I nudged him.

'Five ten and a half.'

'Don't forget the half. Well it's a good height for a surfer. Low centre of gravity.'

'Hey, you really are learning. I'm impressed.'

I shrugged.

'It's my job. I'm paid to know these things.'

I looked over at him and my eyes travelled down to his feet dangling down towards the still water of the lagoon.

'Did you say webbed feet?'

Jason lifted up his bare foot.

'Yep, my dad does too. It must be something in the water.'

I paused to look.

'That truly is quite disgusting.'

Jason grinned.

'No wonder you surf like you do. You don't have gills as well do you? That may be considered cheating.'

Jason brushed his blond hair from his forehead and laughed.

'No, no gills.'

His eyes met mine and flashed as silver as the reflection of the moon in the water below us.

'I enjoy being with you, you know,' he said after a pause, 'I'm so glad you came back.'

'I am too. This is one experience I would not have missed for the world' - I inhaled deeply, the jungle air fresh and alive - 'and I'm glad you've had such a positive start to the year.'

'You were largely responsible for that. You made me realise I wasn't ready to retire.'

I said nothing as I recalled that fateful night in Hawaii.

Jason slid closer to me.

'I have to tell you, Bailey, you look really special tonight.'

The intensity of his tone made the hairs on the back of my neck stand up. I brushed my hand across my neck and looked into Jason's face.

'You're flirting with me,' I said calmly.

Jason blinked.

'Maybe I am.'

He placed his hand on top of mine on the jetty. It was hard not to feel a thrill. Here we were alone in the jungle after a glorious day. It was no wonder surfers and their entourage oozed sensuality. Watery horizons, immense skies, sand between one's toes and fit bodies were infinitely more sexual than stiff suits meeting in a concrete jungle. I pressed my lips together, feeling as if I had been here before. The thought brought me to my senses.

'I am flattered, Jason' – I slowly withdrew my hand – 'but this is not a good idea.'

'But sleeping with Cain was?'

I jolted at the comment.

'That's beneath you, Jason. I am not some object for you and Cain to fight over. Are you sure you're not just trying to prove a point that you can have me too and beat him at everything?'

I pushed my feet into my sandals and stood up. When I turned to leave Jason jumped up and caught my arm.

'Please, Bailey, I don't think of you like an object at all. I'm sorry, I just…'

His voice broke and we stared at each other. Our faces were centimetres apart and when his breath brushed my cheek a wave of desire rushed through me. He was so overtly masculine and delicious but he was also out of bounds. I would not succumb to the weakness I had displayed with Cain. Not even when he lifted his hand and smoothed it gently over my hair.

Damn, what was it with these surfers? Resisting them was harder than I had ever imagined. Cain and Jason were like chalk and cheese yet there was something about them both that stirred me. Cain momentarily but Jason enduringly so.

'I apologise,' Jason said firmly, 'but you look so incredible and we've become so relaxed with each other. I suppose I was in the celebratory mood after today and here you are.'

He stopped speaking and his other hand moved to my cheek. His palm was warm against my skin. His eyes bore into me, silently willing me to melt like a sandcastle succumbing to the rising tide. Somewhere in the undergrowth a monkey shrieked.

The moment was magical but my head was clear enough for me to make the decision to break the spell.

'I am your biographer, Jason. Besides, you have a girlfriend.'

His lips formed a tight line.

'You mean Portia?'

'Yes I mean Portia.' I stepped away from him. 'I heard she was in Australia.'

Jason stepped back and pushed his hands deep into his pockets.

'Did Chuck tell you that?'

'He mentioned it.' I touched a finger to my lips with a quizzical expression. 'In fact I think his words were, the wicked witch followed Dorothy to Kansas to eat Toto.'

Jason's eyes narrowed.

'I didn't invite her there. I didn't want her to be there but she wouldn't leave. She's needy and unpredictable and she won't take no for an answer. I have to be careful.'

'Why?'

'Because she loses it. She can be a bit crazy.'

I arched one eyebrow.

'You think? And here was I thinking inflicting death by Jimmy Choo was normal.'

Jason laughed sadly.

'She wants to be with me but I can't deal with her. She can't take the travelling. She would never have survived that trip you made to get here.'

I smiled wryly, knowing full well that no man would ever ask a precious girl like Portia to make that journey. She would have flown in by private helicopter unless the ocean could have been ironed flat for a perfectly smooth crossing by luxury cruiser.

'Portia likes her comforts. She loves the fame but she hates the groupies. She's so jealous all the time. She thinks I can't talk to a girl without wanting to screw her.'

I pouted.

'Perhaps she has a point.'

The nerve twitched in Jason's cheek.

'Touché, Bailey, but I promise you I'm not like that. The groupies try their best to seduce me, sure, but I don't succumb. That's not what I'm looking for. Not now.'

'Not now?'

He cleared his throat nervously.

'I indulged when I was young and stupid. I was brought up by a dad who thinks women are just docking stations for his dick.'

'Sounds like a pleasant chap.'

'He was all I had so he was my role model until I realised that was not who I was. I made mistakes but haven't we all?'

The silence between us was deafening. I looked down at my feet.

'Sorry if I offended you, Bailey. I'm not perfect when it comes to dealing with women. I guess I could put it down to the fact I missed having a mom around.'

'Really? Do you want mine? She's a fucking nightmare,' I smirked.

A smile spread across Jason's face and I laughed, safe in the knowledge that the awkward moment had passed.

'I guess there's a lot we have to find out about each other over the year,' Jason said.

'Well I have to find out everything about you or this book will be very short.'

He hooked his arm through mine and we turned to head back towards the party.

'I need to know everything,' I said, 'warts and all.'

'Hey I definitely don't have warts.'

'I am talking metaphorical warts.'

'Right. So how about a metaphorical kiss?'

I elbowed him in the ribs.

'Don't push your luck, surfer boy. Now come on, your party awaits.'

California

Eighteen

The next morning, a luxurious speedboat picked us up from G-Land and raced us back to Bali to board a plane to LAX. No bone-rattling bus journey or boa constrictor this time, which was not to say the journey was uneventful. When Chuck heard a strange noise coming from the cabin, we investigated only to discover the skipper had brought along his baby (note: *man eating*) Komodo dragon because, and I quote, 'He gets lonely at home.' If it wasn't for the fact his mouth was only big enough to bite off a finger or two I would have been quite upset. However, the traveller spirit must have rubbed off on me because after tigers and rats, I found sharing my boat ride with a man-eating dinosaur quite amusing. Perhaps it was just as well we were heading for the materialism of Los Angeles or before one could say tie-dye I would be changing my name to Sunshine and converting to Buddhism.

Jason made the flight arrangements en route by calling his travel agent. From the personal tone of the conversation and the swift, book-my-usual orders, it was clear he was not talking to a school leaver at your average travel agent with a qualification in sunbeds. I vowed to one day be important enough to have my own travel agent.

At Denpasar, Oli, the surfers' team manager representing their sponsor, joined Jason, Chuck, Rory, Ruby and I. Oli was a small, rotund man resembling a Weeble with salt and pepper hair growing in a small island on the tip of his forehead. I put his age at pushing fifty but he dressed like a teenager in a hoodie bearing a skate slogan. Oli was pre-programmed to talk to a woman's chest rather than her face. He also had the annoying habit of rolling his eyes and jabbing his tongue inside his cheek whenever a girl walked past who a) was young enough to not remember the early eighties and b) had two legs.

Poseidon, the leading multinational surf brand who paid Jason's seven-figure salary, employed Oli to keep all the team riders happy and organised. A rookie like Rory did not have a personal manager like Chuck so it fell to Oli to coordinate his travels, photo shoots, competitions and promotional events. Jason was the darling of the team and Oli was obliged to tread the delicate line between encouraging Jason to attend events to promote the brand while pandering to his every need. Oli also had to run every request by Chuck, which, as far as I could tell, involved the two managers rucking like two angry tortoises before eventually reaching a compromise and then walking away to bitch about each other like schoolgirls.

'That guy is a dick,' Chuck growled in my ear after one such contretemps in the Denpasar airport lounge.

'He speaks very highly of you too, Charles. Why what's he done this time?'

Chuck flicked his head back and smoothed his hair away from his high forehead.

'Oh I dunno, he wants Jason to model for some hotshot New York photographer with a movie star and a couple of supermodels or some shit.'

'Gosh, sounds awful.'

'For real,' Chuck tsked and wandered away without having the slightest notion I was being sarcastic.

When we boarded the plane to Los Angeles, I automatically turned right, brightly greeting the air hostess in the hope she would appreciate my politeness and not run out of my choice of meal just as she got to my row. Her make-up was so thick her face appeared to jut out from her body as if I were seeing her through 3D glasses.

'Ma'am, your seat is this way,' she said with a laugh that sounded like a crystal chandelier crashing down from the ceiling.

Passengers pushed up behind me like cows ramming themselves through the gate to pasture.

Following the hostess' outstretched arm, I squeezed back through the crowd and pointed at a fold down seat next to the restroom.

'This one you mean? You are joking.'

I thought Jason had given up on the practical jokes.

'DVT is a certainty if I have to sit on that for twenty hours. I'd be better off on the toilet.'

The hostess creased her make-up as she stared quizzically at me.

'In here, Bailey,' I heard Jason laugh.

He poked his head through the first class divide.

'It's Jason Cross,' said voices in a whisper that raced the entire length of the plane like an autumn breeze.

Jason reached out for my bag with one hand, for my arm with the other and pulled me into a world I had never thought I would see. There were sofa-sized seats with enough legroom to do the Can Can. I had my own television, a luxury blanket and socks as soft as silk. A naturally beautiful airhostess who looked genuinely pleased to serve me, deftly poured champagne into a real glass.

'You don't get this in Economy Plus,' I whispered to Jason.

'I wouldn't know,' he replied with a wry smile and I believed him.

'Jason, how much is this flight? I don't think I can afford it,' I mouthed.

'You can't. This one's on me. Now get some sleep.'

I slipped on the headphones and sank back into the comfortable seat. How, I wondered, would I ever be able to return to my normal life when this job ended?

Jason and Rory lived a truly jet-set life between surf breaks and did not seem to have anything resembling roots. They caught flights the way most of us would catch a bus and Jason would probably have thought nothing of hopping straight back on a flight if he suddenly realised he had left behind a favourite pair of shoes. Jetlag did not seem to affect them the way it did most people. The overwhelming tiredness and the feeling of disorientation every morning I awoke in a new location was something I would have to get used to.

Both surfers were booked to tour California before the next scheduled contest, making personal appearances, opening surf shops, appearing on television and radio shows and launching new Poseidon products.

'I need clothes, Oli, can you sort it?' said Jason when we landed in LAX.

From the speed of Oli's reaction one would have thought Jason had screamed – 'FIRE!'.

One urgent phone call later and we were pulling up outside Poseidon's U.S. head office in Irvine, south of

Long Beach. I was exhausted and keen to collapse onto a hotel room bed but I was not even handing out fliers for this show never mind running it. I had no choice but to follow Jason's schedule, but my bottom lip was becoming more petulant by the second.

The California sky was a vibrant blue and the sun sizzled on the bonnet of our black SUV but, after a month in the tropics, I could feel the hairs on my arms standing up in protest against the dip in temperature. The American obsession with air conditioning did not help either. The plush reception area was so cold I could have hung CDs from my nipples.

'Welcome everyone,' the receptionist gushed, bouncing to her feet with enthusiasm.

Her silicone breasts remained perfectly still.

She wiggled out from behind the desk as if she was trying to keep a hula-hoop whizzing around her waist and bent down to air-kiss Oli. Open-mouthed, he happily greeted her breasts before they turned their attention to Jason.

'Jason, how lovely to see you again,' she said in a noticeably higher tone of voice.

'Hey Bambi,' said Jason with a polite nod.

Bambi? I threw Ruby a knowing glance while Bambi tried her level best to flirt and flutter her way into Jason's pants.

We were led through the offices that were steeped in surf culture. Every wall was curved like a wave and hung with stunning photographs of surfers and oceans. High-gloss, colourful surfboards suspended from the ceiling looked good enough to eat. Rock music played over a speaker system in some parts of the building while mood lighting and the sounds of waves drew us into others.

'Is it part of the job description that you have to be gorgeous and a size zero to work here?' I whispered to Chuck as we emerged from a bank of secretaries who could quite easily have been supermodels.

He shook his head, stopped shaking it, stopped to think and then chirped – 'Yep.'

We then entered a vestibule with a high-vaulted ceiling that refracted the sun's rays in a magically kaleidoscopic fashion. The photographs in this room were entirely dedicated to Jason and his glittering career, which was even more glittering when represented by twelve gold world champion trophies and numerous other accolades.

'Is that you?' I gasped, pointing at a photo of an angelic young boy clinging to a surfboard that he could barely get his arm around.

The board had a red lightning bolt running down the centre.

Jason looked thoughtful.

'My first contest victory.'

'Wow, you were so cute.'

'What do you mean, *were*?'

I laughed and reached in my bag for my notebook. This room was like a pictorial condensed biography of all the good parts of Jason's career. The low moments were of course noticeably lacking.

'Pay homage at the altar of Jason Cross the Almighty,' said Chuck, raising up his lanky arms and whooshing his body down into a low bow.

'Give it a rest, Chuck,' said Jason, but I could tell he was proud of his own achievements, which he was entitled to be judging by the glorious display in the room.

I had my head down frantically making notes when Ruby tugged at my sleeve and said - 'Come on, darl', this is the good bit.'

She dragged me off ahead of the others, out of the Jason shrine and across a palm tree-lined atrium towards a set of double doors.

'Do you like shopping?' she said, her blue eyes flashing with excitement.

'No.'

Ruby's face fell.

'Of course I do, Ruby. Why?'

Ruby pointed a bony finger and I turned my head just as Oli opened the double doors with a flourish. I peered into the next room expecting to see yet more tributes to Jason, whose success and marketability had probably paid for the building and its entire staff.

My jaw dropped when I saw the rows and rows of clothes stretching out before me. There was every colour and every fabric a girl could ever imagine. Hawaiian prints nestled between plaids and denim, alongside silks and chunky knits. One wall was entirely devoted to accessories. Luggage, handbags, parasols, shoes, sandals and things for which I could not immediately see a purpose but which looked so adorable I most definitely needed one of each.

'It's an enormous surf shop,' I breathed, as my feet seemed to lift off the ground and float me towards the fiesta of fashion.

'And best of all, it's totally free,' giggled Ruby who was floating along beside me.

'Free? In what way is it free?'

'Like you don't have to pay. You just help yourself, darl'. Show Oli what you've chosen so he can make a list and then it's all yours. How ripper is that?'

'Fill your boots,' Chuck hollered. 'You're part of the team now. Dude, this is like chick paradise.'

'Looks like Chuck paradise to me,' I laughed as Chuck sprinted past me and dived into the male clothing section.

I had never realised I was so superficial but after a gratis shopping spree at Poseidon, during which I selected every desirable item a surf chick could ever want, I really began to like Oli. At least momentarily.

Nineteen

I enjoyed the Californian lifestyle and its spring climate of fresh mornings and warm afternoon sunshine. While Jason and Rory carried out their commitments to their sponsor, Ruby and I power walked on the beach, swam, shopped and spent hours at one of the many cosmopolitan cafes in Newport and Laguna Beach. Ruby was an ideal companion who did not feel the need to fill silences. I wrote while Ruby hungrily read novel after novel, stopping occasionally to comment on our production line. I was writing the books and she was reading them. We were the perfect team. We were not, however, one hundred percent conscientious as it was extremely hard to resist the urge to people watch. We kept a tally of silicone breasts and dogs small enough to be classified as rodents. Many of the latter were clothed in Juicy Couture, as in fact were many of the former and the two were often spotted together. Dogs in baby buggies were everywhere.

The items on the café menus were invariably organic, natural or GM free and all the cakes either resembled lumps of congealed seaweed or solidified horse manure.

'What's that one there?' I asked the girl in our regular haunt.

She was so slim and tanned she resembled a twig in shorts.

'That's a fat free, wheat free, gluten free, dairy free, sugar free oatcake.'

'It sounds delightful,' I grimaced. 'Free of everything. I bet free doesn't stretch as far as the price though.'

'That one's four dollars, Ma'am.'

'Gosh, I hope it's worth it.'

'Of course. It's always worth being good to your body and soul.'

'Yes, quite.'

Was it wrong that that made me want to ask for chocolate fudge cake?

I ordered what emerged to also be a taste free oatcake from the humour free twig, washed down with a caffeine free, sugar free, coffee free coffee and got back to work. It was ironic how the women around us clearly prided themselves on only consuming the most natural of foods while the faces they fed them into were almost entirely fake.

Ruby and I put people watching on hold to attend the final event of the publicity tour; the grand opening of Poseidon's flagship store in Huntington Beach. It promised to be more of a spectacle than the simple cutting of a ribbon. This shop was so expansive it was like the Disneyland of surf fashion. There were televisions larger than many movie screens suspended from vaulted ceilings and a sound system that boomed bass through the floor into the soles of our feet. Parts of the floor were made of glass under which swam tropical fish, giving the shopper the feeling of walking on water. Thousands of glossy surfboards begging to be purchased stood upright in the racks like soldiers standing to attention. On a catwalk runway in the centre of the store, female models swayed their sharp hipbones from side to side in multi-coloured bikinis fashioned for the surf chick to be sexy yet practical for surfing. Ruby had chosen five boy-short bikinis in the time it took me to fetch two glasses of champagne.

Jason was literally drowning in compliments and gifts from the hundreds of adoring fans who had queued, many overnight, to meet their idol. He displayed admirable patience with them all and signed enough autographs to fill the pages of the telephone book. One girl who had hitch-hiked from San Diego presented Jason with a beanie hat hand-knitted from what I suspected to be her own hair. Personally, I would have stamped a restraining order on her forehead and had her ejected from the building, but Jason simply accepted the gift, chatted to the girl for five minutes and left her feeling like she was floating on air. Which she very likely was on the planet she inhabited.

There were a group of terminally ill children from a nearby hospital, many in wheelchairs with skin as yellow as sulphur. Jason talked animatedly with them and hugged them to him. He signed posters and gave every one of the children his mobile number in case they ever wanted to chat. He then ordered the Poseidon staff to kit out the children head to toe in the latest surf wear. The delight on their faces as if they had not a care in the world broke my heart.

In contrast, Jason then met a gaggle of teenage girls who wore T-shirts printed with 'Mrs Jason Cross' across their unfeasibly ample chests. Jason joked with the girls and their aspirations burst into the stratosphere but he took care to keep his comments appropriate. Ruby and I laughed at the girls' giddy reaction and wondered if we had ever been the same as teenagers. Surely not?

There were fans of all ages and backgrounds from all over California as well as visitors from as far afield as England, Australia and South Africa, all hoping for a few minutes of Jason's time, which he gave without question.

While I watched Jason in quiet admiration, a young boy stepped purposefully forward and looked directly at him. The boy's appearance made me step closer for a better look. Judging him against Zac, he was about eight years old, I guessed small for his age, with a shock of white blond hair to his shoulders and skin the colour of caramel. His face was gorgeous enough to send advertisers into a frenzy but his mouth was set in a grim line. I gasped when I recognised the familiar expression of serious determination.

A baggy t-shirt and denim shorts that stopped mid-way down his skinny calves only accentuated his tiny build. His bulky skate shoes made his bony legs look like golf clubs. Jason removed his own cap, which sent a wave of delight coursing through the awaiting fans. Every move he made created a sort of personal tornado that whizzed around every room Jason entered and sent people into a spin. While girls gasped and giggled around us, the little boy remained still and emotionless. When he lifted his eyes and looked directly at me there was no doubt in my mind. His eyes glinted like silver coins.

Caught up in his role as the surf star in attendance, Jason scribbled his well-practised signature on a poster and held it out to the boy. He did not react. Jason lowered his arm

'Do you surf, kid? What's your name?'

'Little shit,' I heard Oli grunt who had just arrived to witness the boy's stony silence.

'Here,' Jason smiled, 'have my cap, I've got plenty more.'

Jason crouched down until he was level with the boy's face and placed the Poseidon cap gently on the boy's halo of hair. The boy stood tall for a moment before he tipped his head towards the ground. Jason's cap fell at his feet and he lifted his giant shoe with a monumental effort to stamp the cap into the floor.

'I don't want your cap, Mister,' he said. 'I got plenty of my own and I don't want your signature neither.'

Jason stood up and tilted his head, unaccustomed to such a reaction.

'Then what do you want, kid?'

The boy ran his forearm underneath his nose and sniffed.

'I dunno, I guess I just wanted to see what my daddy looked like.'

The silence was deafening before Oli slapped his forehead and groaned – 'Fuck me, that's a fucking shocker.'

A hurricane of gasps and whispers coursed around the room and Jason stumbled backwards, his eyes fixed on the boy's face as if an invisible thread connected them. I stepped up to steady Jason. His body felt stiff to the touch. The crowd fizzed, having been privy to such a revelation, while the boy remained rooted to the spot.

'I…' Jason began. 'Who…?'

'Where the fuck are his parents?' Oli hissed as he foresaw the Poseidon publicity machine being outfoxed by an eight year-old boy.

'It appears you're looking at one of them.'

Oli scowled up at me.

'Very funny. Little shit's been put up to this. Probably looking for money.'

'He's a child, Oli.'

'Doesn't stop them bleeding people dry to feel big.'

'Says a man who has to stand on his wallet to feel tall,' I muttered under my breath while Oli wrestled his way into the centre of the confrontation.

'I think we should break this up right now,' he announced.

Jason ran his hands through his hair as he struggled to deal with the moment. The polished professional I had been watching all day was crumbling before the eyes of his public.

'Jason, perhaps we should all go somewhere private to talk,' I whispered.

Jason jolted as if he had just awoken from a sleep walk. He glanced at the dumbstruck crowd that was growing by the second.

'Yes, yes of course, Bailey, you're right as ever.'

Oli muttered something under his breath and threw me another scowl.

Jason crouched back down on his haunches to bring his face level with the boy's.

'What did you say your name was again, kid?'

Unnerved now by Jason's proximity, the boy looked down at his feet and scuffed his shoe along the floor.

'I didn't but it's Harrison. Harrison Evans.'

Jason pressed his lips together.

'And, your mother's name?'

The crowd sniggered and gasped simultaneously.

'Lilia Evans, sir. D'you remember her?'

Jason interlocked his fingers and exhaled slowly.

'I didn't know. I'm sorry, Harrison, I didn't know.'

'Now you do.'

The boy turned on his heel and marched proudly away, the squeak of his rubber soles filling the silence as everybody watched the boy leave and then turned to look at Jason. I half expected Jason to run after him but he slumped as if every muscle in his body ached and silently allowed his son to walk out of his life.

Twenty

We were walking on eggshells around Jason for the next few days while he closed the shutters around him and tried to internally process Harrison's revelation. Ruby and Rory took advantage of the down time to have a romantic break alone in Malibu. Oli's eggshells, meanwhile, were crushed to dust beneath his feet while he stomped around protesting at Jason's attention having been diverted from the objectives of the world title and of making Poseidon money.

'He's just discovered he's a father, dude, that's some pretty heavy shit right there. I mean that is one mega head funk,' Chuck commented.

'It's not the first time some whore's tried to catch him like this,' Oli growled. 'I mean it's a meal ticket, right? I betcha the kid ain't even his.'

'You saw the child, Oli,' I said, 'the likeness was unmistakeable.'

'Whatever. I want tests to prove it.'

'That's up to Jason, I think.'

'I am the boss round here,' Oli seethed, 'and what I say goes.'

I arched an eyebrow and looked down at the primordial dwarf Jason had to deal with as his team manager.

Jason neatly disproved Oli's dictatorship theory when he refused to appear on a live television show that

Oli had planned without his prior consent. The talk show theme was the image of the professional athlete and their responsibilities as role models, which even tactless Chuck realised was a little close to the bone for comfort. Jason explained calmly to Oli that his head was not in the right place for him to be able to paint on his public face and discuss the subject without becoming emotionally involved. Oli listened, nodding his head mechanically and pretending to understand but as soon as Jason left the room, his temper erupted like a burst water main.

'Fucking surf divas!' he yelled, his face tight and scarlet, 'can't fucking rely on them to do anything except surf, bed women and play poker. This is only the biggest motherfucking talk show in the U.S. Like it's not a big fucking deal!'

I peered at his ears in the hope I would actually see smoke come out of them.

'Chill out, Oli man, this is not the way to deal with the situation, you know what I'm sayin'?'

Oli turned a spectacular shade of violet.

'Don't tell me how to deal with this bullshit situation, Chuck. You should be sorting this, he's your fucking client!'

'And he's your top team rider,' Chuck shrugged, clearly enjoying seeing Oli lose the plot.

'If he doesn't back down and agree to do this talk show I swear I will fire his ass.'

'No you won't. No-one fires their number one asset, dude.'

Chuck looked at his nails as if checking them for dirt and sucked in his cheeks. His nonchalance only served to make Oli even more infuriated.

'Which is not to say,' Chuck carried on, 'Poseidon won't fire *your* ass for not getting him to agree to do the show. I mean it's live TV, man, people will notice for real. You're right, that could look real bad for you.'

Jason appeared just in time to stop Oli throttling Chuck with his sausage-like fingers. For someone who had been immersed in personal turmoil for the best part of a week, Jason appeared surprisingly calm and rested. In direct contrast, in fact, to his management team who were distinctly off-balance without Jason's usual clear direction.

I smiled at him, the perfect picture of a well-groomed professional. He wore a black short-sleeved shirt embroidered in silver with the image of the Japanese Kanagawa tidal wave by Hokusai. The sharp, wide collar accentuated the breadth of his shoulders. His black trousers were as crisp as if they had just been removed from their packaging for the first time, which they very likely had. They were cinched in at his slim waist with a smooth leather belt. His blond hair, relaxed as ever, was smooth and shiny. He would not have looked out of place in a Gucci ad.

Jason placed the black leather weekend bag he held on the floor and cleared his throat.

'Where the fuck are you going now?' Oli fumed.

'Not that I have to run it by you, Oli, but I need some headspace before the Tahiti contest so I'm taking a break. Besides, Bailey and I have got work to do on the book.'

I blinked when Oli span around to scowl at me.

'Pack a few things, Bailey, we're going on a trip.'

I clapped my hands.

'I'll meet you in the SUV.' He turned to Chuck. 'You know where to find me.'

Chuck nodded.

'Just with everything that's happened I feel like I need to go home.'

Chuck hugged Jason. He bent down and picked up his bag before walking up to Oli.

'And if you ever threaten to fire me again I swear I will come down on you like a sixty-foot wave at Jaws.'

Lost for words, Oli opened and closed his mouth.

'I didn't know you…' His voice cracked.

'Where's home?' I asked over my shoulder as I headed off to pack.

'You'll see,' Jason smiled. 'It might not be quite what you expect.'

Twenty-One

We drove for three hours, during which we talked about everything from music and movies to food and fashion; everything except the child-shaped elephant in the room. It was his issue, so I let him dance around it. If he wanted to talk to me about his illegitimate son, he would when the time was right.

We were in the remote countryside when we pulled up outside a huge wooden gate painted glossy red. The centre of the gate was branded with the letters RCR burned into the wood. Jason applied the handbrake and hopped out of the SUV to speak into an intercom. The gate slid smoothly across. A winding, dusty driveway stretched infinitely before us. Through the darkness I heard the whinnying of horses.

'Where are we?'

'The Ricky Cross Ranch,' said Jason.

With no further explanation, he pulled himself back up into the SUV and drove on. The gate slid shut automatically behind us. We meandered at a respectful speed through a cosy canopy of gnarled old trees. Ten minutes into the property, I was wondering whether we would ever find civilisation when suddenly the canopy opened out into a clearing lit by fairy lights. A green gypsy caravan sat in the centre of a fenced garden, guarded by a pack of innumerable black and white collie puppies that looked more capable of licking an intruder to death than anything useful.

'Who lives there?' I gasped. 'The witch from Hansel and Gretel or Gypsy Rose Lee?'

Jason laughed and I rummaged in my bag for my camera.

'Actually you're looking at my childhood home.'

I almost dropped the camera.

'You're kidding?'

He shook his head.

'You grew up in a gypsy caravan?'

He nodded.

'But I thought you were the glossy Californian boy next door. How did you ever come from here to be the greatest surfer of all time?'

'That's what you're here to find out. I thought it would be better to show you than just talk about it for the book.'

I whistled.

'Well I'm glad you did. This is something quite unexpected' - I glanced again at the tiny caravan – 'and really quite special.'

'I'm glad you like it and, by the way, thanks for the compliment about being the greatest surfer of all time.'

I playfully punched his arm.

'It was a slip of the tongue. Don't let it go to your head.'

He laughed.

'But I have to admit, Jason, you've come a long way.'

Jason paused before he spoke.

'In some ways yes but' – he touched his hand to his chest – 'in here maybe not so far.'

I smiled and raised my bare feet onto the dashboard, tucking my hands under my knees.

'It can be a wonderful thing to have roots,' I said.

I omitted to comment though that, as in my case, if the roots were rotten the tree could be rather unstable.

We drove on towards a barn stacked to the roof with hay bales like a giant box of Shredded Wheat.

'So,' I grinned when Jason stopped the car, 'are you going to show me your crystal ball?'

'Give me a break, I'm not a gypsy,' he smirked.

We jumped down from the SUV and collected our bags from the back.

'Hello, my loverly, wanna buy a lucky rabbit's foot?'

'Stop,' Jason laughed, 'come on it's this way.'

He picked up my bag and led the way past the barn. The air was an aromatic melange of fresh hay, horse manure and burning wood.

'Hopefully my dad will have the barbecue going.'

'Lovely,' I said as I negotiated my way around gooey pats of what I hoped was mud, 'I should have brought something as a gift. Will he be happy if I just cross his palm with silver?'

The house was breathtaking. It had been fashioned out of local wood and stone and stood reverently on the top of a hill surveying the acres of land that made up the ranch. At the front of the house, a wide, open porch with a huge empty rocking chair took me back to my childhood days reading *Anne Of Green Gables.* I imagined blissful warm evenings spent curled up in the chair, reading a book to the light of the lanterns swinging from the roof beams above. They provided a squeaky percussion to the sound of guitar playing emanating from the west side of the house.

A horse wandered past as naturally as my neighbour's cats that frequented the balcony of my flat. Our feet crunched on the gravel pathway leading to the side of the house, alerting two large Alsatians who bounded around the corner with teeth bared. I yelped and held on to Jason. Hopefully if they were going to eat anyone, they would go for the meatier one of us.

'Mundy, Tav, meet Bailey Brown,' said Jason.

He bent down to welcome the two man-eating wolves that instantly became as docile as a couple of sleepy sheep. They rolled over and allowed Jason to tickle them, their tongues lolling indulgently between their teeth. I bent down beside him and stroked the dogs.

'Which one's which?'

'Mundy's the girl. She's called after Mundaka, my favourite reef break wave in Northern Spain. We'll be going there in the summer.'

'I can't wait. Hello, Mundy.'

'Tav is short for the wave Tavarua in Fiji.'

'Do they realise how international they are?'

'Their names might be but they don't go further than Ojai the nearest town.'

'They seem happy enough. Are they yours?'

Jason nodded.

'You must miss them.'

I stroked Mundy between her front paws and she let out a long sigh of gratitude.

'Don't go getting used to that soppy shit,' said a voice as gravelly as the ground.

I sharply withdrew my hand and just as quickly the dogs scrambled to attention and bowed their heads respectfully. I peered into the darkness. The man who emerged from the smoky air billowing down the side of the house was just short of six foot tall with wide, pointed shoulders and a willowy but toned frame. His clothes hung on him as if he were made of wire. He wore a red checked shirt tucked into well-worn jeans that were held up on his narrow hips by a leather belt with a large, scratched silver buckle. On his feet was a pair of brown leather cowboy boots with heels. A chocolate brown Stetson partially shadowed his face but I could tell he was a ruggedly handsome man in his fifties who could well have been the Marlboro man in his day. His full-lipped mouth stretched slowly into a half-smile.

'How are ya, son?'

'I'm good, Dad, how are you?'

Jason and his father embraced with a stiff hug.

'Dad, this is Bailey.'

A pleasant aroma of musk mixed with fresh cut wood circled my nostrils as I approached Jason's father. He doffed his hat.

'Welcome, Bailey,' he growled, 'I'm Ricky Cross.'

'Hello, Ricky I'm Jason's biographer.'

Ricky looked me up and down and arched his eyebrow.

'He's got a biographer now has he? Well that's a new one.'

We shook hands. His skin was as rough as an old rhinoceros.

Ricky replaced his hat before wrapping his arm around Jason's wide shoulders and leading him away towards the smell of a roasting animal.

'She's a cutie,' I heard Ricky say as I picked my way over the gravel behind them, 'are you screwing her or can I have a go?'

Twenty-Two

We ate crispy spit-roasted pig served with mounds of mashed sweet potato and chargrilled corn on the cob smothered in butter. We washed down the hearty meal with bottles of cold beer. Jason ate as if he hadn't eaten in weeks and Ricky's right-hand man, Jesus (pronounced Heyzoos) entertained us on his guitar while we indulged in sweet pumpkin pie swimming in cream. Ricky regaled us with stories of his youth and of chasing women, which was seemingly his primary hobby. He showed little respect for the fairer sex and I wondered whether he had always been so macho or whether he had become that way after suffering a broken heart.

I quizzed Jason about his father when we took the empty dessert plates into the house. It emerged Ricky had been a champion surfer who was talented enough to be a world-beater until drugs, girls and an injury put his career into free-fall. Jason then explained how his mother had acted like the parachute, rescuing Ricky just before he hit the ground. She had led him towards a new life and, once recovered from his debauched history, Ricky had intended to rebuild his surfing career. However, his beautiful wife then fell pregnant and Ricky had to find a job to pay for his new family. Professional surfing did not have the same salary structure in the Sixties and Seventies as it later came to have for Jason's generation. Ricky put his dream on hold and found temporary work as a ranch hand on the ranch that his own son would eventually buy for him and rename the RCR. The only evidence that remained of Ricky's surfing career was a tarnished and dented cup that Jason showed me. It nestled between family photographs on the thick wooden mantel above the open fireplace in the main room of the house.

'Californian Champion 1966,' I read aloud from the cup's worn engraving, 'Ricky Jason Cross. So that's where you get your surfing genes from.'

'I guess it could be hereditary. We don't talk about it much.'

He doesn't talk about anything except himself much, I was tempted to say, but I bit my tongue and concentrated on the family photographs.

'Did your father resent your mother getting pregnant? Is that why he acts the way he does about women?'

'Not at all. He was totally crazy about her. He fell apart when she died.'

'How did she die?'

'In childbirth. I would have had a younger brother but he died too. It was a horrible tragedy. My dad would have done anything for my mom but he couldn't save her life. Apparently he was the one who wanted more kids so I think he blamed himself.'

I reached out and touched his arm.

'I'm sorry, I didn't mean to pry.'

'You're not prying. I brought you here to show you everything about me so I guess we have to do it.'

I nodded sadly.

'Your poor father. I know how it feels to lose someone you adore.'

Jason brushed his hands back through his hair and took a deep breath.

'Well that is one gene I hope I have inherited. The ability to love as deeply as he loved her.'

I looked at Jason. He was lost in his thoughts.

'You will one day,' I said, 'and she will be a lucky girl.'

His smile was genuine and warm.

I picked up a photograph.

'So who is the boy beside you in these pictures?'

Jason touched a finger to the picture and paused before he spoke.

'That's my brother, Mike. He's a crazy kid. He's caused more trouble than the government.'

'I didn't know you had a brother. You've never mentioned him. Where does he live? Does he surf?'

Jason exhaled towards the ceiling.

'No, there aren't any waves where he is.'

'You don't mean...?'

'No no, he's not dead. He's alive but he's not here. He's in jail.'

'Thank God for that.' I grimaced. 'Sorry, I mean I guess it's better than being dead.'

I pressed my knuckle against my mouth to shut myself up. Jason tilted his head and surprised me by smiling.

'I think I might take my feet out of my mouth and toddle off to the bathroom,' I grimaced. 'Can you point me in the right direction?'

The bathroom was effortlessly and delightfully rural in style. The sink was big enough to bathe sheep in and the bath stood on metal legs that I imagined had long supported many a dirty cowboy after a day spent rounding up cattle. The toilet was in an adjoining room of its own with a warped door that fit the doorframe as poorly as a round peg in a square hole. I sat down and jammed my foot against the bottom of the door. I was just flushing the toilet when I heard the distinctive clunk of cowboy boot heel on the knotted wooden floor outside. When I opened the door, there stood Ricky. He was reclined against the wall with his feet crossed at the ankles and his thumbs hooked into the belt loops of his jeans. His hat was on at a jaunty angle and a smile played on his lips. I smoothed down the back of my skirt, smiled back and turned to wash my hands.

'How's about it then, girl?' he growled. 'You, me and some hot lovin'?'

Did he really just say 'hot lovin'?

I laughed. Ricky's arm flew up to catch his Stetson that toppled from his head.

'What? What are you laughing at?'

He looked genuinely surprised.

'I'm sorry, Ricky, I'm flattered but come on, "hot lovin'"?'

He visibly squirmed.

'It was all I could think of at the time.'

I turned and winked.

'It needs a bit of work, Ricky. You don't have to play this game with me. I'm here to understand you all and I'm guessing that is not who you really are.'

Ricky's eyes met mine. He was wrong-footed. He blushed before he started to laugh. He really had fantastic bone structure and the most peculiar eyes, like lumps of granite with silver specks.

'I've got an image to keep up. Oh well, it was worth a try.'

'I suppose and perhaps if you weren't Jason's father, you never know,' I teased. 'I mean you do have something of the Clint Eastwood about you.'

Ricky gripped his chest like a wounded soldier.

'Clint Eastwood? But that dude is so old.'

'I didn't say you looked the same age.'

Ricky shook his head.

'Man, you English girls really say it how it is.'

'We tend to, yes.'

'OK, that works for me. Jason could do with a girl like you around. You're different, you're interesting. I like that.'

A thought struck me that I had heard the line before. I must have looked quizzical because Ricky stepped back and raised his palms.

'What? What now? Don't go telling me I remind you of John Wayne.'

'No,' I laughed, 'not John Wayne but you do remind me of someone. It's strange but I feel as if I've met you before.'

Ricky shook his head.

'Nope, I would definitely have remembered you.' He led the way back towards the main room. 'Especially with comments like that.'

'Yes I am rather unforgettable.'

We rounded the corner and came face to face with Jason who looked from his father to me and back again with a bemused expression.

'Everything alright?' he asked, slowly handing me one of the beers in his hand into which he had slipped a sliver of lime.

'Everything's great, thank you,' I said.

'Yeah, son, everything's good.'

Ricky nodded and patted his son on the shoulder before clomping away in his heavy, masculine boots.

'Clint Eastwood,' I heard him mutter, 'holy shit, kill me now.'

Twenty-Three

During my time spent on the surfing scene I had learned it was hard to motivate a professional surfer to do anything other than surf, check the surf, travel across the world to surf, write a song about surfing, plan the next surf and occasionally play golf when the surf was not up to scratch. Admittedly if I were paid a million pounds to live on the beach and ride waves for a living I probably would not have been very motivated to entertain the monotonies of life either. However, once immersed in ranch life, Jason showed a real commitment to our book. Away from the hype of the surf world, it was as if he could finally concentrate on the non-aqueous thoughts sheltering in drier corners of his brain.

I enjoyed my most restful sleeps for months in a king size cast iron bed under a handmade quilt that had me dreaming I was Laura Ingalls in *Little House On The Prairie.* We rose early every morning and after one of Ricky's hearty breakfasts of homemade pancakes, eggs, bacon, fresh fruit and copious amounts of strong coffee, Jason and I helped to feed the cattle and horses before taking a drive around the perimeter of the ranch to check all was well on the acres of land.

The climate was hot and dry in Ventura County, turning the fields into a seared carpet of yellow grass. Purple rocky mountains and proud old trees broke up the landscape. A flat field of soil in one sunny corner was a pumpkin patch where, Jesus informed me, the huge orange vegetables grew on the surface in October and November, appearing as if they had been dropped from the sky.

Ranch life was not the place for dainty sandals and designer wedges, which gave me the perfect excuse to go shopping at the cowboy outfitter store in downtown Ventura. Jason introduced me to Jesse and Earl, two ripe old cowboys with paunchy bellies and well-fed cheeks, who had taken the store over from their father and grandfather. Jesse and Earl had known Jason since he was a child who had tried to sell them pumpkins he had pilfered from the ranch. They were fiercely proud of their local champion although they hid the reverence behind their wit.

'Jason have we got some boots for you, boy. These beauties are only five thousand a piece. You probably got that in small change, ain't ya?'

'Betcha he has, Earl, but them white leather boots ain't the done thing to be wearing on the beach now. He'd attract all the wrong sorts in high heeled boots and that rubber suit he wears.'

Jason laughed off their comments.

'I don't need boots, guys, but we need to turn Bailey here into a cowgirl. Show her what you got.'

I was somehow coaxed into Wrangler jeans I would not have been seen dead in back home and a Mexican leather belt with a spectacularly bejewelled buckle. Jason selected a tan beaver Stetson, which he pressed onto my head. I brushed my hair back over my shoulders and tapped the shaped brim of the hat.

'How do I look?'

'Pretty as a picture,' Earl whistled.

'Makes me wish I was ten years younger,' Jesse sighed.

'So you'd be young enough to be her grandpa you mean,' Earl goaded him.

I flicked up the collar of the grey and white gingham shirt I had selected from the racks and smiled. The hat, I had to admit, gave me an air of confidence that only a Stetson can.

'Boots. I need boots,' I said.

'Step this way, Ma'am.'

The cowboy boots were masterpieces of leather workmanship, each one designed for a purpose.

'These here are your work boots,' Earl explained, 'these are for rodeo, the pink ones are your dancing boots and the glitzy ones there with the sparkles on are for very special occasions.' He tapped his nose and flicked his head towards Jason. 'Like a wedding.'

I smiled, largely at the thought of wearing cowboy boots under a wedding dress.

'Well I won't be needing those,' I said with a wink, 'so I'll go ahead and try the work boots.'

I selected a pair of soft leather boots the colour of ginger biscuits with exquisitely contoured heels created from layers of contrasting wood. Despite the length to the knee and the pointed toes, the boots were incredibly comfortable.

'Gosh I can't believe they don't hurt my feet. Boots this lovely should definitely require a certain amount of pain for the pleasure of owning them.'

'They're made for working,' Earl laughed, 'and cowboys work hard.'

I ran my hand over the embroidered leather. Jimmy Choo was a nobody in this town. These boots were exquisite.

I clip-clopped over to the cash register where Jesse's mottled hands were ringing up our purchases.

'Looky here, she even walks like a real cowgirl now.'

Jason, Jesse and Earl looked me up and down and exchanged approving glances.

'It's amazing,' I said, swaying my hips, 'they come with an inbuilt strut.'

'Very sexy, huh, boy?'

Earl winked at Jason who flushed red and pressed his own selected Stetson onto his head to hide his face.

'Cat got his tongue,' Earl said to Jesse.

'Our boots have that effect,' Jesse replied with a chuckle.

Each day when our ranch chores were complete, Jason and I took a drive in the RCR buggy that was like a golf cart without the roof. While Jason drove and at least one of the dogs bounced merrily around on the seat between us, I interviewed Jason about his childhood, his influences and his path to success. It was the perfect setting to delve uninterrupted into Jason's past while taking a well-deserved break from his surfing present. We talked about everything from his first surf to the day his brother went to jail. It was like speed dating in detail. We covered high moments and low moments and with each passing day, Jason trusted me enough to let me inch closer and closer to his true story. I had never felt so passionate about a book before and slowly began to realise that perhaps locking myself away and trying to dredge commercial fiction written to the same old formula up from the depths of my imagination was not where my true talent lay.

I was a good listener; a skill I had practised since my father's suicide with the intention of never letting someone close to me suffer in silence again.

The one subject that was still touchy was Harrison. Jason had not told his father he was very likely a grandfather and he was finding it hard to decide what to do. I offered my opinion once and only once.

'With all due respect, Jason, Harrison is a child. He tracked you down but it's not his responsibility to come and find you again. It's your responsibility to face up to the fact you created a son whether you intended to or not. All you can do now is try to do the best you can by him.'

Jason nodded and said, 'Thank you for your opinion.' I did not broach the subject again.

I soon learned Jason had been younger than Harrison when he first started surfing. Ricky had presented him and Mike with a battered surfboard that was the very board on which he had won the Californian Championships in 1966. The board was still stored in the rafters of the barn, out of place among the horse tack and gun cabinets. The foam beneath the fibreglass had yellowed over time and the deck had suffered war wounds, leaving it cracked and dented. Beneath the wax that had melted and re-congealed in dirty globules, I could make out a red lightning bolt running down the centre.

'This was the board in the photograph of you as a child in the Poseidon head office. Your first contest victory.'

'Well spotted,' said Jason running his hands over the rails. 'Not much gets past you, Bailey.'

I beamed proudly. I was not the clueless surfing virgin I had been at the start of this project.

'The first time I surfed this board, I helped my dad clean the wax off in the sun and then we waxed it up again,' Jason remembered wistfully, 'then we drove over the hills on a rusty old tractor to get to the ocean. Mike was with us but he was really young and he didn't want to do the wax job so Dad let me go first as a reward. He made two marks in the wax where I had to put my feet and before he put the board in the water he held both my arms, looked me straight in the eyes and said – "Son, this is a champion's board so you treat it with respect and surf like a champion". I stood up on my first ever wave and rode it all the way to the beach. I guess I've been doing what he ordered me to do ever since.'

'I had a similar thing with my first pen,' I smirked. 'I held it up the right way, scribbled something and that was that. I've been scribbling ever since. It wasn't really a champion's pen, though, it was a red plastic one my dad stole from the betting shop.'

Jason laughed and climbed up to return the board to its resting place.

'So did Mike like surfing too?'

'Yeah, he had talent, but he was not as motivated as I was. He seemed to have this hidden anger deep inside him that had always been there. Mom could repress it but after she died it slowly bubbled to the surface. He always had a chip on his shoulder about something. I think he wanted to prove that we weren't just nobodies because we lived in a caravan. The thing was, we only had the one board so we had to fight for it and as I was so keen to surf I always won and I got to surf more. While I focused on surfing better and better, Mike concentrated on trying to fight better. That's what landed him in jail I guess.'

I made an O with my lips when I saw the nerve twitching in Jason's cheek.

'It's not your fault you know,' I said softly.

'It is.' He sat down on a hay bale and rested his elbows on his knees. 'He was fighting over me. We were in Florida a couple of years back and one of the Tiger Sharks was bad mouthing me. It got pretty bad and they made threats that they were going to hurt me. Mike took it upon himself to sort it out. He hit the guy and then it was as if something snapped. He just kept going. The guy's head was like a mashed potato.'

My O grew larger.

'He didn't…?'

'No, he didn't kill the guy but still it ruined both their lives. It was my fault; I should've seen it coming. I should have let him surf more, mellowed him out a bit.'

'So that's why you dislike Cain and the Tiger Sharks so much.'

Jason sniffed.

'That and more, yeah.'

We wandered out of the barn and I gently rubbed my hand across his back. The sun was sinking into the ocean behind the hills and the sky was ablaze with the vibrant pink light of a dying day.

We walked to the banks of the ranch's only lake that glistened in the baked earth like a pool of pink champagne. We sat beside each other and stared mesmerised at the surface of the glassy water that was broken occasionally by insects and fish. The only sounds other than the intermittent neigh of a horse and the high-pitched cries of the coyotes known to circle the perimeter of the land was the chorus of frogs hiding in the rushes around our feet.

I breathed in the freshest air I had ever filled my lungs with, leaned back on my hands and closed my eyes.

'You know I used to dream about locking myself away and writing a book in a secluded retreat like this but I always thought it would remain a fantasy.'

'Fantasies can become reality if you try hard enough,' said Jason. He added with a laugh – 'You writers, you have those little dreams in your head all the time, don't you? Do you ever really live in reality full time?'

'Well the dreams are usually better than the reality. Until now.'

I turned to look at him. I felt so overwhelmingly content I feared it was all too good to be true.

I glanced at his handsome face in the dusky light. At the face that had sold millions of pounds worth of surf products and had, speaking of fantasies, filled those of pubescent American schoolgirls and post-pubescent groupies for years.

'Until now,' Jason repeated, 'you took the words right out of my mouth.'

When he said the last word, my gaze faltered from his face down to his lips. By the time they moved back up to his eyes, he was staring directly at me. The hairs on my neck jolted with static electricity and waved as if they had survived an emergency sea landing and were trying to attract attention. It was a warning and I knew I should walk away but I stayed rooted to the spot, my fingers almost touching his in the grass.

'We've talked so much the past couple of weeks,' he said, blinking slowly, 'maybe we should stop talking and see what happens.'

'What do you mean?'

My voice did not sound like my own.

Jason's fingertips touched mine in the cool grass. I tried to move away but the devil on my shoulder pushed me towards him. I watched his lips open. I closed my eyes. His lips touched mine and in an instant my body turned to the consistency of a trifle. The taste was just as sweet.

His lips pressed hard yet they felt as soft as marshmallows against mine. His tongue pushed into my mouth and his warm hand ran up my back. A coyote howled in the distance or was it me howling with desire? The kiss became more urgent and thorough. We tasted each other. My body was almost melting into his. I was more alive than I had ever been but at the same time I felt like I could die from the overwhelming passion flooding through my veins. His hands cupped my jaw, pulling me closer. I opened one eye and saw the sunset reflecting off his cheekbone. I heard the water rippling and the insects chirruping, my senses were so heightened. If being with Cain had felt dangerous then giving in to Jason made me feel suddenly safe.

It was only when Jason paused to catch his breath that I realised I had to stop. Comparing Jason to Cain instantly made me relive the regret I had felt after letting myself give in to that impulse. This time my whole body stirred with a desire I had never experienced before but I had to resist.

'I'm sorry, I shouldn't have done that.'

I pulled away and clambered to my feet. Smoothing down the chest of my shirt, I made to walk away but Jason grasped my hand and pulled me back down beside him.

'Excuse me but I think I did it too. I wanted to kiss you so I did and I would very much like to do it again.'

I suppressed the urge not to let the moment pass. I was too determined not to let a single moment ruin everything the way I had almost done before. I could not mix business and pleasure however incredible that pleasure felt. I had to nip this in the bud. I lifted my chin and looked Jason directly in the eyes.

'And you always do what you want don't you?'

He blinked slowly.

'I guess.'

'You know.' I pulled my hand away and stood up again. 'Not this time, Jason.'

He looked so hurt when he peered up at me that I wavered for a second but then I steeled myself to correct a situation that could destroy everything I had worked for.

'Look it's been an emotional time for you trawling through your past and being so open with me so let's just put this down to a release. A momentary loss of control.'

'Why?'

'Why?'

'Yes why?'

There were so many reasons. Because we had to work together and I needed this job. Because I had made the same mistake with his arch enemy in Hawaii and subsequently found myself on the next plane home to concrete city. Because it was all too obvious. Because that was the effect he had on every woman on the surfing circuit and I did not want to be another notch on his bedpost.

Jason stood up.

'I know what you're thinking.'

I stepped back away from him, not trusting myself to resist.

'No you don't.'

'I do and please, I'm not like the other guys on tour. I don't want you just so I can say I've had you and notch you up on my bedpost. That's not my game.'

Alright so he did know what I was thinking.

'And you're not like the other girls on tour. You're so different. You fascinate and delight me.'

My hand pressed against my chest in a reflex action as I absorbed what was probably the loveliest thing any man had ever said to me. I knew him well enough to know he genuinely meant it.

I swallowed hard and raised my palms defensively.

'Thank you for the compliment and I know you're not like that, Jason but the thing is... the thing is I am not attracted to you. As I said, you're not my type.'

His face fell.

'That's not what it felt like when you kissed me.'

'I thought it was you who kissed me.'

'You kissed me back.'

Where were we, the playground?

'Whatever, we kissed, it was a very nice kiss but that's it, end of story.'

Jason brushed his hair back from his face.

'Do you want to know what I think, Bailey?'

'No but I have a feeling you are going to tell me.'

'I think you are scared of letting yourself fall for any man.'

'Really? So you're a therapist now are you?'

He crossed his muscular arms over his even more muscular chest. I diverted my gaze to concentrate on my feet and took a deep breath.

'Jason I'm sorry, I don't want to fall out over this but I told you in Indonesia I am not going to get involved with another professional surfer. I made a promise to myself and to you if you remember?'

'I don't mind if you break that promise to me.'

I smiled and looked up at him. His smouldering eyes could melt solid gold.

'Let's keep this as a working relationship, OK? You pay me to write your book and that is what I will do but' – I cleared my throat – 'other than that I am not for sale.'

I turned away quickly to avoid seeing the sadness that spread across his face. When I walked away I hoped it was the last time I would have to resist Jason's advances because, judging by the way my entire body still sizzled with the intense emotion generated by his kiss, I doubted how strong my defences would prove to be.

Tahiti

Twenty-Four

The following morning we flew to Tahiti ahead of the contest. Jason had spent the evening studying weather charts and swell predictions and a storm system promised world-class waves at one of his favourite reef breaks of all time, Teahupoo. Enthused by the prediction, it was as if Jason had transferred his feelings away from me and back to the one woman whose whims he incessantly indulged; Mother Ocean. I was glad for the distraction but at the same time a little sad to leave our ranch retreat, say goodbye to Ricky and return to the relative rat race of the world tour.

Teahupoo, or Chopes as it was affectionately known, was one of the world's most terrifying natural creations that had become a necessary rite of passage for the professional surfer. In a similar vein to Pipeline, it was without a doubt one of the world's deadliest breaks yet the contest surfers had no alternative other than to take their chances when the contest was called on, no matter how gigantic the waves on the day. There was no calling in sick to skive in this job.

Outside the contest, when the surf was too enormous to paddle into using human power alone, the surfers towed in behind a jet ski in the manner of a water-skier. This was the new form of the sport that was allowing the surfers who dared take up the challenge to push the limits of the size of wave a surfer could possibly ride. The goal of the respected big wave surfers, of which Jason was one, was to catch the first genuine one hundred foot wave in history. Jason likened the feat to jumping off a ten-storey building into water. It was a better idea, I supposed, than jumping onto concrete but when the ten-storey building then curls over and jumps in right on top of you, the stakes are raised.

Jason and Rory practised towing in on the first few days in Tahiti while waiting for the swell to drop enough for the contest to start. The waves were roughly measured at thirty to forty feet in height and looked terrifying. I could not imagine any human being taking on a one hundred foot wave; it just did not seem physically possible. Watching Jason let go of the towrope and sling himself into a wave that darkened the sky made me feel sick. I did not think I would be able to cope with watching him take on a wave two to three times the size. The swell that we had chased across the Pacific then dropped in time for the contest to a more manageable size of fifteen to twenty feet. Where previously I would have been overawed by the spectacle, I realised I was becoming accustomed to seeing such monsters. I could understand why the surfers felt the need to push the boundaries.

The wave was situated a fifteen-minute paddle out to sea from our island on a concealed coral reef as sharp as shattered glass. The wave formation was unusual in that its base sat below sea level. A sudden and drastic change in the gradient of the ocean floor threw the swells forward at intense speeds, creating a breathtaking sheer wall of water that was as thick as it was high. The wave morphed into a hollow tube with such momentum that, at close range and at its terrifying best, it roared like the engine of a 747.

On the opening day of the competition, Chuck, Ruby and I sat in a boat in the calm channel just metres from the wave. While the surfers risked life and limb, we soaked up the sun and sipped fresh coconut juice straight from the coconut. I had watched the young kitchen hand shimmy up a palm tree in his bare feet to collect the coconuts as effortlessly as if he were retrieving cake ingredients from the top shelf of a kitchen cupboard. He trimmed each hairy fruit back to its bald green skin with a machete and then whipped off the top to expose the flesh and the delicious juice inside.

Despite us being in a Jurassic paradise of jagged volcanoes and spectacular crystal water, the channel was so crammed with jet-skis, boats and surfers it resembled the M25 on a Friday afternoon. The differences being that the occupants of every craft were scantily clad and invariably gorgeous. The latest fad was for the SWAGS to watch their men surf while lying on their fronts on a flotilla of neon pink Lilos, sunning their pert bottoms. They wore eye-wateringly miniscule Brazilian bikini bottoms, which gave as much coverage as an average sized moth splayed out on the coccyx. At first glance, one could have been forgiven for thinking the island was being invaded by a homosexual naval fleet of miniature bald men.

'Look at all those bum cheeks,' I said to Chuck.

'Dammit do I have to?' he said, fanning himself frantically.

The photographers spent more time taking photos of the bottom parade than they did of the incredible scenery.

'Bernard, make sure you get the cover shot, dude,' Chuck said to the French photographer who had joined us in our boat in order to have the prime view of the action.

His name was Bernard and Poseidon had jetted him in especially for the occasion. Bernard was a slim, elegant Frenchman from Biarritz with close-cropped hair and pianist's hands who spent more than half his year away from home shooting surf trips and contests. He had a wife back in France, who was either very understanding or she didn't much care for his company.

'I will try, Shuck. The light it is perfect raght now,' Bernard said from behind the giant lens sticking out from his face like an elephant's trunk, 'if they catch one like dat and pull in I will 'ave the shot for sure, non.'

'Oui oui fer sure you naughty little French man,' Chuck mocked, 'and ve vill pay you one meeelion dollars.'

I leaned across Chuck's lap and winked at Ruby.

'You know I really think he believes he's speaking French.'

Chuck laughed and tapped the top of my head.

'I speak every language in my own way, baby. Now while you're down there. Holy shit!'

I sat bolt upright and lifted my hands.

'What? I didn't touch you.'

'No, not you, B' - Chuck waved his hand at the wave and whistled – 'that Tahitian kid just took the heaviest wipeout I've ever seen for real. I'd be surprised if he came outta that a full human, you know what I'm sayin'?'

Our Tahitian boat driver manoeuvred us closer to the break and every eye in the channel scanned the surface of the water for the unfortunate local surfer.

'Can you see him through your lens, Bernard, is he bleeding?'

Bernard squinted.

'Oui, I see blood. He will soon be shark food, non,' Bernard chuckled.

I shivered and strained to see, feeling as if I was rubbernecking at a car crash.

Chuck whistled to our driver, who span us full-circle and raced towards the injured surfer. He pulled the boat alongside the young Tahitian, who sat astride half a surfboard and smiled crookedly up at us.

He was olive skinned and handsome on one side of his face but the other was red raw and bloody as if he had rubbed it on a cheese grater. The right sleeve of his white rash vest was stained as beetroot as Chuck's hair. Ruby gasped and I covered my mouth.

'Dude, that's like ouch,' said Chuck, stating the obvious.

Our driver leaned over and spoke in French before handing him a bottle of water. The surfer took a sip, smiled merrily and chatted before he handed the bottle back and paddled off to find a replacement board.

'He must be in shock,' I said. 'Shouldn't we take him to a hospital?'

'Nah,' said Chuck, waving his hand dismissively, 'it's just a graze.'

'Yeah, like a lion's been grazing on his face. That looked a bit more than superficial.'

'War wounds,' Chuck shrugged. 'Part of the game.'

'Is death part of the game too?'

'Sometimes, B, sometimes.'

I glanced over at Ruby who was nervously chewing her lip. I tried to think of something reassuring to say to her but nothing seemed appropriate. Her boyfriend's job came with inherent risks, which she was well aware of.

However, seeing the aftermath of a gamble gone wrong was never easy no matter how mentally prepared one was.

Moments later, a tanned hand clutched the side of our boat and Rory pulled alongside on his surfboard. He wore a black impact vest that was a slim life jacket with a built in six-pack.

Ruby reached out and pressed her hand on top of his.

'Be careful out there, darl'.'

He pressed his other hand on top of hers.

'Always, you know me.'

Chuck patted him on the arm.

'Good luck, dude.'

I had to fight the urge to pull him to me like a mother and tell him not to go.

'Wow, you guys look like you're at a funeral,' Rory laughed. 'It's a surf comp, you're supposed to enjoy it.'

'So are you looking forward to it?' I asked to lighten the mood.

Rory pursed his lips.

'Well I don't know if you look forward to Chopes as such, mate. This wave has claimed more lives than any other wave in the world in the last ten years and paddling in is harder than towing in. It's the surfer against the monster and it's a technical wave to ride.'

'Oh and you wonder why we look sombre?'

Rory dipped his head and smiled.

'OK it's pretty gnarly but you just have to approach it with respect. The thing is I could go out there today and catch the ride of my life. And life would be boring as hell if we didn't risk it once in a while.'

'You love this don't you?'

Rory gave me a crooked smile.

'Too right, bring it on!'

He pulled himself up to kiss Ruby and when he paddled away I reached over and clasped her hand.

'He'll be OK,' I whispered, 'and so will Jason.'

Chuck clicked his tongue.

'He goddamn better be. Dead clients ain't too good for the bank balance you know what I'm sayin'?'

Twenty-Five

The first day of the competition was both exhilarating and exhausting. I had done very little except sit in a boat in the scorching sunshine and watch wave after awesome wave but, after a dinner of fresh fish, rice and mango salad, I retired to the cosy wooden hut that was my home for the duration of the contest. In preparation for my arrival, it had been decorated with fresh flowers. Petals had been strewn romantically across the bed. It still smelled like an exquisite box of sweets.

My high double bed was shrouded in a mosquito net, making it look like the bed of a fairytale princess. I sat cross-legged and let the inspiration of the day flood out. My fingers moved effortlessly on the keyboard of my laptop as if I were playing a well-practised melody on a piano. I wrote about the wave, the place and the people. About the smells and sounds and the adrenalin that had been coursing through my veins all day just watching Jason and Rory paddle into perilous waves for a few seconds of glory.

'Hey, Bailey, are you coming to the bar?' said Jason.

I looked up from my work to see his head poking around the door. In just a few days, his hair had turned a whiter shade of blond and his cheeks had caught the sun. He positively glowed. Jason had, everyone had agreed, caught the biggest wave and he radiated the confidence of a man who had spent an extremely good day at the office.

'I'm working right now, Jason, but thanks.'

'I admire your dedication my esteemed biographer but you know what they say about all work and no play.'

'I do but equally all play and no work won't get the job done.'

Jason smiled and kicked off his sandals at the door.

'You have an answer for everything,' he said as he entered the hut. 'May I?'

He lifted the edge of the mosquito net. I nodded and he crawled underneath, settling cross-legged beside me on the bed.

'What are you writing about?'

'You of course. This is your book remember.'

'Right,' he nodded. 'Read me some.'

He tried to read over my shoulder but I quickly lowered the screen.

'Writers are very solitary creatures, Jason. I can only show you my work when I feel it's ready to be divulged. Otherwise it loses its magic.'

He leaned back against the headboard and linked his hands behind his head.

'I understand. As long as you're writing magic, that's fine by me. Now don't mind me. I'll be quiet.'

Jason stretched out on the bed beside me, crossed his legs at the ankles and closed his eyes. I was instantly distracted. His soft grey T-shirt shifted up from the waist of his shorts just enough to reveal a couple of inches of bronzed skin. His firm stomach settled inverted from his hipbones when he lay on his back and a thin caterpillar of blond hair ran up the centre of his belly. The hair on his legs was much darker, almost black in the crevices of his solid blocks of muscle. I glanced at the waistband of his khaki walk shorts then tried to shift my eyes away, but they rested on the hard slab of stomach before travelling up over his broad chest and his latissimus dorsi muscles that spread out from his back to his raised arms like the wings of a flying fox. His biceps bulged against his smooth forearms. From the gentle curve of his Adam's Apple, my eyes moved slowly over the neat, dark blond six o'clock shadow on his square chin to his soft beige bow lips. I gulped and flicked my eyes to his. Thank goodness his lids were closed and he could not see me absorbing every inch of the most perfect body I think I had seen in my life.

I shakily exhaled and shook my head to rid my brain of the thoughts that had preoccupied it since our kiss at the ranch. I could still taste him. Despite the fact we had shared a very intense and passionate moment, we had managed to still be comfortable with each other since arriving in Tahiti. I hoped it was simply because we were mature individuals who were very fond of each other. I suspected, however, it was because deep down Jason knew he was right and that my resistance was not because I did not find him attractive. I sometimes wondered whether he could see right through me and read the thoughts in my head. If he could, he would have every right to feel smug.

I allowed my eyes one more casual journey over his body, momentarily lost myself in a silent fantasy and then returned to my work. Jason fell asleep and breathed rhythmically on the bed beside me.

The first thing I saw when I woke up was the blinking blue light of my laptop on standby. The next thing I saw was the shape of a man's head on the pillow beside me. I blinked in the early morning light and rubbed away the mascara I knew would have smudged under my eyes. I tried to ease myself away from Jason's side as if trying not to wake an angry dog.

'Morning, Bailey,' he said, stretching himself out without the slightest hint of embarrassment, 'so you didn't work all night. Did you sleep well?'

Um, yes, er you?' I pulled the cotton sheet up to my chin. 'I must have dozed off. I didn't know you were planning on staying.'

'I wasn't but sometimes no plan is the best plan. Man, I slept like a baby.'

He sat up and the sheet fell from his shoulders to reveal a naked torso. I gasped and shut my eyes.

Jason laughed.

'Don't panic I'm not naked under here. I just got a bit hot that's all. You can open your eyes.'

I opened one eye and then the other. They say the all-important factor in choosing a property is location, location, location. If the view from my bed was anything to go by, my wood hut had just doubled in value.

Jason reached under the pillow for his T-shirt and pushed the sheet away with his feet. I breathed again when I saw he was still wearing his shorts.

'Don't be shy,' he said, flicking out his T-shirt and hitting me gently with it, 'we're friends.'

'Yes but I don't make a habit of sleeping with my friends.'

'Relax, it was just sleeping. We kept each other company. It could have been worse. You could have woken up next to Chuck or Oli.'

'Eugh,' I shivered.

I twirled my hair into a knot at the nape of my neck and wriggled free of the covers.

Jason pulled his T-shirt on over his head. I heard footsteps on the terrace outside and cringed at the thought of Chuck catching us like this. However innocent we knew it was, it would not look that way. I yanked at the hem of Jason's T-shirt and slipped the material down over his back. He looked back at me and winked.

'I'd prefer you to be undressing me but I guess it will have to do.'

'Get out of here and stop teasing,' I smirked.

We both crawled to the edge of the bed and Jason fiddled with the mosquito net to find an exit.

'Did you write magic by the way?' he said.

'Oh yes, it was utterly magical I promise you.'

'Was it really you motherfucking whore?' shrieked a very distinguishable voice.

I whipped my head around so fast, I overbalanced and tumbled out of bed. The mosquito net caught on my watchstrap and yanked out of its ceiling hook. Jason and I fell to the floor with a crash and flailed around like flies caught in a spider's web. When I worked out which way was up I blinked through the netting at the spindly woman who stood over us like a hungry red back spider ready to kill its trapped prey.

'Portia,' Jason gasped, 'what the hell are you doing here? I thought we talked about this in Australia.'

The barbed toe of her stiletto hit him squarely in the left kidney.

'It was a fucking surprise!' she seethed, her eyes flashing wildly.

She's wearing stilettos in Tahiti. Who wears stilettos in Tahiti? was all I could think, until she let out a war cry.

'I'm gonna kill you, you fucking English whore.'

'Nice to know you haven't forgotten my name. How lovely to see you again, Portia.'

She launched herself at the mosquito net and tried to rip it from us to get at my flesh.

'Bitch, whore, fucking groupie prostitute,' she cried.

'Portia, please stop,' Jason shouted, pulling at the skinny limbs of the wild creature masquerading as a woman.

'Ouch, Jason, just get this lunatic off me.'

When Jason finally succeeded in prising my assailant's acrylic nails from my hair, I had a bleeding lip, a patchwork of bruises and an eye that was beginning to swell like a rising soufflé. I struggled to catch my breath and Jason was fighting to keep Portia's arms by her sides when another female figure appeared at the doorway. In contrast to Portia, Ruby radiated goodness like the fairy at the top of the Christmas tree.

'Bailey, darl', you are not going to believe my news, it's just so amazing… oh. My God, Bailey, what happened to your face? And Jason, what are you…? Oh, it's you.'

Her stern expression looked out of place on Ruby's fresh little face.

'We didn't do anything,' I said meekly. 'We were just sleeping.'

Ruby floated towards me, her simple presence calming the scene. She looked naturally beautiful in a thigh-length white dress dotted with faint pink hearts and a pair of pale pink leather pumps. Portia's cat eyes narrowed as Ruby sailed gently past her, hardly acknowledging her presence. Portia may have been a desirable, sexual beauty but even she could not compete with the effortless prettiness of Ruby. She had one up on Portia in that she was beautiful inside and out.

'You poor thing,' she soothed, touching my bruised cheek. 'Let's get that seen to, darl'.'

I let her guide me towards the door.

'So, what was your news?' I asked.

'It seems out of place now but, oh well, it will lighten the mood I suppose.' She stopped at the doorway and waved the fingers on her left hand. 'Rory asked me to marry him last night and I said yes.'

'Congratulations,' I gasped and pulled her to my tender ribs. 'I'm so happy for you.'

From the unearthly sound that Portia made behind us, one would have thought King Herod's henchmen had just popped round to decapitate her newborn baby. Ruby and I ran from the hut and left Jason to tame the banshee.

'Poor guy,' I said as we ran through the trees towards the restaurant.

'Stupid bloody idiot,' Ruby replied.

'Gosh, Ruby, I think that's the harshest thing I've heard you say about someone.'

'Well it's true. He feels sorry for her and he keeps letting her come back to spend time with him. She just stirs things up with her devil fork and unsettles everybody. She's a bitch and you mark my words, with Portia around we can all forget about Jason's world title.'

Twenty-Six

Ruby's prediction was surprisingly accurate. She may have been a sweet girl who would not ask someone to move if they were standing on her foot but she had also been around the surf world long enough to know how things worked and what state of mind Jason had to be in to perform at his best. Clearly, at least to all of us, a state of mind involving Portia was not it.

The swell dropped for the final day of the competition but the waves were still of such magnitude that by the tenth heat of the day there had been one dislocated shoulder, two grated faces, several broken toes and a 'semi-serious' head injury that would have had the average human taking several month's sick leave.

Of course the unofficial bikini contest in the channel sent Portia in a spin even though she could have given every girl there a run for her money with her naturally toned, petite figure that had been taken beyond perfection by her plastic surgeon. Not that I wasted my breath in telling her so.

'Jason's a good, intelligent guy who hates drugs but that chick is more addictive than crack and more dangerous for real,' was Chuck's summation of the Portia situation. 'Tell him, B, he listens to you.'

'You tell him, you're his manager.'

'But you're his…' – Chuck struggled to finish the sentence – 'He's not sleeping with her but the fact she's here hanging out, does it not bother you, dude?'

'I'm his biographer,' I said firmly, 'and that is all. If he wants to allow some stupid girl to wreck his head then there is very little I can do about it.'

I found it hard to sleep that night. It bothered me. And the fact that it bothered me bothered me even more.

Usually so focused and relaxed when he paddled out to his aquatic office, Jason seemed to go to pieces in Portia's presence. He made tactical errors and simple mistakes, falling on waves that he would usually make with his eyes shut. Unsurprisingly, Jason lost his quarterfinal heat to a young wildcard surfer from France who, at the age of sixteen, looked set to be the youngest surfer ever to qualify for the top echelon of professional surfing. Petit Sylvain, as he was known, was tri-lingual as well as three times better looking than most of the rest of the surfers and supremely talented. He was a sponsor's dream. Poseidon had snapped him up at the age of ten and ever since, Oli had arranged for his family to take their other two children out of day school and move around the world to the best surf spots to guarantee Sylvain's future in surfing. The family's future rested on his shoulders. It sounded like an immense amount of pressure to put on a young man but I had to admit, it seemed unlikely Sylvain would choose to jack in a lifestyle surfing tropical islands for millions of Euros to hang out on street corners drinking cheap spirits with his teenage mates.

Jason was gracious in defeat. He climbed on the back of the jet-ski to make the journey to shore and raised his arms above his head to applaud Sylvain who was beaming like the cat who had got not only the cream but also a big cake to go with it. Back at the camp Jason pulled Sylvain into a hug and congratulated him.

'I am sorry to beat you, my friend,' said Sylvain in a French accent laced with Australian and American. 'I really want you to be the world champion again and I hope this does not destroy your chances.'

'No problem, Sylvain, you totally beat me fair and square. Just do the same against Cain and I'll let it slide,' Jason replied half joking in full earnest.

The photographers went to town taking pictures of the two generations of talented surfers embracing, and then, while Jason sat in a corner of the competitors' area and contemplated his loss and its repercussions for the title race, they snapped endless pictures of Petit Sylvain like paparazzi stalking the famous guests at the Ivy. I glanced over at Jason who had one towel wrapped around his waist and another draped over the top of his head. His eyes glistened with disappointment. My heart sank for him. I wanted to offer my condolences and more than anything to shake him and ask him what the hell he thought he was doing but I dared not for fear of having my throat cut with a diamond-encrusted nail file.

Rory on the other hand, progressed to the semi-finals of this the fourth contest of the year, which jumped him up the rankings and set him in good stead for re-qualifying for the following year. The fact that Rory lost to Cain who then went on to win the final was not enough to wipe the smile from Rory's sunburned lips. He had a solid points score, he had his delicate young fiancée supporting him with the fervour of an army of football supporters and he now had a big prize cheque in his pocket with which to buy her the Tahitian black pearl and diamond engagement ring he had always dreamed he would buy for the indisputable love of his life.

Jason received a cheque and points for his joint fifth place but it was little recompense for having to watch Cain lap up the glory on the podium. It was probably fortunate that Jason had not made it onto the winners' podium because the prizes were presented by a curvaceous Tahitian beauty dressed in a blue flowery mini skirt and a skin-coloured tank top with a yellow flower adorning her luscious black curls. Portia would have executed her on the spot with the winner's trophy, which was a hand-carved wooden sword. Cain raised the sword heavenwards in a manner reminiscent of Arthur extracting Excalibur from the stone.

'I want to thank my ohana the Tiger Sharks,' he boomed into the microphone, 'I love you guys. Thanks to my sponsors and to Sylvain for a great final but I gotta say the best guy won.'

'Dumb prick asshole,' Chuck muttered in his usual loud whisper, causing Rosario, Orca and the rest of Cain's gang to edge a little too close to us for comfort.

Cain exchanged his microphone for a bottle of champagne, which he shook up and sprayed all over Sylvain and the crowd. I could just imagine my mother leaping onto the stage and whacking him around the head with the bottle for wasting valuable alcohol. Cain then returned to the microphone, his mouth frothing with spumous champagne and adrenalin.

'And a big shout out to Jason who we all know is chasing my world title. I'm on a roll now, Brah, so bring it on, baby, bring it motherfuckin' on!'

'What a delightful speech,' I said, 'he should do after-dinner functions.'

After four events Jason was still leading the rankings but, having come runner up to Jason's three wins and now with a win under his belt, Cain was second by only a slim margin. I would hardly describe one win out of four as a roll but he was right in saying the world title race was out of the starting blocks and too close to call. The best eight out of ten results counted towards the world title so there was scope for two less than perfect performances but Cain's confidence was palpable and once he was on a roll, he would be a hard man to beat. I could already feel the happy ending to my book slipping from my grasp and Portia's presence was not helping.

'You gotta help me out, dude,' Chuck pleaded. 'We gotta get rid of her.'

'I don't see how it's my business, Chuck.'

'It is your business. This is all business,' he said solemnly, 'and that witch has the spell to make the share price plummet for shizzle.'

'OK, I admit she's an unwelcome distraction but I really don't see how I can help.'

'You're a woman,' he said with a conspiratorial wink, 'and women can always find a way. I may not be a Casanova with the chicks but I know enough to know that much, you know what I'm sayin'?'

South Africa

Twenty-Seven

The tour moved on like a travelling circus to Jeffrey's Bay in South Africa, seventy kilometres south of Port Elizabeth. The peeling right-hand wave was perfectly suited to Jason and should have guaranteed a good result for him but with Portia attached to him like a ball and chain, Jason surfed way below his best.

'Like if that witch doesn't drop dead of natural causes in the next week I swear I will feed her to the mother-fuckin' tiger sharks. The real ones, you know what I'm sayin'?' Chuck seethed.

Real tiger sharks had been spotted circling the contest, their huge fins slicing through the surface of the water to give an indication of the size of the man-eating giant concealed beneath the surface. I was tempted to help Chuck carry out his threat but if anyone could scare a man-eating shark it was Portia. It was, however, an enjoyable fantasy to pass the time.

The night before the finals, I overheard Portia shouting at Jason in the adjacent room. The argument continued until the early hours and her voice was so loud I could make out almost every word.

'That pathetic little Australian girl has got an engagement ring and I am way hotter than her,' Portia screamed. 'If you loved me you'd buy me a ring. I've supported you for years, you bastard. The diamonds here are the best ever and I could have a totally gorgeous pink one like on *Blood Diamond.*'

I laughed out loud. I think she'd missed the point the film was trying to make. I held my breath when Jason's voice rang out clear and calm.

'But I don't love you, Portia, I've told you a million times. I don't want you here.'

I pressed my hand to my mouth and realised I was smiling.

'I've told you, Jason, if you make me go I will sell my story to the Press and I will ruin you. I promise you that.'

'What with, lies?'

'Of course but lies sell, baby and I have got one hell of an imagination. You need to keep me on side, Jason, or you will regret it. You owe me too much. I will not be thirty-five and single. Who else have you got? That pasty, sarcastic English bitch? How pathetic.'

'Go back to your room now, Portia, I can't stand the sight of you.'

I sat down heavily on the bed and clicked my tongue. I had suspected there was a reason why Jason had not sent Portia home but the mistrusting part of me had put it down to him being a man who could not resist a sexual creature like Portia. I closed my eyes. Jason deserved more credit than I had given him and I knew him too well to really believe he could be so shallow. The truth was, Portia was a dangerous woman who would have been more suited to Cain than to Jason. She was blackmailing him. A man whose public image was everything. I had to help. I had to make her want to leave of her own accord. The problem was the one card I had to play was the one that could in fact ruin Jason's reputation; Harrison. Oli had cunningly managed to suppress the story. However, I had to hope Portia would choose to walk away from the responsibility of a child and would be too proud to reveal to the Press that she had not been Jason's first choice when it came to procreation. The gamble depended on how I played my card. I hated gambling but, for once in my life I knew it was a risk I had to take.

Jason lost the contest in the two to three foot surf of the semi-final, this time and for the first time ever, to Rory whose surfing seemed to be going from strength to strength.

'I'm sorry, mate,' said Rory when they embraced after the heat.

'Don't apologise, you surfed like a champ, he surfed like a chump,' said Chuck with undisguised disgust.

'Are you going to let that asshole speak to you like that?' Portia hissed.

Jason clenched his jaw and nodded. He knew his manager was right and he was not too proud to accept the fact.

Jason then had to endure another winning performance from Cain who defeated Rory with a ten-point ride in the final five minutes of the contest. Rory was secretly delighted with his highest placing yet on the world tour, although he would have liked to have prevented Cain gaining the maximum points if only to assist Jason in his pursuit of the world title. With five contests surfed and five to go, we were half way through the tour and Cain had stolen the lead in the rankings from right under Jason's nose. One year as runner-up after twelve world titles was acceptable but two years in succession was enough to signify a slip into retirement. Loyalty in business was a concept knitted together by delicate silk worms. If it looked like the number one rider was losing his touch, Poseidon would turn their attention to the next big thing, Petit Sylvain or Rory, depending on who was performing better, and all the marketing budgets and support network would be thrown their way. Jason would always be a surfing legend and a wealthy ex-champion, but the surfing limelight he basked in would quickly dim whether he wanted it to or not.

As if to emphasise the point, Oli, who had stayed behind at the head office in Irvine, had a bottle of champagne delivered to Rory. We were all present when he picked it up from reception.

'There is also a delivery for you, Mr. Cross.'

The receptionist handed Jason a similar box sent by Oli. Inside was a bottle of cheap white wine to emphasise his point.

I knew it was time to execute my plan. Time was of the essence if Jason was going to get his title challenge back on track. Short of throwing Portia off the nearby world's highest bungee jump without a cord, I had to resort to a cunning plan. My plan may have more readily qualified as vindictiveness but it was all I could think of under pressure. Otherwise the extensive list of potential book titles I had come up with based around the record thirteenth world title would have been a complete waste of time.

Portia was sipping a cosmopolitan cocktail at the hotel bar when I approached her. She was as immaculately dressed as ever in a black Gucci shift dress and silver Manolos. Her elegant neck was adorned with a choker of huge black pearls. They were a new addition to her wardrobe and an obvious ploy to overshadow Ruby's single black pearl engagement ring. She eyed the barman flirtatiously and slipped her change into her Fendi clutch bag. Her thick eyelashes only stopped fluttering when she saw me approach and her body language became instantly defensive. If I were not so modest I would have come to the conclusion that the girl found me threatening.

I had in fact selected a very unthreatening outfit in which to carry out my task. I wore boot cut jeans, a simple fitted white shirt and my cowboy boots. My hair was in a ponytail and I wore the minimum amount of makeup without baring myself entirely. I had my limits.

The barman gave me a warm smile when I approached the bar and his eyes traced the line of my body approvingly. Portia, however, did not smile.

'What do you want?' she spat.

I nodded at the barstool beside her and slid onto it before she had a chance to protest.

'I love your necklace. Did Jason buy you that?'

Her pointed fingers moved over the pearls.

'Yes, well in a way. I have his credit card. He owes me.'

I was not surprised and I forced my brow to remain smooth.

'I'll have what she's having,' I said to the barman.

'I bet you would given half the chance,' said Portia in a loud whisper.

But you're not having it, I wanted to counter, and anything you are having you're stealing.

'Would you like another drink, Portia?' I said through a forced smile.

She sniffed and nodded. The barman acquiesced.

The cosmopolitan was smooth and tangy. I took several sips to calm my nerves and ran my tongue over the slice of lime. The sourness made my lips pucker. Much like the sour woman sitting beside me.

'So have you enjoyed South Africa, Portia?'

She shrugged a bony shoulder and stared straight ahead. I did not speak again.

'It's alright I guess,' she said after a lengthy pause, which indicated I made her nervous enough that she felt the need to fill uncomfortable gaps in conversation, 'but it's a bit poor and dirty for me.'

'The beach is lovely though. Did you see the pod of dolphins surfing the waves during the final? They leapt over Rory's board.'

'Dolphins are boring.'

I felt as if I was trying to mollify a moody teenager.

'The flamingos flying past were gorgeous. I've never seen flamingos in the wild before have you?'

'What is this, a fucking wildlife appreciation club?'

There was certainly a wild cat on the loose, I wanted to reply, and judging by her body language she was just waiting for the chance to rip me to shreds.

I steeled myself to continue.

'Look, Portia, I wanted to set the record straight. I think we got off on the wrong foot together.'

She finished her drink and glanced down at my feet.

'Maybe because mine fit into Manolos and Choos and you have these big feet that you have to hide in men's boots,' she said with dry laugh. 'Just my little joke, Bailey.'

I laughed even though it pained me to.

'Very good, Portia. Another drink?'

I gestured to the barman. The cost of a few cocktails was a small price to pay for what I intended to achieve.

'I'll have a royal cosmo' this time,' Portia said when he reached for the glass.

I would even pay for the added champagne if it sweetened the pill enough for her to swallow it. I waited for the drinks to be prepared.

'I want you to know, Portia, the incident in Tahiti was completely innocent. My interest in Jason is purely professional. I had been working on his book and he wanted to read some but he fell asleep because he was so tired after surfing Teahupoo.'

She angled herself a little towards me.

'I intend to write the best book I can for both of us. For all of us. I have absolutely no intention of becoming any more involved than I already am as his biographer. I have made a promise not to get involved with any professional surfer in fact.'

Portia tapped her nails slowly against the crystal glass.

'Right so sleeping with people you write books for is professional is it?'

'No and I really must apologise profusely but I can assure you all we did was sleep. We didn't even touch.'

The begging and scraping was sticking in my throat but I ploughed on.

'Come on, Portia, you just have to look at yourself.'

She tapped her fingers more frantically and raised her eyes to gaze at her own reflection in the mirrored wall behind the bar.

'I mean honestly, Portia, why would a man like Jason be interested in someone like me when he has a woman like you?'

I closed my fist around the stem of my glass and squeezed, imagining it was her neck.

Portia paused to reflect before saying – 'Point taken.'

She really was the most hideous girl I had ever met.

'Surfers are not my type anyway, Portia. Men with girlfriends are definitely not my type and' – I paused to take a deep breath before I delivered the blow – 'single fathers with girlfriends and a young son are, as far as I am concerned, one hundred percent out of bounds.'

I heard the unmistakeable sound of Chuck's booming voice in the lobby and knew I was running out of time. Portia turned her sharp knees to face me.

'What the hell are you talking about? Who's a single father?'

'Jason of course. Well not exactly single but he's a father, right? I am so not going down that road. I mean, who wants to be the wicked old stepmother?'

The colour drained from Portia's face.

'I have stayed away because I realise you two needed space to work through this but I have a nephew around the same age as Harrison.'

Portia mouthed the name Harrison incredulously.

'So if you ever want to talk to me about the simple things like the best presents to buy and what they're into then I can help you be the best stepmother on the planet.'

I beamed at Portia and bit down on a cherry. Portia gripped the edge of the bar and stared at me. I wondered what was worse for her; discovering Jason had a son or hearing the news from me. The stepmother thing was definitely, however, the straw that broke the camel's back.

'You're a lying bitch,' Portia seethed, slowly sliding down onto her feet, 'Jason does not have a son.'

'Of course he does, we all know that and he looks so much like him.' I touched my hand to my chest. 'Oh gosh,

Portia, I am so sorry I just assumed Jason would have told you by now.'

A red flush crawled across Portia's face like a rash.

We stared at each other and then my eyes followed Portia's when she turned to watch Jason, Chuck, Rory and Ruby walking towards us. I gulped, feeling immediately sorry for what I was about to put him through but I told myself better one rocky evening than an entire year balanced on the edge of a perilous precipice.

I was either going to hell or to the top of the bestseller chart. Portia had done nothing but condescend to me and dislike me from the moment we met and I was not about to let a girl like her ruin everything I had worked for. The gloves were off, which made writing a damn sight easier.

Jason knew something was up before he reached us. He was certain of the fact when he took a couple more steps and Portia threw her royal cosmopolitan in his face.

'I hate you,' she screamed, 'I'm way too good for you.'

Chuck's head whizzed this way and that as if there was a fire and he was trying to locate an extinguisher. Rory placed his hand on Chuck's arm.

Portia brought her face close to Jason's and pointed her finger at him.

'If you think I am going to play stepmother to some bastard little kid you've fathered with another woman you have got another thing coming. I will not be an old stepmother and I will not be second best to anyone. Oh my God, if people knew about this I would be a mockery.'

A smile touched my lips. My assumptions about Portia, it seemed, had been right.

'I am so out of here. I'm going to find myself a real man who can keep his dick in his pants.'

We all watched open-mouthed as she sashayed across the bar, eyeing every man she passed. Jason then turned back and stared at me. I shuffled my feet.

'Oops, did I say something wrong?' I said.

Jason opened his mouth, closed it again and then wiped the champagne cocktail dripping from his chin.

'No,' he said, 'I think you might have got that absolutely right.'

I smiled, Ruby and Rory did the same and Chuck bounced up and down hollering – 'Ding, dong the witch has gone!'

Jason sat down on the barstool beside me.

'I could not see a way out of that one.'

'I'm sorry to interfere but I had to try something,' I said.

'Just tell me this' – he glanced furtively at me – 'did you do it because you were jealous?'

'No,' I scoffed, 'I did it because this is business.'

'Then why are you blushing?'

'I'm not blushing.'

Chuck's beaming face appeared between us.

'This calls for champagne for shizzle. Now we could all suck on your face, Jason, but I think I'll just order us a bottle. Things are going to get better, dudes. No more distractions.'

Jason and I looked at each other and quickly looked away.

'No more distractions,' I repeated and glugged back the rest of my drink.

California

Twenty-Eight

I called Jon when we landed in Los Angeles and promised to try and make time to meet him while we were in California. It seemed so long since the party that had led to me being on tour in the first place, yet it was only a matter of months. My life, and to some extent I, had changed so much.

'So how is the book?' he asked enthusiastically.

'Great. I'm over half way and honestly I already know it's the best thing I've ever written.'

'I'm so pleased for you, Bailey. Can I have half the royalties for kind of getting you the job in the first place?'

'Kind of getting me the job?' I laughed. 'If I remember rightly you told me not to go anywhere near Jason Cross. Now what was it you said again? Something about not getting involved. About how these guys have groupies in every port and they're glamorous, sexy and dangerous.'

'I must have been right about some of it.'

I pressed the phone between my ear and my shoulder and smiled.

'Actually, Jon, you were right about a lot of things.'

'Uh oh,' he breathed, 'what is that I detect in your voice?'

I cleared my throat.

'Nothing. I'm just saying they are dangerous and glamorous and a bit sexy.'

Jon gasped and I could just picture his mouth dropping open in the exaggerated way it always had.

'Bailey Brown you haven't.'

'No I haven't and I won't. I am far too busy concentrating on the book to have time for games.'

'Thank God,' Jon laughed, 'or do I mean shame? I'm not sure.'

We laughed and made to say our goodbyes.

'Good luck with the rest of the year if you don't have time to see me. I know how you surfy folk jet about on the whims of the ocean.'

'Surfy folk. Am I now one of the surfy folk?'

'I bet you are. Are your toes tanned?'

'Yes.'

'Have you surfed?'

'Lord no.'

'Good, so you haven't been completely sucked in.'

I blushed, thankful we were talking on the phone.

'Thank you for inviting me to that party, Jon, it changed my life.'

'You're welcome. I expect a glitzy invitation in return. And if there are any handsome, gay surfers just send them my way. Good luck, BB.'

I hung up and smiled to myself. We did not need luck. Everything was going according to plan.

That afternoon, Jason drove me to meet his surfboard shaper, Seb. Surfboard design had transformed over the years and much was now done on computer but many of the boards and, indeed all the boards Jason rode, were finished by hand. Jason had an input from the start to the finish of the design and shaping process. The most important test being whether the board responded in the right way when put through its paces in the surf. Jason loved to innovate, trying out prototypes and tweaking designs and according to Seb, Jason had been responsible for some of the most important innovations in board composition during his years at the top. He was never afraid to try something radically different because he was talented enough to turn a risk into a breakthrough.

'This man is a scientist when it comes to his boards,' Seb explained to me through the white mask he wore to protect his mouth and nose from the foam dust that layered the floor like a recent snowfall.

'Seb you sound like Darth Vader,' Jason laughed.

'Luke, I am your father,' Seb wheezed before removing the mask.

Seb was a friendly-faced man in his late fifties with legs too short for his body and ears too big for his head. He chuckled constantly as he spoke as if overcome by so much happiness he had to release it at regular intervals like the valve on a pressure cooker.

His shaping bay was a square wooden room lit by low strip lighting. Sheets of paper showing board dimensions were pinned to the walls in no apparent order. There was no furniture in the room, other than a makeshift wooden bench that supported the surfboard currently being shaped. Instruments such as protractors and templates hung on nails among the dusty reams of paper, alongside the planers and sanders Seb used to turn a crude block of foam into the tools of Jason's trade. The latest album of surfer turned musician, Jack Johnson, played on the stereo, as if to remind Seb of the soulful pursuit behind his work in what could only be described as a soulless wooden box.

It was immediately apparent that shaping surfboards was a dirty, smelly process but it was also abundantly obvious that Seb loved his choice of career. To him it was a vocation. He had been loyal to that vocation since he was a teenager and equally loyal to Jason for two decades. Seb was responsible for the single essential piece of equipment the greatest surfer who had ever lived needed to perform and he revelled in that task. His mission was to keep shaping Jason the best surfboards in the world.

'It's not down to the board, though. Jason would have won all his titles with or without me,' he said modestly but I did not believe his role was as insignificant as he liked to make out.

'Seb is my guru,' said Jason before he wandered off to meet and greet the delighted members of staff who were working with renewed enthusiasm since Jason had walked through the door.

Seb kindly proceeded to bring me up to speed on the science of surfboard shaping.

'The big foam blank is cut down to size by a computer and then I finish the process by hand, sanding the rails,' – he touched the edges of the board which were sharp on the base and smooth on the deck – 'the rocker, which is the curve of the board along its length from the tail to the nose, and the shape of the tail itself. This one's a pintail. It's a rounded point and holds well in the wave. It's used in bigger surf and can handle speed well so won't spin the board out of control.'

I rubbed my nose and tried to concentrate.

'What other tails are there?'

'Oh you get the square tail, the squash tail, the swallow tail, the rounded square, the diamond tail, the...'

'Gosh that's a lot of tails.'

'And boy can I tell you some tales about the boards we've made over the years. See that one' – he pointed out of the door to the opposite wall of the factory on which was mounted a wide board sprayed neon with an eighties zigzag design – 'first board I ever shaped for Jason when he was fifteen. Took him to number one in America. We've been working together ever since, improving, perfecting, innovating.'

'Glad to see your surfboard sprays have improved since then,' I laughed.

'You got to worry when you've been around long enough for spray designs to go out of fashion and then come back in, let me tell you,' he grinned.

Seb picked up the tail of the surfboard he was in the middle of shaping. He closed one eye and peered along the length of the board.

'So enough about me, tell me about yourself. Writing that guy's book must be a big task.'

I glanced around for Jason.

'You could say that. We've had to work hard at it and there have been ups and downs.'

'Like every job,' Seb said philosophically.

'Yes and he can be difficult to pin down when it comes to interviews and concentrating for a long time on the nitty gritty parts.'

'Are you surprised? The guy's never worked anywhere except the ocean his whole life. Never had to be at work at a certain time or ask for vacation leave. Never been the new kid trying to figure out how the photocopier works or where the bathroom is. Never had to kiss the boss' ass to get a promotion. Which is not to say he hasn't worked hard at his thing. We couldn't do what he does, but you see that's how it is when you've got a special gift. I bet it's the same with you.'

I laughed self-consciously.

'Hardly. I'm my own boss, which is great, but I've had to do my fair share of sucking up to agents and publishers and I've also done my fair share of donkey work to supplement my struggling artist's income.'

'Not any more. This will fly off the shelves.'

I pressed my palms together.

'Don't jinx me please, Seb.'

He smiled and returned his attention to the surfboard. I stood beside him and gently touched the foam. The surface was covered in a layer of fresh white dust that was hard and sharp to the touch like tiny crystals of sugar.

'Is this board for Jason?'

'Sure is. This is a board fit for Pipeline. All those boards out there are for him too. Twelve of them.'

I peered out of the door at the dozen off-white foam blanks lined up against the outside wall of the bay like an army of cuttlefish.

'Does he need all those?'

'Trial and error, trial and error. If he rides one and it just doesn't go for him then he puts it to one side and tries another one. This is not an exact science you see so every single board is different. Sometimes two boards might look exactly the same but one feels more responsive than the other.' His eyes twinkled. 'That's the magic of it you see and that's why I'm lucky to have worked with Jason because he senses every little difference. He has animal instinct when it comes to his surfboards. He knows when we've got one just right.'

Seb handed me a soft nib pencil.

'Here, write him a message on this board. Bring the board some luck.'

He traced his finger over the thin balsa wood stringer that ran down the centre of the board, holding the two halves together and giving the finished product its core strength.

'I can't write on there, I'll ruin it.'

'No you won't you'll make it individual and you might increase its value once you go and get all famous.'

We smiled at each other. I liked Seb. He reminded me of Yoda.

I peered closer at the stringer. Already there were dimensions scribbled in pencil beside it, which read 7'3", 18 1/4", 2 1/4".

'That's the length, width and thickness,' Seb explained. 'I'll sign it there when it's finished, a bit like you writing The End on one of your books.'

'I can't wait for that moment,' I said, although my stomach immediately twisted at the thought of all of this coming to an end.

I flicked my hair back over my shoulder and licked the end of the pencil. I tried to think of something to write that would inspire Jason. As a writer, I always felt under pressure to find the right words. Playing *Scrabble* with my family was a nightmare because my mother would mock me if I failed to come up with a triple word score using only four Qs and no vowels.

I licked the pencil again and pressed gently on the foam that felt as soft as butter icing against the nib. *Lucky 13*, I wrote in honour of the thirteenth world title dream.

'Nice work,' said Jason over my shoulder.

I looked up at him and he smiled.

'I better make sure it comes true then.'

'Absolutely. Anything I can do to help just let me know.'

He touched my shoulder.

'You've already done more than you'll ever know.'

When I looked at Seb his brow was wrinkled in an expression of surprise.

Jason shook hands with his shaper and then pulled him into a hug.

'Thanks for all your work, man and thanks for the boards for the programme. I've borrowed one for Bailey too.'

'Always a pleasure to help, Jason now you just take care of yourself and if you have any bright ideas you let me know any time of the day or night.'

'Excuse me but why do I need a surfboard?' I asked with a frown.

Jason clapped his hands together.

'It's time.'

'Time for what.'

'Time to get you wet.'

Both men laughed when I flushed red.

'I beg your pardon?'

'Time for you to go surfing,' said Jason. 'I think it is about time you finally experienced first hand what this is all about.'

I smoothed my hands over my hair and glanced from Jason to Seb. They were beaming like a pair of manic cats.

'But I've learned everything I need to know for the book.'

Seb shook his head.

'You can only learn so much by reading and watching. As the saying goes, only a surfer knows the feeling.'

'And here I was thinking I liked you,' I scowled.

Jason wrapped his arm around my shoulder and led me towards the exit. Seb followed.

'Come on, Bailey, no more excuses.'

'I don't need excuses. I can simply think of a million things I would rather be doing than squeezing myself into a skin-tight neoprene suit and hurling myself into a raging ocean. Eating my own hands would be one of them.'

Seb chuckled.

'You'll love it, you'll see. Let me know how you go.'

'You will, you'll love it,' said Jason when he opened the door of the SUV for me. The back was stacked high with rounded nosed surfboards.

'Will everyone stop telling me I will love it. I won't love it because I am not doing it. I told you I will stick to the writing and you stick to the surfing.'

We waved goodbye to the staff and Jason drove out of the parking lot.

'Bailey, you can't write about surfing if you've never tried it.'

'Believe me, Jason, I can. People write about serial killers and they don't go out on a strangulation binge just to know' – I made quotation marks with my fingers – 'the feeling.'

Jason threw his head back and laughed.

'It's hardly the same thing, Bailey.'

'It is,' I huffed, 'almost. It could quite easily involve death. The only difference being I will be the one who dies.'

I pulled down the visor mirror and applied a coat of lip-gloss.

'Whose benefit is that for, the dolphins?'

I pursed my lips.

'I am not going surfing, Jason.'

'Yes you are.'

'No I am not.'

'Yes you are.'

'I don't want to. I can't do it.'

Jason clicked his tongue.

'Now we're getting somewhere. I can't is something different from I won't.'

'Is it?'

He turned to me and arched one eyebrow.

'I can't means you're simply scared and that we can work with. I will show you some people who will make you never say "I can't" again.'

'I don't believe that's possible but go ahead. Knock yourself out.'

'I will,' Jason grinned, 'and if it doesn't work for any reason then you still have to go surfing or else you're fired.'

'That's cheating.'

We glanced at each other and shared a smile.

'O.K.,' I said, 'we'll see if you can convince me once I've met these people you're talking about but I very much doubt it.'

Twenty-Nine

The well-built boy with waves of blond hair down to his bony shoulders had been accidentally shot in the eye by an air rifle fired by his best friend when they were both seven years old. The same age as Zac. He, Ben, was now thirteen and almost completely blind.

'I see clouds, Ma'am,' Ben said with a faint smile on his disconcertingly serene face, 'that's all I see.'

Ben's friend, also thirteen, was a Mexican girl called Izel who had lost both parents and both legs below the knee in a devastating car accident. She sat on the sand with one hand firmly clasped around Ben's and looked up at me with a smile as bright as the sun's rays on an exquisite summer's morning.

'I'm his eyes and he's my legs,' Izel said matter-of-factly, the words tripping off her tongue with a singsong Central American accent. 'I like your sandals Ma'am.'

They were pretty sandals. White leather dotted with tiny blue crystals; this season's must have at Poseidon. Sandals that this little girl had no use for. I swallowed the lump in my throat.

Jason was engrossed in a conversation with a young man in his twenties who was paralysed from the chest down and was in a wheelchair specially adapted for the sand. He had a face and body like a youthful Steve McQueen and he was dressed in a clean white vest and red board shorts. He looked every part the surfer other than the fact his arms and legs refused to move.

'Hey, B, stoked you agreed to come surfing, dude.'

Chuck bounded across the sand towards me, waving his long arms like an enthusiastic octopus. In contrast to his usual eclectic mix of fashions, Chuck was dressed only in a pair of black and white board shorts with a tessellated diamond design. The shorts were pulled in tight at the waist but were having trouble staying up on a body the shape of a pencil. His vibrant hair was covered with a big brimmed trucker cap emblazoned with the words *Live To Surf, Surf To Live.* Seeing Chuck somehow always made me smile, even today.

'I did not exactly agree but I'm here at least,' I said with a grimace.

'Cool. Come meet Wyatt, he's a blast.'

Wyatt was the handsome young man in the wheelchair. He had been one of the west coast's most promising young surfers and had just signed a lucrative contract with Poseidon when he fell victim to a freak accident. While free surfing a hollow shore break wave with his girlfriend who was also a sponsored surfer, Wyatt crashed headlong into his fate.

'It was a small day but the wave was smashing down onto the sand,' he told me, recounting the story I was sure he had told many times, perhaps wishing he could rewrite the ending. 'I pulled into this tube that was super fast and I remember seeing daylight. I thought I could make it out but the barrel shut down, flipped me over and smashed my head into the sand. I heard a click and that was it. So easy, so fast, so dumb but so final. But hey there's nothing I can do to change it. I was an instant quadriplegic so like

I couldn't even swim to shore. Get this, my chick had to save me. How bad is that for a guy's ego? Dragged me out of the shorey and called the lifeguards but it was too late.'

I bit my lip.

'Gosh, how awful, Wyatt. I don't know what to say.'

He smiled a crooked, cheeky smile.

'What is there to say? Not much. Wish I hadn't taken that goddamn wave, wish I'd pushed through the back of the barrel. I've said it all like a zillion times but it's bullshit. If I was there tomorrow I'd still go for that wave, the barrel was sweet.' He smiled indulgently at the memory of the tube ride then blinked slowly and repetitively to bring himself back from the moment. 'Right, enough of the cry baby shit, shall we surf?'

'Let's do it,' said Jason.

'How?'

I looked from the boards lying in the sand on the deserted beach like a deck of cards fanned out on a table, to the ocean stretching out before us.

'How are these kids going to surf?' I whispered to Jason.

'Just watch,' he smiled, 'this is something we do often. Then you can join in.'

My heart beat faster.

'A word of advice, Jason, tales of paralysis by surfing are not motivational for complete beginners,' I whispered again.

Jason screwed up his face.

'I guess you're right but' – he waved his hand dismissively – 'don't worry about it, Bailey, you will be sweet I promise. After all, you've got the best teacher in the world.'

I looked over each shoulder.

'Where?'

'Ha,' Chuck laughed, 'you better live up to your own hype, dude. If she breaks her neck now it is like totally your fault. She'll sue for everything you've got.'

'Thank you, Chuck,' I groaned, 'now run along and play with the sharks.'

Ben, who was well built for his age, carried Izel into the water while she called out constant instructions about the approaching waves and currents. Izel gripped the bodyboard tightly with one hand and paddled with the other arm, while kicking what little was left of her legs. The determination that she would catch more waves than the boys was apparent in her coffee-coloured eyes. Jason took Ben's board out to him and Izel counted aloud the gap between the waves in each set so that Ben would be able to predict when one was about to hit. Izel also called out whether the wave was a right or left hander so that Ben would know which way to turn his board once he had eventually caught it.

'Steep take off,' she directed. 'That one's a close out. Leave it, leave it. Go for this, Ben, go!'

Izel always stayed close, warning Ben of obstacles and unseen dangers and soon the two of them were paddling around like a pair of playful turtles.

'My balance is off today,' Ben tutted when he fell off a wave half way along it.

He wanted to be perfect and showed no fear. Taking on the ocean was bad enough when one could see the waves approaching but surfing it blind was, in my opinion, nothing short of petrifying.

Jason and Chuck concentrated on Wyatt who needed to be carried into the water. They positioned him gently on a ten-foot orange longboard resembling a baguette that had been sliced in half and smothered with marmalade. It looked beautiful but Wyatt was unimpressed.

'It's a kook's board and a hell of a lot different to the ones I used to ride but I guess this body isn't built for skinny contest boards like Jason's anymore.'

Jason ruffled his hair and turned Wyatt to face the horizon. The waves were rolling consistently onto the beach as gentle as ripples on a windy puddle but still the thought of being out of my depth made me shiver. While keeping a watchful eye on Izel and Ben who were shrieking delightedly at every wave and wipe out, Jason manoeuvred Wyatt into position and pushed him into the best wave of each set. Wyatt lay flat on the board with his head lifted and whooped as he flew along the waves with the speed of a missile. When he reached the beach Chuck was there to catch him and push him back out to Jason.

'Be careful,' I warned when he rolled off and landed in a heap on the sand at my feet.

'Why?' he replied, hooting with laughter. 'It's not like I have to worry about breaking my neck is it?'

I sat beside the board Jason had borrowed for me, buried my bare feet into the warm sand and watched with fascination as Wyatt, Ben and Izel's grins grew wider by the second. They looked so free and blissfully happy that I swung between laughing out loud and welling up with tears.

'Come on, Ma'am, come join us,' Ben called out.

He couldn't see me but he could obviously smell a scaredy cat landlubber at twenty paces.

'Yes, Ma'am don't be scared,' said Izel.

'Scared? I'm not scared, I'm just...'

They all looked at me and chuckled amongst themselves.

'I'm just not sure I'm altogether waterproof.'

I walked uneasily into the waves, gripping the board at my side and squeaking with discomfort as the water crept up to my waist chilling each vertebra one by one. Izel whizzed past me on her bodyboard, wiggling her body and laughing uncontrollably. Ben was on the next wave, standing tall and proud. Next came Wyatt, carried towards the beach on a magic carpet of white water. I put my head down and kept wading ever deeper while coaching myself to show no fear.

'Ready?' asked Jason.

'As I'll ever be. I can't believe I am actually doing this'

He tapped the deck of the board and I pulled myself up onto my belly. Jason grasped the rails of the board.

'I can and I'm proud of you. Now hold on.'

Before I had time to ask for instructions, Jason pushed the tail end of the board when the wave rushed up behind me. I felt myself being picked up by the force of the ocean and catapulted towards the beach as fast as if I were careering down an icy mountain on a toboggan. I had control of neither my speed nor my trajectory and my fingertips burrowed into the rails of the board for dear life.

'Where are the brakes?' I shrieked.

'Jump up!' I heard the group cry in unison when I finally emerged from the agitated ball of foam that had enveloped my ears and found myself on a relatively smooth wave.

'Jump, Bailey,' Jason and Chuck hooted.

My laboured motion would not have been classified as a 'jump' in any language but before I knew what I was doing, my body was clambering into an upright position, like the progressive illustration of Neanderthal man to the Homo Sapien. My eyes were transfixed on the deck of the board, marvelling at the two feet firmly planted across the wooden stringer that looked very much like my own. Blue Chanel nail varnish and a small mole on my right little toe. They were indeed my feet and they were holding firm.

My support crew cheered, my fingers released their iron grip, my body unravelled and the wave carried me aloft on the shoulders of very gentle white horses – white ponies perhaps - that tended towards a courteous trot rather than an angry gallop. I breathed in the salty mist settling above the waves. My lungs filled with the comforting scent of the ocean and the fresh, clean air pumped through every muscle in my body. I lifted my eyes towards the beach to where Chuck was bouncing up and down punching the sky. My arms unwittingly did the same and the wind whistled past my ears, blowing every cobweb away to the horizon. I was standing. I was standing on a moving surfboard on a wave on the ocean. I was really doing it. I was surfing.

I was hooked.

I caught so many waves I lost count before the sun plunged into the sea and spread across the surface like an egg being cracked into a hot frying pan. I had never felt so exhausted yet I laughed more than I had laughed in months. Any worries that had clouded my mind vanished in a flash and were washed away in a whirlpool, leaving me feeling free and nothing short of ecstatic.

It was true what they said; only a surfer knows the feeling.

Just before the blanket of darkness fell and as the tide came in, Jason lay on top of Wyatt's legs and paddled the two of them further out to sea where there were bigger waves forming. Izel described the whole scene to Ben in detail even counting Jason's paddle strokes. In the distance we could just make out Jason paddling Wyatt into the wave of the day. Their facial expressions were indistinguishable but their chorus of laughter and cheers carried towards us on the late onshore breeze was enough to let us know Wyatt was in his element.

'You were incredible!' I shrieked, kissing Wyatt's dripping wet cheek when he returned to shore in the arms of Jason and Chuck.

'I am aren't I?' he winked.

'Hey, Bro, she's too old for you,' Jason sniggered.

'Well thanks very much, I'm not that old.'

'Surfing keeps you young and fit,' said Wyatt, 'stick with us and you'll be young enough for me soon.'

I smiled down at his angelic face and my heart melted. I tried to push the ball of tears down into my throat by swallowing hard but it welled up like a burst water main. The mixture of exhaustion and emotion was too much to contain and a heavy tear dripped down my face, running through the fine layer of salt that had encrusted on my cheek. I blinked and tried to turn away but Ben reached out and touched my arm. He sensed I was crying.

'I'm sorry, I don't know what's wrong with me,' I sniffed.

'We have that effect,' Izel shrugged unperturbed.

'Don't feel sorry for us, Ma'am,' Ben said softly. 'Sure I still see clouds but today the clouds are bright. Today life is swell.'

'Sure is,' Wyatt beamed, 'and we're stoked you shared it with us.'

'I'm *stoked* too,' I replied, 'thank you for showing me what surfing is all about.'

When I said surfing, what I really meant was living.

Thirty

The following morning I came down to breakfast puffy-eyed but gleeful in the knowledge I had written some of my best work for years. Energised by the experience of surfing with Wyatt, Izel and Ben and inspired by seeing Jason give his time freely to such a worthy cause, I had stayed awake until four in the morning typing like a woman possessed. Still buzzing from the consumption of far too much coffee in the early hours, I bounced into the breakfast room and up to the table where Oli had joined Jason, Chuck, Rory and Ruby.

The waitresses were wiggling around Jason like worms after a rainfall on freshly dug soil. Jason's glass was full, I noticed, while the others contained nothing but the sticky remnants of orange pith.

'Morning everybody.'

'G'day, surfer girl,' Rory and Ruby chirped yet despite their friendly smiles I sensed the mood was sombre.

I took a seat between Chuck and Ruby.

'What's happened?'

'Earthquake,' said Ruby, while Oli growled, 'Tsunami.'

Jason shook his head.

'It's terrible.'

Chuck, in his usual avalanche of words exclaimed, 'The motherfuckin' ocean has almost sunk the Maldives, dude, it's bad, you know what I'm sayin'?'

My hands stopped mid-air as I was tearing open a hot croissant. Crumbs of flaky pastry floated down into my lap.

'Oh my goodness, when did this happen?'

'Last night,' said Rory. 'Seems there was an earthquake off Indo that sent tsunamis to the Maldives and Sri Lanka. Some islands are underwater although it's not like the one that smashed Sri Lanka in 2004.'

'That's terrible news.'

'Sure is. The Maldives are so low lying they can't take surges like that.'

'They'll be gone one day the poor bastards,' said Chuck philosophically.

'Well that's a comforting thought.'

I put down the croissant and looked at Jason.

'So what does that mean for you guys?'

'No Maldives comp,' he shrugged. 'It's too dangerous because it could happen again.'

He stopped speaking and sat back while a brunette refilled his coffee cup. Her eyelids fluttered so fast I thought she might be having some kind of fit.

'Thanks, Danni.'

He already knew her name. I bristled and then kicked myself for even caring.

'The fault lines could be unsteady so the surfing authorities won't send us into the area.'

'Will they go elsewhere?'

'Doesn't sound like it. I think they might just cancel the comp and give us a break until France, so the title will be decided on nine instead of ten contests.'

I sipped yet more coffee while Oli and Jason discussed the benefits and disadvantages of not having a contest in the Maldives. Apparently Cain had had a good run of luck in the Maldivian reefs over the past couple of years because the contest was held at a consistent left-hander off the island of Lohifushi, which favoured Cain's goofy-foot surfing. Taking the contest out of the tour was effectively removing one of Cain's strongest performances, which could only be positive for Jason's assault on the title.

'It's a bit of a bummer. I really wanted to check it out for our honeymoon,' Ruby sighed.

'The way these tsunamis keep happening the Maldives might not be around for your honeymoon for real,' said Chuck, raising his eyebrows dramatically.

'The poor locals,' said Ruby. 'I wish we could go there and help clean up.'

'Take a mop and bucket and a fucking big sponge,' Oli chortled.

'Turn that up. Can you turn the TV up, Danni?' Jason called out, pointing up at the images of the tsunami-hit region on the television in the breakfast room.

If Danni had moved any faster I would have expected her to burst into flames and vanish like the DeLorian in *Back To The Future.* We watched the news report while Chuck took a telephone call from the television network who wanted Jason to appear to discuss the after-effects of tsunamis on the ocean. I grabbed a pen and paper and began to note down any facts I might need about the event. I was somewhat embarrassed by my own lack of knowledge on the subject while everyone else around the table discussed the causes and facts and figures as fluently as if it was their chosen subject on a quiz show.

The television images that had begun to filter through from the tsunami zones filled me with dismay for the people in the worst affected areas and with awe at the brute force of the Indian Ocean. A grainy film taken on a mobile phone by the shaky hand of a tourist in the Maldives captured the moment the wave washed ashore. I had been expecting the sort of mythical tidal wave I had seen in films, peaking in a one hundred foot crest above the buildings. Instead the tsunami was a dramatic surge of water wider than the island. It rushed onto land with the speed of an avalanche, consuming all in its path. The tourist, who was thankfully filming from the relative safety of a tall building, shrieked in horror when he saw cars and people being picked up and carried away in the flood.

'He'll be telling that story till he dies,' said Jason.

Chuck handed the phone to Jason. Moments later we saw his name and a still photo of the man sitting at our table appear on the television screen. Jason discussed the current tsunami and the formation of waves with the newscaster while behind him Danni's eyelids wafted a breeze across the room.

'Contrary to public opinion, the kind of waves we ride are not created by wind blowing on the ocean but by weather systems,' I heard Jason say. 'We chase swells that we can predict in short by looking at where the low and high pressure systems are and where the swell will hit. The wind is a factor because offshore winds smooth out the ride. The earthquake, though, created this tsunami. The tectonic plates shifted under the ocean and if you imagine one drops or one rises, that creates a difference in water levels in the ocean and creates this kind of surge that devastates when it hits land.'

'It's a seismic sea wave,' Rory whispered to me while I continued to take notes. 'The tsunami is really long so when the front of the surge hits shallow water, the back, which can be kilometres behind, keeps racing forwards until it all piles on top of itself like a train derailing.'

'It's so fast,' I gasped, pressing the nib of my pen into the paper as I watched in horror.

'Too right. They can travel at like five hundred miles an hour. You can't outrun that thing.'

The television network continued to flash up pictures and film of the aftermath of the tsunami and the reported death toll rose like the water level. It became apparent that the devastation would not reach that of the Sri Lankan tsunami that had killed tens of thousands but neither was there much in the way of good news to report.

I had a sudden thought and my hand shot up to my mouth.

'Oh my God, we could have been there. One more week and we would have been.'

'I know,' Chuck snorted, 'how rad would that have been huh?'

'Thanks, Bill, and I hope we can all coordinate a fast and efficient response to this disaster. I am pledging a substantial sum to go towards the rescue effort and I hope other people listening who are in a position to do so will do the same,' Jason concluded, bringing his interview to a close.

We all sat quietly and drank our coffee knowing that the inhabitants of the Indian Ocean islands would be searching for loved ones and trying to recover from the life-changing assault by the forces of nature. It hit me how strange it was that Jason and Rory could not go to work because an earthquake and subsequent tsunami had toyed with their office and made it off limits, which was not something I had ever had to factor into my working life before. It was also desperately ironic to think how the day before I had witnessed the power of the ocean in bringing pleasure and meaning to peoples' lives only to see its power of destruction less than twenty-four hours later. One thing was certain, no matter how much we got to know and love the ocean, it was always in charge.

'Are you going to eat that French donut?' asked Chuck, breaking the silence that had engulfed us like a fog.

'French donut? You mean this croissant? Honestly, Chuck, don't let the French hear you calling their patisserie delicacy a donut when we get to Hossegor,' I said with a smirk, passing him the plate with the uneaten croissant.

Jason excused himself from the table and it was only five minutes later that I realised Danni had also mysteriously disappeared from the breakfast room.

'Our waitress has done a disappearing act,' I huffed.

Chuck leaned closer to me while munching on the croissant.

'Don't worry, B, she won't be *doing* Jason. She might try but she's not his type you know what I'm sayin'?'

I blushed when I saw Rory and Ruby exchange knowing glances.

'I'm not worried,' I said hotly, 'I just want to get some work done with him today that's all. While we have some spare time.'

'Yeah yeah sure.'

Chuck beamed and shoved the remaining pastry into his mouth.

Oli slapped the tabletop.

'Guess I better get back to the office,' he announced. 'I'll make arrangements for France. We may as well get over there early and Jason can do some promos. Plus there's a whole lotta French totty to get through.'

Ruby tutted.

Oli stood up and stretched his stubby arms above his head. His belly jutted out from under his hoodie like that of a woman in her third trimester of pregnancy.

Ruby and I exchanged looks of disgust.

You want him, I mouthed childishly.

You've already had him, she mouthed back.

We stifled our sniggers and forced ourselves to look serious.

'Hey cheer up folks it's not all bad news,' Oli said with a sniff while one hand rubbed the rug of greying hair above his waistband, 'the ground shift from the earthquake might shake up the Indo reefs and make somewhere like Nias fucking amazing to surf. We could get radical new waves from this.'

I tilted my head and frowned up at Oli.

'What are you, a tsunami salesman? Tell that to the poor sods who are looking for their houses that have been washed five hundred miles down stream, I'm sure they'll be rushing for their surfboards.'

Oli shook his head and waddled away muttering, 'Chicks, man, they just don't *get* this shit.'

France

Thirty-One

'What's that?' asked Chuck.

He tentatively held up the shellfish as if it was likely to crawl out of the shell and bite his head off.

'I think it's a bulot or whelk,' I said, upon hearing which, Chuck threw the offending creature over the edge of the terrace railing and into the swimming pool below.

It sank to the bottom to join the blossoming community of giant prawns, mussels and razor clams that had already been granted their freedom from Chuck's iced seafood platter.

'What's that?' said Chuck.

'It's a cockle.'

'A cock what? Man that's nasty.'

Over it went.

'Chuck stop hurling them in the pool,' said Jason, 'they're dead already.'

'Are you sure, dude? I think I just saw that one wink at me for real.'

'Where's its eye?'

'I dunno, B, that's the problem with this shit, it could be its asshole. Have they never heard of like *cooking* shit in this country?'

'It's supposed to be cold, it's a French speciality.'

Chuck looked disbelieving at me and gulped his champagne.

'Well their speciality sucks. Man I need a burger. What's that?'

We had all been invited to the Waterman's Ball, a glittering event celebrating the surfers and important members of the surfing industry who had achieved greatness over the previous year. The ball was held in a private Basque style mansion house in the sprawling foothills of the Pyrenees. The house had been lovingly refurbished by Poseidon's European Managing Director to be contemporary in design while maintaining the traditional white and red walls and red roof of the local architecture. The L-shaped main house hugged an Olympic sized swimming pool that danced with colour-changing lights and Chuck's emancipated shellfish. A stage fit for Glastonbury had been constructed on the other side of the pool, the backdrop being the moonlit ocean that lapped the visible shores of Biarritz, St. Jean de Luz and San Sebastian. The mountains of the Pyrenees stood sombrely behind us in the dark like silent bodyguards.

I already adored this region of France nestled in the crook of the elbow-shaped coastline joining France to Spain. The sun had greeted us every day of the trip from the moment we had stepped off the plane onto the sizzling tarmac at the modest airport in Biarritz. The evening skies were a mass of stars and the air was so fresh I felt as if I were breathing in twice as much oxygen than usual.

All we had done over the previous weeks was eat and drink in between working and surfing. How the French women stayed so skinny while being constantly tempted by indulgent cheeses, buttery pastries, rich chocolates, sugary almond macaroons, flaky baguettes, rich meats in even richer sauces and sumptuous wines was a mystery. I suspected the wealth of slimming treatments that filled an aisle in the supermarket and the national refusal to denounce smoking as a health hazard were key factors. If it had not been for my daily beach walks and regular surfs in the temperate waters with Ruby, I would have been having to replace the surfboard I was borrowing with my very own super tanker by the time we left France. I now understood the true meaning of both gourmand and gluttony and embraced both with equal fervour.

The evening's celebrations at the Waterman's Ball had opened with a buffet of canapés that would have cast a shadow over any Buckingham Palace garden party. There were platters of fresh fruit kebabs, tapenade-topped blinis, stuffed olives, hot caramelised nuts, fresh pitta bread and homemade hummus, anchovies in oil, Spanish tortilla, stuffed peppers, squid in ink, scallops wrapped in cured Bayonne ham, calamares, rustic crackers spread with rich camembert and reblochon cheeses, red lump caviar, black lump caviar, miniature filo pastry tarts filled with glazed fresh fruits, tuna empañadas, avocado salad, tomato and mozzarella salad and freshly baked breads all lit up by flickering candles.

'What no chips and dips?' I quipped to Ruby, who then proceeded to defy science by consuming more than her entire body weight in canapés.

The indulgence did not stop there. Above iron fire pits, bearded Basque men with biceps like bowling balls manually turned several whole pigs on spits. Bars around the gardens offered 1998 Perrier-Jouët Fleur de Champagne as well as exquisite cocktails and Pastis, the drink of choice of the old men who played boules in the region's villages. I had partaken of two glasses of Patxaran (pronounced pacharan), a sloe-flavoured liqueur that gave one's taste buds a hearty punch before sliding delightfully down to warm the stomach and twist the head. Suitably relaxed by the Patxaran and with the possibility of the contest being called on the following day due to a (rather untimely for the revellers) swell, I was now restricting myself to a couple of glasses of chilled rosé wine from a nearby Basque vineyard that perfectly complimented the seafood.

I was sharing a round table fit for King Arthur's knights with Jason, Chuck, Oli, Ruby and Rory. Ruby was avoiding the seafood, although with decidedly more decorum than Chuck. She had, however, wolfed down almost an entire baguette since taking her seat. I was sure she had a tapeworm. Oli, whose shirt collar was so tight his head resembled the inflated Violet Beauregarde in *Charlie and the Chocolate Factory*, spent the entire time taking very loud business calls on his Blackberry. After each call he would then argue at even greater volume with Chuck about public appearances and French TV and radio shows he wanted Jason to do.

'But it's the top French radio station and it's a big deal.'

'I don't care, dude, he ain't doing it' said Chuck while holding up a clam. 'What's that?'

'But we promised.'

'You promised, dude. We didn't make no promise so you better unpromise you know what I'm sayin'? Anyway, Jason don't speak French you dumbass.'

'They'll have a translator, dipshit.'

'I don't care, he ain't doing it.'

'OK he can have a new fucking car if he does it.'

'Whatever, he's got enough cars.'

'Fifty grand.'

'Peanuts.'

'One-fifty.'

'Keep climbing little man.'

It was a tasteless game of ego tennis. Jason meanwhile ignored the pair of them and did not even blink when his fee rose to a figure that made me choke on my wine.

After a dessert of warm tarte tatin with homemade vanilla ice cream washed down with a syrupy Sauternes wine, the live band began to play. They bravely performed a medley of English language songs sung by a French man who had no grasp of English pronunciation. The Fray's *How To Save A Life* sounded suspiciously like *Have To Shave A Wife*, John Lennon's tearjerker *Imagine* was apparently written about a girl called *Imogen*, Oasis' *Don't Look Back In Anger* became *Dork Likes Black In Wrangler* and my personal favourite, Lulu's *Shout* was simply *Shit*.

'Let's dance,' said Ruby suddenly.

She was positively bursting with energy, which was hardly surprising considering she had consumed enough calories to power the entire Australian army.

Chuck did not need convincing.

'Yeah, dawg, let's boogie,' he whooped, leaping to his feet and contorting his lanky body towards the dance floor like a drunk uncle at a wedding.

Rory escorted Ruby with a little more class, the pair of them giggling conspiratorially when they looked back to see who I would be lucky enough to dance with between Oli and Jason. I knew Jason was not big on dancing at public functions. I just hoped Oli did not consider himself to be the next John Travolta but it would not have surprised me in the slightest if he did.

Before Oli could speak, I rose to my feet and offered my hand to Jason. He raised his silver eyes and smiled but the smile quickly shrank into a frown when his eyes were diverted behind me. I made to turn around just as a very drunk Cain careered into me, sending the delicate crockery on the table and a half-drunk bottle of Perrier-Jouët crashing to the floor. Jason pushed back his chair and leapt to his feet while I struggled to move Cain off me. The Tiger Sharks surrounded our table like a cordon of riot police.

'Leave us alone, Cain,' Jason warned. 'You'll only humiliate yourself.'

Oli cowered behind a silver candlestick.

'Don't you tell me what to do, Brah, you ain't the boss of me,' Cain shouted, waving his arm wildly as if he was trying to stay upright in a gale.

'But I'm the boss of him,' Oli stammered, pointing at Jason, 'and I'm telling you to step back.'

Oli did not stand up.

Jason and Cain both looked at Oli and then back at each other.

'Shut up, Man, this ain't your battle,' said Cain.

He then turned to me and draped an arm around my neck. His muscles contracted around my throat as he yanked me towards him. I gasped. His breath was flammable and his eyes rolled manically. He was high, drunk and dangerous.

'I wanna feel that soft English ass move like it did when I screwed you, Sista.'

Soft ass? The cheeky bastard.

He grabbed my bum and squeezed hard. I fought to break free of his grasp but he was strong despite his willowy frame. The Tiger Sharks roared their approval and barricaded Jason's way as he battled to reach me.

'Get off her, Cain or I swear I will…'

'You will what? WHAT?'

Cain let go of my backside and gestured at Jason who was being held by Rosario and Orca. I could tell the situation was on the verge of becoming even uglier than Cain's crew.

'Leave it, Jason, I'm fine,' I pleaded breathlessly. Cain's arm tightened on my windpipe, 'I can fight my own battles.'

'This is not your battle, Bailey, this is our battle. Cain just likes bullying people weaker than him but this is all about me.'

Cain laughed a gravelly laugh.

'Oh I dunno, Brah, we could make this about her if you like yeah. How about you give me her tonight and I'll give you a wave in the contest? The way you're surfing you gonna need my help.'

Jason growled and wrenched his arms to break free of Orca and Rosario. Oli was now nowhere to be seen. I gasped for air and managed to turn my head towards Cain.

'If Jason surfs so bad then why does he get to you, Cain?'

His hand stopped on my left breast.

'You what?'

'I said why does Jason still get to you if he's no threat in the surf? Or are you just trying to rattle him tonight because deep down you know that he is better than you'll ever be?'

'You bitch. You think you're so clever huh, Sista?'

Cain's mouth twisted horribly and he relaxed his arm enough for me to push myself away from his side. His black eyes narrowed and made me shudder.

'You got a big mouth,' he seethed, grabbing me by the wrist and twisting until my bones hurt.

I clenched my jaw and held his gaze.

'And you've got a big ego for someone who has to hide behind thugs, beat up girls and threaten people to get what you want. Chinese burns are for playgrounds.'

He squeezed tighter and I could not help but cry out in pain.

'Get off her!' Jason yelled so loud the music stopped.

A sudden war cry froze us where we stood and all I saw was a shock of aubergine hair as Chuck hurled himself into the mix. Rosario landed face first in a half eaten tarte tatin on the table and Orca lost his footing and tumbled over the railing into the swimming pool where he sank to join Chuck's discarded seafood colony. Jason was loose and gunning for Cain while Oli bounced up and down at a safe distance.

'Stop, Jason, please don't do this,' I cried out, positioning myself in the middle of the world's top two surfers.

'Get out of the way, Bailey, this punk needs to learn a lesson.'

Cain squared up to his rival and growled – 'There ain't nothing you can teach me, Brah. And I'm no punk. You think you're better than me, huh? You and your Hollywood crew. You dare to look down on me.'

I flinched when Cain thumped his chest with both hands. On my other side, Jason's chest rose and fell rapidly.

'But you can't look down on me when I'm the champion of the world and that is the way it's gonna stay, Brah. I am better than you. I am the best.'

I wiped Cain's spittle from my cheek but I remained firm, refusing to move. If life without a father had taught me anything it was how to stand up for myself and be as stubborn as a mule. They could be as defiant as they wanted to be but I could always be more so.

'A punk like you doesn't deserve to be World Champion. It's an honour and you don't live up to the title.'

Cain laughed.

'It's an honour that I won, man and I will win it again.'

With my hand pressed against his chest, I turned to look Jason in the eye.

'Rise above this, Jason. You have to be the better man here. Then you will have won this battle. The rest you will have to do in the ocean.'

My eyes moved towards the mesmerised crowd that had gathered around us. Jason's eyes took my lead and when he looked back at me I knew I had won him over. Ever the consummate professional, Jason valued his public image too much to fight his rival hand and fist in front of his peers and the surfing industry's movers and shakers. I felt his breathing deepen while Cain twitched on my other side like a man possessed.

Jason finally spoke, calmly and assertively.

'I will not let you win this title again, Cain but I will do my fighting in the water. Let's leave this to Mother Ocean. May the best surfer win.'

The disappointment was visible on Cain's face. He was positively itching for a physical confrontation and once again Jason had taken the higher ground and denied him what he wanted. This made Cain hate Jason even more; I could see it in his eyes.

Chuck placed a hand on Jason's shoulder and we moved away from Cain and a rather waterlogged Orca who was regrouping the Tiger Sharks.

'The best surfer will win,' Cain yelled after us. 'Let me tell you the ending to your book, haole girl. Your hero goes down. There ain't no happy ending here.'

'I hope the contest starts tomorrow,' said Chuck as Cain's words drifted in the air around us, 'then that drunk fucker might just go drown himself.'

'No I don't wish that on Cain, Chuck. I want to see that punk's face when I take his title away from him.'

Jason shrugged on his jacket then turned and wrapped mine gently around my shoulders. Rory and Ruby caught us up, both of them pulling us into a silent hug.

'Sorry, mate, I couldn't let Ruby get caught up in that so we held back,' said Rory with an apologetic bow of his head.

Jason gripped his shoulder and smiled.

'No worries, I think Chuck had it covered.'

'For shizzle,' Chuck beamed proudly before bounding off to find our driver.

Rory and Ruby followed on behind. I slowly buttoned my jacket. Jason stepped towards me and took my hand from the top button.

'Thank you, Bailey.'

'What for?'

He softly touched my wrist that had risen up with red welts.

'For bringing me to my senses when I was about to kick his ass.'

I smiled and touched my other hand to his cheek.

'And risk ruining a handsome face like that, why bother?'

Jason blushed.

'Besides,' I added with a shrug, 'I need a great photo for the book cover and a broken nose really wouldn't cut it.'

Jason threw his head back and laughed.

'Oh my God you're sounding more like Chuck by the day.'

'If I start dressing like him then you should worry,' I winked.

The car pulled up at the kerbside and Oli yawned exaggeratedly behind us.

'Can we go now before this turns into *Gone With The Fucking Wind*?'

Jason opened the car door to let me in. Before he closed the door behind me I heard him turn to Oli and say coldly – 'Let's get one thing clear, Oliver, you are not my boss. You work for me. The ocean is my boss. She's the only one who can tell me what to do. Just remember that.'

I smiled to myself. Jason Cross was back in control, which was exactly where I needed him to be.

Thirty-Two

As Chuck had hoped, the contest began the following morning on Hossegor Beach in the comparatively flat Landes region north of Biarritz. The beach stretched before me like a ribbon the colour of a Golden Retriever and covered around two hundred kilometres from Hossegor to Bordeaux, with only slight interruptions for rivers to filter into the ocean. The contest site had been specially built for the occasion on the beach and would vanish afterwards as efficiently as it had arrived. Four glass-fronted cabins made up the judging towers and Press centre and two grandstands had been erected on either side, one to house the competitors and the other for corporate hospitality. International flags representing the surfers' nations flapped in the offshore wind that whipped the scent of the nearby extensive pine forest towards the beach. There were the flags of Hawaii, USA, Brazil, France, Australia and South Africa. The Union Jack to represent Rory's place of birth only made an appearance in the flag of Hawaii. I guessed the French would resist as best they could flying the British flag on their beaches.

The main contest area was fenced off from the general public. Burly security men, who looked as though they had been genetically engineered for the purpose, guarded the gateways as seriously as if their lives depended on it. Which they very likely did considering the enormous PR stunt the pro contest appeared to be. Poseidon's logos were on everything from the rash vests worn by the surfers to the limited edition bottled water. The company wanted nothing to go wrong that could tarnish their event.

A separate tented village sprawled across the beach for the general public, selling contest memorabilia, drinks and French snacks. All of the latter were a variation on the theme of baguette and cheese - baguette and brie, baguette and emmenthal, baguette and camembert, baguette and brie and emmenthal and so on. Every stall was manned by skinny French girls not much wider than one of the baguettes, dressed in skimpy bikinis and hot pant style board shorts.

Unlike the reef breaks we had thus far visited on tour, the French waves broke on a sand bar making them less predictable because they shifted around according to the sand deposits. A frighteningly powerful shore break smashed onto the sand like the arm of a road worker crashing a sledgehammer onto concrete. On occasions the resulting surge of water soaked unsuspecting tourists up to their waists and even washed a bewildered dog off all four paws. I kept my distance from the water's edge and followed our entourage to the VIP area.

We checked in with the security guard who gazed longingly at the smooth brown skin of Ruby's legs. Only an impatient cough from Rory snapped the man from his fantasy, at which point he caught sight of Jason Cross in our midst and genuflected dramatically. The guard then attached colour-coded bands to our wrists of the type worn by hospital patients. Mine and Ruby's were green and declared us to be a '*SURFER FRIEND*'. The yellow bands were for the '*SURFER*', red for '*VIP*', white for '*PRESS*' and black for '*STAFF*'.

'These are a status symbol in Europe would you believe?' said Ruby.

'Really? You're kidding?'

'Nope, I'm serious. You see guys who have managed to get hold of a band pretending to be competitors just so they can pull girls. And the girls aren't much better. To them a band is a ticket to all sorts of delights.'

I looked down at the shiny plastic band on my wrist.

'Gosh, you mean this is a sex ticket?'

'Bailey!' Ruby giggled. 'Well I guess you could look at it like that.'

I waved the band in the air.

'I suddenly feel like I'm sporting De Beers diamonds. Perhaps we should have our own security.'

'You bet. Never underestimate the power of the band.'

Right on cue a group of stunning French girls caught my attention from the far side of the crowd barriers. I moved towards them.

'Mademoiselle, can you get us a band?' asked the first girl who wore a yellow and black polka dot bikini too itsy bitsy to have a whole song dedicated to it.

I clutched the band protectively.

'Oui, Mademoiselle, comme celle-ci, exactement, yes.'

'I'm sorry girls but I can only get one for me.'

'Give it to me,' said another of the girls fiercely.

With her smooth black hair and thick black kohl around her eyes, she looked like she should either be gracing the cover of *Vogue* or drinking vials of blood.

I narrowed my eyes and made to walk away but the first girl delved in her Chloé handbag (that I would have considered inappropriate for a sandy beach) and brandished a wad of Euro notes.

'I buy it from you, please.'

I looked at the fistful of notes and marvelled at the effect a few inches of reflective plastic could have on a woman's pride. Mine and theirs alike in inverse proportions. I then waved my emerald bracelet in the air and skipped away, calling over my shoulder – 'Sorry, Ladies, no can do. You have to be a surfer friend to get one of these beauties. Have fun out there.'

The VIP treatment was going to my head.

'They're the BB girls,' Ruby explained when I took my place beside her at the top of the grandstand.

'What does BB stand for?'

'The Bombshell Beach girls. They are the renowned French Pro Hos' - She silently mouthed the last two words – 'They set out to get what they want and they usually get it, at least temporarily. They come to every contest day and every party of the European leg and every year they are all single just before the surfers roll into town. Last year two of them dumped their local boyfriends and one dumped her husband just the week before the event.'

'Poor guys.'

'Well what did they expect?' she said with mock seriousness. 'If you're not on the world tour and you're with a BB girl then you're on a short lease if you get my drift.'

'Wow, so they're feminist in the way they know what they want and cast men aside to get it but then they're setting feminism back years by making a pro surfer they don't even know their life's focus. Perhaps it's the new form of feminism. SWAG feminists. They don't burn bras, they make sure they can afford the most expensive damn bra they can find without lifting a finger to work for it.'

We both laughed and peered over the railing to see the vampire BB girl draped around the neck of a young pro surfer from South Africa. She had her tongue in his ear and from the smile on his face it was fairly clear what she was offering.

'I don't think I'd have the energy to be a BB girl, Ruby. Licking a salty stranger's ear at nine a.m. looks exhausting.'

Ruby laughed and wandered over to the table set up behind us that was loaded with croissants, pastries and fruit-filled tarts. I smoothed sun cream onto my face and neck and closed my eyes to breathe in the coconut aroma that always made me think of holidays. I was drifting off under the pleasant warmth of the early morning sun when I heard the beach erupt and I looked out to see what resembled a cartoon sandstorm with arms and legs buzzing towards us. Behind me, Jason stood up to check out the commotion.

'Here comes trouble,' I said when Cain emerged from the hysterical ball of fans and strutted proudly into the contest area.

His eyes were masked by sunglasses so large they covered most of his cheeks but, as the sun was shining, he could avoid being accused of having a hangover. The other competitors pushed forward to see the potential confrontation, having either witnessed or heard the rumours of the previous evening's fracas between Cain and Jason. Cain's jaw was rigid when he reached the top of the stairs and came face to face with Jason. I held my breath and glanced at Chuck who had appeared beside me, a vision in red, white and blue.

'Punch him, man,' Chuck hissed to himself, smacking his fist into the palm of his other hand.

'Wouldn't that be bad for Jason's image?' I whispered back.

'Uh yeah, B, you're right. OK, take one on the chin.'

'Wouldn't that make Jason look weak?'

'Right, for shizzle so we want him to walk away. Just walk away, dude.'

'Bad competitive spirit,' I teased.

'Man, you've gone and got me all confused.'

A nerve twitched in Jason's cheek, which was the only visible sign he was riled by Cain's outward arrogance. A smile spread across his face before he offered his hand for Cain to shake.

It was Cain's turn for his cheek to twitch. I looked at both men who stood just inches from each other and considered how alike they were despite the polar differences in their images. They were both fiercely competitive, hugely confident, fit, startlingly good-looking and supremely talented and only the man they were facing stood in the way of world domination.

'Glad you could make it, Cain,' said Jason calmly. 'I hope you last the day.'

Cain accepted the handshake and squeezed so tight Jason flinched.

'Oh I'm goin' all the way, Brah. Just glad you and your little posse' – he flicked his head towards Chuck and I – 'could be here to see me stand on that podium as the best in the world.' He let go of Jason's hand and sniffed the air. 'I smell blood, Man, and it damn sure ain't mine.'

Thirty-Three

I had never seen so many people crowded into one stretch of beach. The rabble of enthusiastic fans was so immense it made the Pipeline event seem small in comparison. On the road into Hossegor, cars were wedged in to the most unlikely gaps, abandoned on roundabouts and central reservations by laissez-faire French drivers who would not let a small inconvenience like the Highway Code cause them to miss the finals of the competition that set the whole region alight for a fortnight each September.

By the start of the first quarterfinal all the surfers from the event who had already been eliminated had crowded into the competitors' area to watch the action unfold, along with their wives and girlfriends and the many children who followed their fathers on tour.

'What a life for little ones,' I commented to Ruby.

'The kids never used to come on tour but the surfers earn more money now so they can afford to take their families with them. They might not get a conventional education but they learn languages and cultures and they stay healthy at least.'

'You sound like you're trying to convince yourself,' I winked.

Ruby blushed.

'It's a bit bohemian perhaps but I think it works.'

'I'm just teasing, you're right. International beach travel at the age of six or sniffing highlighter pens at an inner city bus stop, I know which one I'd choose.'

The noise in the competitors' area was overwhelming. Unlike the other events on tour where the surfers took the first flight out of town as soon as their luck ran out, the French Poseidon Pro was immediately followed by a contest at Mundaka just two hours south in a picturesque village in Northern Spain. With many of the surfers basing themselves around Hossegor for the duration, they were on site to watch the finals and to make the atmosphere even more electric than usual. With news of Jason and Cain's bitter rivalry rife, everyone wanted to witness the showdown.

Jason kept himself to himself in a corner, his ears covered with huge headphones, his eyes fixed on the surf as if he were hypnotised.

'Surfers in the next heat please collect your vests,' announced the beach marshal. 'Jason Cross in red and Luis Roberto in yellow. You may paddle out in five minutes.'

Jason stormed through the crowd of well-wishers and hagglers that were his peers, collected his vest and ran down to the water's edge fully concealed behind a wall of security guards while fans tripped over each other in the deep sand to catch a glimpse of or sneak a touch of their idol. Thirty minutes, ten waves, some awe-inspiring aggressive manoeuvres and one solid victory later, a now wet Jason was back in his corner with his headphones on and a furrowed brow as if he had simply popped to the restroom and not just annihilated a very able Brazilian competitor in huge, rumbling surf.

'He's not surfing like himself but if he keeps surfing like this angry machine he'll win the final for sure,' Oli commented to Chuck.

'Bring it on,' Chuck whooped, rubbing his hands together. 'Cain's done us a favour.'

'He must be tired approaching every heat with such aggression,' I said with concern. 'I just hope he doesn't peak too soon.'

Ruby and Rory nodded their agreement while Oli tutted disapprovingly and wobbled off to wish Jason luck for his semi-final against the wildcard and local favourite, Petit Sylvain.

'I'm backing you all the way, Jason,' Oli said, giving him a manly pat on the shoulder while Jason kept his eyes on the ocean. 'We need this win.'

Not five minutes later I overheard Oli giving his young hopeful, Petit Sylvain, a rather similar pep talk.

'I'm backing you all the way, Sylvain. We need this win.'

His sincerity was touching.

The surf continued to build throughout the semi-final until the sets were a definite ten feet, dwarfing the surfers on the face of the wave. The wind also switched onshore as the land heated up in the blazing sunshine, turning the waves into frothing, voluminous mountains of water.

'Last wave of Sylvain a nine-point-eight,' announced the commentator who was a local pro surfer, before repeating the same in French, Spanish, Portuguese and Basque.

'That was no nine-point-eight, you're kidding me!' Chuck hollered. 'What is this, every French man for himself?'

Many of the surfers around us agreed and even with my limited knowledge of the judging system I suspected

Jason was struggling against Sylvain's local advantage. Cain, who had already qualified for the final and was watching intently to see who he would have to surf against, roared with laughter.

'Your boy's letting it slip away, Brah,' he shouted to our group. 'I can smell the success already.'

'I can smell something you asshole,' Chuck hissed, 'and it ain't your motherfuckin' success.'

However, to the chagrin of perhaps one third of the fans on the now heaving beach, Jason beat Petit Sylvain in the dying seconds of the semi-final with a superior display of surfing that surprised even those of us in Jason's camp. Oli bounced up and down.

'Good job you were backing Jason all the way, hey Oli?' I said coldly. 'We needed this win.'

Oli narrowed his eyes at me. I smiled at my small yet satisfying victory.

'The final you have all been hoping for, ladies and gentlemen. Cain Ohana our current world champion from Hawaii and Jason Cross who is chasing his heels for a thirteenth world title, from California, the champion of the people. Let's hear some noise for our finalists.'

The roar from the beach was loud enough to dislodge an avalanche of sand from the dunes. Cain and Jason avoided each other before paddling out, heading for the ocean from opposite sides of the contest site like two gladiators entering an arena. The ocean was the lion, waiting with frothing jaws for the attack. I had never wanted Jason to win a contest more than I did at that moment.

'Stand away from the water's edge,' the commentator warned in five languages as the overhead waves violently pounded the shore.

However, the now hysterical fans continued to surge forwards for a better view.

For the first half of the heat, Cain and Jason matched each other wave for wave. They both put super-human effort into each ride, pulling off apparently impossible manoeuvres in enormous waves that were neither smooth nor predictable. The onshore wind closed down the sort of tube rides we had witnessed at Teahupoo so the surfers adapted their approach. They performed big, snapping turns off the lip of the wave and awe-inspiring floaters. They carved graceful yet aggressive cutbacks, aerials and full three-sixty degree turns that were over in the blink of an eye. Both had an unassailable desire to prove they were the best surfer in the world and both surfed better than they had for months as a result.

After each nail-biting ride, Cain and Jason had to claw their way back out to the peak to beat the other one and gain the priority that would allow them to then choose the wave they wanted from the next set. When their talent was so closely matched, tactics such as priority and wave selection would make the difference between winning and losing.

Chuck gave us all a running commentary of the heat over the commentary on the loud speaker above our heads, while I furiously scribbled facts, descriptions and details of the proceedings so as not to miss a moment.

'Jason Cross takes the lead and priority…'

'Cain re-takes the lead with that last phenomenal ride, ladies and gentlemen…'

'If the result stays the same Cain will have a commanding lead on the world circuit…'

'A huge floater from Jason Cross. He free-falls and he lands it, he's lost in the foam but no there he is. That has to regain him the lead…'

'The surfers are fighting to get out the back. They're almost there; it's too close to call. The judges award the all-important last priority to Jason Cross with one minute remaining.'

Jason had priority and could choose any wave he wanted, thus putting Cain at a tactical disadvantage. Rory was on his feet and Ruby gripped my arm. Cain splashed the water angrily and threw his arms in the air when the priority call was announced. He then gave the judges a two-fingered salute that would very likely cost him a five hundred dollar fine. With the final hooter approaching, Cain needed a score of seven-point five to retake the lead.

I put down my pen and concentrated on the action. This was more than just a contest; this was a battle for pride. Jason looked like he was about to paddle for a wave but pulled back. Cain hit the water again and was forced to wait. On the next wave Cain tried to push Jason out of position but a defiant Jason would not budge. The minute ticked by, Cain grew increasingly frustrated and the Tiger Sharks to my left began to make the sort of noises one would only expect to hear at the zoo. When Jason stroked into an awesome wave and jumped lightly to his feet just as the final hooter sounded, Cain's screams were carried to the beach on the strong onshore wind. Jason attacked his final ride with the power of a man who knows he is a winner. His turns were bigger and more powerful than ever and a precocious aerial carried him into the arms of his fans on the beach. They beat the security guards to reach him and Jason offered no resistance when the fans lifted him onto their shoulders and carried him to the podium where his trophy and cheque were waiting.

'Jason surfed that last wave so aggressively I thought I was watching Cain,' Ruby said and she was right.

When Cain reached the beach, he was still screaming so loud the fans backed away in fear. When a small boy naïvely approached his hero to ask for an autograph, Cain threw his surfboard onto the hard sand and rammed his foot into the base of it, snapping the board in two. He then handed the bewildered child the fragments before storming up the beach in a rage. There were no more autograph hunters brave enough to make their requests.

Ruby, Rory, Chuck and I took our positions on the top of the grandstand and looked proudly down on Jason who soaked up the adoration on the podium. He thanked the contest organisers, the fans and his sponsors before spraying the delighted crowd with a magnum of champagne. There would, I was sure, be plenty more of that during the evening. Jason had narrowed the gap between himself and Cain with just three contests remaining. Cain was forced to accept his second prize on the podium and Jason took great delight in shaking his hand.

'The best surfer won,' I overheard him say.

'It ain't over yet,' Cain replied through gritted teeth.

'Look at Cain. Man he's pissed,' Chuck laughed, wrapping his arm around my shoulder.

'It must be awful having to stand there watching your nemesis lap up the glory.'

'Yeah.'

We looked at each other and Chuck thrust out his hand for a hi-five.

'I think we're back on track, Bailey Brown, whoo hoo. Life is good.'

A piercing wail down below us suddenly silenced the crowd and even Jason stopped celebrating to see where the noise was coming from.

'Aidez-moi, s'il vous plaît, c'est mon mari, aidez-moi, please, HELP ME!'

The woman fought her way through the crowd screaming and crying so hysterically I thought she might collapse. Her body visibly shook and her face was dripping wet with tears. Her eyes held an expression of genuine terror.

'Her husband is drowning,' somebody shouted. 'The lifeguards are off duty now.'

Before the mêlée could assemble into some sort of order, Jason had leapt off the podium and was already sprinting towards the ocean. The woman ran with him pointing wildly at the spot where she had last seen her husband before she stumbled with exhaustion and fell as heavily and as suddenly as if she had been shot in the back. Chuck and I clambered down the stairs and followed the thousands of people to the water's edge. People were shouting directions and straining to see any signs of life in the water. When we reached the sloping shoreline, the waves breaking in front of us were so huge and created such a haze of spray that our view was limited. Tyler dived straight in without missing a beat.

Every so often I saw Jason's arms pounding through the water in a front crawl motion as he was lifted up on the swell before dropping from sight again behind the waves. Before long, a pack of surfers including Rory had joined him in the search and were paddling around the area on their boards. The woman, who had regained her footing, stood to our right held up by a man and a woman who looked at a loss at how best to help her. The wails coming out of her mouth were spine chilling.

'He was swimming during the final so nobody saw him when he got into trouble,' said the Chinese whispers.

'He should never have been out in these conditions, the beach was red-flagged all day, which means no swimming.'

Which was fair enough in hindsight but wasn't going to help the poor, desperate woman whose heart was breaking into pieces as the minutes ticked by.

How quickly the mood had changed from jubilation to trepidation. How cruel the ocean was to have us adoring it one moment for bringing Jason the waves he needed to win and then hating it the next for taking this woman's husband as payment.

After the effort and emotion of the day, Jason was clearly exhausted but he refused to stop searching, diving frequently underwater and following the current that hurtled down the long beach towards Spain. When his arms grew fatigued, he borrowed a surfboard from a local man and paddled along the coast with Rory until the sun vanished into the water. The crowd thinned as time passed, people glancing with a mixture of embarrassment and sorrow at the woman who maintained her vigil on the beach. The lifeguards had been rallied from the nearest emergency station and the helicopter that had whirred above us during the now-forgotten contest scoured every inch of the water like a hawk scanning the fields below for an unsuspecting mouse. Ruby joined Chuck and I on the beach and we stood in a line, holding hands and barely speaking except to say repeatedly – 'That poor woman.'

I did not even know the woman but found myself crying silent tears. Her grief was so overwhelming it made me want to hurl myself in the water and find her husband myself, but the waves were so large and ferocious I did not stand a chance. Only men like Jason and Rory who lived their lives by the tide had a hope of staying alive in the conditions, which made us all the more aware that the woman was very likely now a widow.

As I stood staring at the ocean that had swallowed the man with the sound of the grief-stricken woman ringing in my ears, I thought of my own father's death and how I had not seen my mother cry a single tear for him. She had shown only anger; at him for leaving her in such a way, at me for being the teenager she was left to deal with alone and at herself for giving her life to Bob Brown. At the time I felt I could not turn to my mother, even though my own heart felt as if it had been shattered like a mirror dropped from a great height onto a stone floor. I had held the pain inside and as I had fought to rebuild my heart, I had secretly vowed not to let it be broken again.

I wondered whether my mother had grieved like this woman in private. Or whether she had not loved my father the way this woman loved her husband. I wondered whether this woman would be able to see that life could carry on without him or whether she would find it impossible to live. She was a stranger but I was privy to her most raw emotions. I wanted to reassure her that she would survive as darkness settled around us like a veil and her husband had been missing for over two hours. However, I knew the only thing keeping the woman on her feet was the irrational hope that at any point her husband would emerge uninjured from the sea. That he would comment on his refreshing swim before wrapping his arms around her and taking her back to what may have seemed like a humdrum reality before she had been forced to entertain the thought of living it alone.

When Jason and Rory returned to dry land, it was so dark we could barely make them out against the silhouette of the waves. Ruby said nothing but gave my hand a tight squeeze as if to say *thank God my own man is here.* Jason looked crestfallen and fragile when he trudged up the beach towards the woman, dropped the surfboard onto the sand and then pulled the woman into his arms. She screamed until her throat could take the strain no more and she fell limp in his arms. Tears of despair mixed with the salt water on Jason's face.

'I'm sorry,' he repeated over and over again. 'I'm sorry I couldn't save him.'

Spain

Thirty-Four

There was no champagne that evening. Instead we made a silent pilgrimage to the Basque village of Mundaka where the next contest was due to begin the following morning. In the big scheme of things, Jason's moral and physical victory over Cain did not seem quite so important and we were all dealing with issues the disaster on the beach had unearthed from our consciences. The deathly silence in the car was only broken by Oli cursing his own bad luck at having a man drown during his company's contest.

'Oli,' I said after an hour of hearing him complain, 'next time someone offers you a penny for your thoughts, sell.'

We checked in to the intimate little hotel in the centre of the village that overlooked the cheerfully painted red and green fishing boats bobbing merrily in the harbour. In direct contrast to our day, the setting was beautifully idyllic and peaceful. From my white iron balcony that made me feel like a tragic Juliet waiting for her Romeo, I could just make out the moonlit left-hand wave peeling along the point outside the protective harbour wall. Mundaka was a world-class surf break and the discovery of such surf in this picturesque village had brought a new wave of tourism that kept the town alive. When the local authorities had, just a few years before, made the mistake of dredging the river that flowed into the bay at Mundaka, they had temporarily destroyed the wave that relied on the shape of the sandy bottom for its perfect formation. That year, the surfing contest had been cancelled and the top surfers had stopped travelling to Mundaka. The tourism suffered and so began a fierce campaign to put things right. The story made me realise how much the sport had become an intrinsic part of the culture in these parts of Europe.

'It's amazing here isn't it?'

Jason was also taking in the view from the adjacent balcony.

'Stunning. That church on the cliff top is gorgeous. It looks like its keeping watch over the ocean. Shame it wasn't around earlier.'

'So tragic,' Jason said in what was almost a whisper.

We paused. The sound of the rumbling surf filled the silence.

'It's so quiet and quaint I feel as if we've gone back in time.'

'It may be quiet now but believe me, Bailey, these Basques know how to have a good time. On Sundays the generations crowd the streets, from the babies to the grandparents, the older ones drinking Sangria and eating pintxos until dark.'

'Pintxos?'

'The tapas.'

He raised his hands to his mouth like a mouse nibbling on a piece of cheese.

'Tortilla, calamares, all sorts of little sandwiches, anchovies, patatas bravas. I think it's the food that makes me win when I come here.'

'Let's hope so.'

Jason smiled weakly. Since trying to save the man, he had visibly shrunk in stature as if the stuffing had been knocked out of him by the experience. I sensed he felt some responsibility at not having been able to save the woman's husband. It was an irrational guilt but I could tell it was eating Jason up inside.

I smiled supportively and rubbed my stomach. None of us had eaten for the past few hours. Other than Oli who would not let a little thing like a terrible death interrupt his eating habits.

'My stomach does feel like a raided biscuit tin now you come to mention it.'

Jason's face lit up for the first time in hours.

'Give me a minute and I'll sort us out a picnic.'

'A picnic? But it's too late. The shops are all shut. Look, it's a ghost town.'

Jason tapped his finger against his nose.

'The Señora who runs this hotel has a bit of a soft spot for me.'

'Don't they all, Jason,' I laughed.

'Meet me outside in ten and I'll take you somewhere special. If you think that church is gorgeous wait till you see this.'

'What about the contest tomorrow?'

He shrugged one shoulder.

'I couldn't sleep now if I tried.'

'OK, I'm in. What about the others?'

'Maybe just give Rory and Ruby a knock when you're coming. Chuck and Oli lack a bit of culture for this adventure.'

We smiled at each other across the balconies as if we were Montagues and Capulets conspiring to elope. While

Jason sneaked off to work his charm on the lady of the house, I pulled on a pair of faded jeans and a soft grey cashmere jumper that would have washed out my skin tone several months before, but which now complimented my tan. The air was heavy and warm but a wind had started to gust from the north, warning of a potential storm. I pulled my hair into a smooth ponytail, slipped on a wool beret and a pair of seaweed green ballet pumps and tiptoed down the corridor to knock on Rory and Ruby's door.

We drove west on narrow mountainous roads, passing the port of Bermeo and snaking on towards Bakio. Ruby, Rory and I had no idea where we were going but all of us were glad of the distraction. I knew the minute I closed my eyes in bed, my ears would ring with the sound of the woman on the beach. I would rather have stayed awake all night than hear her cries of pain and grief again.

Jason suddenly pulled the car steep right down a vertiginous slope that took us to the base of the sea cliffs. In the moonlight I could just make out an island peninsula attached to the mainland by a sinuous stone pathway. The four of us breathlessly climbed and counted over two hundred steps that took us over the water and up the steep side of the island to the lone building at its summit.

'This is the monastery of San Juan de Gaztelugatxe. See this bell' – Jason pointed to the huge bell suspended above the enormous wooden chapel door – 'this used to warn the sailors of approaching storms.'

He pulled the rope beside the door and the surrounding cliffs resounded with the sound of the hermitage bell.

'The sailors would bring votive offerings here as thanks for having avoided a storm. And down in the caves at the bottom of the peninsula I heard they locked up women who were suspected of being witches.'

'Ooh careful, Jason, some of your exes might still be down there,' I said.

Rory doubled up with laughter.

'Ha, at least someone tells him how it is.'

Jason opened and closed his mouth before saying - 'Come on let's eat.'

We sat at a stone table that had been worn smooth over the centuries. I could imagine monks having dined there, eating chunky slabs of bread and cheese washed down with jugs of cider. Jason had brought along a picnic of bite-sized bread rolls filled with cured Serrano ham, thick cheese, pickled peppers and chorizo. There were also pots of olives, a vegetable pasta salad, a tub of anchovies swimming in oil as if they were still alive, and peppers stuffed with white fish and vegetables. He had even thought to bring four plastic beakers into which he poured fruity sangria from a leather flask. We held our beakers aloft.

'Salud,' said Jason.

'Salud!' we replied enthusiastically.

After eating, our funereal mood had lifted and we climbed around to the side of the monastery facing the horizon. The sky above us was bright and inset with stars like sequins on a ballroom dancing dress, but out to sea a storm front was slowly advancing. We sat on the grassy cliff top and watched the heavy clouds gathering like an angry mob. Purple forks of lightning began to split the sky, piercing the surface of the ocean that was growing more agitated by the minute.

'The storm's still a while away,' said Jason.

Rory agreed. They spent many hours studying weather charts to predict wave patterns so I felt confident in their judgement.

'We better leave enough time to get back to the car,' said Rory. 'I don't want Ruby falling down those stairs.'

Ruby tutted and patted his arm reassuringly.

'I'm fine, darl', don't fuss.'

I lay back on the damp grass and looked up at the stars. Sitting exposed on the rocky peninsula sandwiched between an expanse of ocean and an electrified sky I suddenly felt vividly alive. I reflected how easy it was to rush through days, barely taking in the scenery and never stopping to savour a special moment. The man who had drowned that afternoon had very likely not paused to appreciate the vast undulating beach or stopped to take in the beauty of his wife before entering the water for what would be his final swim.

'What will happen to that man?' I said so quietly I could barely hear myself.

Jason pulled a long grass from the soil and stuck it in the corner of his mouth, chewing on it pensively. He looked like his father, a reflective cowboy.

'The current will have taken him to Capbreton or maybe even Spain,' said Rory, brushing back his curls from his grave face.

'How awful,' Ruby sighed.

'He'll wash up eventually,' said Jason so matter-of-factly I shivered. 'At least it's not Hawaii where body *parts* wash up after the sharks have had their fill.'

'Oh my goodness.'

'Yeah they say it's bad for tourism.'

'I'd say it's bad for the poor bastard who becomes fish food.'

'Right. So they like to find them before anyone else does. It's often a surfer out for a dawn patrol who finds the body. We're like the dog walkers of the ocean. Us and fishermen.'

'I hope he didn't suffer.'

'Who knows? But at least he died somewhere idyllic and not crashed out in a chair in front of the TV with a microwave meal. When I go I want it to be in the ocean.'

'Jason don't.'

'What? We're all going to go sometime. Talking about it won't suddenly remind God you're here.'

'I was thinking this afternoon,' said Rory, tipping his head towards the sky, 'what do you want God to say to you when you get up there?'

'Assuming there is a God,' I said.

'Yeah, assuming there's someone who gives a hoot how we lived our life, what would you want him to say at the end of yours?'

Rory looked at me and I grimaced.

'Me? Well, I don't know. I don't really like thinking about stuff like this but maybe something like, "*Bailey Brown, I've read all your books. Your last book was a masterpiece.*"'

'I might have known yours would be about work,' Jason laughed.

'How did you know that?'

'Because it's how you measure yourself.'

I tilted my head in surprise at Jason's insight.

'What about you, Rory?' I asked.

Rory scratched his head.

'I think I'd like him to say – *"Aloha, Rory, great last wave, dude".*'

'Ha, I love it,' Jason laughed. 'I think I'll copy that one. I heard about a guy recently who had a heart attack in the biggest barrel of his life. Now that would be the way to go.'

'Ruby?'

Ruby looked at me and shook her head.

'No I can't think about that. Not right now.'

Her eyes glistened in the moonlight.

'Let's go ring that bell again,' said Rory, jumping to his feet and holding out his hand to Ruby, 'warn the sailors about the incoming storm.'

They clambered over the low wall and wandered off towards the front of the monastery. I sat up and watched the dagger-like lightning dancing on the horizon. The gusts of wind were growing stronger. I wrapped my arms around myself and pulled my sweater tighter against my skin. Jason and I sat in companionable silence, lost in our own thoughts. It was a full five minutes before we turned and smiled at each other.

'Thank you for this, Jason, this is very special.'

'I knew you'd like it. I love this place, it's so spiritual. Just what I needed after what happened today.'

'You were very brave.'

Jason shook his head.

'No I wasn't brave. It was nothing.'

'You exhausted yourself for someone you didn't even know, Jason, and you took a risk swimming into those waves to try and find him. It was not nothing.'

'I just did what I had to do but I failed.'

He strained his broad neck to look over the cliff at the ocean below. I shifted onto my knees and crept cautiously towards the edge of the cliff where I lay on my stomach and gazed down at the white water crashing against the peninsula.

'The ocean looks angry,' I said.

'You're right. Maybe it feels bad about what it did to that woman.'

In Jason's world the ocean was so alive it was as if it had a soul.

'You know, Jason, I still don't understand how you do what you do, taking a risk every day you go to work.'

Jason joined me and dangled his arms precariously over the edge.

'What's wrong with risks? Risks are fun.'

'Are they?'

'Sure. I take a risk because I love what I do. If I didn't risk the consequences of dangerous waves I wouldn't be living.'

'I remember Rory saying something like that at Teahupoo. He said life would be boring as hell if we didn't risk it once in a while.'

'I quite agree.'

Jason chewed on another long grass.

'So why don't you do risks, B? Something about your father wasn't it?'

I swallowed the ball of emotion that burst into my throat. On a usual day I would have changed the conversation but the conversational limits seemed to have shifted after the day's tragic events at the beach. Slowly, I took the key hidden somewhere close to my heart and unlocked the door that kept my father's memory neatly secured where grief couldn't find it.

'My father was a risk-taker, a gambler.'

I cleared my throat when my voice broke.

'And what happened?'

'The inevitable I suppose. He lost everything. All we had. On a stupid lame horse. I think it made it out of the gate but then it got a whiff of someone's picnic and trotted off in the wrong direction in search of sandwiches.' I forced a laugh to stop the tears. 'My father was in so much debt by that point to loan sharks that he knew the game was up. God my mother was so angry with him. I remember her screaming the house down while I hid in my bedroom.'

My voice sounded so distant. The lightning flashed in front of my eyes and thunder rumbled ominously above us.

'I remember vividly I had a Walkman with these grey ergonomically shaped headphones that I thought were so cool. They probably weren't but then I was never what you would call a style icon.'

'I don't believe that for a minute.' Jason tapped my hat.

'My father had bought them for me with the winnings from a bet he had incredibly won the week before. A horse called Baileys and Cream won him the jackpot so he said I was his lucky charm. "For my lucky charm" he said when he gave me the Walkman, "you'll always be lucky".'

Tears began to drip down my face but I was too caught up in the memory to wipe them away. I ploughed on, my thoughts flashing between the past and the images of the woman on the beach earlier that day. She had grieved, she wasn't afraid to show how much she loved someone.

'I turned up the music really loud and I remember it was George Michael singing *Father Figure.* You know the one, *I will be your father figure, put your tiny hand in mine…*'

Jason nodded and reached out to hold my hand.

'I tried to listen to the song while my mother screamed at my father for being a loser, for throwing our life away, for not loving her enough to want to give her a good existence, for loving me too much and spoiling me, for everything. She beat him down just like she tries to do to me but then I guess she felt justified. He had acted like an idiot and betrayed her trust.'

'Did he shout back?'

I shook my head.

'My father didn't have a temper. He kept things inside. Like I do. My mother lets it all out, screams and hollers and eventually we all switch off and don't listen any more.' I took deep gulps of fresh air. 'I suppose he felt he had no-one left to turn to but I would have listened, I would have. Instead he gave up. He thought he had ruined everything for us and he decided we would be better off without him and so he did the most selfish thing I think anybody can do and took his own life.'

A sob escaped from my throat. I had said it out loud. My secret was in the air, flying around my head like a pet bird suddenly free from its cage that does not know which way to fly.

'My God, Bailey, I'm sorry.'

'I loved him so much. He was the only man in my world and then he left me and I found him dead in his chair. And do you know the worst thing? He was smiling. He died smiling as if he was happy to be leaving us. Is that love? Letting the one person who adores you find you dead?'

'Bailey, I'm sorry, I wish I'd known.'

I didn't respond and just allowed myself to cry endless, silent tears. My mind whirled with all sorts of emotions; anger, despair, self-pity, confusion but when Jason pulled me into an embrace, I realised I felt better. Emotionally drained but strangely better. Jason just held me and said nothing, which was exactly what I needed him to do. There was nothing he could say that could change the story or make it make sense.

The sound of the hermitage bell clanging behind us made me sit up and wipe my eyes on the sleeves of my jumper. Jason smiled tenderly at me.

'Storm approaching.'

'I think it already hit me. Gosh what a rollercoaster of a day eh?'

'You bet.'

I gasped and slapped my hand against my mouth.

'Oh and we didn't even toast your victory. You're only a whisker behind Cain now with three contests to go.'

'Ah it's not that important.'

'Yes it is,' said Rory, appearing behind us with Ruby, 'you did the business, mate.'

I collected the four plastic glasses together and poured what was left of the sangria into them. I handed a glass to everyone and raised my own.

'To Jason.'

'Hear! Hear!' Rory cheered.

'Salud,' said Jason. 'What's the matter, Rubes, don't you like the sangria?'

'Hmm?'

We all looked at Ruby's glass. Her and Rory exchanged meaningful looks before Rory nodded and a smile burst on to Ruby's face as stunning as a sunflower turning to welcome the dawn.

'You're pregnant,' I gasped before she said anything.

Rory and Ruby nodded in perfect synchronicity.

'Oh my goodness that's wonderful news!'

We hugged and the boys shook hands before giving in to the hugs and the tears that were now tears of joy.

'I'm so happy for you guys. You'll be great parents. Congratulations.'

'Thanks, Jason and we want you to be godfather if that's OK?'

Jason looked choked.

'Me? I don't know if I can.'

'I won't take no for an answer,' said Rory.

Jason hugged his friend again.

'Thanks, Man, really I am honoured.'

'You and Bailey will make the perfect godparents.'

I laughed, then frowned and then cried again when I realised Ruby was serious.

'Gosh, one life ends and another begins.'

We downed the last drops of fruity wine while Ruby unwittingly rubbed the place where a bump would grow on her tiny frame.

'Rain,' said Rory when droplets as big as buckets of water began to smack the ground around us.

'Uh oh.'

The four of us raced to gather our things and began to run towards the two hundred and twenty-nine steps we had to descend to get us to the car. Rory held Ruby's hand tightly and we shrieked with a mixture of delight and shock as the heavy rain drenched our clothes until they felt like a second skin. We reached the car and tumbled in, soaking the leather seats and instantly steaming up the windows.

'We'd better get back to base,' said Rory.

He started the engine but did not move the car until Ruby had fastened her seatbelt. I wondered whether I would ever find what they had. I had resisted real love for a long time but suddenly I felt as if I was almost ready.

Thirty-Five

Jason came second in the Mundaka contest to none other than Rory who seemed to have grown from his mentor's young hopeful into a confident contender since getting engaged and discovering his fiancée was pregnant. Mundaka was a consistent, peeling left-hander that suited Rory's style as a fluid goofy-footer. Jason was surfing backhand on the wave and displayed his usual ability that made the crowd cheer and gasp in disbelief. His first wave of the final was a perfect ten but he then struggled to find a suitable back up wave for his second score, while Rory notched up two high eights to win. It was Rory's first ever contest victory on the dream tour and represented his coming of age as a professional surfer.

Some camps suggested Jason had thrown the final to allow Rory to claim the prize money but, as much as Jason adored his friend, I knew he did not have it in him to lose on purpose. He was a natural competitor who lived for winning and, as much as he loved Rory, a man like Jason always wanted to be number one.

Cain, still seething from his defeat in Hossegor, had not regained his composure. He had apparently suffered a mental-block with the wave at Mundaka for years and this year was no exception. He finished fifth, which gave Jason a slim but important lead in the rankings. Personally I put Cain's poor performance down to the vast quantities of alcohol and cocaine I had seen him consuming in the bar of our hotel the night before the final. Later that night while Jason and Rory were fast asleep in preparation for the competition, Cain was having loud, drunken sex with a too-young-groupie in the alleyway below my balcony. His regime was not what I would call a lesson in professional abstinence.

We prepared to leave Europe at the end of October with a true feeling of triumph in our team. Jason was back at the top of the world rankings and I was two thirds of the way through his book, which was proving to be a pleasure the more I got to know the subject of my work. Rory had leapt up the world rankings into the top eight and had seventy thousand dollars in his pocket to pay for a wedding at the end of the year and to put money aside for his baby's future. He wore a constant expression of fulfilment. Jason also took Oli aside and negotiated a new contract for Rory. As the greatest surfer in the world heading towards a record world title, Jason was too valuable to Poseidon for them to deny his requests. He could probably have asked for Oli's head on a plate at lunchtime and had it delivered on a silver platter with an orange in his mouth by dinner. Ruby did not reveal the details but from the excitable buzz in the air around Rory and Ruby, I suspected Rory's new salary was substantially more than the last.

Chuck also had a glow about him that money and success tended to bring to his face. Now that Jason was back on top and looked likely to remain so if he maintained his form, Chuck spent much of his day fielding calls with offers of guest appearances and requests for interviews. He filtered out the worst of the bunch and only approached Jason with about ten percent of the demands.

'Jason, do you wanna throw the first pitch at the Dodgers game?'

'Nope.'

'J.C. do you wanna go on the new *Temptation Island*?'

'Nope. I live on temptation island twenty-four-seven, Chuck, I don't need to go on a show.'

'CNN live link to Hawaii?'

'Yup.'

'Ad for shampoo?'

'Nope.'

'But it's two hundred thousand k, dude.'

'Still no.'

'Motherfucker. I'm never gonna get me a Hummer at this rate.'

'I'll buy you a Hummer if you stop trying to make me do shampoo ads.'

'Love you, dude. Front cover of *Men's Health*?'

'I'll think about it.'

'Live on stage with Jack Johnson for two songs at some environmental gig?'

'Of course. The guy's great. I'll do it.'

'For real? But it's charity, man, I don't get commission from that.'

'I'll do it.'

'Shoot.'

'Call me a motherfucker again and I'll downgrade your Hummer to a push bike.'

'Love you, Man.'

And so it continued daily.

Chuck lived for the buzz of being the centre of attention, even if that spotlight only landed on him thanks to his famous client. Chuck was on such good form he even decided he would make an effort to get on with Oli. That lasted about three hours until we reached the airport at Bilbao and they had a fight about whether the team manager or the personal manager had the greater right to the last chocolate and almond pastry. Jason solved the problem by eating the pastry himself.

To the delight of the fans in the airport, Jason then took out his guitar and began to strum a Hawaiian song.

His voice was as creamy and sumptuous as Ben and Jerry's and the women in the boarding lounge leaned towards him like cobras under the spell of a snake charmer. I had discovered over the months that there was very little Jason was bad at. His surfing talent surpassed all others, he had a golf handicap of three, he played a perfect poker face, he sang beautifully, and he spoke Spanish and Japanese. Thank God he did not write like Shakespeare or I would have been out of a job.

Ruby and I exchanged weary looks while Jason sang and every woman in the vicinity dreamed of being alone with him.

'I'll just run to the toilet before we board,' I whispered. 'Back in a sec'.'

I hummed Jason's tune merrily to myself as I washed my hands. We were off to Hawaii. To the single most idyllic place I had visited on tour and to the setting for what would hopefully be a fairytale ending to the year. The previous year in Hawaii, I had known so little about the surfing world. Now I was an intrinsic part of that world and I was confident in my own role within what was essentially an intimate community whose names and faces were now so familiar to me.

The sound of a man coughing made me look up and the face staring back at me in the mirror was one I had not expected to see in the ladies' toilets in Bilbao airport.

'Cain. What are you doing in here?'

I span around. He was resting against the toilet cubicle with his ankles crossed and his fingers hooked into the belt loops of his jeans that were pulled loosely around his hips with a studded belt. He smoothed his hand over his shaved head and lowered his chin but never took his eyes from me. I had a sudden feeling of déjà-vu that unsettled me but my thoughts were distracted by the menacing figure of Waipahe standing guard at the door. I noticed he had a new tattoo of a spider's web that covered his neck and spread across his chin like a beard.

'I think you pretty boys have got the wrong room,' I said as confidently as I could.

'Think you're smart don't you, Sista?' said Cain, moving closer towards me.

I pressed my back against the sink unit and glanced around for something to hit him with but a block of yellowed soap was not going to do the trick unless I lathered him to death.

He was now so close to me I could smell the alcohol on his breath and the stale scent of cigarettes absorbed into the cotton of his black T-shirt.

'Been drowning your sorrows have you, Cain? Looks like you're letting yourself go a bit for a world champion.'

He pressed his lips firmly together and leaned even closer towards me until I was forced to look away. However the sight of Waipahe cleaning the gaps in his teeth (and there were many) with a flick knife made me look back at Cain.

'How did he get that through security?'

Waipahe laughed like a drain.

'I don't bow down to bullies so just tell me what it is you want. I've got a plane to catch.'

'Yeah me too, don't worry. We're on the same flight. All one big, happy family hey, Brah?'

He smiled at Waipahe who spat some molar detritus onto the floor and grinned lopsidedly back.

'Do they allow him onboard or does he have to fly freight with the other animals?'

Cain placed his hands either side of my hips. I leaned back against the sink until my lower back muscles began to complain. Cain's groin pressed hard against me.

'The thing is, Sista,' he said breathily, 'I don't wanna have to listen to Jason fuckin' Cross playing guitar and singing about my fuckin' beaches, you get me?'

I nodded and held my breath.

'And when we get back to Hawaii, to my islands, I don't want no motherfuckin' haole messing up my world title. Are you hearing me, Sista? Hmm?'

'I thought you agreed to let the surfing do the talking,' I muttered.

Cain moved his face dangerously close.

'I don't go making deals with men like him, you get me? In Hawaii, I rule. What I wanna happen, happens.'

I struggled to move but his body had me pinned so tight against the unit our bones were grinding together.

'You get me?' he hissed again.

'Yes,' I gasped. 'I'm not missing a word at this distance.'

'So we got an understanding, yeah?'

'Not exactly. What does this all have to do with me? I'm just writing Jason's book.'

He flicked the side of my head.

'Ouch.'

'Yeah so you get to decide how it ends.'

'Well not exactly because it's fact not fiction.'

He pressed a finger hard against my lips.

'Then I'll tell you how it's gonna end. Jason. Don't. Win.'

'That would be *doesn't* not don't.'

He lowered his hand against my hip and stared into my eyes.

'And how do you expect me to stop him winning exactly?' I carried on.

Cain shrugged and pulled back until I could stand upright once more. I exhaled and started to breathe again when he walked slowly away and wrapped his arm around Waipahe's neck in a mock stranglehold.

'You work it out. Everybody says he listens to you. I can see you have this' – he jabbed his fists together – 'connection. So either you stop him winning or my Tiger Sharks will.'

Waipahe pounded his fist against the hand-dryer, denting the metal without even flinching. I swallowed.

'You're serious? You don't want to win fair and square. You want to bully your way to the top.'

Cain ground his teeth together and for a moment I felt genuine fear.

'I've had to fight my whole motherfuckin' life, not like that asshole. He's had it easy.'

I chose not to argue otherwise.

'I will win this world title one way or another, Sista. So I just wanted to warn you. We don't wanna go breaking legs but we will.'

Waipahe nodded enthusiastically like a dog that had just heard the words 'walkies' and 'biscuits' in the same sentence.

Cain ran his tongue along his lips, blew me a kiss and opened the door.

'I knew when I met you you would come in handy, Sista. Bitches always do. Aloha.'

'Aloha,' I growled as the door closed behind them and I grasped the edge of the sink to steady myself.

Cain was not playing games. Jason had told me he had been threatened before and the threats had led to his brother's incarceration. I feared this time the threats could materialise into something dreadful. Cain's pride had been dented after the confrontation in France and two subsequent defeats and he was determined he would not lose face in front of his own people in Hawaii. However, if I told Jason what had happened, it could distract him and have the same effect as if Cain had attacked him personally.

While I fought to regain my composure, the euphoric cloud I had been travelling on began to evaporate around me and all I could picture was a fall from a great height. Something bad was about to happen and I did not know how to stop it.

Hawaii

Thirty-Six

'This is where we'll have the ceremony,' said Ruby, skipping along the beach.

She was as tiny as a nymph but with the early signs of a baby bump that gave her body the silhouette of a small snail clinging to a twig.

'It's stunning,' I sighed. 'Fairytale. Are your family coming?'

'My parents and my brother and Rory's mum and step-dad and you guys. We want it cosy, you know, just the people we love.'

'I'm honoured, Ruby.'

'Then I hope you'll do me the honour of being my bridesmaid.'

'Me?' I gasped. 'But…'

'No buts and no, "but you hardly know me", blah blah. I know you, I love you and I want you to play a special role.' She held my hands gently. 'I've had the best year of my life, Bailey, and part of that has been sharing life on tour with another girl who is so great to be around. You've really added something to our team. So will you?'

'OK I will. Just don't make me wear big sleeves or one of those flower halo things. Although I might agree to kiss the best man if he's cute.'

Ruby clapped her hands and laughed.

'I promise and it's Jason so I'll leave that up to you,' she winked.

In just under a month Ruby had achieved the incredible task of planning almost an entire wedding without turning into the bride of Frankenstein. The only other wedding I had been involved in was Joanna and Gerry's, before which Jo had metamorphosed into a psychotic individual obsessed with every detail. She had insisted on dressing me like a demented Disney princess and shortly before the big day had become nothing less than certifiable as she ranted and raved about rearranging seating plans and about her shoes having being dyed white with a hint of cucumber instead of with a hint of saffron. In my reserved opinion, if she had spent less time worrying about the details and more time concentrating on whether she was marrying the right man, the whole situation would have righted itself.

Ruby and Rory had restored my faith in wedding preparations. Ruby was marrying the man she adored and she did not need a cake the size of the Empire State Building to prove it. The ceremony would be held on Sunset Point, the tip of the famous Sunset Beach on Oahu. Ruby had purchased a cream suit and a tasteful purple Hawaiian shirt for Rory and an empire line cream chiffon dress for herself that hid her bump and would certainly bring a tear to Rory's eye on the day. Talented local women had been entrusted with the task of hand-making the orchid leis for the wedding party and a hand-tied bouquet for Ruby. It was promising to be a simple, beautiful celebration.

The wedding date was set for the week after the season ended so there was the small matter of two very important contests to get out of the way first, but Jason and Rory had been free-surfing for hours on end all over the North Shore while waiting for the first contest to get underway. They were fit and mentally prepared, which was exactly what the challenging surf in Hawaii required. Cain, meanwhile, confident to the point of cockiness in his own ability in Hawaiian surf, spent more time studying the form of the local girls, which kept him and Jason apart. At first I was anxious every time Jason went surfing for fear of Cain's threats coming to fruition, but over time I relaxed. Cain was arrogant and aggressive but, even if he did meet Jason in the water, I hoped he was not stupid enough to attempt to hurt his rival while hundreds of free-surfers and photographers looked on.

With my mind somewhat at rest, I concentrated on my work. The book was nearly done, although having written fiction up until that point, it was unusual for me to not yet know the ending. In some ways it made the project more exciting but I hoped I would not be in for a nasty surprise. Waking up every morning in a cornflower blue beach house with the tropical ocean just metres from my bedroom window was the perfect inspiration and I wanted the story to reflect the beauty of the setting. However, having the final chapter in sight brought with it mixed emotions. Even though I was delighted to have almost completed my book, as any writer would be, the year on tour had been the most glamorous of my life. I was dreading the thought of it all coming to an end.

'And this,' said Ruby, flinging her arms wide, 'is our house. Jason's wedding present to us. Crazy huh, darl'?'

I clasped my cheeks and stared at the perfect beach-front home. It was a white wooden house with a pointed roof and a wall of sparkling windows looking out at the

Pacific Ocean. A plumeria tree covered in yellow and white porcelain-like flowers formed an arch in front of the door and orange hibiscus flowers framed the decking and lawn. A white picket gate divided the neat little garden and the fine sand of Sunset Beach. The ocean was just a hop, skip and a jump away.

'Lovely pond you've got,' I said, nodding at the ocean.

A whale shot a celebratory fountain into the sky half-way to the horizon. We then watched mesmerised as a turtle the size of a generous coffee table crawled out of the whale's playground and settled into the sand in front of us for a sunbathe.

'This is paradise, Ruby. I never knew people actually lived like this.'

Ruby sighed happily and linked her arm through mine.

'I can't quite believe it myself but I think we're going to be really happy here, Rory, bubba and me. In a few weeks we will be Mr. and Mrs. with a baby on the way and a house of our own. It's funny how life works out.'

I tilted my head against hers.

'It's wonderful. The perfect end to a perfect year. I needn't have worried about Cain and…'

'What about Cain?'

Ruby tilted her head to look at me. I turned sharply away so she would not see my cheeks redden. The last thing Ruby needed was the stress of knowing Cain was threatening to destroy our run of luck in any way he could.

'Nothing, you know just the battle for the world title and everything but it seems fine now.'

I tossed my hair and forced a smile.

'Bailey, is there something you're not telling me?'

'No.'

'But you look worried. Has something happened with Cain?'

'No,' I croaked, 'nothing really.'

I glanced nervously at my watch.

'Oh quick, Ruby, we're late. The heats will have started, we better get a move on. You don't want to miss Rory surfing at Sunset Beach in the second last contest of the year.'

Mentioning Ruby's darling fiancé did the trick. Her expression changed and she waved her hands in the air with a grin.

'Pom-poms a go-go. Let's get a move on.'

Thirty-Seven

'How long is left?' I asked anxiously of Chuck while biting my nails and hopping from one foot to the other.

'Five minutes.'

'Damn, come on, Jason.'

Five minutes left in round two of the Sunset Beach competition and Jason was in danger of being eliminated by a relative unknown local from Velzyland. He was a seventeen year-old recent recruit to the Tiger Sharks and had been surfing Hawaiian waves since he could walk. He was extremely talented but to defeat Jason Cross in the first elimination round of the penultimate contest of the world tour would turn him from a promising young professional into the harbinger of the apocalypse.

'Four minutes, dude,' Chuck warned.

Either side of us, cars honked their horns either in support of the local giant killer or to notify Jason that a set was approaching from its journey across the Pacific. Jason knew what score he needed and had been waiting patiently for a wave to arrive that had the right scoring potential. However, after almost half an hour, he was still waiting. Luck was an important factor and if it was not on our side, the outcome of the year could change in an instant.

The wave at Sunset Beach was visually awesome and a popular tourist attraction. It broke far out to sea so the surfers had to paddle for ten minutes before they even reached the waves but the peak was generally of such magnitude, the surfer's ride made for quite a spectacle even at a distance.

'Set coming,' said Rory, leaping to his feet.

'Three minutes,' Chuck growled, 'what the hell is up with him, man?

'Nerves maybe?'

'Nerves? He's twelve times world champ, B, he don't do nerves.'

'That's easy for us to say but we're not the ones under pressure here.'

Chuck clicked the bones in his neck.

'My wallet will be under pressure if he doesn't pull his finger out and catch a wave. One minute.'

'Stop counting. Time flies by when you count.'

I glanced across at Cain and his followers who were now standing on the roof of Cain's truck howling at the sky while Jason's hopes of regaining the world title slipped away.

'Quick, get on the roof. Rory, get up here. Ruby, maybe not you. Everyone else who is not growing a baby, on the roof.'

Rory and Chuck scrambled up to join me and Ruby sat on the bonnet.

'Now wave your arms and shout as loud as you can.'

'Set approaching,' Rory hollered, jabbing both arms straight up towards the cloudless sky, desperately trying to attract Jason's attention.

'Go, Jason, go!' I yelled.

Ruby joined in then surprised us all when she stuck two fingers in her mouth and whistled like a construction worker.

'Man this is like totally embarrassing for real,' Chuck muttered when half the beach turned to watch us instead of the heat in the water.

I leaned towards Chuck and as I did so I saw Cain staring over at me with eyes of fire. I ignored his stare and whispered to Chuck - 'Thirteenth world title, book deals, film deals, big commission, HUGE commission, a great big shiny Hummer.'

'CATCH THE GODDAMN WAVE MAN, I LOVE YOU!' Chuck screeched.

The commentator began the ten-second countdown and the crowd on the beach joined in.

'Ten, nine...'

A twelve-foot wave swung wide onto the west peak of Sunset Beach. Jason's rival was out of position, sitting too deep on the point to be able to catch the wave.

'Eight, seven...'

Jason's head spun around and he saw us leaping up and down on the car.

'Six, five...'

Jason dug his arms powerfully into the water and propelled himself up to speed.

'Four, three...'

The crowd whooped and whistled, Cain roared, we inhaled sharply.

'Two, one...'

Jason took off.

The hooter sounded the end of the heat.

'Our judges have to agree that Jason's hands both left the rails of the board before the hooter sounded or else this wave will not count ladies and gentlemen,' Rock O'Rafferty announced, his voice quivering with anticipation. 'This wave is smooth as glass. Look at Jason go. It's four times overhead and the drop is endless. Jason cuts back into the foam and then a huge re-entry and another and a massive slash. He's approaching the shallow inside bowl. The wave barrels. He's gone from view, he's looking for the exit. He's trying to find the doggy door out and BOOM there he is. Yeah! Give that man a round of applause, show your appreciation, come on!'

Jason stood on his board and sank slowly into the ocean. He held his head and sat motionless in the still water of the channel while he awaited his fate from the judges. He needed an eight-point ride to make the next round. Even I could tell the ride deserved more than eight points but essentially if the judges decided Jason's hands had still been attached to the rails of the board when the hooter sounded, the wave would not count as part of the heat.

'Please, please,' I prayed.

'Motherfucker, motherfucker,' Chuck repeated anxiously.

Jason turned to look at the beach. Chuck jingled the change in the pocket of his lemon coloured shorts. I mentally held tight to the final chapter of my book that I had placed on ice.

'Jason's hands did leave the rails, ladies and gentlemen and the judges awarded that powerful ride a nine-point-nine-five!'

'YES!' we all cried, jumping up and down and hugging each other.

Jason was as ecstatic as if he had just won the entire world title race. He punched the sky, stood up on his board and somersaulted into the water. It was a small victory but it was a significant one. The race was so close at this point that the slightest slip up meant certain defeat. It was endless pressure from now until the end of the Pipemasters.

It took Jason half an hour to traverse the fifty metres of sand between the ocean and his car as fans hounded him for autographs, photographs, hugs and kisses. He even signed a little white dog with a black marker pen at the owner's insistence.

'Aren't there laws against that kind of thing?' I laughed when he reached us.

'It wouldn't be the strangest thing I've signed, believe me.'

I raised my palms and laughed.

'Don't tell me. That's a whole different book.'

Jason pulled his red rash vest over his head and exhaled his relief towards the sky. His chest heaved, the wet tanned skin sizzling in the sun.

'Phew that was damn close.'

'Too damn close,' Chuck nodded. 'You were killing me out there, man. What's up? You look distracted for real.'

Jason shook his head and droplets of cool water landed on my skin.

'I don't know. I guess I was freaking,' he shrugged, 'with the year nearly over and everything. It was suddenly real.'

'Win first, freak later, dude.'

Chuck and Jason shook hands and patted each other on the back.

'Thanks for your support, guys. Seeing you all making fools of yourselves on the car brought me to my senses. I couldn't let you all down.'

We all smiled proudly and I was taken by surprise when Jason pulled me into a tight hug. The light golden hair on his chest pressed softly against the naked skin above my bikini top.

'Thank you,' he said, holding the embrace longer than I expected.

I hugged him back. His body felt tired in my arms. When we parted I noticed Ruby looking at us with a broad smile. As for the female fans behind her, well if looks could kill…

I handed Jason a towel that he draped over his head to shield himself from the thousands of prying eyes watching his every move.

'Make yourself decent now,' I smiled. 'I'll take your rash vest back to the beach marshall if you like. I could do with the exercise.'

Jason thanked me and pulled himself into the passenger seat of the car where he rested his head in his hands. I meandered along the pathway at the top of the beach holding the wet jersey. I felt both concerned and relieved. Something had unsettled Jason and I wondered whether Cain had had some part to play. However, I was worried about broaching the subject in case I was wrong and Jason's distraction was simply down to nerves. Suddenly I felt someone grab my elbow and pull me between the monster trucks parked beside the path. Cain's breath hit my face.

'Cain. Like a breath of stale air in my life as ever.'

'You're not doing what I asked,' he hissed.

I made eye contact and held it despite the ball of dread in my throat.

'And I won't. That much I can promise you.'

He ground his teeth, his eyes searching my face.

'Then I can promise you, this ain't over. Have your little party now, Sista because it is gonna end real soon.'

Waipahe stepped up behind Cain. As if he needed a bodyguard. Waipahe had another new tattoo, this one on his forehead that read 96712, the postcode of the North Shore.

'Is that his serial number at the pound?'

'What? What she talkin' 'bout, Cain?'

Cain waved his hand.

'I know you make jokes when you're scared, Sista. I know I get to you. I just hope you don't think I'm not a man of my word.'

I bit my lip.

'You know, Cain, you're in the wrong sport. You should have taken up boxing or professional playground bullying. Surfing is far too soulful for the likes of you.'

He bared his teeth in something resembling a smile without the warmth.

'Surfing is a tough game now. Some day soon we'll be riding one hundred foot waves for breakfast but don't worry your pretty head, Jason will be well finished by then, yeah. This sport ain't for pussies now, girl.'

As he said the 'p' word, his hand moved quickly down towards my crotch. I gasped and fell as I heard a smack and Cain reeled backwards clutching his shoulder.

'Get your filthy hands off her.'

Rory reached out to help me up with his other hand still raised. Waipahe whistled for the Tiger Sharks who assembled with surprising speed for such bulky men.

'You're a dead man, Aussie boy,' Maika'i announced with a glottal growl.

Maika'i and Waipahe moved forwards threateningly but Cain's laughter stopped them in their tracks.

'Hey, Brahs, looks like we gone and got a new big guy on tour huh?' he mocked. 'Jason's little protégé just went and grew up. Now this is gonna make things much more fun.'

The Tiger Sharks laughed along with their leader. I suspected half of them were wondering what protégé meant.

Cain looked coldly at Rory and then brushed down his left shoulder.

'Welcome to the game, Rory boy. When this gets out, Brah, you won't even be able to buy a wave on this island.'

Rory clenched his jaw, wrapped his arm around me and said nothing.

Cain turned away and clicked his fingers for his gang to follow. Seconds later a group of bikini-clad female fans accosted them. Money and power could, it seemed, buy love, because it was certainly not dashing good looks and sparkling personalities that got the Tiger Sharks laid.

I exhaled.

'Thanks, Rory. I just can't seem to avoid that guy. I just wish I'd never got involved with him.'

'He's a bully. He would have got to you eventually. Anything to try and upset Jason's team.'

At the mention of Jason, my eyes flickered from Rory's face to my feet.

'What is it, Bailey? Has he threatened you?

'Not me exactly.'

'Jason then?'

I nodded sagely.

'He threatened to hurt Jason to stop him winning the title.'

'Why didn't you tell us?'

'I didn't want either of you to worry. Threats from the Tiger Sharks were what ended up sending Jason's brother to jail and I didn't want to open that can of worms.'

Rory rubbed my shoulder.

'You're a good friend to Jason and to me. Thanks for your concern but we'll be fine. Jason is way stronger than Cain and besides he's got me to watch his back.'

'Well you did a good job of watching mine. I hope I haven't got you into trouble. Winning the title in Hawaii means everything to Cain. I am worried.'

Rory shook his head.

'Cain is not a problem, Bailey, he's just an angry man who needs attention. He likes to feel powerful. Anyway, the title will come down to the best surfer between him and Jason on the day. Other than a very public attack on his rival, which would be far too obvious, what else can he possibly do?

'You're right, Rory. I suppose I'm still quite new to all this.'

I felt somewhat reassured.

'It will be fine, Bailey. And all any of us can do is help Jason prepare for the finals. The rest is down to him. Now, put Cain Ohana out of your mind and let's enjoy the last weeks of the year as a team.'

Thirty-Eight

Much to my disgust, Cain won the Sunset Beach contest in spectacular form, scoring a combined total of nineteen-point-eight out of a possible twenty. Despite having upped his game to progress to the final, Jason appeared to run out of steam like an old engine approaching the brow of a very steep hill. Where usually he had the balance of a cat, he fell on the most simple of manoeuvres. All was not lost for the world title but Jason had made the task much more difficult for himself with everything resting on the final event, the Pipemasters. Just as it had the previous year when Cain had snatched the title from under Jason's nose.

The stress was beginning to show in Jason's usually calm demeanour. After a year of competition there was the slimmest of margins separating Cain and Jason and the Hawaiian surfer definitely had the home advantage at Pipeline. Jason had committed everything to winning the world title and I could tell the thought that he might throw it away at the final hurdle to his Nemesis was killing him. Chuck concentrated on making Jason's life as uncomplicated as possible. He filtered all requests from the media and let very few through the net. He put all interviews on hold until after the Pipemasters and chased cameramen from the garden, leaping like a spindly gazelle after them if they dared to try and encroach on Jason's down time. He turned down appearances and only allowed the prettiest groupies through his imaginary cordon to ask for autographs, each of whom went away with Chuck's phone number.

With the tension in the house palpable, I often wrote outside on the lookout post overhanging the beach. It was easy to become blasé about my surroundings after almost a year spent on beaches but the thought that I could very soon be working back at my desk in England made me determined to enjoy the moment. Writing longhand in the sunshine with the Pacific Ocean as my motivational soundtrack made work a pleasure. I could hardly get the words down fast enough.

'Read me some,' said Jason. 'Please.'

I lowered my bare feet from the chair in front and clasped my notebook to my chest. Keeping his eyes fixed on the ocean, Jason held his ankle behind his buttock and stretched his quad muscle. He was dressed in just a pair of blue board shorts the colour of the ocean.

'OK,' I sighed, 'I wouldn't usually until I have edited it but I guess you've got to read it sometime and I'm particularly proud of this part.'

I shook my hair and smoothed down the pages. Jason pressed his hands into his kidneys and bent backwards. His body was so supple he could have been a contortionist.

'Jason, Can you stop bending yourself in half in front of me? I'm starting to feel quite nauseous.'

'Sorry.'

'Now, take a seat and I will read to you.'

I cleared my throat and then cleared it again. No matter how many books I had written, reading the words out loud always felt painfully personal. The words were about

Jason but they were *my* words and, just like a schoolchild handing in her homework and waiting for the reaction of the teacher, revealing my words to people made me feel exposed.

'Jason Cross is an inspiring example of a child growing up in poverty who chased his dream, fulfilled it and now lives it every day,' I began softly. 'From the moment Jason's father, cowboy Ricky Cross, pushed his son into his first ocean wave, Jason was hooked. The freedom and detachment the ocean afforded him from a somewhat harsh reality became a passion that drives Jason to chase swells around the world and even to risk his life to catch that perfect wave. His office is the ocean and his life is a beach. To wake up every day and have a job to do that one would happily do for free is a rare opportunity and Jason Cross knows he is lucky. However, he also knows it was not so much luck that brought him to his paradise but a burning desire to be the best and to never take no for an answer. The philosophy of this surfing legend appears to be, if you visualise it, it will happen. You can get there. You just have to believe.'

I looked up from the page and closed the book.

'And be supremely talented,' I added with a wink.

Jason lowered his head onto his clasped hands and sighed. I took a deep breath of warm, island air.

'Do you like it?'

'Do you have to ask?'

When he looked up at me, his eyes were glistening.

'You make me sound too good.'

'Well that's what I'm paid to do,' I smirked, adding seriously, 'and believe me it is not a hard task because everything I have written is true.'

Jason reached out and pressed his big hand on top of my small one.

'Thank you. You are a very talented woman.' His fingers tapped the back of my hand. 'And these hands do write magic. You should get them insured.'

I laughed and pulled my hand away, wriggling my fingers in the air.

'Now that sounds like a plan. I could be rich.'

'You will be,' Jason said so firmly it made me stop laughing. 'I know you'll be a success.'

The fact that my success relied on his success made me uncomfortable. In fact, Jason was wholly responsible not only for the ending of my book and its potential in the bestseller charts but he also carried on his shoulders Chuck's financial success, Oli's job, the interests of Poseidon's Board and shareholder's, Rory's career and the hopes of every one of his millions of fans. When a sportsman reached Jason's level, it was no longer just a question of personal achievement and winning to please himself. How he did not collapse under the pressure I did not know. It was little wonder Jason had seemed tired as the year drew to its climax.

'Is everything alright, Jason? Is something bothering you?' I waited a beat. 'Or someone?'

Jason brushed a lock of hair back from his face. It flopped instantly back to settle on his long eyelashes.

'What do you mean by someone?'

I wanted to tell him about Cain's threats but the words stuck in my throat. If I said the wrong thing and Jason lost the world title as a result I would never forgive myself. I shrugged.

'Nobody in particular. I just thought you seemed preoccupied, a bit off the boil, that's all.'

Jason nodded and wrapped his arms across his naked torso. Living among surfers I had become somewhat accustomed to seeing the men around me half-naked with rigid six-packs, but it was still a daily pleasure.

'You're very intuitive.'

'I just don't like to see you keeping your troubles locked up internally, especially if it starts to affect your performance. We all want you to win and if I can do anything to help you, just tell me. You don't always have to act like our invincible leader.'

I raised an eyebrow and smiled softly. Jason ran his tongue slowly over his top lip.

'It might sound stupid.'

'Try me.'

The ocean sent a haze of spray into the air between us, setting the moment in soft focus. Jason inhaled and crossed his hands on the top of his head. His chest expanded, the muscles rippling across his ribs. I tried not to stare and turned away to look at the ocean. Four waves were ridden at Pipeline before Jason spoke.

'I think I'm scared.'

'Of what?'

I instinctively knew he was not talking about the waves he had to surf in order to win the world title, which were terrifying to the average human being but not to a man like Jason.

'Of failing?' I suggested.

'No not really, if it happens it happens. I'm actually more scared of winning.'

I glanced at Jason and the confusion was written on my face.

'You see, I told you it would sound stupid.'

'Not at all, I just don't really understand.'

Jason looked around as if checking for spies and pulled his chair closer to mine. We huddled together in the manner of children plotting to run away.

'The things is I've been thinking so much about myself since we started writing this book. Far too much about myself, which is not healthy, believe me. A man could get an ego.'

He tried to laugh. I smiled and waited for him to carry on.

'After all that reflection, I summed up my life and what have I achieved? A dead mother, a brother in prison, a father I hardly see and when I do we don't talk about anything that matters. We talk about women and waves.'

'Hey, they matter,' I joked.

'Sure they do but I don't have a wife or a woman to care for. I'd love to be doing all this for someone and have a person to share it all with. I've got a son I've seen for all of five minutes that I didn't even know I had.'

His voice trailed off. I watched his shoulders slump and wrapped my arm around them.

'You have had unprecedented success in your career. You've brought pleasure to millions of people. You have friends who love you.'

'I know but tell me, Bailey, is that really success?'

His usually smooth skin creased into deep lines around his eyes and on his brow.

'So, if I win at Pipeline, if I get this record world title, then what? I have put years into this dream and I'm almost there but what happens afterwards?'

'I hadn't really thought about it to be honest. I suppose you enjoy the glory and then decide whether you want to carry on.'

'I hadn't thought about it either until we got to Hawaii and the last leg of the race. Suddenly I'm thinking what am I going to focus on if I achieve everything I dreamed of? I've only got my career.'

I bit my lip, recognising instantly that Jason and I were very much alike. I had been focusing on my career for as long as I could remember and all I dreamed of was the moment I knew I had made it as a bestselling author. If truth be told I had never thought about the far side of that mountain. Once I, *if* I, reached that summit, what then? Was it a lonely descent that awaited me? I swallowed hard and rubbed my hand against Jason's warm skin.

'I don't know how to answer that, Jason. To be honest, I didn't have the foresight to think about it.'

'Me neither but I'm nearly there and the truth is, it scares me.'

This was the most vulnerable I had ever seen Jason. Over the time we had worked together we had shared many special moments and memories but Jason's defences were well and truly down and he had chosen me as his confidante.

'You could stay up at the top for a while and look at the view before you decide where to go next. I'm sure things will look bright once you've achieved everything you dreamed of.'

He nodded slowly.

'When you put it that way, it sounds less frightening.'

'Good and you could set yourself a new goal. Why don't you try and track down your son? It's not your fault you didn't know he existed and it's never too late to try and be a father if you want to be.'

'What if I mess it up? I don't want to ruin the kid's life.'

'I doubt that would happen as long as you didn't steamroll in without thinking. You're an amazing person. What about the mother? How long were you together?'

Jason raised his head and a look of embarrassment flashed across his face. His mouth twitched.

'About twenty minutes.'

We looked at each other for a moment, which was all the time we needed for any awkwardness to pass. We both doubled up with laughter.

'Oh dear, Jason, and here was I imagining she was your lost first love.'

'I was young and she was a pretty groupie who was a friend of a friend and…'

I raised my hands defensively.

'You don't have to go into the details. I get it.'

'I'm a changed man, I don't do that anymore.'

Jason slapped his hand against his forehead.

'Dammit, what must you think of me?'

I tapped the top of my notebook.

'You know what I think of you; it's written in here. Although,' I said with a smirk, 'I may have to make some changes now.'

Jason blushed and a smile settled on his soft lips.

'I can't believe I just admitted that to you.'

'Don't worry about it, I'm your friend. I won't judge you.'

'Is that all you are?'

For a moment I was knocked off balance.

'Well I am your biographer and friend.'

'I know but' - he shook his head - 'as we're being so honest, I was wondering whether you could ever see us being anything other than friends.'

I pressed my lips together and my stomach flipped. Jason clicked his knuckles.

'I know it might be the wrong time to bring it up what with me just admitting *that* and all but I've been thinking a lot about it and well,' he sighed, 'now I'm getting tongue tied.'

I watched his tongue as it traced the line of his lips.

'You have been doing a lot of thinking, Jason.'

I scribbled on the cover of my notebook. The blood rushed so fast through my veins it filled my head with white noise.

'I remember what you said to me at the ranch and then everything we talked about in Spain when you told me about your father and so I know it might take some time for you to open up to the idea but' – he inhaled slowly – 'I just want you to know how I feel. Now I guess it's just the thought of you leaving when this book is done. Completely selfishly, I don't want you to go. I can't imagine being without you.'

I blinked.

I can't imagine being without you, I wanted to say in return. It would have been such a release to just admit it but the words stuck in my throat.

My eyes searched his face. He was so handsome and so vulnerable I was drawn towards him and memories of our kiss flooded my thoughts. It had been the most overwhelming kiss of my life but I had pushed the experience into a dark corner of my mind where it could not be dangerous. Jason was a beautiful man, inside and out. He was no Cain

Ohana and one special woman would have a wonderful life with him but I told myself we had a relationship that worked. He respected me and I him. I had almost completed the best work of my life. It was something solid and tangible. The heady dream of romance was not. He was in a vulnerable place, looking for security but who was to say whether that would last?

I closed my eyes and fought the urge inside me to just let myself fall into his arms. I searched for the right words.

'Jason, I'm sorry, I…'

'Hey, Jason, are you coming for a wave at Pipe?'

I opened my eyes. Rory was standing a metre away waving his surfboard happily.

'Not now, Rory,' Jason snapped.

'Come on, mate, you've got to get out there if you want to be on top form for the contest. This isn't the time for slacking off.'

'Like I don't already know how Pipe works? Give me a break, Rory.'

The smile faded from Rory's boyish face.

'What's up with you two, did somebody die?'

'We're talking,' Jason said impatiently.

'Sorry, Jason, I just thought we could have a bit of fun free-surfing and work on some contest tactics,' he said sadly.

'Rory, if you need the practise, you go, I don't need to babysit you.'

I glanced apologetically at Rory who shrugged. His smile quickly returned when a blossoming Ruby walked up behind him, wrapped her arm around his waist and reached up on her toes to kiss him.

'Love you, darl',' she said.

Rory touched her slightly rounded belly and grinned.

'Love you *two.*'

Jason watched them, his expression grim and without another glance in my direction, he marched across the grass towards the house.

Thirty-Nine

Ruby and I sat in companionable silence at the lookout post. I tried to concentrate on my work but attempting to take my mind off Jason while writing about him was a struggle. I wanted to confide in Ruby but she was too close to the situation to involve her. My mind raced.

The awesome waves at Pipeline were a welcome distraction. The swell was building every half hour and was now three times overhead. Ruby looked up frequently from her knitting (she was, as she put it, in her unfashionable nest-building phase) to search for Rory in the line-up, which was not an easy task. We had counted over seventy surfers crammed like sardines into the small take-off area at Pipe. Catching a wave involved not just positioning and strength but a battle of wills. Those in contention paddled aggressively, the war cries audible from land. Boards touched and arms bashed against each other. Leashes were pulled and locals laid claim to the best waves. If, heaven forbid, a surfer dropped in recklessly on another surfer's wave, all hell broke loose with fights on and off land, because to encroach on another surfer's ride at Pipeline could be a matter of life and death. If a wipeout did not kill you, the surfer you had crossed probably would.

Ruby and I observed like the crowd at a firework display.

'Ooh,' we gasped when an over-excited surfer took off too deep on a wave and fell lifelessly from the lip.

'Aah,' we sighed when he popped up dazed but still conscious.

'Ouch,' we cried when one surfer's board was snapped clean in two.

My attention was only drawn away from the action when I heard a cheer from the Tiger Sharks' house and Orca, Rosario, Waipahe and Maika'i strode down the beach with boards under their arms.

'There's Rory on a wave,' Ruby chirped.

I forced a smile but my stomach churned when I realised the Tiger Sharks were watching him too.

An hour passed before Rory came close to catching another wave. Wherever he paddled, the bellicose members of the Tiger Sharks tailed him and whenever he turned to go, at least one blocked his path. Cain's threat rang true. Rory would have struggled to buy a wave at Pipeline that day.

Ruby was oblivious to the conflict unfolding just metres from where she sat, occasionally resting her knitting on her knees and looking out to pinpoint Rory's location. I never took my eyes off Rory's curly haired silhouette as the sun moved behind the surfers and made its journey towards the horizon. I prayed for the ocean to send Rory a wave. I prayed for darkness to fall prematurely. I prayed Rory would admit defeat, swallow his pride and paddle in.

The swell continued to increase and the waves began to visibly warp when they hit the Pipeline reef. At six o'clock, the lifeguards packed up their equipment and either went home for the evening or paddled out to catch some of the waves they had been forced to watch all day. When Rory paddled for one of the more monstrous sets of the day, he looked to be in the perfect position. I bit down on my knuckle and watched his arms stroke through the water.

'He's going for this one,' said Ruby but at the last second, Rory's board jerked backwards when Rosario grabbed his leash and prevented him from catching the wave.

Rory splashed the water in anger, his frustration visible.

'Why did he do that to Rory?' Ruby gasped. 'What's going on out there?'

'Macho stuff,' I croaked.

I glanced back towards the house, wondering whether I should explain to Jason what was going on just outside the safety of our private garden.

'He's paddling again,' Ruby informed me. 'Oh, he let that girl have it.'

Chivalrous by nature, Rory pulled back on the only wave that he had had a chance of catching for over two hours to allow one of the local girls to surf safely to shore. Petite against the huge wall of water behind her, the Hawaiian surfer girl put me in mind of a Barbie Doll with bendable joints. She looked both graceful and powerful as she rode the wave to its end, hopped down onto her stomach and belly-boarded the white water into the beach. Cursing Rory's manners under my breath, I returned my attention to the line-up.

Dusk was settling around the surfers and the ocean surface had developed a bruise of purple and orange. The night was still and the beach was almost deserted except for surfers watching the dying minutes of the action at Pipe. The catcalls from the Tiger Sharks' house pierced the air, the decibel level rising in correlation to the size of the swell. Ruby and I sat forward in our seats and watched open-mouthed when a set pushed through that was bigger and more menacing than anything we had seen at Pipeline so far. As the new powerful ocean swell overtook the old swell, the wave mutated and crashed down onto the reef with a ground-shaking explosion.

Even the Tiger Sharks scrambled anxiously over this first wave to escape and position themselves for the wave behind. Ruby's stomach rumbled.

'Come on, Baby, me and bubba are getting hungry.'

'He's paddling. Yep I think he's on this one, Ruby.'

I strained my neck to see as Rory raced Maika'i towards the take-off spot. Rory looked set to be first out of the starting blocks until he suddenly jerked backwards with obvious force and Maika'i took off, slamming his fist back towards Rory as a sign of defiance.

'They pulled his leash again,' Ruby cried out.

She placed her knitting down on the decking.

'They're playing a dangerous game out there,' I hissed.

'That is no game.'

Ruby was up on her feet, her hands supporting the small of her back.

I could wait no longer. Cain had clearly meant every word of his threats.

'I'm going to get Jason. Keep an eye on Rory.'

'What's happening, Bailey? Is Rory in trouble?'

Ruby's questions carried on the air as I sprinted across the now cool grass to the house.

'Jason, come quickly. Rory needs you.'

I kicked off my sandals and threw open the screen door.

'Jason, where are you? Please, come quickly!'

I stumbled through the door.

Jason looked embarrassed at first but then sensed the urgency in my voice.

'What is it? What's happened?'

I grabbed his hand and struggled to catch my breath.

'Please come. It's Rory,' I gasped.

Jason let me pull him into the garden.

'The Tiger Sharks have him cornered out there' – I pointed frantically towards the ocean while we ran – 'he can't get a wave. Cain made threats. Said he wouldn't be able to buy a wave when he finished with him.'

'When did this happen?'

'At the Sunset contest. We didn't want to worry you.'

Jason's brow was set in a deep furrow by the time we reached Ruby. He rested his hand on her back and lowered his head.

'Can you see him, Ruby?' he said with surprising calmness. 'Is he doing OK?'

I clasped my chest and felt it heave. Perhaps I was exaggerating the danger. Rory was an incredibly capable surfer after all. Maybe I overestimated what Cain was capable of.

'There he is.'

We followed the line of Ruby's arm and saw Rory crossing arms with Rosario in a desperate struggle to catch the wave. Orca paddled in front of Rory in an attempt to block him while Waipahe and Maika'i were caught unawares by the voluminous wave that wrapped onto the reef at a disjointed angle. Rosario was heavy and strong but not as fast as Rory. Rory put his head down and dug deep for every last ounce of his strength.

'Go, darl',' Ruby urged.

My heart was in my throat and my head throbbed as Rory propelled himself into the wave. Orca blocked his path but at the last moment, Rory yanked his board to the left and flew past Orca, taking the wave at a precarious angle. He freefell and crumpled deep into his legs at the base of the wave. For a moment I thought he was too off-balance to make the essential turn but Rory absorbed the impact and righted himself. The wave stood up, its tube as misshapen as a Dali clock.

'Thank God.'

Ruby exhaled and bent down slowly to collect her knitting. My eyes drifted to the Tiger Sharks who were punching the water and each other in the line-up for having allowed their plaything to escape.

'No, that wave is ugly,' Jason said, almost to himself.

He held his hands up to his face. He strained to see, moving from one foot to another as he gradually edged closer to the beach.

'Don't go for the barrel, Rory, straighten out.'

The anxiety in Jason's previously calm voice caught Ruby's attention and mine. I watched the expression on Jason's face flash between concern and fear.

'What is it, Jason?'

'He didn't make the barrel,' he said in a monotone that made me shiver.

Ruby flicked her head back towards the ocean.

'But he made the take-off.'

'That wave was ugly,' Jason said again.

My eyes scanned the ocean but the dusky light hampered my vision. My hand reached out of its own accord and came to rest on Jason's arm. I could feel him shaking.

'I don't think he made the barrel. I can't see him.'

Jason moved quickly towards the beach entrance.

'Stay here,' he pointed firmly at us. 'I'm just going to check. Stay here.'

Ruby's knitting needles clattered to the ground.

The anxiety in Jason's tone was enough to make us do anything but stay where we were. I took Ruby's hand and followed. The cold hands of fear strangled my airway.

'What's happening, Bailey? He's alright isn't he?'

Ruby's hand trembled in mine.

'It's fine, Ruby. Jason just couldn't see him. I bet Rory's walking towards us as we speak. He'll be starving by now.'

My voice sounded like a distant chatter. The next few seconds seemed to move in slow motion when we reached the beach and all three of us stopped dead in our tracks. A small crowd had gathered at the shore, their fingers pointing at an abandoned surfboard bobbing around in the shallow waters. The board lilted towards us on the swell and Rory's Poseidon stickers reflected in the dwindling light of the day.

'Where is he, Jason?' Ruby said in a ghostly whisper.

It was Rory's surfboard but there was no sign of Rory.

Jason's eyes were ice when he looked at us, his face as white as if every last drop of blood had drained to his feet. A tear ran down my cheek before I could stop it.

'Where is he?' Ruby said again.

Ruby and I stared at Jason as if he had the power to rewind time. He said nothing before he span on his heels and raced along the sand, stumbling in holes and tripping over exposed reef as he desperately tried to reach the board.

Jason threw himself fully dressed into the water and half-swam, half-ran out towards the surfboard, which he grabbed with both hands and yanked into the air. Half a leash hung lifelessly from the tail of the board where it had snapped under strain. The other half would be attached to Rory's ankle.

Ruby and I held hands and ran as far as the shallows. When I stopped at the water's edge, Ruby just kept on going. She dragged her legs through the water as if she hardly noticed she had left the beach. She fell and smashed her knees against the razor sharp reef but just got up again and kept ploughing on. The voices of the small crowd made no sense to me.

'Ruby,' I shouted, 'please, Ruby, come back. Jason will find him. Ruby!'

I grasped my head to stop the throbbing in my brain.

What was happening? Was this a vivid nightmare I would awake from, soaked in sweat rather than the salt water of the ocean?

'No, please no, not Rory,' I said over and over. 'Please, no.'

I was reminded of the first Pipeline contest I had watched at this very spot the December before when Jason had lost the world title to Cain. Jason survived, I told myself, and so would Rory. The same fear gripped me although this time it was much more intense because these people had become my true friends. I loved Rory like a brother and the thought of something happening to him was unimaginable. I would not let myself imagine the worst.

I plunged into the water and tried to run against the current to help Ruby, to get away from the thoughts in my own head. My legs ached and my progress was as slow as if I were attempting to run through treacle.

'SURFER DOWN!' Jason hollered from the water.

Those on the beach who had not yet realised what was happening sprung to their feet. Some grabbed surfboards and ran down to the water. Others still stood in groups whispering and shaking their heads. The few surfers remaining in the line-up turned sharply towards Jason who was paddling out on Rory's board, his eyes scanning the water. Every surfer paddled towards Jason. Every surfer that was except the four Tiger Sharks, who paddled straight to shore and made their way towards their house under the cover of the enveloping darkness. Now was not the time to deal with Cain's henchmen.

I reached Ruby and grabbed her by the shoulders. She was not crying. She had a look of unstoppable determination etched on her face.

'Let me go,' she wheezed. 'I must find him.'

Waves lapped over the reef towards us, hitting Ruby in the stomach and knocking her backwards. She was drenched as far as her chest. Her breathing was shallow and fast.

'Ruby, don't do this,' I pleaded. 'Please come back to shore. You have to think of the baby. Please.'

In deeper water, Jason dived beneath the surface and swam into the maze of caves that provided a lethal foundation for an already deadly wave. I was exhausted but pumped with adrenalin as I tried to stop Ruby sacrificing herself and her unborn baby to the power of the Banzai Pipeline.

Jason and the surfers tried to scour every inch of the ocean surface but darkness was closing in fast. I remembered the sound of the screams of the woman who had lost her husband in Hossegor but the fact that Ruby was neither crying nor screaming filled me with a greater fear. She was already in a deep state of shock and her body was as hard and immovable as stone. I struggled to move her onto land while the shore break waves smashed against us with terrifying force.

'Over here!' I heard a high-pitched voice cry.

The Barbie girl surfer was waving her arms in the air.

'Come, Ruby, quick, they've got him.'

Ruby moved her neck mechanically and relaxed enough for me to guide her back to the safety of the beach. Her body began to shake and she fell every couple of steps as we stumbled along the sand. I squinted in the darkness but was afraid of what I would see.

I could just make out the prone body of a man lying on the surfboard that Jason, the girl and three other surfers were pushing forcefully through the water. When they reached the shallows they lifted the board aloft like pallbearers with a coffin and carried the body to the beach. An arm tumbled off the side of the board clutching the Velcro strap of a surfboard leash in its hand. My heart flipped with joy. Rory had managed to rip the leash off his ankle, he had saved himself and he was still alive. The sound of sirens shattered the peace of our tropical paradise.

'He's going to be alright, Ruby,' I breathed, holding her tightly.

We pushed gently through the onlookers.

Jason crouched over Rory's body while the girl pumped his chest with astonishing force. I clasped a hand to my mouth when I realised Jason was giving Rory mouth-to-mouth resuscitation.

'Don't you dare leave me,' Jason shouted every few breaths. 'Don't you fucking dare.'

'Let me through,' said the paramedic who swept through the crowd with his partner and brought an instant sense of reality to the situation.

The paramedics opened bags and set machines in motion and spoke a language to each other that might well have been Slovakian for all the sense it made.

'What's happening?' Jason asked over and over, his breathing heavy in the silence of the sombre crowd.

The paramedics did not respond.

I held Ruby tight and refused to let her go. She stared at the ground in front of her as if in a trance. Unable to bear the sight of Rory's lifeless body, I looked up and saw the figures of Cain and the Tiger Sharks some distance away on the beach. They were too afraid to come any closer.

Suddenly Ruby clutched her stomach and fell from my grasp onto her knees. Jason and I reached out to catch her but she lurched forwards and flung her hand past the paramedics and onto Rory's naked chest.

'NO! I love you, Baby,' she screamed erupting into sobs that came from somewhere deep inside. 'I don't want you to go.'

The very next second, one paramedic sat back and pressed his face into his hands. The other let out a long breath and turned the switch on a machine that screeched in the darkness like a vampire bat. A tear ran down my cheek and dropped into the sand. Jason wrung his hands and howled at the sky.

'I'm sorry, we did all we could, but he's gone.'

Ruby rested her head on her fiancé's shoulder and pulled her petite pregnant body into the curve of his arm that still clutched the fragmented leash. Rory's eyes stared up at the sky, empty and cold. Darkness swallowed up paradise and time stood still.

Forty

A stunned disbelief settled on our pretty blue beach house as if we were shrouded in a freezing fog. The colours had faded from the scene and a stale smell filled the air. At times I felt as if I could hardly breathe. At first nobody dared set the funeral wheels in motion because to do so would be to accept that Rory was truly gone from our lives. I remembered the same suffocating panic when my father died. The fog of death seemed to seep through every crack and crevice, reaching me wherever I tried to hide. As a teenager I had thought if I pretended hard enough my father was still alive he would come back to me. A man with such a colourful spirit could not simply cease to exist. I had refused to play the Grim Reaper's rules until enough time had passed to make the pretence no longer possible.

Now, as grown adults, we were all playing the same game. Rory was young and handsome, adored and talented and he had been about to start a new wonderful life as a husband and father. It just did not make sense that Rory's death could be part of the greater plan. It was simply not fair and we were not willing to believe it was true. Of course it was not a choice we had the power to make. Rory was gone and all we had were memories. Every one of us replayed his last days. Each of us wracking our brains to desperately remember details of the last words we had exchanged with him and what he had looked like and whether he had been smiling. Jason unfortunately could recall all too well their final exchange. Regret, the emotion he had refused to entertain before, was strangling him.

I remembered the terror I had felt when I could not recall my father's final words to me, as if they held the key to his memory that would vanish completely without those closing moments. I lay in my bed at night staring at the ceiling just trying to recall as many of Rory's words as possible. I even wrote them down.

I quickly realised I had to accept responsibility for my dear friends. I had been there before and I was more equipped than most to deal with the emptiness and to ensure the living continued to live.

I took on the horrendous task of informing Rory's mother and stepfather, whom I had spoken to only for a matter of minutes before in the sort of meaningless, chirpy telephone conversations that do not forge any lasting relationships. Their cries haunted me until I saw them in person at Honolulu airport, broken people among the colourful holidaymakers in the arrivals hall. I arranged for Ruby's parents to fly in on the next available flight from Perth along with Ruby's brother, Tim. Jason paid for first class travel but none of them would have relished the comfort. Ruby's parents took charge of their daughter in the way only parents can and I immediately worried less about the health of her baby. Ruby refused to leave Oahu and begged to be allowed to move in to the beach house she had dreamed of sharing with her new husband. Chuck and I unpacked the furniture Ruby and Rory had ordered together and prepared the rooms in the impersonal manner of a hotel. The setting was soothing but displayed none of Rory's identity. Ruby was not yet ready to live among happy memories of the man who had been her "One".

With Ruby taken care of by the people who knew her best, I turned my attention to Jason. He was crumbling before my eyes.

'Why did I not go surfing with him?' he said over and over. 'I could have prevented this. If only I hadn't said no. If only I had been a better person to him. If only I...'

If only. All of us dwelled on those two words. If only Rory had never paddled out that day. If only the Tiger Sharks had left him alone. If only I had told Jason about the threats. If only the wave had been more gentle. If only... It was a pointless exercise but it was inevitable. We would all have changed things if we could have but in wishing *if only* we were deceiving ourselves into thinking we had the power to change the course of Rory's life.

The day after Rory died, Jason displayed a calm strength that carried us through the first few painful hours. The second day he closed himself off to the rest of us and sank into a silent turmoil. On the third day, Jason was angry, which only increased on the fourth and fifth days. At first the anger was directed at himself, then at Cain and the Tiger Sharks whom he held responsible for the accident. An inquiry had been launched into the incident and Jason reported his beliefs to both the police and the North Shore Lifeguards. The problem was Orca and his crew had not actually held Rory underwater until the life drained out of him. We had seen them berate him and interfere with his attempts to catch waves but that happened often, if to a lesser extent, in the surf. There was no doubt they had upset Rory, probably to the point of exhaustion, and their bullying had caused him to take a wave he might otherwise have avoided, but the final decision to take the wave had been his. None of us could prove Rory's death was as a direct result of their actions and it soon transpired that no independent witnesses were willing to point the finger of blame at a gang who were apparently capable of causing something as unthinkable as the death of one of the world's best surfers.

On the fifth day, Jason's hatred turned on the one thing he had always loved; the ocean. I immediately realised this threatened to destroy everything he had ever worked for. With eyes as black as Cain's, Jason told me he could not allow himself to forgive Mother Ocean for what she had done and he was resolute in wanting nothing more to do with something that could be so destructive. He tied himself in knots wondering whether if he had managed to save the man in Hossegor, Rory would also have been saved. He dwelt on every negative, mulling over the aftermath of the tsunami and Wyatt's life-changing accident that had left him paralysed.

'But Wyatt isn't bitter about what happened,' I tried to gently argue. 'He adores the ocean to this day. He loves surfing and being in the water is what helps him carry on.'

'Do you really believe he's happy being like that?' Jason hissed. 'The ocean did that to him and now he has no choice but to surrender to it because his body is fucking useless on dry land.'

'You would not say that to his face,' I replied firmly. 'He's an inspiration to you and you to him. You had great fun together the day you first took me surfing. What was it again, only a surfer knows the feeling?'

Jason said nothing.

His hatred for the very thing that had brought him self-esteem, wealth, success, fame and a purpose in life frightened me. I knew Jason was lost without his best friend but to also lose the passion that had driven him out of a hard life and around the world's most beautiful beaches would destroy him.

I called his father in the hope that the man who had instilled in Jason the passion for surfing would be able to do so again in time.

'Jason lost one brother in childbirth, the other is in jail and now the young man who had become like his third brother has gone. He is devastated, Ricky. He is trying to be strong but at a time like this I think he needs family. He needs you.'

'I don't think I can come, Bailey,' Ricky said after a pause, 'I've got the dogs and cattle and the horses and it's expensive and...'

I was surprised by his unwillingness.

'Jesus will look after the ranch and I can arrange the ticket for you. Please, Ricky. I don't know who else to turn to.'

Ricky made no promises. All I could do was buy his ticket and hope he would appear. Hoping at the same time that I had done the right thing.

When a surfer dies the tradition is to hold a paddle out memorial service in the ocean. Rory's memorial was scheduled for exactly a week after his death. The news had shaken the entire surfing community, reminding each of them who surfed of their own vulnerability and, indeed, mortality. We received phone calls, emails and cards from thousands of surfers as far afield as Chile, Australia, New

Zealand, Reunion Island, Barbados, Ireland and Scotland. Chuck and I thanked as many people as we could for their thoughts and prayers, informed them of the memorial arrangements and put every message no matter how small aside for a time when Ruby would be able to find comfort from the reaction to her beloved fiancé's death.

'How is she doing?' I asked her mother the day before the memorial.

'She's like a flower that's been left out in the sun with no water. Still pretty and delicate but wilting and dying in front of our eyes,' her mother admitted sadly.

I assumed Ruby would not be strong enough to attend the ceremony.

On the evening of the sixth day, while Jason and I were preparing the flowers and palm leaves to scatter in the ocean at the memorial service, Jason finally broke down.

'I miss him so much,' he sobbed. 'How can this have happened? I don't understand.'

I had no answers. Words of consolation were useless. I held him, just as he had held me in Spain. I felt the big, strong man tremble like a child in my arms. We cried until we could cry no more. We opened a bottle of rum and let the neat liquor burn our throats in the hope it would warm our hearts. We talked and we sat in silence. We held one another as if the world was about to end and then we fell asleep in each other's arms.

Forty-One

When I awoke, I was still locked in Jason's embrace. I opened my eyes and watched him sleep. His eyes were shut so tight he was frowning as if he was concentrating on shutting out the world. His breathing was shallow and occasionally a nerve twitched in his cheek. I pressed my body against his. I had never felt so protected and safe in my life.

It was, however, I who had to find the strength for the two of us that morning. Jason stared at the orchid leis and tears welled up in his eyes.

'I don't think I can do this,' he said.

'You can and you will because Rory deserves nothing less.'

I handed him his board shorts and a garland of flowers. It was not the usual funeral attire but this was not the average funeral. Surfers had their own way of celebrating life and, in death as in life, they very rarely followed the norm.

The air was still and silent when the enormous crowd filtered onto the beach from all directions. The main Kamehameha Highway from Haleiwa was gridlocked for miles and people had abandoned their cars in the traffic jam to walk the remaining distance to the beach at Pipeline. The first crowd formed a circle and then the people after that formed a circle surrounding the first until the entire circumference of the circle was thirty people deep. There were hundreds and hundreds of people on the beach and yet more were still visible in the distance walking silently along the sand to pay their respects. Over two hundred surfboards stood vertically in the sand in the centre of the circle, resembling tombstones in a graveyard.

Chuck and I greeted people and thanked them for coming but the numbers were so overwhelming I felt exhausted by the time Jason appeared with his board under one arm. He walked purposefully with his head down and the crowd parted respectfully to let Jason place his surfboard in the centre. He gazed around at the collection of boards and paused for a moment before raising his eyes and scanning the circle. When he spotted Cain and the Tiger Sharks on the opposite side of the gathering dressed in black shorts and T-shirts, he visibly stiffened and hatred flooded onto his face.

'You're not welcome here,' he spat, marching across the sand towards them.

I ran to intercept him.

'You did this. You and your gang of evil bastards did this to my friend. Get out of here.'

He stopped just inches from Cain, who firmly held his ground. I stopped beside Jason and gasped for air.

'Please, Jason, this is not the time.'

Jason and his Nemesis faced each other unblinking.

'I had nothing to do with this, Brah,' Cain hissed. 'I wasn't even in the water when he took that wave.'

'Maybe not but these animals of yours were and I'm not stupid, Cain, I saw what they were doing.'

I touched Jason's arm.

'Let's deal with this later.'

Cain glanced at me and his steely gaze momentarily flickered. He knew I had witnessed his threat to Rory. He knew I could pull the rug from under his feet in front of all these people. The temptation was there but I also knew it was not the right time for hatred and blame.

'We're here to honour Rory,' I said quietly, 'and I will not let anybody ruin that so let's put the egos to one side and get on with celebrating his life shall we?'

Jason lowered his chin onto his chest and paused to take a few breaths before turning and walking away to the other side of the circle. I left Cain with a look that said *I know what you did* and then joined Jason. It was time to begin.

I held the notes I had made in both hands to stop them shaking. I could have tried to blame it on the wind but the air was as still as if God had switched off the wind machine and sent it in for a service. The ocean was also uncharacteristically still, with Pipeline glistening like the millpond it became during the summer months when the swells switched to the south. Even the palm trees had stopped rustling and a pair of old turtles that had been labouring along the tide line were now motionless beside the water. The only sound in the air was the occasional sniff and suppressed sob from those who were already overwhelmed by the occasion.

Petrified that if I waited any longer I would lose the strength I had taken all morning to muster, I began.

'I only got to know Rory this year but this life on tour is intense, so in that time I came to love him as a very special friend. Rory was caring, kind and loving. He adored Ruby, his fiancée, with the sort of love many of us will never have the pleasure of experiencing. Rory doted on Ruby and when he proposed and Ruby accepted, the happiness they both felt was infectious. That happiness became something unquantifiable when Ruby discovered she was pregnant and all of us know Rory would have been a fantastic father. I believe his spirit will stay with us to ensure his child grows up aware of how beautiful and talented a person Rory was.'

I looked up to try and compose myself and to stop the tears falling onto my notes. As I did so, someone delicately touched my arm. It was Ruby. She wore a pink dress and a cream flower in her hair. She held a hand-tied bouquet of the tropical flowers she had chosen for her wedding day. Her feet were bare. Ruby looked even more petite than usual and as breakable as porcelain but the pink gloss on her lips and her perfect oval bump gave her a glow that reassured me she would survive this. I pulled her into my arms and hugged her tighter than I had ever hugged anyone before.

'Thank you, darl',' she whispered in my ear, 'please continue.'

I nodded and turned back to the circle. People were either staring at the ground, lost in their own thoughts, or looking at Ruby with mixed emotions of sympathy and fear as if any minute she might self destruct in front of their eyes.

'Rory was selfless,' I continued, 'and always ready to protect his friends and family. He stood up for what he believed in and he tried to guide those around him with a delicate touch. Likewise, he was guided by his mentor, Jason Cross, whom he loved like a brother.'

Jason did not move. His chest rose and fell and his arms were rigid at his sides. I pressed on.

'Rory loved life and just before it was taken from him, he was on the verge of achieving everything he had ever dreamed of. We can question fate, we can be angry and full of hate for the invisible forces that caused this to happen, we can cry and dwell on the tragedy and we can drive ourselves to distraction trying to find a reason for something so truly awful.'

Jason's fists clenched and opened and clenched again beside me.

'But this turmoil, this overwhelming grief, this crippling fear of life, is this what Rory would have wanted for those he left behind? I don't think so. Rory died doing the very thing that made him the man you all loved. To Rory and to many of you, surfing is not a hobby or a sport or just a job that you have to do because you are paid to do it. Surfing is what drives you. It's your lifeblood and it drove Rory. It is what got him out of bed in the morning and made him race through the house to see the ocean before he even had a cup of coffee just to check what the waves were doing. It filled his waking thoughts and it filled his dreams. It was his passion and even though it came with obvious risks, Rory took those risks on board and carried on regardless. He was not reckless but the chance of catching a wave that surpassed all others was enough to spur him on. I remember Rory once telling me – "Life is all about risk. It can be dull as hell if you don't risk it once in a while." – and he was right. He took risks and in the end it may seem as if he lost but Rory truly lived. Look around at all the people here his short life touched.'

The heads of the crowd lifted and they acknowledged each other. I recognised pain in their tear-stained faces but some were smiling, already letting Rory's memory become a positive thing.

'Rory knew life would not go on forever and just recently Rory shared with Ruby, Jason and I how he would like to be greeted at the gates of heaven.'

A tear rolled down my cheek and I paused when Jason gently took my hand. Ruby then took the other and we all squeezed hands before looking up at the clear blue sky above us.

'Aloha, Rory,' we called out in unison, 'great last wave, dude.'

The crowd howled their appreciation and almost instantaneously a wind whipped up the sand around us and began to blow so strong it almost knocked me over. It felt as if all the angels had put their fingers to their lips and blown. I gasped to catch my breath.

'He's answering us,' Ruby laughed tearfully. 'He always had to have the last word.'

Ruby squeezed my hand tightly. The wind had brought colour to her cheeks and a smile played on her lips.

'He's really talking to us,' she said with a sparkle in her eyes I had been scared would never return.

I did not know whether she was right but it definitely felt as if there were greater forces at play.

Rory's parents stood beside us looking completely overwhelmed by the outward display of love for their son. Slowly the surfers stepped into the circle and retrieved their boards from the sand. They held flowers and palm leaves and wore leis around their necks. One by one they made their way to the water's edge. Cain and the Tiger Sharks paddled out first. Jason pulled off his T-shirt and then pulled me into his arms.

'Thank you,' he breathed.

His heart pounded heavily against my chest.

When he moved away a shadow passed across his face. This would be the first time Jason had been in the ocean since Rory died and I could tell he was struggling with the prospect. He wanted to honour his closest friend but he was afraid to go back in the water. Perhaps it was the danger or perhaps, as I suspected, it was because he wanted to carry on hating the ocean but knew as soon as he surfed again he would be hooked once more.

'I don't think…'

I reached up and placed the plumeria lei he had been gripping in his hand over Jason's head and let it drop onto his shoulders.

'You can do it, Jason. For Rory.'

'It's not the same paddling out alone.'

'Maybe you won't have to.'

I nodded to the slim figure walking from the house with a board under his arm. He wore a cap pulled down so the brim hid his face but the board was unmistakeable. It was yellowed and dented with a red lightning bolt running down the centre. It was the board that had won the Californian Championships in 1966 and it was the board on which Jason had caught his very first wave.

'Dad,' Jason gasped.

'Hello, son,' said Ricky, glancing furtively around, 'I'd be honoured if you'd paddle out with me.'

Father and son followed the other surfers out into deeper water where they once more formed a circle sitting astride their boards. Jason and Cain sat far apart, as they were in life and in character. The wind whipped up the surface of the water like a cappuccino. Ruby and

I held hands at the water's edge with her parents on one side and Rory's on the other.

'This is amazing,' Ruby's brother Tim said.

'Just like Rory,' Ruby sighed.

She was serene as she watched the surfers bow their heads and toss their flowers and leaves into the ocean where they dispersed on the currents, carrying with them the memories of Rory. I threw my flowers and leaves into the shore break and closed my eyes. Ruby then held up her flowers and breathed in their sweet aroma before hurling them into the water. We silently watched the bouquet that should have been thrown by the bride at the end of a wedding celebration drift out towards the horizon in the rip tide.

After a minute's silence, the surfers began to splash the water with their fists and shout at the top of their voices. I could not make out the words but the energy and emotion was unforgettable. They then broke the circle and paddled towards the waves. They rode them sometimes four or five abreast, attacking the ride and laughing when they fell. Ruby's face was soaking wet with tears but still the smile touched her lips.

'I wish he could see this,' she said.

'Maybe he can.'

Eventually the only two surfers remaining were Jason and Ricky Cross. They sat beside each other, Ricky a slighter version of his well-built professional surfer son. When the best set of the day approached, they spun their boards around, paddled together, jumped lightly to their feet and rode the wave with Jason just inches behind his father. At the end of the wave Ricky kicked off and tumbled into the water and Jason dived in beside him. When they emerged from under the surface, Ricky swam towards Jason, stopped for a moment and then opened his arms to hug his son. They were too far away for me to make out their faces but I sensed they were smiling.

I watched and then I reached a hand to my cheek and realised I was crying. I wiped the tears away and caught sight of Cain standing staring out to sea. For an instant I was caught off-guard and the look of despair on his face made me sad. His head was lowered when he approached me and when he reached my side he stopped.

'I'm so sorry,' he said quietly before walking on.

Forty-Two

Rory's body was repatriated to Australia two days later. Ruby planned to spread his ashes at his favourite wave in Margaret River, the place where fate and a chocolate muffin had first brought them together. We had a tearful goodbye.

'I want him to be able to surf that wave forever. He'll be happy there,' Ruby explained, her eyes glistening with tears.

'I hope you can be happy again too, Ruby.'

I held onto her, wishing she did not have to leave. She pulled slowly away and squinted up at me.

'Promise me you'll be happy, Bailey. Don't let life and love pass you by.'

I gave a half-smile.

'What do you mean?'

She touched her hand to her heart.

'You have a lot of love in your heart. Let it out.'

I looked at my feet.

'I'm fine, Ruby, honestly.'

'You're more than fine, darl', you're wonderful. We all think so. I just want you to promise me you won't go through life being blinkered. There is more to life than work you know.'

Her eyes scrutinized my face and I suddenly sensed that the girl I had felt the need to care for over the previous year had enough maturity for both of us.

'I loved Rory with all my heart and I lost him and yes the pain is excruciating but' – she wiped a tear from her cheek – 'if I could do it all again I would. I would suffer all this pain for one day with him because the love we had was worth it. What is it Shakespeare said? "Better to have loved and lost than never to have loved at all".'

'I think it was Tennyson,' I said with a smile.

'There you go that's why you're the writer, darl'.'

She nudged me playfully with her elbow and we laughed through the tears.

'Just think about it, Bailey.'

I nodded.

'I promise, Ruby and you remember I will always be at the end of the phone for you. Don't be lonely.'

Ruby gently rubbed her bump.

'I won't be. I've got a part of him right here.'

I watched her leave. She was so petite she looked like a child as she stepped hesitantly across the sand but in a week she had become a woman with knowledge of the highs and desperate lows of life. There were more stages of grief to come for Ruby but I had faith she would cope. She might have been as delicate as a little bird but she was stronger than most of us had given her credit for.

Less than a week later, the organisers of the Pipemasters event held a vote among the surfers, which Jason did not attend, and made the decision to run the event. I was then relieved Ruby had left before she had to witness life slipping back to normality on the dream tour without Rory's presence. The contest Director, Munroe Stores, came to inform Jason in person.

'Everybody wants to get home for Christmas and a good swell is predicted. Too much is riding on the final result to cancel it. I'm sorry.'

A nerve flickered in Jason's cheek, just as it did in his father's when he felt anxious.

'So ego comes before respect for our dead brother does it? Cain knows I would take the title if we cancel so he's pushing for the comp to run, is that it?'

Munroe looked like a man who was not easily rattled but the way he shifted his feet and averted his gaze indicated his mission sat uncomfortably upon his shoulders.

'Cain shouts and we all jump, is that it, Munroe?'

Munroe ran his hand through his thick white hair and sighed.

'Believe me it's not like that, Jason. Rory was a totally respected and loved member of the tour but you gotta understand there are too many sponsors involved and too many surfers trying to re-qualify for the tour in this last event and, well, great surfers die every year. We can't just stop because of a tragic accident.'

Jason stood up so quickly Munroe flinched.

'I think you should go, Munroe. I won't surf this event and if that means I forfeit my title to Cain then so be it.'

'NO!'

Chuck jumped to his feet.

'Dude, I so can't let you do that.'

Chuck wrapped his long arm around Munroe's shoulders and guided him to the door.

'Thanks for coming, man, just let us deal with this.

'You got three days,' said Munroe sadly.

'I'm not doing it,' Jason said firmly and left us to ponder how we could change the mind of a man who was more determined than anyone I had ever known.

THE END

I stared at the two words on my laptop screen and sat back against the headboard of my bed. My book could not end like this. Rory dead, Jason retired, Cain the unworthy winner of the title by default. I could not let it happen without a fight.

To give him his credit, Chuck had tried everything he could think of to convince Jason to compete in the contest. He had tried the sympathetic approach and the aggressive approach. He had tried bribing him with cars and holidays and new sponsorship opportunities. He had even offered to fix him a date with the world's highest paid supermodel because he knew her 'people' and they owed him a favour. Finally Chuck had shocked us all by offering to donate his entire year's salary to a charity of Jason's choice if he just competed one last time. Judging by the way Chuck began to shake as if he were in an earthquake when he made the offer, I think every ounce of his being was praying Jason would see the error of his ways and compete without accepting the bribe. Jason thanked Chuck for his efforts but still refused.

'Man what is up with him?' Chuck growled. 'I mean if you can't bribe a dude with chicks and cash there is definitely a problem, you know what I'm sayin'?'

Chuck had never really grasped the concept of principles.

For Poseidon, Jason's choice to withdraw from the title race was nothing short of a commercial disaster. They had already invested a huge amount of time and money in a marketing campaign celebrating the thirteenth title that Oli had assumed his superstar surfer would be bringing home. The fact that Rory was a Poseidon rider and had died so publicly was also a blow. Oli was sympathetic in his own way in that he cursed both surfers regularly and sympathised only with himself. He had neither the tact nor the inclination to read Jason's mood and work out how to convince him to compete.

Ricky had tried to work on Jason by regaling his son with tales of their early surfs and playing classic surf movies on repeat. He tried desperately to stir the passion for the ocean in Jason but it was as if a light had been extinguished inside him. Even his eyes had dulled from silver to grey.

I was emotionally drained after the events of the previous fortnight and I was dogged by the selfish fear that my book would be a failure if Jason retired on a low. Life stretched ahead of me like a dusty track with no road signs. In frustration I jabbed my finger on the cursor key of my laptop and ran through the pages.

'All this bloody work and for what?' I muttered. 'I might as well let Tristan know he's got space on his books for a new author. Damn it.'

My finger released the key and my eyes focused gradually on the words filling the screen as if trying to see through a window blurred with condensation. At the same moment my eyes found clarity, so did my brain. I knew what I had to do.

Forty-Three

I lay my head back and closed my eyes. Outside my window just metres away on the beach were the sounds of the final event of the pro surfing tour getting underway. Rock O'Rafferty was warming up his commentary microphone and attempting to rouse the crowd that had been gathering since early that morning. The hooter boomed intermittently like a fog horn on a stormy night with the organisers testing the equipment to make sure the event ran as smoothly as possible. There was a buzz in the air, which stopped dead at the door of our house. While I listened, I nervously wiggled my fingers above the keys of my laptop. I then highlighted the words **THE END** that I had written previously and pressed delete. I was the writer and there would be no ending until I said so.

'The swell is a perfect west swell, the trade winds are smoothing out the Banzai Pipeline like glass,' Rock announced. 'It's eight feet this morning with a bigger swell expected. I know you're all waiting for the Cain Ohana and Jason Cross showdown but right now, ladies and gentlemen, I'm sorry to announce Jason Cross has still not confirmed his entry.'

A groan of dismay coursed through the crowd.

'Jason is listed in heat number eight and there is no loser's round two in this event, guys, so if he misses that first heat that means instant elimination and bye-bye world title.'

I surveyed the beach that was packed with spectators and checked the time. I had just over three and a half hours to convince Jason to compete. The heats flew by as if on fast-forward. In contrast to the other nine events on the tour calendar, the Pipemasters was run with four surfers in each heat rather than two. As a result the contest was completed in less time to ensure the North Shore's famous wave was not monopolised and other surfers prevented from surfing there for longer than strictly necessary.

Petit Sylvain won his heat, which allowed Oli a brief moment of happiness but two other Poseidon surfers were eliminated in heats four and five, one consequently failing to re-qualify for the tour the following year. This surfer left the water with his head bowed and a quivering lip.

'Poor guy,' I sighed, 'and just before Christmas too. Could it be any worse?'

'Fucking loser,' said Oli, spitting his gum at my feet. 'Well he can forget his fucking contract for next year that's for sure.'

Apparently it could.

Worse still was yet to come when I heard the gate to the driveway sliding open. I ran through the garden, my veins bursting with adrenalin, to greet Chuck but the flash red Mustang in the driveway made me stop short. I peered at the darkened windows, holding my breath when the door opened and a Jimmy Choo with a silver heel appeared on the end of a slim ankle.

'Portia. What are you doing here?'

She was spooned into a gold dress that highlighted her neat waist and tiny hips. Her caramel skin looked flawless and her yellow gold bracelets and necklace glinted in the sunshine. The reflective bronze lenses of her sunglasses concealed the expression in her eyes as she slithered towards me, her hips swaying dangerously.

'Bailey, what a pleasure as always,' she hissed. 'Have you gained weight?'

'No I think perhaps you've shrunk, it happens to people when they age.'

A beetle wandered casually past Portia's foot. She stabbed it with the chrome heel of her shoe and took pleasure in grinding it to a pulp.

'Oh I'll miss your British wit,' she pouted.

'Really? Leaving so soon?'

Portia stepped towards me and brought her face up to mine.

'It's not me who's leaving, honey, it's you. End of the tour, end of the book, right? Goodbye, Bailey Brown. Portia is here to stay.'

Portia addressing herself in the third person was not a good sign.

She ran a talon down my cheek.

'I let you get to me and play your little tricks, but not any more. Jason needs a good woman right now after everything that he's been through and I am that woman.'

Engulfed in a cloud of perfume, I coughed.

'What about his son?'

'I've been following him in the magazines and I ain't seen any sign of a child. I think you played me.'

Her eyes narrowed. I moved back.

'What you're really saying is you couldn't find yourself another man so you thought you'd do a quick backtrack while he was vulnerable and pounce like a cat on a mouse?'

Portia threw her head back and laughed at the sky.

'Jason ain't no mouse, girl, he is all man. It's just such a damn shame you'll never get to find out. You were right about one thing though, girlfriend' – she looked me up and down – 'why would he look at someone like you when he can have me? You are so not his type.'

I swallowed and watched as she swayed past me and headed for the house. I was not about to get involved in a catfight over a man but Portia's games were the last thing I needed, blowing into the camp like a tornado and pulling up the invisible guy ropes that were just about keeping us secured with her evil tongue and feminine wiles. I dragged my hands back through my hair and let out a cry. Fixing Jason had just got a whole lot harder.

'Ricky, you have to help me,' I pleaded. 'I need you to deflect that girl who just arrived. Where did she go?'

Ricky flicked up the rim of his cowboy hat and nodded towards Jason's bedroom. I glanced in the direction and saw Portia's arms slide around Jason's waist before she kicked the door shut with her foot.

'Well she didn't waste any time.'

'She's a fit piece of ass, pardon my French. Who can blame him?'

'You stupid men,' I said in exasperation, 'when will you ever learn?'

I left Ricky with a look of disgust.

Chuck made it back from the airport just as Cain's heat entered the water. Jason was due to surf in under thirty minutes but he had been holed up in the bedroom with Portia for over an hour. I was in a foul mood and very confused. I felt like telling Jason where to shove his world title and his book for that matter, but I had already got other people involved. It was too late to turn back now even if I did end up looking a fool. I sincerely hoped Chuck's passengers had not made a pointless journey.

Ben was the first to emerge from the car. He shook his shoulder-length hair, smiled at the sunshine hitting his face and then turned to wave at me. His damaged eye was hidden under some very trendy sunglasses.

He helped Izel out of the car. She was wearing two prosthetics and stood with the support of crutches that bent her arms backwards uncomfortably at the elbow. Ben held a hand protectively behind her back but did not touch her as he was well aware how feisty the thirteen year old, petite Mexican girl could be if she felt she was being condescended to. Wyatt was in the front passenger seat. Chuck opened the wheelchair and helped Wyatt into it. The three new arrivals beamed like cheerleaders.

'I'm so happy to see you all.'

I forced a smile.

'We wouldn't miss this for the world,' said Wyatt.

'After all,' giggled Izel, her accented words rolling in the back of her throat, 'we have been coaching Jason all year.'

'We want to make sure he's been listening,' Ben stepped in with a laugh.

'So, B, where's the man of the moment?' Chuck chirped.

I could tell from his expression that he was in no doubt our plan would work.

'I'm afraid there's been a slight hiccup,' I said.

Forty-Four

I shielded my eyes when Chuck burst into the bedroom.

'What the fuck?' Portia screamed. 'Get this asshole out of here, Jason.'

'Are they naked?' I mumbled, not wanting to look.

'No,' Ricky replied with a note of surprise.

I stole a glance at Jason. He was standing facing Chuck, while Portia sat fully clothed on the bed. Her hair was still pulled into a tight bun and I could tell she had been crying.

'Get out of here, all of you,' Portia yelled, her face an angry flush of colour. 'This is between me and Jason.'

'There is no you and Jason, Missy,' Chuck spat, 'if he's got any sense.'

We all looked intently at Jason.

'Just give us a moment, please,' he sighed.

'We don't have a moment, dude. This is it now. Time is up. Are you going to do the comp or what?'

'No he isn't,' Portia hissed at Chuck whose hands closed into tight fists. 'He's coming back to L.A. with me.'

'Over my dead body, bitch.'

'Then so be it, Chuck.'

'Stop it, both of you!' Jason shouted. 'I am here. I'm not some asset to fight over like you're in the divorce court for God's sake.'

'Eugh like I'd be married to a loser like him.' Portia rolled her head dramatically. 'It's you I want, Jason, you know that and you want me too. I can tell.'

'No, Portia' – Jason dropped his head wearily – 'I don't want you. I haven't wanted you for a long time. That's what I've been telling you for the last hour, you just won't listen. I think you should go.'

My heart leapt unwittingly and before I knew it a smile had spread across my face.

'What the hell are you grinning at, you English freak? You think he wants you? No way, bitch.'

Portia hurled herself at me and only Chuck's quick thinking saved my eye from being pierced with a stiletto heel.

'Funny,' I laughed, 'I suddenly feel as if we've come full circle. I'll say one thing for you, you're consistent.'

'What? What are you talking about you whore?'

While Portia struggled in Chuck's tight grasp, I reached out and took Jason by the elbow.

'I've had enough of this. Come here, Jason, I want to show you something.'

He let me lead him to the front window and we looked out across the lawn to see Ben, Izel and Wyatt making themselves comfortable at the lookout post. They were visibly thrilled at being so close to Pipeline and their laughter carried on the breeze. Jason swallowed.

'What are they doing here, Bailey? Did you do this?'

I nodded.

'Yes. Yes I did. I wanted to remind you of the people you have inspired with your surfing. To bring you your very own fan club who could help you through the day.'

'This is blackmail.'

'No. This is the only way I knew how to show you what you were throwing away. You give people hope, Jason and you encourage them not to quit, yet here you are quitting at the final hurdle. You're not even going to try to jump it because you're scared of what's on the other side.'

He shook his head vehemently.

'You're wrong. I just think surfing Pipe would be disrespectful to Rory.'

'I don't believe you.'

Our eyes locked together and for a moment I saw anger burning inside him but I carried on. I had nothing to lose. I would be leaving in a few days regardless and if Jason disagreed and still refused to surf, we would all be in the same position as we currently were. I had to risk it.

'If you want to know what I think...'

'I get the feeling I'm going to find out whether I want to or not.'

'I think Rory would be so angry with you if you let the year end this way.'

Jason swayed at the mention of Rory's name.

'In fact as far as I can see you will be disrespecting him a lot more by turning your back on the very thing that Rory lived for. He loved surfing, Jason. He also loved you and he would hate to see you throwing away your world title and handing it on a plate to Cain.'

Jason bit his lip.

'Don't let Cain win, Jason, please. Don't let Rory down. Do this for Rory or for those kids out there or' – I paused – 'just for yourself.'

A sigh left Jason's lips and he grasped his head as if he was in pain.

'And as for what's on the other side of that hill,' I said softly, 'let's get to the top first and enjoy the view before we worry about that shall we?'

Jason began to chuckle. He stood taller, pulling back his shoulders to look out towards Pipeline.

'How do you do it?' he breathed. 'How do you read me so well?'

When he turned to look down at me I knew I had done what I had set out to do.

I shrugged.

'I've always had a passion for reading and, besides, you're my character. I have to know you well or else my book would be very shallow.'

'You know this is the second time you've talked me into going for the thirteenth title. Do you remember?'

'I remember.'

How could I forget? It was the night Jason found out about Cain and I.

'What would I do without you?'

I shrugged.

'Maybe relax and put your feet up?'

Jason laughed and then his face turned serious once more.

'Promise me you'll be there with me at the top.'

He offered me his hand. I took it.

'I promise.'

Jason beamed and took several deep breaths before spinning on his heel.

'I'll do it,' he said.

I followed him out of the door and across the grass towards the lookout. Chuck met us halfway. I gave him a thumbs up and Chuck's hair stood on end with excitement.

'The witch is over there cooling off,' he warned. 'I said she could stay if she behaves.'

I glanced nervously at Portia who was staring at Ben, Izel and Wyatt. Her hands were raised protectively against her chest as if she might catch quadriplegia if she moved too close.

'I'll get your board ready,' Chuck beamed.

'No need, here use this one.'

Ricky appeared behind us with the lightning bolt board on which Jason had experienced his first thrilling wave ride.

'You fixed it up,' Jason gasped.

'Just a bit of cleaning and ding fixing,' Ricky sniffed as if it was nothing.

The board had been lovingly restored to its former glory.

'I've been working on it at night. I don't sleep much being a ranch owner.'

Ricky shoved his hands into his pockets.

'I hoped you would change your mind.'

Jason slipped the board under one arm and pulled his father into a tight hug.

'Thanks, Dad and you know it means the world to me you being here to watch. This is the first time since I joined the tour.'

'I know, son and I apologise for that but I couldn't risk people seeing me…' – his words disappeared as the hooter sounded.

'Your heat!' I gasped. 'It's started already.'

Jason leapt into action. He pulled off his T-shirt and Chuck bounded off along the beach to find the competition rash vest. Ricky waxed the board and Jason quickly greeted his delighted fan club before running back to me to attach his leash to his ankle.

'Thank you, Bailey,' he said and bent down to kiss me on the cheek.

There was a scream and before anyone could stop her, Portia had wrenched the board from Jason's hands and hurled it to the ground. She jumped up and down on the deck, her metal heels piercing the thin layer of fibreglass and sinking deep into the foam. When she had finished and slumped to the ground, Ricky's prize-winning surfboard resembled a cardboard box pierced repeatedly with a fork.

'What have you done?' Jason's voice was laden with shock. 'Get her out of my sight. For good.'

The colour drained from Portia's aesthetically stunning face. She might have had the most naturally beautiful features I had ever seen, but all at once we saw her for the ugly person she truly was.

Forty-Five

Jason and Ricky raced to the board room and unwrapped a new board suitable for Pipeline. Jason's hands shook as he applied the wax and he protested when Chuck wrenched the competition rash vest over his head until we realised his neck was stuck in the armhole.

'You need a leash,' Ricky called after him as Jason sprinted across the grass.

'No time,' he called back.

Ricky stopped at the edge of the garden and slowly lowered the leash that he gripped tightly in his hand. The sight of it made my spine tingle. The last time I had seen a leash held tight was in Rory's hand. It had been apparent that the leash had held him underwater, probably wrapped around a coral head, and Rory's attempts to unhook it had failed. He had finally found the strength to rip the Velcro fastening from his ankle but it had evidently taken his last ounces of energy to do so.

'He doesn't need a leash.'

I touched Ricky's arm. He was shaking.

'Run, son,' he coached from a distance.

'Shall we run to the water's edge?' I suggested.

Ricky shook his head.

'No. No I think I'll just watch from here.'

As it turned out there was nothing to watch. By the time Jason wrestled his way through his well meaning, adoring fans, stumbled over the sharp reef and paddled out through pounding surf to the line-up, Rock O'Rafferty had begun the countdown for the end of the heat. The three other surfers in the water stared gobsmacked at Jason who had never been known to miss a heat, such was his professionalism. Missing the most important heat of his life was unfathomable.

'Five, four, three, two, one.'

The hooter sounded.

'It's a tragedy, ladies and gentlemen. Jason Cross did not get the chance to catch a wave. We don't know what happened there but we will get that story for you.'

The roars of celebration drowned out Rock's commentary when the Tiger Sharks realised the enormity of what had just occurred. Cain Ohana was the world champion. He was through to the next round and on points alone he could not be caught. The final competition result was irrelevant.

I hugged Izel who burst into tears. Ricky and Chuck hung their heads. Wyatt and Ben consoled each other, their pain real.

'It's not fair,' said Ben. 'It can't just end like this.'

'Contests aren't fair,' said Wyatt soberly. 'That's life.'

I walked away from them, past Oli who was screaming into his Blackberry. His pain was real but it was pain for himself. Jason was an asset that had just plummeted in value and Oli, his team manager, would be held responsible.

I stopped under the shadow of the front porch and rested my head back against the cool wood. I closed my eyes, suddenly overcome by a feeling of exhaustion. For the previous fortnight I had been negotiating a fierce rollercoaster of emotions, which all at once closed in on top of me. I had tried my hardest to help Jason through the gloom and we had almost made it, but it was over. There would be no world title and no glorious showdown. I slid down the wall, curled up against my knees and let the tears flood out.

'I let you all down.'

Jason awkwardly lowered his surfboard down beside me. I glanced at the writing scrawled along the wooden stringer in the centre of the board.

Lucky 13.

It was the board I had signed in the shaping bay with Seb.

'I jinxed you,' I said with a weak smile.

'No, you tried to inspire me and you did. I just took a bit too long to catch on.'

He slid down beside me and held onto his knees. His skin was dripping wet.

I laughed weakly.

'Funny, I always wanted to inspire people but I thought it would feel better than this.'

'But you do inspire people, all the time,' said Jason. 'I'm sorry. It was me who messed up.'

I rubbed his knee.

'Don't be. You gave it your best shot.'

'But that's not what I'm about. I'm a winner, just like you.'

'Like me? I don't feel like a winner right now.'

'Bailey Brown, I haven't seen you be self-pitying before.'

'It'll pass,' I shrugged. 'Just let me indulge myself for a moment. It's been a tough year.'

'It's not over yet.'

Jason leapt up and outstretched his hands.

'There is one more thing we can try.'

'Really? Because I am out of options.'

'Luckily,' Jason winked, 'I'm not.'

He took my hand and almost dragged me back towards the beach. His face was animated when he spoke.

'When I was out there in the water I could hear Rory cursing me for being such a fool. "You dickhead," he was saying, "after everything we've been through. How can you just give up?" He was there with me. I could feel it.'

'Great,' I said in bemusement, 'could he just throw the big man upstairs a couple of quid to turn the clock back?'

Jason laughed and held my hand tight as he forced his way through the crowd.

'Sorry, I can't sign autographs right now but I'll be back,' he said politely to the adoring faces around us. 'I will be back.'

We stepped up onto the judging tower and I stopped to catch my breath above the sea of fans.

Jason gazed intently at me, his eyes flashing.

'Unlike Cain I have been professional and respectful my whole career. Now I am going to see if all that respect has done me any good. Are you with me?'

I smiled up at his youthful looking face and felt a thrill when I realised Jason was indeed back and more determined than ever.

'I have absolutely no idea what you are talking about,' I beamed, 'but yes I'm with you.'

Munroe pulled his shock of white hair back from his face and frowned.

'I'm sorry, guys, I really don't think I can bend the rules on this one. It's too important.'

'Exactly, Munroe, it is important. Too important to stick to the rules. Come on, you don't want to let the people down and not give them the showdown they're all waiting for, do you? A damp squib of a finish to a world title race is hardly great for publicity.'

Munroe scratched his head in the manner of Laurel and Hardy and sucked air through his teeth.

'You missed your heat, Jason.'

'I know. For the first time ever in my career. I have never caused you guys trouble, Munroe. I have never questioned the decision of the judges, even though sometimes they get it wrong.'

Munroe smiled wryly and Jason continued.

'And I realise I'm asking a hell of a lot but our team has been through so much in the last couple of weeks and we just lost it for a minute there but we're back. All of us.'

Right on cue, Chuck stumbled in the door dragging Ricky behind him. Our motley crew huddled behind Jason and watched Munroe pleadingly. He shifted his eyes.

'You want me to reinstate you, which means the next heat will have five surfers. They might not like that especially when I tell them who it is. You're not easy to beat.'

Jason blushed and struggled to find an answer.

'Why don't you ask them?'

Everybody looked at me.

'Yes, put it to a democratic vote, Munroe. The surfers voted to run the contest so why don't you ask them to vote on whether Jason can be given a second chance? That way you wouldn't be stepping on anyone's toes.'

'Yeah, dude, let's have a vote,' Chuck hooted. 'I vote yes!'

Munroe chewed his lip and scratched his head again before he slowly began to nod.

'I guess it can't hurt. We'll have a break at the end of the next heat and take a vote. I guess the public will be happy if you're allowed back in. And I do mean if.' He shook hands with Jason. 'Good luck and between you and me, I hope they let you surf.'

'Thanks, Munroe. I guess I'm about to find out how popular I really am.'

Forty-Six

Munroe's office behind the judging tower was crammed with every surfer and official from the world tour, reflecting the international nature of the professional surfing circuit.

The burly Brazilians congregated in one corner talking over each other at top volume in their native tongue. Their exchanges always sounded like furiously heated arguments until they doubled up with laughter and then continued with equal vehemence. The stylish French surfers, which included Tahitians and surfers from Reunion Island, surrounded Petit Sylvain who had qualified for the following year and was their clear leader despite his youth. They were smartly dressed to a man, well coiffured and lean. The Australians were a rather more rowdy bunch with relaxed beach hair and stubble. They tended to swear every second or third word and spent most of the time before the meeting comparing stories of bikini girls they had spotted that morning. Two South African surfers, one of whom had enjoyed an ear lick from the BB girl back in France, sat alone engaged in a serious discussion about the democratic process about to take place.

The Americans were a divided collection of Californians, Floridians and tattooed Hawaiians. Jason was surrounded by those from the west coast, including the big wave surfers from the San Francisco area who were a more tenacious bunch than their sprightly So-Cal peers and the fresh-faced locals of Daytona and Cocoa Beach. The Hawaiians were another breed entirely, their bodies buff and thick-skinned enough to withstand daily punishment in some of the world's most violent waves. Despite being California born, Cain held court in the centre of the Hawaiians, his skin burned darker than almost every one of his brothers.

Every face in the room was familiar to me now and I found comfort in being surrounded by all the people I had come to know over the year. We were a close-knit community, which was not to say we all saw eye to eye all the time. Like a dysfunctional family we travelled the world's beaches, changing each other's lives along the way. I would miss it terribly.

Cain's face was set in a grim line when Munroe got the proceedings underway by announcing Jason would make his case and then the surfers would vote by a show of hands. Chuck, Oli, Ricky and I stood at the back of the room quite literally with our fingers crossed. Ricky had his cowboy hat pulled firmly over his eyes and appeared nervous among the surfers. I wondered whether he was feeling regret for not having been able to follow his own dream as a talented young surfer to compete at this level.

Jason's tone was resolute when he took the floor.

'I realise I am asking a big favour of you all. I won't go into the fine details of why I missed the heat today. I admit I have been suffering since Rory died. We all know how it feels when a fellow surfer dies. We are reminded of the dangers of our career and of how close we are every day to surfing our last wave when we paddle out in waves as perilous as we do for this tour.'

A murmur of acknowledgement spread around the room. Cain glanced around and lowered his head.

'I'm afraid when Rory, my closest friend, lost his life at Pipeline I focused on those negatives. I felt the fear and I lost my direction. I failed to focus on the reason we do this job and that is because ultimately the ride is worth the risk. Rory told me that over and over and when I paddled out there today I heard him reminding me of that fact.'

Jason took a minute to gather his thoughts. Cain, meanwhile, shuffled his feet impatiently.

'I was a mess this morning,' Jason carried on, 'but my team' – he nodded at me and I blushed when every face in the room followed his gaze – 'they got me going. I was not prepared, I broke a board, and my back-up board wasn't ready. I missed my heat. The first heat ever.'

'Shame,' Cain sniffed.

'Quiet,' ordered Petit Sylvain firmly.

Cain's mouth dropped open but he said nothing.

'I am asking you for the chance to let me honour my friend by competing for the title at Pipeline as I should have this morning. I am asking you to bend the rules just this once. I know whoever I come up against will have to surf a five-man heat but there is no other way around this. I am asking for your support. That is all I can do.'

Jason sat down on the edge of Munroe's desk and Munroe took the stand.

'Does anybody have anything to add?'

Cain raised his hand.

'Yeah, Brah. Cain Ohana, current world champion,' he said sarcastically, 'I have something to add. I won that title fair and square and I don't see why we suddenly go changing the rules because Jason's a bit upset.'

'The circumstances are extenuating,' pointed out a surfer from San Francisco.

'Hey we've all had people die,' Cain replied. 'So we're gonna let a guy back in when his dog dies huh?'

Two of the Australians jumped to their feet.

'Take that back, mate, you're disrespecting one of us.'

The Tiger Sharks stood up to retaliate but the rest of the Australians joined the confrontation.

'Yeah, in fact disrespecting is all you guys ever do,' one of them hissed.

The Brazilians were next to stand.

'Yes you look down on all of us who are not in your gang,' one growled, 'and we won't stand for this anymore.'

'Hear hear,' the South Africans added.

'Jason has always played fair,' said Petit Sylvain, 'and he is a worthy champion. We want to see him surf.'

'Oui!' his friends shouted.

Cain banged his chest.

'I am a worthy champion. I won this fair and square. I fought for this.'

'You got that right,' tutted a Floridian, 'you fight. That's what you do. You don't know what fair means.'

Cain panicked when he realised he was losing the one fight he needed to win. A fight involving words instead of fists was not his forte. He glanced back at the Hawaiians.

'Back me up, Brahs.'

The Hawaiian surfers who competed on the circuit were not the Tiger Sharks. In fact, Cain's henchmen did not have the right to vote.

I held my breath when the largest of the Hawaiian locals, a man whose arms were entirely covered in tattoos, which was a significant surface area considering the size of his biceps, stepped forward and placed his hand on Cain's shoulder.

'I respect you as Kama'aina,' he said in a voice so deep it sounded like thunder, 'and we respect you as a champion but here in da islands, surfing is in our blood.'

'It's in my blood,' Cain protested.

Beside me, Ricky clenched his fists. He related to the theory.

The Hawaiian moved his eyes slowly around the room, taking in every person in front of him. The discussion had become a dangerous melting pot of issues based on personal relationships and national pride. I was worried the pot was about to boil over but the big man's voice had a calming influence. One by one the surfers sat back down to listen.

'In Hawaii surfing is the sport of our kings, of our ancestors. We must not let that sport be tarnished by violence and fighting. We do not want the sport that founded our culture to be based on threats and intimidation. The waves are intimidating enough, huh?'

A murmur of agreement buzzed around the room.

He placed his other hand on Jason's shoulder. His biceps flexed.

'There is much talk of what happened to your friend.'

Cain's face twitched with nerves. His eyes were fierce.

'And we will never know for sure whether the rumours are true or whether Hui, our God of the ocean, decided it was Rory's time. Whatever, I believe we owe it to our surfing brother to honour his name and end this year with a fair fight. A fight in the water. I say we let the waves decide.'

Cain struggled under his grip. Jason smiled gratefully and shook the Hawaiian's hand. I pressed my hands together and prayed when Munroe faced the surfers and said – 'Shall we take a vote? All in favour of Jason Cross being reinstated please raise your hand.'

Chuck fidgeted beside me, his hand jangling the change in his pocket. Slowly the French surfers raised their hands, followed by the South Africans and the Australians. Cain grimaced when the Californians and then the Floridians followed suit. When the Hawaiians then raised their arms, he slammed his hand against his chest and let out a deep cry. When Waipahe, who had obviously been struggling to follow the debate, raised his hand, Cain yanked it down and punched him full in the face.

'The vote is passed,' Munroe announced, the relief audible in his voice. 'Jason Cross will surf in a special five-man heat.'

I cheered and hugged first Chuck and then Ricky who smiled sheepishly.

'Isn't that fantastic, Ricky?'

Ricky bowed his head.

'Yeah,' he croaked, 'great.'

I felt a hand on my shoulder and Jason spun me around.

'We did it,' he cried, pulling me off my feet and into his arms.

'You did it,' I laughed, sliding down his body and placing my feet between his.

The rest of the surfers were filtering out of the room and the Press vied for the scoop at the door.

Jason glanced over his shoulder and with his hands still around my waist, pressed his forehead lightly against mine.

'Cain did it,' he smiled. 'I didn't have to say anything. He talked them into supporting me with his big mouth. That guy does not know when to shut up.'

'Likewise,' Cain hissed behind Jason's back.

Jason let go of me and I stepped back against the wall when I saw the expression of hatred on Cain's face, which turned his handsome features as frightening as one of his ugly Tiger Sharks. He jutted out his chin.

'You think you beat me, huh? You and your' – he jerked his head at me – 'interfering bitch here.'

Jason raised his arm in front of me like a barricade.

'I've warned you, Cain, you leave her out of this. Like you should have left Rory out of this.'

A smile flashed across Cain's lips.

'Yeah, was it worth it?'

'Worth what?'

Jason swallowed hard. His face moved closer to Cain's.

'Worth sacrificing your friend's life for your own cause?' Cain seethed.

Jason clenched his fists.

'How fucking dare you?'

I began to slide towards the door. I could hear Chuck's voice like a loudhailer outside celebrating the small victory and I suspected I would be in need of back up.

'You let your friend die for you, Brah,' Cain carried on, driven by the anger of having every one of his peers turn against him. 'You sacrificed him so you could get what you wanted and then when it went wrong you used him as your sympathy vote.'

'You evil bastard.'

Jason's breathing was heavy. I reached out for the door handle.

'You want this title so much you would do anything,' Cain spat, 'just like me. You're just like me, Brah, you just won't admit it to yourself.'

'I am nothing like you, you said it yourself.'

Jason grabbed Cain's T-shirt at the chest. Cain laughed in his face.

'Oh yeah you're like me except at the end of this day I will still be the world champion and all this will have been for nothing. Your friend will have died for nothing. Hey, Brah, try not to think about him when you're catching waves in the place he died.'

I burst out of the door when Cain's horrible laughter filled the room.

'Chuck, Ricky, I need your help. Quick!'

The sounds of fists hitting skin and bone escaped from the doorway.

'Quickly, they're killing each other.'

Chuck had to physically drag Ricky into the room and slam the door shut to keep out the Press whose ears had pricked up at the word 'killing'.

Jason had Cain on the floor and his hand was pressed against his throat.

'Jason, no!' I cried. 'Stop it, don't do this.'

Jason's face was emotionless. He stared at Cain and squeezed tighter. A gurgle escaped from Cain's throat and he struggled to release Jason's steely grasp.

Chuck dived at the pair and released Jason's grip only to receive a hefty punch to the nose when Cain struggled free. Chuck fell backwards onto the floor and hit his head. He groaned in pain. I shouted at Ricky to get between the two surfers who were too strong for me to separate, but Ricky was rooted to the spot.

'You're a bloody cowboy' – I grabbed his arm – 'do whatever it is cowboys do. Don't just stand there like a useless lump.'

'I can't,' he sighed.

I groaned in exasperation and rushed to prise Jason's hands from Cain whom he now held up against the wall. Jason was like a robot programmed to kill and nothing I said or did succeeded in interrupting his mission.

'Jason, he's not worth it, please.'

'Maybe not,' he answered mechanically, 'but Mike is worth it and Rory was worth it. This punk deserves everything he gets.'

Just as Cain's face turned a dangerous shade of red, he swung his arm and caught Jason on the side of the face. Jason let go and reeled backwards clutching his eye. I screamed and the next thing I knew, they were back wrestling on the ground. One moment Cain was on top punching Jason as if he were a soft pillow, the next Jason had the edge and he was pummelling Cain as if kneading dough.

'Help your son, Ricky,' I pleaded, 'stop this please.'

Chuck was unsteady on his feet and stumbled towards the door to prevent the photographers entering. They could smell a valuable shot a mile away.

'You sent my brother to jail and the only other brother I had in my life, you sent to his death. I'm gonna kill you,' Jason hissed.

Cain cried out when Jason's hands squeezed his throat. I felt a chill of fear and any sense of victory following the surfer vote was erased. Jason was about to lose everything, not just his world title.

'That's enough. Let go of him, son,' Ricky said with chilling calmness.

Jason looked up at Ricky and hesitated long enough to let Cain get the upper hand. Cain scrambled to his feet. Jason followed. Cain swung his arm and Jason ducked. Cain's fist connected with Ricky's hat, which fell to the floor. Ricky ran a hand through his hair and slowly raised his head. Mid-swing Cain's other fist stopped in the air as if someone had pressed pause. He stared open-mouthed at Ricky. Jason looked from one to other in confusion.

'You,' Cain gasped.

His arms dropped lifelessly against his sides.

I stared first at Cain who looked as if he had been mortally wounded. My eyes then moved to Ricky and then to Jason. My hand shot up to my mouth. Instantly I saw what had been nagging at my conscience all along. If Cain was the yin, the black, and Jason was the yang, the white, Ricky was the combination of the two. His body was as lean as Cain's but as defined as Jason's. His eyes were a mottled marble of black and silver. The webbed feet all three of them had and the nerve that flickered in their cheeks. The incredible natural surfing ability that surpassed every other surfer who had ever existed in the world and was as rare as if it was indeed the product of genetics. Cain's shaved head that probably concealed a shock of blond hair he thought would have hindered his acceptance in a Hawaiian gang. I had looked into the eyes of all three at close proximity and felt an uneasy sense of déjà-vu and now I knew why.

'You didn't lose your only other brother, Jason,' he said sadly, 'you're looking at him.'

Cain cried out and Jason fell backwards in shock. Ricky stood between the world's two best surfers and hung his head like a prisoner resigned to his sentence.

'Your younger brother didn't die, Jason. I gave him away when your mother died because I couldn't face looking into the eyes of the child that had stolen her from me.'

'No.'

Cain bit hard on his lip and tears welled up in those very eyes.

'I know it was not your fault, son,' said Ricky, 'but the mind does weird things when you lose someone you truly love.'

Now that I could understand.

'I can't believe this,' Jason stuttered.

'You know from experience that love hurts but look what hatred does. It just creates more hatred. Don't let that hatred destroy you. It destroys the very soul of life if you let it.'

Cain and Jason were speechless, as was Chuck, which was the first time since I had met him.

'Holy crap, this is radical shit,' he mumbled eventually, leaning back against the door nursing a split lip.

'You boys are natural surfers, you have soul. I'm sorry for the lies and deceit but twenty years had passed before I knew it' – Ricky looked sadly at Cain – 'I always followed your life, boy. I never forgot you. I sent you a photo. Did you get it?'

Cain nodded mechanically. He had suddenly changed from an angry warrior into a lost child. I felt a surprising surge of sympathy towards him. Jason may not have had the most luxurious of childhoods but at least he had roots. Cain had been sent away from his brothers through no fault of his own and had gone on to unwittingly destroy one and become the fierce rival of the other. I wondered how different his life would have been if he could have grown up surfing with Jason by his side.

'That's why' – Ricky turned to Jason – 'I never came to watch you because I knew I would meet Cain. I knew I would see both of you so close yet so far apart and it would kill me.'

I screwed up my eyes as one might do when waiting for a balloon to pop but there was no explosion. There was nothing except a stunned silence that engulfed us all.

It was the booming voice of Rock O'Rafferty over the P.A. system that broke the spell.

'The contest is about to re-start, ladies and gentlemen and I am happy to announce the reinstatement of Jason Cross.'

A huge cheer erupted from outside the room.

'Maybe we will get the showdown we all hoped for after all and I would like to bet, ladies and gentlemen, that this will be the biggest showdown yet.'

'Ironic,' Chuck tittered to himself, 'I like it.'

Forty-Seven

There was no time for questions and recriminations. Minutes after finding out they were the closest of blood relations just as they were about to spill that blood, Jason and Cain had to walk out of the room to face their fans, the Press and each other in the most important contest of their lives. Jason had fought to surf the contest and could not delay the proceedings any longer. I suspected neither Jason nor Cain quite knew how to handle the bombshell Ricky had just dropped on them. Surfing a challenging wave like Pipeline where the mind had to be completely focused on the task offered escapism from dwelling on reality. It was nevertheless the ultimate test of their professionalism.

Pipeline was at its dramatic best. By the time we returned to the beach the left-hand barrel was a sheer glass tunnel of noisily churning, fast flowing water. The 'morning sickness' created by early morning winds that unsettled the shape of the waves had passed and Pipeline was putting on a show for the crowd of thousands on the beach and millions around the world.

Chuck, Ricky and I helped Wyatt, Izel and Ben down to the high tide line on the beach where they made a camp for the day. They were determined to stay as close to the action as possible and all three were sporting caps they had designed at home with JC13 scrawled across the front. Ricky stayed with them. He had avoided watching his sons in person throughout their careers and, although I was sure he felt tempted to run from the confrontations that would undoubtedly occur after the final, he fulfilled his duty to stay and support. Whom he was cheering for I did not dare ask.

I had been concerned Jason would run out of steam after the extreme events of the day and the previous weeks, but when he took to the water it was as if he was operating on autopilot. He surfed every heat with a perfection that surpassed any of his performances throughout the year. His surfing was both fluid and aggressive as if he was throwing every emotion he had into a melting pot to create a recipe for the ultimate surfer. He was focused and careful not to make the kind of mistake that had cost his best friend his life, but he was also powerful and confident. Jason was completely absorbed in the task and, as a result, the spectators and the judges were in awe of his performance. He scored perfect ten after perfect ten. Rory's memory could not have been honoured to a greater degree.

Cain, however, was clearly struggling to pigeonhole the life-changing information he had just received in order to concentrate on his technique. He made costly mistakes and scraped through heats by the skin of his pure white teeth, often relying on his adversaries to make mistakes. Luckily for him, Cain's reputation as a fierce competitor preceded him and was enough to make the other surfers nervous. By the time they had realised Cain was not at his usual best, the heat was almost over and Cain had done enough to proceed. At the end of a close-run semi-final,

Cain stepped out of the water, dropped his board on the sand and bent over to rest his hands on his knees. Fans crowded around him, jostling for autographs and kisses. I strained my neck to see and caught sight of Cain just as his legs crumpled and he fell heavily onto the sand.

'Cain Ohana's in trouble!' Rock shouted to the life-guards but by the time they reached him with a stretcher, Cain was back on his feet.

He refused assistance and marched determinedly up the beach as if he had been sent to single-handedly invade a nation.

'Man, that guy doesn't know what to do with himself,' Chuck whistled, cracking open a beer.

Her offered me the bottle.

'No thanks.'

My stomach twisted nervously. Jason was set to face Cain in the final and we all knew what Cain was capable of when he was angry. I just wanted it all to be over.

'Be careful, Jason.'

Jason turned to me with his board under his arm and smiled. We were the only two people left in the garden while Chuck and Oli played a game of who could make the loudest and most important sounding telephone calls in the house.

'You sound worried,' he said. 'I have been doing this a long time you know.'

I nodded and smiled in an effort to appear carefree. Jason stepped back onto the lookout and gently touched my arm with his free hand.

'I know,' I shrugged, 'but you've been through so much. I just want you to be careful out there.'

Jason blinked and my heart surged when I realised how much I would miss looking into the most stunning eyes I had ever seen. We stared silently at each other for a moment before Jason blinked again and shook out his already wet hair. The droplets of seawater glittered in the air around him like a halo.

'I better go. The final waits for no man.'

I crossed my fingers. Jason leaned forwards and I offered my cheek. Before I knew what was happening, he lifted his hand to my chin and turned my lips to meet his. I succumbed to the salty kiss, which was brief but intense enough to send jolts of electricity through my body. When his lips left mine a gasp escaped from my mouth.

'Thank you for caring,' he breathed. 'I will miss you.'

I felt as if we had said our final goodbye.

This was it. One more heat and my year on tour was over.

I stood on the lookout watching Jason run through the excited throng of people on the beach. They chanted his name and patted him on the back. He acknowledged their wishes of good luck but did not stop, ploughing on through the sand towards the terrifying, majestic waves of the Banzai Pipeline.

One year previously I had stood on the same lookout and watched a contest I knew nothing about. Now I knew so much about surfing: the technical terms, the science of wave formation and surfboard shaping, the judging system, the internal politics, the history of the greatest surfer of all time, his deepest secrets and the deep-rooted motivation stirring within him that had driven him to succeed from his humble beginnings. I had travelled the world. I had shared a boat with a komodo dragon, I had surfed with turtles and seen sharks in South Africa. I had watched the sunset in Indonesia and the moonrise in Spain. I had slept in a jungle hut and a tropical Tahitian dwelling. I had lived like a cowboy. I knew to shuffle my feet in the shallow waters of tropical places like Tahiti to prevent myself stepping on a deadly stonefish and I knew how to say hello and thank you in Indonesian. I had learned how to say 'good waves' in French, Spanish and Portuguese.

I had suffered the shock of seeing a woman lose her husband and then felt the wrenching pain of watching our friend die just metres away. I had made friendships with Ruby and Chuck that would endure I hoped for a lifetime. I had tolerated Oli and, as I now accepted but would not admit to anyone but myself, I had fallen in love with the man who had made all of the above my reality.

I smiled to myself. I was proud of what I had achieved. If someone had told me when I flew out to meet Jon to escape my waning career and I was dragged unwillingly to the party in L.A. that my life would change to such an extent, I would have laughed. I was then a writer of moderate success who was losing direction and sliding onto the slush pile while fighting to keep a grip on my career. I was now about to write the final chapter of a book I was desperately proud of, whether it came within sniffing distance of the bestseller charts or not. I had become so engrossed in the subject, the story had taken on a life of its own and almost written itself. I had never thought that was possible. The realisation that some of that passion came from the fact that Jason had captured my heart for real was nothing to be ashamed of. I had learned to love and I could do so again. I had also fallen in love with a world I never knew existed and, even if I never felt the Hawaiian sand between my toes again, I was thankful for the life-changing experience. I would do it all again if I had the chance. As Ruby had said, it was better to have loved and lost than never to have loved at all. I had loved and I had also lived. I had not lost. It had all been worth the risk. I lifted my watery eyes towards the vivid blue sky. My father would be proud.

'Are you coming down on the beach, B? We should watch this one with the true fans, for shizzle.'

I wiped my eyes and span around to smile at Chuck. Dressed in a yellow shirt, shorts and sunglasses with his shock of heliotrope hair, he resembled a giant matchstick.

'For shizzle,' I beamed and left the detached haven of the garden to cheer alongside Ben, Izel, Wyatt, Oli, Ricky and a congregation of devoted fans.

'Here we go.'

I crossed my fingers on both hands.

'Cross mine for me, will you?' said Wyatt.

'I wish I could cross my toes too,' Izel said, laughing at her own joke.

'Yeah I wish I could cross my eyes,' Ben smirked.

Chuck threw back his head and howled with laughter.

'Man are we a motley crew or what?' He clutched his chest. 'Hey, Ricky, how many sons you got in this final, dude? If the other two have got anything to do with you, you better come clean now.'

The frown lines on Ricky's weathered face smoothed out and we all laughed our way into the start of the most important heat of the entire year with the ice broken and the sun in our hearts as well as on our skin.

Forty-Eight

At the start of the final, Jason and Cain sat astride their boards on opposite sides of the break like east and west on a compass. The perfect set waves were approaching every five or six minutes and when the first ten-foot waves barrelled onto the reef, the crowd leapt to their feet to get a better view of the surfers. The surfer in blue from Brazil paddled for the first wave and fell on the take-off. Everybody held their breath until he re-emerged in one piece and paddled out for the next set. The surfer in white from Australia made the drop on his choice of wave and pulled into the tube but did not make it as far as the exit. Both scores were nominal. There were murmurs of confusion when Jason and Cain remained steadfastly sedentary on their surfboards. They did not even attempt to paddle.

'What's happening, Ma'am?' asked Izel who looked like she might burst into tears.

I crouched beside her.

'Don't worry, Iz, they're probably just taking a moment to steady themselves.'

'As long as they don't take too long,' said Ben, who was relying on Izel for his commentary, 'the final will be over in a flash.'

'There is a huge set approaching,' Rock announced. 'Those of you at the water's edge mind you don't get too close. We don't want to be coming in rescuing you when the final heat of the year is in the water.'

On this set, both the Brazilian and the Australian caught waves that took them to Backdoor, the right-hand wave that mirrored Pipeline. Blue scored a very respectable seven and white a six-point-two. Cain and Jason did not move.

'I really don't understand what is happening here,' Rock marvelled. 'It's as if our two champions are waiting for the other one to start the proceedings. Let's hope one of them bites the bullet.'

When the third set passed without Jason or Cain even attempting to paddle, Chuck began to get even more fidgety than usual.

'What the hell is he doing, man?'

'I don't know,' Oli spat, 'but he better do fucking something or I will kick his goddamn ass.'

'Language, Oliver,' I scolded, tilting my head at Izel and Ben.

'Sorry,' he sniffed, 'I meant butt not ass.'

I raised my eyes skywards.

Ricky thrust his hands into his pockets.

'I've ruined them,' he said under his breath, 'I should never have told them.'

'Told them what?' Izel frowned.

'Nothing, honey,' I smiled, 'now come on, let's start cheering as loud as we can OK?'

Chuck started waving his arms in the air and whooped as loud as he could. Wyatt cheered, Ben joined in and Izel and I chanted loudly. Oli pouted like a petulant child and Ricky stayed impartial. The crowd around us joined in the commotion until we resembled a horde of crazed tribesman doing a rain dance under the baking hot sun.

Jason looked around and I could tell he was smiling. He glanced down at his board and ran his hand across the decking where I had written *Lucky 13*. He flicked his wrist and looked at his watch, as did I. Only ten minutes remained until the final hooter sounded. Somebody had to win.

Jason lay on his board and began to paddle but not towards the waves. He stroked his arms through the water and paddled in Cain's direction. The Tiger Sharks hollered but Cain's head was down. He seemed completely unaware of his surroundings and of the millions of people watching in disbelief as he sat motionless throughout the final of the Pipemasters.

Despite his threats and his steely exterior, I felt sympathy for Cain. Having seen the regret in his eyes at Rory's memorial, I honestly believed he was not a bad person at heart. He had faced a struggle through life and he had erected a façade that had helped him survive as he had fought his way to the top. His methods were misguided but he had to be admired for his perseverance. Now Cain sat like a lost little boy. His proud, muscular body looked devoid of its usual power. Cain had lost his fighting spirit. Jason was not someone he could easily hate. He was his brother and without hatred, Cain was finding it hard to function.

Ricky clenched his jaw and stared out at the ocean.

'I wish I was out there with them,' he sighed.

'I don't,' I said when a wave positively exploded on the coral reef. 'In fact if you paid me one million dollars I would not paddle out there with them.'

I shivered and turned back towards the action. Blue and white were paddling around merrily as if they had been given free passes to Disneyland on a day when nobody else was admitted. I strained my eyes to see when Jason reached Cain's side and sat up on his board. Their broad backs faced us while they both looked towards the horizon.

'Looks like our two champs are having a discussion,' said Rock. 'We can only guess what they are saying.'

Not in a million years, I thought to myself.

'Oh man this is gonna kick off,' said Chuck, sucking air through his teeth.

I suspected otherwise.

After a short discussion, the two surfers turned to face each other. Jason offered Cain his hand and the crowd gasped. Cain stared at the outstretched hand. The crowd held their breath. Cain accepted the handshake and the loudest cheer I had ever heard sent shivers through my spine.

'Holy shit,' Chuck yelped, 'the Press are gonna love this one. Yeah, dude, I feel a bonus coming on.'

The handshake lasted until the surfers pulled their boards together and embraced in a hug. The rowdy Tiger Sharks fell deathly silent; a silence that was more meaningful than any word I had heard them utter. I glanced back at the Tiger Shark camp and laughed. Watching Cain hug Jason must have been like watching a shark jump through hoops for a trainer. Their leader would have some explaining to do when he returned to base.

'The heat is on,' I grinned.

'About fucking time,' Oli growled.

'Language, Oliver.'

'What? What the fuck did I say now?'

Jason and Cain lay down on their boards and paddled side by side into the impact zone. The other two surfers knew their free passes had been rescinded. The greatest surfer of all time and his fiercest rival and current world champion were ready to compete. The others may as well have left the water immediately.

The first wave rose up when the swell hit the reef and the surfers let it pass. The second wave was smoother than the first and built until it was four times overhead on an average human. Izel commentated every second that passed for Ben. I was in danger of biting my nails to the quick and Chuck was frantically chattering his teeth despite being on a tropical beach. Wyatt was as calm as ever, his eyes dreamy as he watched his old life played out in front of him.

Jason and Cain paddled themselves over the lip of the wave that crumbled and a crest of white topped the green wall like cream on a cake. The wave peeled in both directions and jumping effortlessly to their feet, Jason and Cain split the peak, Jason travelling left while Cain travelled right. The wave was majestic, as was their surfing and they carved along the glass-like water in perfect synchronicity. The similarities in their surfing were profoundly apparent, as were their differences. Cain still surfed with a natural aggression while Jason was more graceful and quietly self-assured. At the end of the ride, the spectators were electrified. Jason and Cain turned and paddled back out to the line-up, both being awarded nine-point-five.

'Not a bad start,' I winked at Chuck.

'This is the best goddamn heat I have ever seen and you know what, I don't think I care who wins when they're surfing so awesome.' He paused. 'Actually take that back, if Jason wins I am gonna be rich. I hope he kicks Cain's ass.'

The clock ticked by. There was only time for one more set of waves. Blue took the first, which closed out along the face. He straightened out to avoid the explosion of white water that chased him as far as the beach. White took the second wave. He rode it well but the wave did not open up to offer him the chance of a barrel. He too headed for dry land.

Jason and Cain glanced at each other. Two waves remained. Cain sat up and gestured for Jason to take the first. Jason paddled, pressed his chest into the board, placed his hands on the deck and took off. The rail of the board jammed into the face of the monstrous wall of water like a curved saw cutting into a tree. Jason dropped to the bottom, his arms raised like wings. He pressed deep into his knees and turned the board then sank his arm into the wave face and this time was enveloped in a barrel so hollow and so deep he disappeared from view for what seemed like minutes. I clasped my hands together and prayed. We all exhaled when Jason briefly emerged before seeking and finding the second tube on the wave that was even longer than the first. A ball of water burst from the end of the tube and Jason shot out at breathtaking velocity. He threw his head back, covered his face with his hands and pointed his fingers to the sky, dedicating his ride to his beloved friend, Rory, who should have been there to witness the moment.

When Jason kicked off the wave, he span around and sank into the water to watch Cain take off. Cain paddled and made the drop that was horrifyingly steep. He manoeuvred into position and stalled for the tube. Cain crouched as if to slot his lean body inside a barrel so vast it could have accommodated ten of him. He vanished and then reappeared before pulling into the second tube and then the third. He shot out, pushed down on his fins and performed the most impressive front-hand turn I had ever seen. The nose of the board smacked the lip of the wave beyond vertical and then Cain yanked the board around to complete the perfect turn. Cain raised his arms modestly for a man who had been known for swearing and gesticulating wildly in past heats. Jason also raised his arms and as Cain surfed past his bitter rival he reached down with an outstretched hand and the two men hi-fived each other in a very public display of respect. The atmosphere in the Tiger Sharks' house was now as sombre as a graveyard.

The last exchange of the final was later heralded as two of the best waves ever ridden at Pipe and the most memorable display of sportsmanship surfing had ever seen. Jason and Cain had made history in more ways than one. The crowd surged into the water to greet the surfers when they paddled towards the sand. When the final hooter sounded, they were both hoisted onto the shoulders of their fans and carried onto the beach. When they reached land, both rides were awarded perfect tens by the judges. No lesser score was justifiable. It was a dead heat, the first ever in a Pipemasters final.

'This is an unprecedented situation, ladies and gentlemen,' said Rock, his voice breaking with the euphoria of what we had all just witnessed. 'I'm not sure what will happen here. There may be a count back to all the scores awarded by every judge rather than just the average. I will let you know as soon as I know. Wow, this is incredible.

We could have two winners for the first time ever here in Hawaii.'

The latter was already true. After everything they had overcome, Jason and Cain were both winners.

'What happens now?' Chuck squealed. 'Does he win the title?'

'I don't know,' I laughed giddily, 'I'm confused.'

'I don't care,' Ben laughed, throwing his arms around Izel, 'this is the best day of my life.'

'Mine too!' Izel cheered and planted a kiss on Ben's lips.

Their blushes made us all laugh.

Oli patted Ricky on the back and then shrieked when Chuck lifted him up and kissed him on his balding head. Oli wriggled and swore but I could tell he was enjoying the moment as much as the rest of us.

'Oh my God, my toes moved!' Wyatt suddenly shouted out.

I fell to my knees beside him in the sand.

'You're kidding, Wyatt, really?'

A grin spread across his handsome face.

'No, I'm only joking but that sort of thing happens in the movies.'

I jabbed him playfully.

'Gets you able-bodied folk every time,' he winked. 'Mind you, right now I feel like I could stand up out of this wheelchair and run over to hug Jason myself. Do it for me, Bailey.'

I nodded, stood up and began to walk across the sand towards the swarm of fans holding Jason aloft. He saw me and tapped their hands.

'Let me down a second, guys,' he said.

The crowd lowered him to the soft sand and parted to let me through. I beamed at Jason and he beamed back, his face sparkling with a mixture of water droplets and euphoria.

I opened my mouth to speak but Rock's voice filled the air.

'The count back changes nothing, ladies and gentlemen. The Pipemasters is a dead heat between Jason Cross and Cain Ohana. We have two worthy winners.'

I clasped a hand to my mouth. I knew what that meant.

'And as a result Jason Cross is the new world champion by the smallest of margins, twelve points. Show your appreciation for the new world champion, record breaker and thirteen-times winner, JASON CROSS!'

I shrieked with laughter and covered my ears when the fans erupted with the force of a volcano. They jumped up and down and cheered and Jason and I were forced together.

'You did it,' I laughed, my body pressed up against his.

'We did it,' he laughed back and wrenched me off my feet into a hug.

I kissed him quickly and then let the spectators carry him away to join Cain on the podium. It was Jason's moment, one to share with his fans around the world. We could celebrate later.

'I want to dedicate this world title first to my best friend, Rory, who passed away at this beach so recently. His spirit was with me today. This is for you Rory.' Jason stood in the centre of the podium and lifted the trophy towards the sky. 'Secondly I want to thank my crew who make all this possible for me. I may be the one out there surfing but believe me a lot goes on behind the scenes to get me there.'

'For shizzle,' Chuck sniggered beside me.

'My manager, Chuck who is a ball of energy and a great friend. My team manager, Oli, who...'

'Is a pain in the goddamn ass,' Chuck murmured while Oli strained to hear his praise.

'My father who was the man who took me surfing in the first place. I would be nothing without you.'

Ricky bowed modestly, while on the podium Cain watched him with a curious intensity.

'My young friends over there Iz, Ben and Wyatt who may think I inspire them but in truth they inspire me more than they will ever know.'

Izel was already crying with happiness.

'And,' Jason breathed, 'my biographer, confidante, friend and rock, Bailey Brown, who came into my world a year ago and made it a better place. You have her to thank for me surfing today. It's a long story and she will tell it much better than I can, believe me.'

Not used to such public praise, I swallowed the ball of emotion in my throat and nodded at Jason to say thank you while the crowd broke into enthusiastic applause.

'Next,' Jason turned to face Cain, 'I want to thank Cain. You all know we have had feuds over the years and we have both been through ups and downs in our careers but if I had not had a surfer as incredible as Cain to compete against I would never have reached this level. His awesome ability made me have to dig deeper to beat him. We have both had a profound effect on each other and today, well today we learned to respect each other too.'

Cain smiled, which he rarely did in public and shook hands with Jason.

Jason paused and took a deep breath before he spoke again.

'Finally I want to announce my retirement from competitive surfing.'

The crowd gasped and Chuck almost fell over.

'I have competed for a long time and I have finally won the record thirteenth title. That is all I ever dreamed of and I want to thank all of you, my fans, for supporting me and being loyal to me for so long.' He raised the cup to his chest and gently kissed it. 'The reality is even better than the dream and I am so thankful for all of this. I won't disappear completely but now' – he glanced back at Cain – 'now it's Cain's turn. He is the new generation and the man to beat and I wish him luck. Thank you and goodbye. For now.'

Forty-Nine

I made some calls. In just a matter of days I would be back home and it was about time I reconnected with my real family and my agent.

'Twistan is in the earwy Monday morning meeting,' said the receptionist, Lolly, which she unfortunately pronounced 'Wowwy'.

I had already been on hold long enough for the soundtrack to complete a full circuit of a Patagonian panpipe CD.

Thankfully I was calling on Jason's free phone or I may as well have been throwing dollar bills out of the window.

'Who shall I say called?'

'As I said, Lolly, I'm Bailey Brown, one of his authors,' I said through gritted teeth.

'Baiwey Bwown,' she said.

I suspected the apparent pressed-lip concentration was actually focused on the application of nail varnish while balancing the telephone on her shoulder.

'Is his assistant available, Lolly? I'm calling from Hawaii to let him know I have finished my book.'

Little Miss Brain Bypass failed to react to the triumphant news and put me on hold for a further infuriating panpipe rendition of *Greensleeves,* while she very likely filed her toenails and gave herself a spray tan in the Ladies.

'Vewonica is in the earwy Monday morning meeting too I'm afwaid.'

If I were Lolly, I'd be afraid of my head floating off my shoulders like a helium balloon.

'I could twy Audwey for you.'

'Who's Audwey? I mean Audrey.'

'She's Vewonica's assistant.'

The assistant to my agent's assistant. I did not realise how far down the pecking order I had slipped in a year. Out of sight, out of mind, out of favour, out on my ear. I kicked myself for not having kept Tristan up to date with my progress.

'Don't worry, Lolly, I will arrange a meeting with Tristan when I return to London with the manuscript. If you just let him know I called, thanks.'

'No pwoblem. Now what was your name again?'

'J.K. Rowling,' I growled and hung up the phone.

My next call was to my mother. I had been thinking about her and my father almost daily since Rory died. My mother had lost her husband in the most painful and guilt-ridden way I could imagine. It was no wonder she was bitter. I had decided to try and rebuild our strained relationship when I got home.

'Mother, it's Bailey.'

'Bailey, what are you calling so bloody early for? Where's the fire?'

'Sorry, Mother, I'm calling from Hawaii.'

'My heart bleeds.'

I took a deep breath and pressed on.

'I just wanted to call and let you know I will be home soon. I just finished my book.'

My mother sniffed.

'I'll shampoo the red carpet shall I?'

I sighed.

'Is that Auntie Bailey? Is she a big, famous author now?'

'Zac?'

Joanna took the phone. I doubted my mother put up much of a fight. She had never been one for recreational telephone use.

'Mother had a small accident with a cigarette and a sofa,' Joanna explained without even saying hello.

Her voice was heavy with weariness.

'I was on the school run with Zac but we had to make a detour.'

A lump formed in my throat as Joanna ploughed on with the story. It was as if she were explaining the sorry tale to herself, trying to fathom the whole point of her having got out of bed that morning.

'I've finished my book,' I said eventually.

My reason for calling seemed irrelevant now.

'Congratulations.'

'So I will head home soon.'

'Why on earth would you want to do that?'

'To see you all. To meet my agent. To get back to normal.'

My voice trailed off.

'You don't sound thrilled at the prospect, Bailey.'

I could not pretend otherwise.

'If you want my advice,' Joanna said sadly, 'stay as far away from here as possible.'

I was stunned by my sister's candour when she was usually so sensible.

'This is not "normal", Bailey, this is just one way of living and if you can find a way of living where the sun shines and you find sand in your pockets and you have beautiful, happy friends, why not stay there? Don't come back here because of guilt or misplaced loyalty. Live your life, Bailey. Don't make the same mistake I did.'

I was speechless. A tear rolled down my cheek, which flowed into a river of tears when I heard Zac say he loved me in the background.

'I love you both too,' I said, masking a sob.

'Send us a signed copy,' said Joanna, adding with a soft laugh, 'and get one of those handsome surfers to deliver it will you? I haven't seen a six-pack in the flesh for years.'

I laughed. If I had had a dollar for every six-pack I had seen over the year I would have been a rich woman.

'I have to go, Bailey. Mother is trying to light a cigarette on the gas fire. I hope we don't see you soon if you have any sense.'

It was officially the strangest sibling conversation I had ever had.

'What are you doing?' said Jason. 'You're missing the party.'

I looked up from my laptop and smiled at the boyish grin on his sun-kissed face. Despite the dramas of the day, Jason looked so happy and at peace with himself. His salty blond hair flopped over one eye. He blew it back and walked into the room. He was still wearing the fresh flower lei from the prize presentation and he was holding two flutes of champagne, one of which he handed to me.

'Cheers,' I said, clinking my glass against his and taking a sip.

'Is it done?'

I nodded, words suddenly escaping me. Which was hardly surprising when I had just typed three thousand of them in one sitting.

'Oh,' he said quietly, the smile fading from his cheeks that were already tinged with a champagne induced glow, 'that's good I guess. Time to get this baby published, huh?'

'Mmm,' was all I could muster.

We both sat and stared at the laptop that contained the story of Jason's life we would tell to the world.

'So we're done then?' he said.

'Yes we are.'

We looked at each other, a loaded silence between us.

'You haven't written "The End" yet,' he said.

I lowered my champagne glass onto the bedside table and reached out for the keys but Jason clasped my wrist.

'Wait a minute. What about the next chapter?'

'There isn't a next chapter. I'm done.'

Jason blinked.

'There's always another chapter.'

Jason pulled me up from the bed. The champagne fizzed on my tongue, matching the buzz I felt inside whenever we were alone together. Jason stopped at the bedroom door. The victory party was in full swing outside if the sounds of music, chattering voices and laughter were anything to go by. Wyatt was singing along to an acoustic guitar, his voice as clear as the champagne bubbles in my glass. Chuck's voice boomed above them all of course as if he had a megaphone permanently stapled to his lips.

'Let's go out of the window.'

'What? We're not fifteen years old.'

Jason winked.

'Then let's pretend we are. Come on, I want to escape the party for a bit. I've had a long, hard, very confusing day.'

We climbed out of the ground floor window, giggling at our own immaturity. When my dress caught on the window latch, Jason unhooked it and lifted me gently to the ground. His eyes ran swiftly over my exposed flesh as he did so. I smiled and followed him through the palm trees and down onto the beach.

In the peacefulness that moonlight brings, one could have been forgiven for thinking an ocean as calm as the Mediterranean was lapping the beach but I would forever recognise the profound rumble of Pacific swells hitting offshore reefs. The ebullient waves were only visible by the dark shadow they formed in the distance, outlined with a crest of white foam. If the mythical white horses really existed, they were galloping as merrily by night as they had done by day.

I had bare feet and relished the sensation of my toes sinking into the fine sand. Joanna was right; I would never tire of finding sand in my pockets and in my shoes. My feet were naturally exfoliated and even my little toe sported an impressive tan. The sand beneath the surface was cool to the touch as we walked cordially along the shore.

Eventually my curiosity got the better of me.

'What did you say to Cain in the water, Jason? What was happening out there?'

Jason pushed his hands deep into the pockets of his jeans.

'I said we don't have to hate each other to compete against each other.'

'And what was his reaction?'

'He was so confused, Bailey and you know, for the first time ever, I felt sorry for the little punk.' He laughed quietly. 'I mean I've hated this guy and been wound up by him and beaten down and I suddenly thought, jeez, that's exactly what a little brother's meant to do.'

'You were acting like siblings all along.'

He nodded and I glanced across to see his smile as white as the moon.

'Weird huh? He's done some bad stuff but then I admit he's had it tough. At least I knew where I came from and didn't feel unwanted. I had a family, even if we were dysfunctional. He realised he had been involved in sending his own brother to jail and I think it all became too much for him. He looked completely lost. So I said, come on, Bro', let's give these people what they came to see. Let's surf our socks off and may the best guy win. Our dad's watching. I think a draw was the fairest result.'

'Wow, that's big coming from a man who wins for a living.'

I too pushed my hands into the pockets of my dress.

'I can share the glory just this once,' he winked. 'The crazy thing is, when Cain caught that last wave, it's the first time I've ever seen him smile in the surf. He didn't need aggression to surf like a world champion, he just needed passion.' Jason paused to reflect. 'I think we might see a different Cain Ohana from now on.'

We stopped beside a giant turtle that was fast asleep on the tide line.

'Now that is something I won't be seeing much of back home.'

Jason bent down and gently ran his hand over the turtle's domed shell.

'So what will you do now, Bailey?'

'Me? I don't know. Get this book on the shelves and start to think of the next one I guess.'

'You know this is going to be a bestseller, don't you?'

I pressed my lips together and nodded.

'Yes,' I heard myself say with a confidence that had previously eluded me in my career, 'yes I do.'

'So then before the world goes crazy for you, maybe we should take a holiday,' Jason suggested shyly.

I crouched down beside him.

'Have I not just been on a kind of permanent beach holiday for the past year?'

'People might think so from the outside but it's not all fun and games is it?'

I shrugged. My hair fell over my shoulder and tickled the bare skin of my arms.

'No it's not all fun and games but it's wonderful. I will miss it.' I now paused to reflect. 'And how about you? What will you do?'

Jason sat back in the sand and rested on his arms. He tilted his head to look at the sky. His angular cheekbones sent shadows across his face.

'I guess I will enjoy my retirement. Track down my son and try to be a father to him. After seeing what being fatherless has done to Cain, how can I not accept my responsibility?'

'I think that's a very admirable goal, Jason. I really hope it works out for you.'

'Thanks' - He cleared his throat - 'and beyond that I want to settle down in a beach house somewhere, maybe Hawaii, with my perfect girl. I will surf for fun and maybe look for new challenges. Chase big waves, do some movies maybe.'

I rested back on my arms beside him.

'Sounds dreamy.'

'Yeah it does. I'm just hoping this dream turns out to be reality.'

'It will, as long as you find the right girl.'

The stars twinkled above my head. The sky looked so expansive it seemed to be twice the size of the sky back home.

'I've found the right girl,' said Jason, 'she's my perfect ten. In fact, if I could score her a fifteen, I would.'

I turned my head towards him. His head was turned towards me. We stared at each other. His eyes shone brighter than any of the stars and took my breath away.

'You told me when we got to the top of the hill we would look at the view and see where to go next. Well I'm looking and the only thing I can see is you.'

Jason rolled onto his side and gently reached out to touch my cheek.

'I know I'm not perfect, Bailey but this year has been the most valuable of my life for so many reasons. I have learned so much and I've realised what I truly want. I want you.'

My breathing became more rapid when he brushed his hand through my hair and moved closer.

'When we first met, you said we were polar opposites.'

'Did I?'

I was surprised he remembered things I had said to him a year before. The thought he had dwelt on my words made me tingle.

'You did and maybe we are but I agree with what Chuck said back then, that we are the perfect team. Look how much we've achieved since we met. Together, we could do anything we put our minds to. I'm sure of it.'

His face was so earnest, I was almost convinced.

'But I promised myself I wouldn't get involved with a professional surfer,' I said.

'I'm not a professional surfer,' he smiled. 'I've retired, remember?'

'Don't tell me you did that for me,' I gasped.

'Bailey, I would do anything for you. The thought of being without you is too much to bear and when I saw you had finished the book I panicked. If I had to trade my world title just to spend another year with you, I would. You mean everything to me.' He took my hand and held it tight like he never wanted to let go. 'I think deep down you feel the same way. Don't go, Bailey. Don't say this is the end.'

I opened my mouth to speak but no sound came out. My mind raced with all the reasons why we would not work and why I should not take the risk but my heart was fighting my head all the way, desperately urging me to succumb to the magnetic attraction.

I looked into the eyes of the most beautiful man I had ever seen and finally allowed my heart to thaw. The tropical breeze blew over my skin as my body arched into Jason's and our lips melted together. I felt gravity release me and I floated on air. The kiss was even more intense than our first and I was completely lost in the overwhelming emotion. Yet at the same time I was completely found. For the first time in my life I was exactly where I wanted to be.

When we came up for air, I tilted my head and looked into his stunning silver eyes.

'I'm sorry, Jason, I have to write "The End" tonight,' I said softly. 'The book is finished.'

His face fell.

'But you were right,' I smiled, 'there is another chapter. Chapter one of a whole new story.'

Epilogue

Three years had passed since the party with Jon in L.A. and now I was back in the city of angels to attend the glitzy premiere of the much-anticipated surf movie, *SWELL*. The red carpet had been altered for the occasion to a blue one inset with sparkling wave patterns. Flaming torches lit the way to the theatre that had been lavishly decorated with aquariums. Beautiful girls swam in the tanks dressed as shimmering mermaids. We all sat in the back of a luxury limousine sipping champagne and waiting for our cue.

'I'm so glad you didn't listen to me,' Jon whispered while we waited anxiously to make our journey past the world's Press. 'Look at you. You're gorgeous and radiant. You're a successful writer and now you've got your very own book adapted into a Hollywood movie. Damn, why didn't I grab you for myself when I had the chance?'

'Because you're gay,' I suggested with a laugh.

'A minor obstacle.' Jon clinked his glass against mine. 'To you, Bailey Brown. Thank you for keeping your promise of a glitzy invitation and thank you for not listening to a word I said about *Jason*.' He mouthed the last word.

Jason grinned and wrapped his arm around my shoulders.

'So what did you tell her about me, Jon?'

Jon blushed as red as the usual premiere carpet.

'Nothing.'

'Really?' I raised an eyebrow. 'As I remember it you said men like Jason are glamorous, dangerous, adrenalin-fuelled, mmm what else was there?'

Jason laughed and raised his glass.

'If only I was that exciting. Well, thank you for bringing this woman to me, Jon, she changed my world.'

It was my turn to blush.

'No I just came in and shook it up a bit.'

'A bit? Bailey, you were like my own personal tsunami.'

The limousine pulled to a stop at the end of the carpet, music began to play and the audience that had gathered to meet America's surfing sweetheart, Jason Cross screamed with excitement. The screams and cheers followed us wherever we went these days. I was thinking of investing in earplugs.

I touched Jason's firm thigh that had powered him along millions of waves and most recently to his fourteenth world title. I had known retirement would not suit a man who simply loved competing, so, after a year's break during which he explored new waves and new opportunities, I encouraged him to return to the dream tour. Why retire when he was still the best? The title had been a close-fought battle against his brother, Cain, who had become an acquaintance if not a friend of Jason's. Cain would be in the audience at the movie along with his fiancée, Portia. She could not, it seemed, resist the Cross genes and was much more suited to Cain than she ever had been to Jason. They fought like cat and dog most days and thrived on the excitement. Rumour had it that Portia, the queen of the tiger sharks, kept all the boys in line with her armoury of stilettos.

I leaned my head against Jason's shoulder.

'You go ahead, darling, they want to meet their hero.'

'Come with me.'

I kissed him on his full lips that I would never tire of kissing.

'I'll follow at the end with Ruby. I just need a bit of time to settle myself.'

Jason, the love of my life who adored me as much as my father had and made me feel as if I could achieve anything I wanted, stepped out of the limo to the flashing of cameras. The noise that erupted from the gathered crowd was deafening.

'Are you nervous, Auntie Bailey?' asked my nephew Zac who had grown into a handsome, confident boy.

He was sitting across from me with Harrison who became more and more like Jason every day. Harrison preferred skating to surfing and I could already see he would grow up to be as determined and unstoppable as his father. Their relationship had developed steadily over the three years with Jason having to earn his young son's trust. For a man who had won world title after world title, Jason found becoming a good father the most difficult and thrilling challenge of his life and he had grown as a person through the experience. I even enjoyed being the wicked stepmother (only without the wicked part).

'When I'm nervous playing football, Auntie Bailey,' Zac continued, 'I just try to think what Ronaldo would do. He just grits his teeth, puts his head down and runs because he knows he has done all the preparation.' He sniffed and looked at my stunning bejewelled heels. 'Just maybe don't do the running part.'

Joanna and I looked affectionately at Zac who bubbled with confidence due to the changes in his own life.

My sister finally plucked up the courage to leave Gerry, despite feeling guilty about her only child joining the statistics of children from 'broken homes'. Zac, however, had thrived, as had my sister. Zac was very likely to become the first professional footballer who also had a solid grasp of algebra.

'Let's go, dude,' said Harrison, pulling Zac by the arm. 'I wanna catch dad up and granddad Ricky is saving us a seat inside. He don't like all the cameras and fuss and,' he whispered loudly, 'he sneaked off to meet one of the cute mermaids who asked for his number.'

I laughed. Ricky would never change, other than the fact that he now travelled to watch both his sons compete on the dream tour as often as he could leave the ranch. Ricky liked to think of himself as their coach and burst with pride every time one of them won. Which was often.

Joanna followed. She turned as she exited the car, her long hair falling loosely over her shoulders.

'I'm so proud of you, Bailey. Dad would have loved this moment.'

I pressed my lips together in a smile and prayed my waterproof mascara would hold firm all night.

I would like to say my mother was sitting beside me thinking the very same as Joanna but of course she was not. She regularly asked me when I was going to get a 'proper job' and alcohol was still her best, in fact her only friend. My mother would very likely never change and I had accepted that. I visited her as often as I could but damn how I loved the feeling I had when I left her dismal home, breathed again and returned to Jason's colourful world.

'Come on, Jon, let's leave these chicks to do their lipstick and all that chicky stuff,' Chuck chirruped merrily.

He beamed at Ruby and I and bounced up and down trying to catch sight of himself in the reflective partition between the driver and us.

'You look a picture,' I said with a wink at Ruby.

'For real? Cool beans, Bailey.'

'A very colourful, slightly abstract picture,' I laughed when the surfing world's most successful manager bounced into the limelight in a bright turquoise suit with hair to match.

'See you in there, B,' he said over his shoulder. 'Enjoy the moment. You deserve it.'

He blew me a kiss and lolloped away with Jon in tow who looked like he wanted the ground to swallow him up in case people thought Technicolor Chuck was his date.

Ruby and I turned and looked at each other. She had blossomed into a stunning woman since becoming a mother to my godson, Rory Junior, who was an identical mini version of his father. Ruby was as petite and elfin as she ever was, but the strength she had displayed since Rory's death was astounding. Jason and I visited Ruby and our godson as often as we could in their idyllic Hawaiian beach house. Ruby had tried to live in Australia but she said she felt close to Rory whenever she looked out of the window at the Pacific ocean. She could not bring herself to hate the waves that he had so adored.

'It will be strange to see Zac Efron playing my Rory on the big screen,' she said with a bemused smile.

'I think he'll do him justice.'

Ruby lifted my hands from where they were twitching in the lap of my exquisite designer dress that was the colour of Jason's eyes. She held them between her own.

'You did him justice, darl'. You are the only girl who could have written about my Rory and brought him back to life with your words.'

'Thank you, Ruby, you don't know how much that means to me.'

I had received many compliments and rave reviews about my book *Lucky 13*. Not least, but most surprisingly perhaps, from my agent, Tristan who read it in one sitting and immediately called me himself. No 'Audwey' or 'Wowwy' calling me on his behalf this time. At last, it seemed, I was worthy of his expensive breath. Tristan soon scribbled me back into his books when he realised I had written a potential worldwide bestseller. A bestseller that would, he told me excitedly, appeal not only to surfers but also to anybody who had dreams, to anybody who was seeking a bit of escapism and to anybody who had loved and lost or simply loved. I thought that pretty much covered almost everybody.

'This is bloody marvellous stuff, darling,' he gushed when I met him in his office, his fingers tapping furiously on the manuscript as if he were subliminally adding up the profits he would make on an imaginary calculator. 'You couldn't make this stuff up.' Tristan paused, his jowls wobbling. 'You didn't did you?'

'Not at all, Tristan. This is how these people live. It's all true.'

'Good Lord. Really and truly? You mean the women and the waves and the women and everything?'

'Everything.'

'Unbe-bloody-lievable. Not a bad life is it? Apart from the killer waves perhaps but all in all, good Lord, I never knew this world existed.'

'Neither did I, Tristan, neither did I.'

Lucky 13 was more successful than I could ever have imagined and I was very soon on my own world tour signing books and making appearances. It was everything I had ever dreamed of and, best of all, I had someone to share it with.

Jason and I worked our schedules so that he could be by my side when I needed support and vice versa. We even returned to Bali together and delivered a book to Wayan in his restaurant on Jalan Legian. If having an unknown author dine there had been lucky for Wayan, having the world's greatest surfer and his published biographer pop in for a banana jaffle was, judging by Wayan (and Made, Ketut, Made, Wayan and Ketut's) reactions, akin to Buddha himself dropping by. It was an eye-opener how much of a seasoned traveller I felt in Bali the second time. My horizons had broadened over the year I had been on tour. My world felt much bigger and more exciting than it had once been.

Ruby and I quickly did the girl thing and reapplied our lipstick for the fifth time that hour and then exchanged nervous glances.

'Shall we, darl'?

'We shall,' I smiled.

Ruby and I stepped out of the limo and walked towards the blue carpet. Just before I reached the bank of photographers, a couple of British tourists dressed head to toe in Disney merchandise stopped me, unperturbed by the cameras flashing in our direction.

'Excuse me,' said the man from beneath a hat with Mickey Mouse ears, 'can you tell us what the excitement is all about?'

'It's a film premiere,' I replied politely.

'Goodness, isn't that Zac Efron?' the woman yelped, slapping her hand to her Pluto sweatshirt.

'And are you two actresses?' the man asked.

'Of course they are, Terry,' his wife said, 'look how pretty and slim they are.'

Ruby and I laughed and she nudged me in the ribs.

'This,' said Ruby, 'is the girl who wrote the totally amazing book on which the film is based.'

Terry's ears fell off. By which I mean his mouse ears not his real ones.

'Gosh so you're a writer,' he gasped. 'She's a real live writer, Gwen.'

'I know, Terry. I heard. Isn't that wonderful?'

They leaned towards me while a cheer erupted for Zac's arrival.

'And have you written anything we would know?'

I paused and savoured the question I had so dreaded in the past.

'Yes,' I replied with a confident smile. 'Yes I have.'

THE END

8602200R00232

Printed in Great Britain
by Amazon.co.uk, Ltd.,
Marston Gate.